Better Angels

Better Angels

Harold W. Peterson

Library of Congress Control Number:		2012905517
ISBN:	Hardcover	978-1-4691-8946-8
	Softcover	978-1-4691-8945-1
	Ebook	978-1-4691-8947-5

To order additional copies of this book, contact:
Xlibris Corporation
1-888-795-4274
www.Xlibris.com
Orders@Xlibris.com
111989

For my mother, Rosanna

Chapter One

May 1985

A warm suffocating air settled upon my face. My breath drew shallow, and I nearly remembered. Then they came, the intoxicating worms devouring deep into my brain, numbing their way to the memory. I heard them hiss and then suck before slithering off into the empty darkness.

"Daddy?" a child whispers. The voice he knows but is sure he has never heard before. His eyes open. A small dark-eyed girl stands before him. He blinks, trying to focus—to understand.

Is it a dream?

"Emily?" he says so easily.

It is a dream.

"It's me, Daddy," she says. Beams of moonlight flickering in from a window play their ethereal tricks. She is there, then is not, and then is there again.

"What, honey?" he says.

"Can I sleep with you?" Her smile is as light as her words.

He knows why she has come.

"The trees outside are making noise," she says.

"Making noise, huh?" he says.

"Up!" she says. And then, raising her arms over her head, she leans into him.

He lifts her onto the bed where she wiggles up into his arms. She rolls her eyes up at him and smiles.

"Good night, Daddy," she whispers.

Drenched in sweat, my neck and shoulders throbbing, I awoke staring down at the dashboard of my truck. It had to be late afternoon the way the sun was blazing through the windshield. There was no telling how long I had slept—an hour, maybe two. I had driven nonstop from Lansing, Michigan, yesterday evening. The once-empty rest area was now bustling with commuters. I thought about using the facilities, but couldn't invoke a need.

Back on the interstate, for no good reason, I took the second of the three Omaha exits and soon found myself driving west along Dodge Street. Then, for no good reason, I made a right on Fifty-Second Avenue where I pulled into the first motel I saw.

The two-story, pool-less but cable-ready *Ever-Rest Inn* was the answer to my whimsical callings. It didn't take me long to secure a room from the perky little blonde at the desk who, with her perky little smile told me where I could find a bar.

"It's called *Cliff's!* It has a jukebox! And it's fun!" she said in her perky little way.

The room stunk of cigarettes and air freshener. I threw my backpack and duffel bag onto the bed and switched on the television. Nothing interested me, but I did see that the White Sox had run the Tigers out of Comiskey. What a difference a year makes—fuck the Tigers. I switched it back off and headed out the door. I wanted to get drunk.

Cliff's Tavern, as the small wood-burnt sign read, wasn't far from the motel, but if I hadn't of been looking, I would've surely missed it. Squeezed between an empty antique furniture shop and what looked to be an abandoned office supply store, Cliff's appeared to be the only open business on the block.

The place was dark, smelled of sour booze, and the few scattered patrons appeared annoyed by the sunlight that followed me in. The bar ran along the far wall where blood-red neon illuminated mirrored glass and bottled liquor. A constellation of shrouded candles burning from the half dozen tables cast their light in broken patterns about the grimy crushed velvet walls. And there, opposite the bar, just as Miss Perky had promised, stood a glowing jukebox softly playing some old Bobby Darin tune.

I climbed up on the nearest barstool and ordered a rum and Coke from an ancient bartender who I assumed had to be Cliff himself, as nobody would be pouring drinks at his age if he didn't have a proprietary interest.

"You Cliff?" I asked.

"Yep," he grunted, and then slid the rum and Coke at me.

Without another word, Cliff hobbled down to the other end of the bar where he sat staring vigilantly at the door. I gulped down the drink and called for another. Cliff looked irritated but gimped back over. This time, I ordered a double, figuring I'd let the old guy sit a spell.

All at once, sunshine sprayed the barroom, and a middle-aged woman entered, sporting a leopard-spotted shirt and brown too-tight leather pants. She paraded herself and her veil of pungent perfume past me.

"Hey, honey," she hollered at Cliff while peeking over the top of a pair of dark sunglasses. "If you're going to play this sappy-sad music all night, then me and my girlfriends are going elsewhere!"

Then twirling around haughtily, she strolled back toward me where she straddled the barstool next to mine.

"Hi, honey!" she said to me before rummaging through an oversized purse, an unlit cigarette dangling from her lips.

"Give me a High Ball and some change for the box, sweetie!" she hollered back at Cliff.

She lit her cigarette, gave it a lengthy drag before throwing her head back and blowing smoke at the ceiling.

"You're cute," she said, raising an eyebrow to me. "But you're definitely not from around here."

I nodded to her before taking a slow sip of my drink.

"Passing through then, on I-80 I bet?" she asked.

I nodded again.

"All right, now wait a minute. Let me guess," she said, her bar-lit eyes giving me the once-over. "You're from . . . wait, don't tell me. You're from up north somewhere, Canada maybe. Am I right?"

"Close," I said. "Michigan."

"I knew it," she said, taking another drag from her cigarette.

Cliff slid the High Ball at her and slapped down some change on the bar. She shot him a wink and then turned her attentions back to me.

"Now don't tell me, let me guess. You're on your way to . . . wait, don't tell me. You're on your way to . . . California!" she blurted.

"Alaska," I said.

"I was really close," she said with a self-approving smile. "I can always tell," she added before blowing more smoke at the ceiling.

"Sure," I said, thinking, why quibble over a few thousand miles?

"The name's Connie, sugar," she said, flashing me a lipstick smile. "What are you drinking?"

"Name's Henry," I replied, "and I'm drinking rum."

———————————

Five minutes later, Connie and I were sitting at one of the small tables having a drink. Five minutes after that, Connie was sharing her life's story—a story that was neither short nor interesting. But she had bought me a drink, and I felt an obligation.

I didn't want to hear that she had been married for nearly sixteen years and had been only recently divorced, or that she had a teenage daughter, Amber, and an ex-husband, Roy. I couldn't care less that Roy was a good father but a lousy husband, or that Roy *bored her to death* and cared only about his *Trans-Am*. And I certainly didn't want to hear about how she'd found herself a *slick lawyer* and had taken Roy to the proverbial *cleaners*—although apparently, the court did award Roy sole custody of the Trans-Am.

Perhaps it was her bleach-treated hair, her "hyp-noxious" perfume, or the way her stories only required from me a bare minimum of responses—but the more she went on about Amber, Roy, and the Trans-Am, the more fascinating she became to me. As alcoholic currents began trickling down through my mind, so too did her alluring presence until, before long, I wanted her.

"Bev and Marisa should be here by now," said Connie, glancing quickly around the barroom and then down at her sporty tennis watch. "It's nearly six. They both get off at five—it's Friday for heaven's sake," she added.

She then did another scan of the barroom, as if they might've instantly appeared in the few seconds since her last look.

"Probably working late again—they work downtown for this asshole accountant. He's always keeping them late!" she huffed.

"A real workaholic, eh?" I said.

"A real *alcoholic!*" she replied and then laughed at her own cleverness. "The guy drinks constantly and puts everything off until the last minute. I don't know how he stays in business. We all used to work for him, but finally, I had enough. I work at the courthouse now. Nobody there works past five." She laughed again, this time placing a hand on my shoulder. "You never told me anything about yourself. So what's it that you do?"

Connie leaned back, as if to get a better read from me, but before I could answer, the barroom door swung open and two women walked in with the sunlight.

"Over here!" Connie shouted at them.

All three women exchanged high-pitched pleasantries and then sat down around the table.

"I want you to meet my friend," said Connie. "This is Henry. He's on a trip to California," she said, glancing at me. "From Minnesota, right?"

I went with it and nodded, then introduced myself to the two women.

"Bev and Marisa both work for that asshole I was telling you about," said Connie. "Did he make you work late again?"

"Of course," said Bev, rolling her eyes. "The prick!"

Marisa snickered and then, waving at Cliff, she shouted, "Honey, bring me a Bud Light and a martini for Bev!"

"Now what is it that you say you did?" Connie asked me.

I smiled at both Bev and Marisa but didn't answer.

Connie frowned then playfully hit me on the shoulder.

"Come on now, sugar, tell me," said Connie.

"I'm in sales," I lied. I had found that people didn't ask much of salesmen. Perhaps it was because they worried a salesman would try to sell them something—or worse, they'd have to buy something from you.

"What kind of sales are you in?" asked Bev, twisting her diamond ring around the base of her bony finger. She was a gaunt woman with a twiggy frame, sunken eyes, and a turned-up nose that gave her a slightly snobby air.

"Automotive parts," I lied again.

"On vacation?" asked Bev.

"Something like that," I said.

"Interesting," said Bev, glancing over at Connie. "As soon as we get my Richard off to Princeton, the three of us girls are heading to the islands for a vacation," she said.

Bev lit a cigarette, took two quick drags, and then crushed it out in the ashtray.

"I'm trying to quit," she said to me.

"You're always trying to quit, Bev," said Marisa, lighting one of her own.

"Well, at least I'm trying," said Bev.

"So, when exactly are we going, Bev?" asked Connie.

"This fall, for sure," said Bev.

"You always say that," said Marisa, shaking her head. "But just because you're free doesn't mean the rest of us can go, or afford it," she added.

"We'll pick a good time for everyone," Bev said, waving at her dismissively. "We'll figure out something that works—financially," she added.

"What do you mean by that?" said Marisa sharply.

"Nothing, just that we'll work it out, that's all," said Bev with a shrug

"How long will it take to get your *precious* Richard off to Princeton, anyway?" snarled Marisa. "I thought he was accepted for last fall. Is the *brilliant* Richard playing hard to get? Oh no, that's right, he waited a year to *find himself*. Where did he go again? Oh yes, that's right, *rehab*. Has your little angel *found himself* out of rehab yet?"

Bev's sunken eyes flamed as she glared at Marisa.

"You . . . you are a wretched thing!"

"And you're a *pretentious bitch!*" fired Marisa. "I'm not going anywhere with you. It's bad enough I have to work with you day-in and day-out, but I don't have to listen to you during my time off! And I certainly don't have to go on vacation with you!" Marisa stood up and pulled her purse from the back of her chair. "I'm sorry, Connie, and . . . *Henry* is it? I'm not going to do this tonight! I'm not going to stay here and listen to her shit anymore! You know, it's not as easy for some of us! We all don't have a big house and the rich ex-husband and a perfect son . . . well, *nearly* perfect anyway!"

"Come on now, ladies," Connie pleaded. "We're all friends here. We don't need to . . ." She hesitated and then grabbed each of their arms. "We're all friends here."

Marisa looked away while Bev stared at her coldly. Then Marisa ripped her arm from Connie's grasp and, without another word, marched out of the barroom.

Bev's stare shifted to Connie where it softened some.

"What did I say?" Bev said to Connie. "This isn't my fault, you know. She's been in a mood all day. She wants everyone to be as miserable as she is. Can I help it if she married an *impotent* piece of shit?"

"No, Bev," cried Connie, a mix of tears and mascara streaked down her face. "It's not your fault! It's never your fault! We used to be such good friends, all of us, and now it's always like this!"

"Please, Connie, you're overreacting. This is nothing new with her—she's always this way. She can't have a child and despises those who do," said Bev, lighting another cigarette. "You know she despises you for it too?"

"What?"

"That's right. She talks about it all the time. About how you're making life difficult for Amber. About how you sabotaged your marriage because you were feeling restless, and Amber has suffered because of it. And about how you . . ." She paused.

Connie shook her head. "About how I what?"

Bev looked away, took a long drag from her cigarette before her eyes settled back on Connie.

"Well?" said Connie.

"Well *what?*" replied Bev with a shrug.

"About how I what?"

Bev shrugged again.

"It's no secret. Everyone knows you *cheated.*"

Connie put her hand over her mouth.

"Oh my god!" she cried out. "I don't believe it! But I didn't—"

"Oh please, Connie!" said Bev. "Remember who you're talking to. I know—half of Nebraska knows about you and Judge Lamb, so spare me the perfunctory denial. The thing is, I don't care. I've never thought much of Roy anyway, the little piss-ant. And as for Amber goes, she's getting along fine, so what's the big deal? My point is that Marisa hates her life because she can't have a kid, so she wants us to hate ours."

"I'm not sure what you or anyone else thinks they know, but I can assure you that you don't know anything," said Connie, her voice low but firm. "And I am shocked that neither of you ever said anything to me before."

"Fine, have it your way. It's none of my business. I really don't care what you do or who you're with," said Bev, glancing quickly over at me. "I don't need this, nor do I have time for it. Call me next week, Connie."

Bev crushed out her cigarette and moved around the small table.

"Nice to meet you, mister auto parts guy," she said to me as she passed.

Then she too was gone.

I sat silently waiting for Connie to say something, but she only stared vacantly in the direction of the jukebox.

"Can I get you a drink?" I asked.

Connie looked at me and then smiled. The smeared mascara around her eyes made her look like a ballplayer.

"That would be wonderful," she said.

When I returned from the bar with fresh drinks, all traces of her sadness were gone.

"I'm sorry you had to witness that," she said. "I want you to know that that stuff about—"

"Don't worry about it," I said dismissively. "It's nothing, really." Reaching over the table, I took her hand and squeezed it. I didn't need her to explain anything. In fact, I didn't need her to talk. I only wanted her to stay there and sit with me, so I didn't have to be alone.

For the next few hours, neither one of us said much. Cliff brought round after round as we sat close together, listening to the music.

"You want to get something to eat?" Connie asked as George Jones whined from the jukebox—something about being drunk at four in the morning.

"Sure, but I walked here," I replied.

"Are you saying you *walked* all the way from . . . where was it? Missouri?"

"No, I *walked* all the way from the *Ever-rest Inn*," I said, grinning. "And I've never even been to *Where-was-it*, Missouri."

Connie threw back her head and laughed before hitting me playfully on the shoulder.

"Then I guess I'll have to drive. Do you like Mexican food?"

"Sure," I said.

———————————————

Aside from a dumpy Latino waitress, a couple of sombreros, and a few strategically placed maracas, *La Siesta's* was about as authentically Mexican as a Dairy Queen. I sat across from Connie in a pink plastic booth, pretending to read the oversized pink plastic menu until she decided we should order the *Nachos Grande* and a couple frozen margaritas.

We were already well into our second margarita by the time the nachos arrived. While Connie's big appetite slowed our conversation, the tequila rapidly enhanced our fascinations for one another, and soon we were racing toward the motel in her dark Cutlass.

Connie drove around to the backside of the motel and parked discreetly beneath the quivering glow of a broken streetlamp where the car couldn't be seen from the street. I knew then, this wasn't her first time.

We got out, and Connie met me at the front of the car. I took hold of her waist, and she kissed me. Her mouth tasted of cilantro and cigarettes. I slid a hand beneath her shirt, probing my way up her torso, below her bra, and over her shallow breast.

Metal popped and snapped beneath us as I brought her down on top of me. I let her weight smother me against the warm hood of the car. I rolled over on top of her, grabbing at her leather pants and peeling them from her legs.

"Now!" she moaned while tugging violently at the fly of my jeans. "Right now!"

She threw her head back and I caught a glimpse of her face—wanting but all at once unfamiliar. A surge of heat rushed from beneath us, high into my chest and throat, dry and suffocating. I tried to back away, but she held me tight between her legs.

"What?" she cried out. "What is it?"

"I can't," I said, shoving her down hard against the hood of the car. "I don't . . ." My voice broke and then the world went spinning around me. My only thoughts were that I had to get away. I ripped myself from her grasp and made for the distant lights of the motel, but didn't get far before I stumbled and fell fast to the ground.

"What the hell? What did I . . ." She paused. "Fuck you! You *impotent piece of shit!*" she then shouted from behind me.

Somewhere, I had heard the words before. I scrambled to my feet, but after only a couple short steps, I fell again. That's when I realized the pants around my ankles. I heard an engine rev, followed by the dull spray of dirt inside a fender.

"*Asshole!*" she screamed as the car went whooshing by.

From my knees, I watched the taillights brighten, dim, and then vanish into darkness. I stood, pulled my pants up, and staggered around to the front of the motel where I spied my truck and room.

I fumbled with the key in the lock but managed to open the door and thrust myself inside the stuffy room. I collapsed onto the bed where I lay shaking uncontrollably. My mind hurried with scattered visions of *her* . . . always *her*. If only I could reach her now, talk to her . . . She'd understand. She always understood.

Crawling over my duffel bag, I reached for the telephone and dialed the familiar number. There was a static click and then it rang. Once . . . twice . . . three times . . . then another static click.

"Hello?" a man's voice answered.

Surprised, I didn't reply but held the receiver tight to my ear.

"Hello?" the man said again. "Who is this?"

"Let me talk to her . . . please," I gasped.

"Who is this?"

"You know who it is," I said. "Now let me talk to her."

"She's sleeping," said the man. "We're all sleeping."

Another static click before there was a cold dial tone. My head pounded, my stomach churned, and I lunged at the sink and got sick.

Back on the bed, I rummaged through my duffel bag until I found it—its stainless steel shimmering expectantly in the low light. I slid the clip easily into the handle, cocking a cartridge into the chamber.

"Lock and load!" I said to no one.

I sat down on the floor, leaned back against the side of the bed, and closed my eyes. Was there anything in this life left to live for?

Slowly, I lifted the Colt upward until the barrel touched my chin.

Don't do it, Bronco! came an echoing voice. *You hear me, don't you go and do it!*

I tapped lightly at the trigger.

Please don't leave me here, Hen! I'm so scared!" came another voice.

I opened my eyes, searching for faces. There were none. I lowered the Colt and shut my eyes again. Finally they came—the numbing worms hissing and sucking through to the memory until there was nothing left but the darkness.

Chapter Two

June 1961

"Hey there!" a voice hollered from behind me. I spun around into a brilliant sun.

Shading my eyes, I made out the wiggle of a silhouette atop the hulking pile of tailings. It bounced once or twice before bounding down toward me. A girl, a woman, or something in between, cast out from the sun itself. She skipped up to me, a figure tall and curvy and as pretty as I had ever seen. She set her hands on the back of her hips, stood glaring at me through dark eyes sharp and ready for a fuss.

"Well?" she said hotly.

Too stunned to speak, I stared blankly at her. She was my age, perhaps a bit older—fifteen maybe. Despite her intense look, there was a subtlety to her features—something in her aspect set off by the harshness in her eyes, something manifest in her lips, something on the verge of a smile but not quite.

"What are you, one of them dumb-mutes?" she said fiercely. Then she smiled, and all at once, she seemed shy.

She brushed an unruly strand of light brown hair from her face, tucking it neatly behind her ear as she bounced up and down on the toes of her washed-out sneakers. She wore a plain white tee shirt tied high on her waist and tight faded jeans rolled above her knees, exposing plenty of suntanned skin, much too dark for so early in the spring.

"Is that your dog?" she said, pointing up the road behind me.

I glanced back over my shoulder.

"Yeah, that's Saucy," I said weakly when words finally came.

The dog pranced up beside me with a welcoming wag in her tail. She inched up to the girl, sniffing inquisitively.

"It's okay, she doesn't bite," I said.

"She's pretty," said the girl, offering her hand. Her eyes softened with her smile. She allowed Saucy to lick her palms. "You're a pretty girl, aren't you?" she said, stroking the dog's black coat.

I wanted to say the same about her, but I could only watch as Saucy let the girl rub her back and shoulders.

"She likes you." It was all I could think to say.

"I like her," the girl giggled. "What kind of dog is she?"

"She's part shepherd, part Siberian . . . I think."

"Siberian?"

"Siberian husky," I said.

"Oh," she said, continuing Saucy's rubdown. "Do you live in that house with the little trailer in front?" She pointed over my shoulder again.

"Yeah," I said.

"Name's Jessie." She stuck a hand out at me. "Jessie Mason. Daddy and I drove up from Michigan about a week ago. We live with my granddaddy in a cabin back up the Steese a ways."

"I know it," I said, taking her hand and giving it a good shake.

The cabin was a real hole. Built in the typical Alaskan fashion—part log and part whatever happened to be lying around—it had all the comforts of a toolshed. Surrounded by heaps of junk was everything from ball joints to backhoes. Folks said that Spenser could have one of the largest salvage yards in the state, if only he could part with any of it. My stepdad always referred to it as *The Shit Towers* because he said you can see the shitpiles from the highway.

"So ole Spenser is your grandfather."

"Yeah, do you know him?"

"Not really, but I know who he is."

I had never met the old man personally, but he was notorious for his misfortunes in the gold mining business. An early pioneer and prospector, old man Spenser's struggles had become folklore in these parts. It surprised me to learn he had a granddaughter. I had always thought him for a loner.

"I've heard the stories anyway," I added.

"What stories?" she said, brushing from her eyes another lock of insurgent hair. She again tucked it neatly behind her ear. "I don't know much about it. I only met him a week ago myself."

"You know, the stories about him getting *swindled* and . . ." I hesitated, thinking perhaps she didn't know.

"What's it all about?"

The sourness in her tone made me wonder if I should've kept my mouth shut.

"Oh, nothing really." I shrugged.

"You say he got *swindled*?"

Now I would have to tell her.

"Yeah, his partners cheated him out of his claim—so the story goes. Your grandfather was a partner in this gold mine. It's just up the way." I pointed in the direction. "If you'd like, I'll show you sometime."

"Sure," she said, her eyes uneasy.

"They say he got taken by his own partners—say they sold the claim right out from under him and then skipped town. They ran off with all the cash and his wife too. At least, that's the way I heard it."

"I guess I do know something about that last part. Daddy told me his momma left him when he was just a babe—raised by his aunty back in Flint. That's where we came up from, Flint."

"I don't know about any baby," I said.

"Seems like a shit thing to do," she said, shaking her head. "Say, I didn't get your name."

"Henry Allen," I said.

"What do you do for fun around here, *Henry Allen*?" she said, bouncing me a smile.

"I don't know," I said, as nothing immediately came to mind. This was Fox, Alaska, for crying out loud. "I'm on my way to cut wood for old man Spooner. He lives up the road a ways," I said, pointing.

"Seems everything is up that road a ways." She laughed. "You work, swell," she said, picking up a rock from the ground. She began rubbing it between her hands. "You doing that all summer?"

"Yeah, old man Spooner has me over a couple times a week to cut his winter wood. I get two bits an hour. He's a little kooky, but all right, I suppose. He taught me how to fly-fish. There's some pretty good fishing around here."

"Neat, me and Daddy fish sometimes," she said, looking beyond me at something across the road. She then placed her arms behind her back and stood staring at it intently. "At least, we did back in Flint," she added.

Then arching her back, Jessie lifted her arms over her head and her left leg high in the air, and all once, she fired the rock across the road, where it sailed dead center between twin birches connected at their base.

"Strike!" she shouted and then nodded toward the trees.

"Pretty good," I said, impressed.

Saucy was too, as she jogged off after the rock.

"Where did you learn to do that?"

"Daddy taught me. He taught me just about everything there is to know about baseball. It's only the greatest game ever invented." Her eyes scanned the ground for another rock. "Me and Daddy love the Tigers."

"*The Tigers?*"

"Yeah, the Detroit Tigers." She wrinkled her nose at me. "The baseball team!" she shouted. "Say, I thought Alaska was supposed to be a state now, not an island." She laughed. "You mean you never heard of *Al Kaline, Harvey Kuenn,* or *Jim Bunning?* They've got their eyes on the pennant this year."

"I've heard of them," I lied. I'd heard of the Yankees, and maybe the Tigers, but *Al*, *Harvey*, or the *Bunny-man*? And what was a *pennant*? Was it the same as the World Series? I wondered.

"I do like the Yankees," I said.

"The goddamned Yankees!" she shouted. "For Christ-sake, you're a damn Yankee fan! Don't tell me that! Please don't you tell me that!"

Jessie began shaking her head and flapping her arms like a mad woman. Never before had I witnessed such fussing and cussing from anyone, let alone a girl.

"You can't like the Yankees! We can't be friends if you're a fan of the *Pen-stripers!*"

"The *Pen-stripers?* I'm really not a baseball fan or a Yankee fan," I quickly confessed. "I did hear the Yankees were in the World Series not long ago, that's what I meant."

"That's good, I suppose," she said calmly but with skeptical eyes. "It's true, the Yankees are in the Series a lot. Hang around me, though, and I'll make you a Tiger fan."

Jessie stared intently across the road again and then fired another rock at the birch trees.

"Strike two!" she shouted. "You *do* play baseball."

"Well, I'm no Joe DiMaggio," I said. He was one of the few baseball players I did know.

Jessie scowled, and I thought she was about to have another fit, but then her face softened and she shook her head.

"Figures, he's a *Yankee*," she said.

She picked up another rock, examined it, and then tossed it at me. "You try," she said.

I bobbled it but caught it before it hit the ground.

"I don't . . ." I hesitated. "It's really not my—"

"Come on. Let's see you throw, *DiMaggio!*"

Jessie stepped backward to give me some space.

"All right," I said. After all, how hard could it be?

Gripping the rock tightly, I brought my arms up over my head while at the same time lifting up my left leg the way she'd done, except that's where the similarities ended. After that, my arms and legs appeared to have minds of their own, moving awkwardly and in a manner defying all semblances of order and purpose. The rock flew from my hand, disappearing into the spring day as I tumbled to the ground. And although I didn't actually see it (as it was explained to me later), the rock soared skyward into the air where it eventually reversed its flight, plummeted downward, and struck me squarely on the back.

"Ouch!" I cried out. I felt the rock skip down the length of my spine. My pride and I lay on the ground, routed and hoping, at that moment, I would be swallowed into the earth. Jessie stood over me, her hands to her mouth, laughing. My face burned red.

"That may bruise," she said, her laughter now hysterical. "What a *rube!*"

"A *rube?* What's a *rube?*" I asked, shooting her a shameful look.

"You are!"

Then, without hesitation, Jessie knelt down beside me, slid her hand under my shirt, and began gently messaging the spot on my back where the rock had hit me.

"There, there. All better?" she said sweetly.

No one other than my mother had ever touched me like that before. It felt different, but good. It tingled and sort of tickled.

"Are you going to be okay?" she asked.

"I'll be fine," I whispered.

Jessie glanced away. "Your house is big," she said.

"Yeah, Tom built it," I said.

"*Tom?*"

"My stepdad," I said. "*The Big Shitbox*, he calls it, on account of it's so square. He built the toolshed, the pigshed—"

"*Pigshed?* You've got pigs?"

"Nah," I said dismissively. "That's just what Tom calls it, on account of it's always a mess. He built everything here, except the old boathouse. It was here when we got here."

"*Boathouse?*"

"Yeah, you can't see it from here, but it's down by the creek."

"You got a boat?"

"Nah," I said. "It's because it's so long you could store a boat inside—that, and it's sliding into the creek." I laughed. "At least, that's what Tom says. He's a flight mechanic in Fairbanks. He flew choppers in Korea, you know. He's teaching me to fly them. He's already taught me a few ground-school things."

"You mean them *whirlybird* thingies?" she said, wrinkling her nose.

"Nobody calls them whirlybirds!" I barked and then said calmly. "They're called choppers."

"Sorry," she said with a shrug. "My granddaddy does construction now. He and Daddy are framing houses in Fairbanks."

"How did you end up here?" I asked.

"My parents got divorced, and Daddy decided to come here to work for Granddaddy. I just up and decided to come with him."

"You wanted to come here?"

"Sure," she said. "It sounded fun, like an adventure."

"You might change your mind once winter sets in."

"So how do you like it here so far?"

"It's all right. Daddy and Granddaddy are gone most of the time. After breakfast, they leave me to tend the cabin until they come home for dinner, but I never know when that's going to be. I've been getting pretty bored hanging around the house all day, so I decided to see if there was anyone around. That's when I came across you."

Jessie flashed me an easy smile.

"You know," I said, "I don't have to cut wood today. I can always make it up tomorrow. The old man lets me keep my own hours. We could do something else."

"Like what?" she asked.

"You want to fish?"

"Don't have a pole with me," she said, showing me her hands.

I was going to tell her she could use one of mine, but then I had another idea.

"We could check out the beaver pond," I said.

"What's a beaver pond?" she asked, wrinkling her nose at me again.

"It's a pond about a half mile downstream from here," I said, pointing back toward the creek. "The beavers dammed it up in three places, so now it's really a series of ponds. It's swell," I said.

"If you really don't have to work, I'm game. What happened to Saucy?" she asked, glancing around.

"Oh, don't worry about her, she's around. Believe me, she knows exactly where we are."

"I'm glad for that," Jessie said, laughing, "because I'm not sure I do."

A thicket of high grass and quarrelsome brush had swallowed the trail down to the beaver pond, but I did my best to stomp out a pathway for Jessie. When we finally broke through the dense undergrowth, we were welcomed with an explosion of blazing sunlight. We suddenly found ourselves standing a few feet above the near shore of a sparkling pond stretched between two enormous beaver dams.

"Wow," whispered Jessie. "It's fantastic."

"Yeah," I said, happy to have thought of it.

A rustling sound came from behind us, and suddenly Saucy leaped out from the trees behind us, startling Jessie. Saucy quickly brushed up against her apologetically, panting hard, her tongue dangling from the side of her mouth.

"I told you she was around."

Jessie patted Saucy on the top of her head.

"Hey girl," she said.

The dog nestled her nose into Jessie's hand and began licking her fingers. All appeared forgiven.

"I see you've made a new friend, Sauce."

Jessie rubbed Saucy hard under the chin and then, kneeling down, she dipped a hand into the pond water.

"It's warm!" she announced and then, standing up, she gazed out over the pond. "We should go swimming!"

Swimming this early in the summer had been the farthest thing from my mind. Although, the thought of swimming with Jessie anywhere, at any time, excited me—the way the girls' underwear section of the *Sears & Roebuck* catalog did.

"It's really a lot cooler once you get in," I said, "but a week from now, it'll be all right."

"What do you mean? Let's go now, the water's fine!"

The excitement in her voice fueled my own, and I would agree to anything.

"All right," I said, but we'll have to get our suits."

"Suits, why, we can just *bare ass it!*"

"*Bare ass it?*" I said, not sure if I heard her correctly. "You mean . . ." My voice faded as I watched her untie the tee shirt from around her chest.

"What? You've never been skinny-dipping before?" She raised an eyebrow as she peeled off the tee shirt and tossed it at my feet.

I stood hypnotized, doing all I could to contain my enthusiasm but still staring shamelessly at the light blue brassiere that was doing all it could do to contain a good-sized pair of breasts—or *tits,* as Tom often referred to them.

"Uh . . . no," I mumbled. But before I could stumble over another word, she removed the bra and tossed it next to the tee shirt. Never before had I beheld such a sight. My insides suddenly wanted to be outside, and everything about me felt awake and alive.

"Come on, it'll be fun," she said, her breasts bouncing along with her words.

She then slid her jeans down over the subtle curves of her hips. I now understood precisely what she meant by *bare ass it*. My heart raced, my mouth watered, and I found it suddenly difficult to speak.

"I . . . uh . . ." Unless I was subconsciously speaking in tongues, I had lost even the basic verbal skills, but my eyes worked splendidly as they boldly cast themselves down to her most precious part: a vision I had only envisioned until now. Frozen—my eyes wide, mouth agape—I nearly fell over.

Then all at once, Jessie sprang from the shore, diving headlong into the pond, the raucous splash ripping me from my enchanted state.

"Whew!" she screamed as she came bursting from beneath the water. "It's not exactly warm, but it's all right!" She shook her head, wiped her face, and then yelled back at me, "What are you waiting for? You chicken?"

What I was waiting for had less to do with being chicken (although I was petrified) than it did with a certain physical presence that I was all at once self-conscious of, which was surely doing everything *it* could do to go in after the naked girl.

With my clothes strewn along the shore, I—along with my resounding manhood—dove cannonball into the pond. The splash was exhilarating and went a long way to cool my internal flame. When I surfaced, to my surprise, I found Jessie only a few feet away from me, an impish grin on her face.

"You know what's really fun?" she said.

"What?" I replied uneasily.

"This!" She let out a wicked scream before lunging at me. Her slippery body engulfed my head and shoulders, pulling me downward into a distorted world of sunlight and shadows. I didn't struggle, but instead surrendered to her weight and warmth. I let her pin me to the muddy bottom of the pond. The need for air eventually brought me gasping and coughing to the surface, wishing I were a fish or any creature that could breathe underwater.

"You'll pay for that!" I sputtered, splashing pond water into her face.

"Oh yeah?" she cried, returning a splash before disappearing again into the pond.

I dove after her, seized her shoulders, and drew her to me—my hands touching, probing, and clutching any part of her slick body that I could take hold of. All the while, my lungs were screaming for air.

But not for exhaustion, I could've stayed in the pond forever. Even suffocation seemed a small price to pay for grappling and groping beneath the cool water with Jessie. But after a while, we both staggered up the bank on the other side of the pond, breathless and tired.

"Over there," I pointed to a sandy spot in the sun. I was less self-conscious, but still sat down quickly and pulled my knees tight to my chest.

Jessie sat down next to me and leaned back on her elbows, not in the least shy about displaying to me all she was as a woman.

"So Joe?" She grinned.

"*Joe?*"

"Yeah, aint you Joe DiMaggio?" She giggled.

"I don't think so."

"Yeah, you're more of a *rube*," she said sharply, but then smiled.

"I don't even know what that means."

"It's funny," she said, shaking her head. "My daddy, he hates the Yankees like me. I mean he really hates them. But he tells me that the year I was born, in '47, the Yanks won the pennant by twelve games over the Tigers. But he says the Tigers had won the Series in '45, so he wasn't so sore about it. Anyway, in '47, he says, Teddy Baseball, because that's what they call Ted Williams . . ." She hesitated, then stared at me curiously.

"Say, you know Ted Williams, don't you?"

"Sure, Ted Williams," I said, trying to sound confident. I had heard the name. Still, my mind was on other things.

"Well, Williams won the Triple Crown that year. You know—average, homers, and RBI's?"

23

"Sure," I lied. She might as well be talking French for all I could understand, as I sat staring wantonly at her breasts.

"Daddy says it was pretty amazing because Williams also won it in '42. But here's the thing—*DiMaggio* won the MVP that year."

"*MVP?*"

"Most Valuable Player," she said, rolling her eyes.

"Oh, yeah." I nodded. "That makes sense." Of course, now, I barely knew my own name.

"The way Daddy tells it, DiMaggio was the greatest clutch hitter there ever was. And in '47 he won the MVP, even though Williams won the Triple Crown, and that takes some clutch hitting, boy. Daddy hates the Yankees, but he loves *The Clipper* as he calls him. And sure as shit, you bring up DiMaggio." She shook her head and gave me a pleasant nod.

"Yeah . . . well, he was great," I said, pleased for having brought it up, but more pleased with Jessie's naked body stretched out beside me. I watched as a tiny bead of water rolled from her pink nipple down along the outside of her breast and disappeared into her armpit. I wished we were back in the pond. I wanted so much to touch her again.

"That's what Daddy says, but I don't know. I'll take Al Kaline any day." She nodded. "Of course, Daddy says I never saw DiMaggio," she added.

"Say," she said, squinting at me. "What's that?" She pointed to my neck.

I felt for my necklace. I forgot it was even there, and I was happy I hadn't lost it in the pond. "Oh, this." I pulled it over my head and handed it to her. "My mother gave it to me."

"It's pretty," she said, examining it closely. She then rubbed it between her fingers. "It looks really old."

"It might be—not sure. My mother got it off an old native friend of hers. Supposed to be a piece of moose bone. That's a raven's head carved on there," I said, pointing at it. "Tom drilled the hole for the strap. I've had it a long time—paint needs to be touched up a bit."

"No, I like it all faded and old. It's like them totem pole thingies you see around. It's neat," she said, handing it back to me.

"My mother says it's supposed to bring me luck." I slipped it back over my head.

"Does it?"

"Does it what?"

"Bring you luck?"

"Oh . . . well, so far." I smiled, my eyes racing the length of her body.

"Daddy says that you should never lose a good luck charm. Otherwise, you'll have bad luck."

"Yeah, why's that?"

"I'm not sure, but he also says that if you have it long enough, it will hold all your luck—becomes a little part of you," he says.

"Yeah, well where's your good luck charm?"

"Don't have one." She smirked.

"Why not?"

"Because it's a lot of bullshit." She laughed. "Daddy, he's full of it most of the time. Don't get me wrong, I love him, but he's full of shit." She laughed again, but then suddenly, her eyes turned serious. "Say, Henry, you hiding something from me?"

"What d-do you mean?" I stuttered, knowing precisely what she meant.

"You're hiding something, all right." She placed a hand on my knee and tried pulling it from my chest. "Let me see," she giggled.

"See what?" My face warmed.

She pulled harder at my knee, but I wouldn't budge. Then suddenly, her eyes softened, and so did her grip.

"You know something, Henry? You're pretty cute, even with your skinny little arms and that choppy crew cut."

I glanced down at my arms, which suddenly did look somewhat sticklike. I remembered my last haircut. *High and tight!* Tom had said to the barber—but choppy? I supposed I had never thought about it before, but now I couldn't stop thinking about it. I began to sense her eyes upon me, burning my face and the back of my neck. Anxiously, I pulled my knees tightly into my chest with all the strength my stick-arms could muster.

"Come on, Henry, let me see," whispered Jessie, her eyes staring directly into mine. Then, sliding her hand down the outside of my thigh, she giggled. "I've already seen it," she said softly, "and I don't bite."

I wasn't altogether convinced, but the sweetness to her tone was beyond reproach. All I saw was her dark brown eyes staring back into mine. She had me—there wasn't anything I wouldn't do for her now. Releasing my knees, I leaned back onto my elbows and extended my legs, exposing to her all I was as a man.

Without words or removing her eyes from mine, she moved her hand across my waist and gradually downward where, gently, she took my most intimate part into her hand. Then leaning forward, she kissed me lightly on the cheek.

"I should go now," she said, releasing me. "I never know when Daddy will get home."

All my manly sensations began gathering themselves at the lower center of my body as I watched Jessie stand up and walk gingerly down the rocky bank to the edge of the pond.

"It's really cold now," she announced after taking a couple tentative steps into the water. "Aren't you coming?" she said, glancing back at me.

When she looked away, I quickly skipped over to her. Jessie stood holding her arms tight to her body. When she saw me, she leaned her head against my chest and rolled her eyes up to mine.

"I don't want to go back in," she moaned.

"That's okay," I said, wrapping my arms around her. "I know another way across."

"What way?" she said with a curious scowl.

"This way!" I shouted. Then, lifting her up, I charged us out into the pond.

"*Rube!*" she screamed before we both went plunging beneath the water.

Chapter Three

August 1968

"Blackjack 105, this is Blackjack 5, two minutes out, over!" came the squelchy call from the ship's radio.

"Blackjack 105, roger, out," I said into the headset. "One minute out, boys, and don't ask me about the LZ, because I don't know!"

I scanned the horizon searching for the landing zone, but all I could see was jungle.

"That's some of the thickest triple canopy shit I've ever seen!" I shouted at my copilot, Ho. "You see anything?"

"I don't see shit," Ho shouted back. "Suppose to be bomb crater, right?"

"Yeah, they cut out an LZ especially for us."

"We'll find it," Ho said assuredly and then, after careening his head in all different directions, he pointed down at a slow-rolling river snaking its way through the jungle.

"Well, fuck me! That's the *Hodrai!* We're in damned Cambodia!"

"Blackjack 105, this is Blackjack 5, one minute out, over," the radio blared again.

"This is 105, roger," I replied, "still no visual, out!"

"I don't see shit, and we are definitely in Cambodia!" yelled Ho.

"I knew this mission was FUBAR," I shook my head. "Every time we get rangers this shit happens, damn it!"

Peering out my portside window, I saw Flanny's chopper in formation next to us.

"I wonder if he knows what the hell we're doing in Cambodia," I said to Ho. "Hey, who's the new peter with Flanny, anyway?"

"Covey, I think," said Ho.

"Yeah, Covey, right. I sure as hell—"

"Blackjack 105, this is Blackjack 5, thirty seconds out. The LZ is hot, repeat, the LZ is hot, over," screeched the radio.

"Blackjack 105, roger out," I replied, my stomach suddenly jumping into my throat. "Damn!" I quickly switched on the intercom. "Thirty seconds, boys, and we're hot. So look sharp," I said to the crew.

"Blackjack 105, this is Blackjack 5, ten seconds out. Do you have visual, over?"

I couldn't see shit, so I glanced over at Ho, who only shrugged and shook his head.

"This is Blackjack 105, that's a negative, negative—" But before I could say more, there it was, a tiny hole carved out of the dense jungle resembling a neat little bowtie. "That's it?"

Ho shrugged again.

"Let me get this straight. We're dropping these ranger bastards under fire in that skinny little shithole?"

"Must be," said Ho.

"You'd think they'd at least let us drop them on the treetops and have them climb down—they'd probably have a better chance!"

"I don't think so," Ho said.

Sarcasm was wasted on Ho.

"Blackjack 5, this is 105. I have a visual, but the angle's no good. I'm going around to the south, over!"

"Blackjack 5, roger! You got the lead, 105. Out."

I looked out the window at Flanny's ship and then at the horizon. The best approach was probably from the south, but I couldn't be sure. Perhaps viewing it as an hourglass instead of a bowtie, I might be able to take advantage of its length. I wondered what Flanny might do. He'd probably suggest a high overhead approach or "spiral" as he called it, but I hated that kind of slow and gradual "get your ass shot off" approach. So screw it. I had the lead, and it wasn't like I had to land the ship. I just had to get them close to the ground.

"Blackjack 5, this is Blackjack 105. We're going in, over."

"Blackjack 5, roger, out."

I dropped the nose of the chopper down, diving toward the tiny hourglass. Flanny followed.

"A little steep, sir?" my crew chief's voice chirped over the intercom. "Our ass is a bit high!"

It was true, the ship's nose was almost pointing straight down. The scorched brush and splintered trees of the crater's bottom were fast approaching. I pulled back on the stick in an effort to dump some air speed, but we were still coming in too fast. All at once, machine-gun fire ripped through the windshield a few inches above Ho's head, exploding onto the cabin floor between us.

"Shit! That was close!" I cried out. "Hold on!"

Instinctively, I worked the stick, throttle, and the foot pedals, swooping the big metal bird down and flaring it out a few feet above the bottom of the crater, the rotors barely missing a fallen tree. The chopper lurched upward, and then losing airspeed, it plunged downward toward the bottom of the crater.

"Whoa!" shouted Ho. "We come in hard!"

"Too hard," I barked. "We're going to have to land!"

Landing in this shit was the last thing I wanted, but I had come in too fast and everybody knew it. We were already too low. The crater was a tight fit, full of all sorts of debris—the worst of which were the downed trees and the turned-up boulders. Pulling power and tilting the chopper slightly to the right, I was able to avoid a large mound of what looked to be dirt and rock.

There was a sharp snapping sound as the tail rotor slapped at a small tree—fortunately, too small to cause them any serious damage. Sliding forward wildly on the landing skids, all I could do now was watch and pray as clumps of dirt and shattered trees slashed along the chopper's nose. Finally, we lunged forward on the tips of our skids, swayed to a stop, and then slowly rocked back to the ground, the main rotor screaming but not hitting anything.

"Get them out!" I yelled into the intercom.

Over my shoulder, I watched Jake, my door-gunner, burn round after round from his .60-caliber machine gun. One by one, the half a dozen rangers jumped from the deck to the ground where they charged halfway up the steep edge of the crater before huddling behind a cluster of elephant grass and tree stumps—pinned down and drawing fire. Then in an eruption of swirling smoke and dust, Flanny's ship came thundering overhead and then soared off in the direction of South Vietnam.

Flanny was already gone, and I needed to get us the hell out of here, fast. But before I could do anything, I felt and heard the rhythmic popping sound of machine-gun bullets slamming into the side of the chopper.

"Go, go, go!" Jake's static-ridden shouts came blaring into my headset.

Looking back, I saw the last ranger—a mountain of a man—leap from the deck, stumble, and then fall face-first to the ground. He tried several times to get to his feet before rolling over onto his back, holding his leg.

Then more bullets hit the side of the chopper, causing Jake to duck down behind his gun. He glanced back at me—the question on his mind went straight to his face.

"Hell no!" I shouted back at him. "Leave him! We're out of here!"

Turning to Ho, I signaled that we were taking off and immediately hit the throttle and then the collective, but when I pushed the stick, expecting lift, I got nothing.

The chopper only rocked forward on the tips of its skids, the main rotor nearly digging into the ground in front of us. I quickly cut power and brought the chopper back down flat on its skids as another burst of bullets slammed into the side of the chopper, the last bullet ricocheting off the deck.

"We're taking hits back here!" Guy's voice came blasting over the intercom.

"All right, all right!" I shouted back at them. Again, I tried to lift off, but the chopper remained stuck on it skids.

"Blackjack 105, 105," the call came over the radio, "this is Blackjack 5. What the hell is going on down there? Why are you down, over?"

"This is 105," I replied. "We're down, goddamn it! We're taking hits! Need cover west, cover west, over!"

"Roger 105, we copy. Bug out of there ASAP, out!"

Again, I tried to get the chopper off the ground, but again it only wanted to dance on the front of its skids.

"Easy!" Ho shouted at me. "I think we're stuck on something!"

"You think so?" I said, glaring at him, again my sarcasm lost. Once more, I dropped the chopper back down hard on its skids and then again tried taking off, but to no avail. Repeatedly, I rocked the chopper back and forth, desperately trying to break it free from the earth as more bullets pounded into the side of the chopper. A thunderous explosion then came from high off to the right, shaking the ground beneath us.

"Take that, you fucking commie bastards!" cried Jake. And then at the big ranger, he shouted, "Stay down, motherfucker! Stay down, goddamn it!"

Jake squeezed off more rounds over the man's head. The ranger hadn't gotten too far and was on his hands and knees, crawling up the side of the crater toward the huddled rangers some twenty feet away. All at once, he staggered to his feet and stood gazing vacantly up the hill at his team.

"Get down, you dumb son of a bitch!" Jake yelled at him.

The ranger looked disoriented, like a dog that didn't know whether to fetch or stay. He gave the chopper a quick glance and then, turning back, he took one wobbly step toward his team before a foray of machine-gun fire cut through him. Blood spurted from his face, chest, and stomach as he dropped to his knees and fell forward.

"You dumb motherfucker!" Jake shouted at him before showering the tree line with more bullets.

"We got to get out of here, sir!" yelled Guy from behind me. "We can't hold out much longer!"

Bullets continued to pour into the side of the chopper forcing me to set it back flat on its skids. It was only a matter of time before we'd be ripped to shreds. I had really fucked us this time. The chopper felt heavy, I felt heavy, my chest felt heavy. It was suddenly hard to breathe—I couldn't do anything but stare hopelessly down at the stick in my useless hand. A bullet smashed through the windshield whizzing a few inches from my head. And with it came the heat—it came from everywhere—from the jungle, from inside the chopper, from beneath my helmet and from inside my mind. It was overpowering making it hard to move and even harder to breathe. My eyes burned from sweat and I couldn't keep them open. The heat was suffocating and I couldn't escape it—I couldn't get free.

"What about him, sir!" shouted Jake, pointing to the downed ranger. "He's hit, we can't leave him. He's a dumb motherfucker, but we can't leave him!"

I knew I had to act, but I could only observe. I understood what to do, but I could do nothing. The heat was unbearable, burning me from the inside out. I could think of nothing but death—my death and the death of the crew. My chest heaved for air and my body yearned for anything cooling—anything to extinguish the fire within me and around me. I blinked rapidly, trying to keep my eyes open, but all I could see were flames, their fiery reds and blazing yellows scorching the back of my eyelids and rolling upward into my brain.

"Sir . . . sir?" a far-off voice was calling me. It was Guy's voice. And then I saw my crew chief, his helmeted head next to mine. "Sir, I think our left skid is caught on something. Maybe a tree or a root or a rock or something, I don't know. Let me take a look!"

I could only stare at him blankly, slowly rocking back and forth in my seat. "Yeah," I mumbled, but my mouth and lips burned as I spoke.

"Do it!" Ho shouted. "If you need help, signal!"

Guy disappeared, and then reappeared at the nose of the chopper. Through the windows, I could see only parts of him pounding an ax at something near the left-side skid. Suddenly, Guy's head popped in front of the windshield. He was waving his hands.

"Be right back," said Ho. He quickly freed himself from his seat and was gone. A few seconds later, I saw sections of legs, arms, and hands pulling and pushing wood, dirt and other debris from beneath the chopper.

The staccato snaps of covering machine-gun fire and the smell of cordite filled the air inside the cockpit while my insides were still burning up; I feared I would melt into the seat of the chopper. I had to get out. I had to get free. The heat was swallowing me, strangling me, paralyzing me. I had to get out of here. Closing my eyes, I saw only the searing flames. I was helpless, and I knew I was going to die.

Then all at once, darkness shrouded me, and I could see or hear nothing. I thought I must be dead. I was no longer hot . . . but instantly cool and wet, as though I were floating beneath water in a world of shadows and murky bottoms. Above me, standing beyond the surface, a form, the sunbeams refracting brilliantly off white skin as it rocked with the ebb and flow of the water. An angel—an angel come to take me from here. I tried moving toward it, but couldn't. I tried to speak to it, but couldn't. But it spoke to me. I could hear her voice.

"It's a go, sir . . . sir." The voice got louder. "It's all go! It's a go! Go!"

Opening my eyes, I stared down at my hand, which was tightly gripping the stick. Looking around, I saw Ho in the seat next to me fastening his shoulder strap.

"Let's go!" Ho shouted. "You okay?"

"Yeah, okay, where—"

"We're all clear, sir," Guy's voice roared from behind me. "The left skid was wedged in pretty good! It's all bent to shit, but it'll work! We've taken some hits, but we're all right! The tail is clear too! And for now, Jake and our ranger pals took care of Charlie!"

Immediately, I hit the power and nosed the chopper forward and instantly, I felt the floor lift beneath me—precious lift. We were light and moving fast, up and away from the hell, from the shit. The wind in the chopper felt cool on my sweat-soaked face. When we were well above the tree line and out of harm's way, I gazed out my portside window and watched the tiny bowtie LZ disappear into the triple canopy jungle.

But before reaching maximum speed, a bitter and metallic scent overwhelmed the cabin—something frightening and familiar. At first, I thought it might be the cordite from the machine guns, but then it struck me. It was blood—fresh blood. I glanced down at the floor and saw the dark streams below my feet, pouring in with the pitch of the chopper.

"Blood!" I cried out. I looked over at Ho. "Who's hit?"

"The ranger," said Ho. "Jake pulled him in before we took off."

"Can't we stop the bleeding? He's losing a hell of a lot of blood back there!"

"No point," said Ho, shaking his head. "He dead."

"Allen!" Flanny shouted from the doorway, "You all right? Shit, you had me worried! What in the hell was that all about anyway? I thought you guys were goners. You know you weren't supposed to land there, don't you?"

I didn't answer. I didn't want to talk right now. I sat on my bunk staring blankly down at the floor. Flanny grabbed a campstool leaning against the wall of the hooch and sat down in front of me. I could tell he wanted to talk.

"You missed one hell of a debriefing," he said.

"I froze," I said softly, "I couldn't move a muscle. I nearly killed everyone on the slick. I fucked up. There's my debriefing."

"Hey, you're alive aren't you?" said Flanny dismissively. "Don't be a puss—nobody likes a pussy AC, Allen." He reached over and slapped me across the knee. "Now get your pussy-ass up and let's go back to my hooch. I've got some cold pops—Bud-flavor I think."

"I got scared, Flanny, real scared. I nearly couldn't fly. I've never been so scared in my life. I couldn't . . ." My voice broke suddenly.

Flanny stared at me, his ocean-blue eyes warm but calculating. After a long pause, he said, "Get over yourself! Now let's go. I got some whiskey that will brave your pussy-ass right on up!"

He got up and headed for the door, but I didn't move, causing him to begrudgingly come back and sit down.

"Listen, puss," he said, placing his elbows on his knees and leaning in toward me, "I'm only going to say this once. My tour's nearly over, and I have been flying the better part of three years for old Uncle Sam. I've flown hundreds of missions in this godforsaken country—some were a piece of cake and some were not. Hell, you've flown a few of the tougher ones with me yourself. And there wasn't one mission where I wasn't scared shitless."

I didn't look at him. I didn't want to hear any of this.

"The problem with you, Allen, is you're still flying like you're some pussy peter sitting right-seat to me. You're a good pilot, start acting like one!"

He slapped me across knee again and stared at me coldly.

"In case you haven't noticed," he continued, "people die around here. And not just on some crazy night mission or on account of some hot LZ, but all the time and because of the strangest shit. A few weeks ago, remember that crew chief—took it in the face from a rotor blade, just because some asshole pilot got his ship too close to a flagpole. Shit like that's always—"

"Hey, *Bronco!* I hear you were riding the rodeo today!"

Lieutenant Broadway stood at the doorway of the hooch, his shirt unbuttoned, exposing his massive chest, a towel slung over his shoulder.

"Up and down, up and down, up and down. They said it was like you were riding a damned *bronco,* yee haw! Ride 'em, cowboy!

Yippee!" he squealed and then went hopping skipping around the hooch on what I guessed was an imaginary bronco.

"You're just in time, Lieutenant," said Flanny. "I was just talking about *asshole* pilots."

Broadway stopped in midgallop, his face now serious. He came over and squatted down in front of Flanny.

"Fuck you, Flanagan! You see this?" He pointed to the gold bar on his lapel.

Flanny grinned.

"What's that, your little butter bar, Broadway? Am I supposed to be all hot and bothered because of *that*, or the *shitbag* wearing it?"

"That's fine, Flanagan, just fine. Keep it up," said Broadway. "It means that I outrank you, motherfucker! And it means that if you piss me off, I can make your life a living hell around here."

"Really, Lieutenant?" said Flanny, smirking. "I was just telling Mr. Allen here that my work in this lovely country has nearly come to an end, and I will be leaving it to fine young officers like you, Lieutenant. And if my disrespectful or irksome behavior were to somehow land me some tedious campside duty instead of risking my short-timer ass chasing down VC in my chopper, then I would be happy to spend my last days here pissing you off."

Flanny reached over, grabbing Broadway by the lapel, pulling him close to his face. Flanny wasn't a large man, especially squaring off against the likes of Broadway who looked the giant next to him. But something in Flanny's voice demanded a respect. I could see it in the lieutenant's eyes.

"You see, Broadway, your butter-bar ass has only been in-country for a short time. And since command wouldn't let you fly an ash-and-trash mission across the mess hall by yourself, they're going to make sure my last days are spent flying missions important to the cause, whatever that is, while you and your little butter bar here get your feet wet, or . . ." he paused, "get dead!"

Broadway jerked himself from Flanny's grasp.

"I'm watching you, Mr. Flanagan," said Broadway coldly. "Remember, I'm watching you!"

Broadway stood up and sent us both an icy glare before storming out of the hooch.

"How did you ever land a hoochmate like that?" asked Flanny when Broadway was gone.

"He's all right," I said. "We went to flight school together. He's just a little abrasive at times, but quite harmless."

"Career guy, eh?"

"Yeah," I said. "How'd you know?"

"Career guys are always harmless, and they're always pulling rank—like the rank makes the man or the rank is the man. It's always important to them that they outrank someone. It's why they make it their career. The problem is that both get killed at the same time."

"*Both?*" I said.

"The rank and the man," he said.

"You don't think Broadway will make it?"

"Ah, shit," said Flanny. "He'll make it. He'll probably be a goddamned general some day. Guys like that always do. You got to think about yourself to survive this place. You always have to be watching your own ass first. And watching his own ass is what Broadway does best. It's probably what will get him promoted. The minute you start thinking about somebody else's ass is the minute yours gets fried. Besides, Broadway is too shitty of a pilot. They'll never send him out on anything too important."

"But then how can you be a good pilot and still watch out for yourself, since they're always giving you FUBAR missions?"

"Remember, Allen. You may not be a goddamned general, but you're the swingin'est dick on your ship, so act like it. You see, this is a learn-as-you-go war. And don't think command knows what the hell they're trying to do. Look at us—we're flying rangers into Cambodia for fuck sake."

"It's fucked up," I agreed.

"Hell yeah. I had this mission two weeks ago. Major Whipple sends me and another slick out in the boondocks with a couple of gunships. They want us slicks to fly treetop over this place near Plei Djereng where they suspect VC activity. Get this—we're supposed to fly over trees all slow like until the VC bastards started shooting at us. And when we got shot at, we couldn't fire back. We had to call in the gunships."

"Did you get shot at?"

"Hell no, but that's not the point. It's a really fucked-up mission when you have to use your own guys as bait. It really got me thinking about things. I won't do it again. They can do what they want to me, but I don't have much time left, and like I said, I'm officially on the lieutenant's plan of looking out for number one. It's time for this soldier to go home."

"But what about guys like me, Flanny?" I asked. "What should I be doing?"

"Well, *Bronco*," he said, snickering. "And that's what they're calling you now. For starters, you can quit worrying about it. Guys that worry about dying all the time are *AD* for sure."

"*AD?*" I asked.

Flanny laughed and then gave me another slap across the knee.

"Already dead," he said.

Chapter Four

May 1985

"Emily!" he shouts from the deck. He doesn't see her, so he shouts again. "Emily, come on in, honey. It's getting nasty out here!"

It's springtime, but winter's wake is still biting as even the newly sprouting birch leaves cling to their branches and cower beneath icy raindrops.

"Okay!" she answers, barely audible through the swirling wind. Suddenly her tiny head pops out from around one side of the rain-slicked mound of freshly dumped topsoil. "I just got one more to put in the oven, Daddy!" she says assuredly. She has been busy baking fresh mud pies—a new family favorite since the dirt arrived.

Darting from behind the mound of mud, Emily bolts across the lawn, her ears and cheeks wind-reddened.

"Take your boots off outside!" he hollers down to her.

"I am, Daddy!" comes her reply.

Stepping back inside, he waits for her to appear at the bottom of the stairs. When she does, he can see the front of her bright orange tunic is sopped in mud.

"Take off your Indian dress before you come up here, honey. It's filthy!"

"It's called a kuspuk, Daddy!" she yells up at him.

"Well whatever it is, it's filthy, so take it off before you come up. Your mother will have a fit if you get mud up here!"

"I am! I am!" she yells before disappearing again.

She reappears atop the stairs.

"You need to wash your hands—your fingers are caked with mud."

She glances down at her hands. "Okay," she says, nodding. She quickly makes for the kitchen, and he watches her climb the stool in front of the sink.

"Daddy?" she says, peering up at him sweetly.

"Yes, honey," he said.

"Are you going to fly the whirlybirds tomorrow?"

"That's right, honey. Daddy has to fly the helicopter tomorrow."

"Can I go with you, Daddy?" she asks. "I want to fly in the whirlybird."

"Someday you will, but Daddy has to fly for work tomorrow, and he can't take little girls."

"Please, oh please, Daddy. Can't I go with you?"

"I'm sorry, sweetheart, not this time. But sometime soon, okay?"

"Yeah, okay," she says. "But someday soon—okay, Daddy?"

"Soon, I promise," he says, hating to disappoint her.

———

My eyes opened and caught the glimmer from the stainless steel Colt lying on the bed only a few inches from my head. The bathroom fan growled defiantly at me until, at last, I got up to shut it off. There, I threw up a couple times before crawling into the shower. For a long time, I sat in there, letting the warm water spray over me until I could muster enough energy to wash myself. Then I scoured my neck and head and then my face, chest, and stomach. I scrubbed hard and furiously, the washcloth grating against my skin. I washed my back, groin, legs, and feet—every inch of my body, rubbing away the dirt and grime that clung so wickedly to me until my skin stung red.

Stepping out of the shower, I instantly felt the foulness of the motel room affixing to me, contaminating me until I was dirty again. I dug out some clean clothes from my duffel bag—a tee shirt and a pair of faded jeans. I put them on but felt dirtier still.

On the way out, I caught a glimpse of myself in the mirror. I was thin, pale, and looked every bit of fifty years—which would've been fine had I not just turned forty last month.

It was a little past 6:00 a.m. when I checked out of the motel. My next stop was Fort Hood, Texas, which was a little more than eight hundred miles away. But if I pushed it, I could be there by nightfall.

I made it as far as Wichita before sleep caught me and I had to pull over. I rolled into a small city park not far off the interstate and nosed into a shady spot next to the restroom. I spread out my sleeping bag in the back of my Ranger pickup and settled in for a late afternoon nap.

I awoke to the peaceful blue of a cloudless sky. Birds melodiously chirped their springtime tunes—mocking me.

My watch told me I had slept for the better part of twenty minutes. I got up still tired, but I knew I wouldn't sleep.

The small park wasn't much different than any other city park in small-town America. It was scattered with oak and maple trees and had the requisite amount of picnic tables and restrooms. It had a running fountain and an information board. The only real difference was its cleanliness—it was probably the cleanest park I had ever seen. The lawn was tidy, the restrooms spotless, even the trashcans shone vibrantly.

I washed my face and brushed my teeth in the sparkling sink of the orderly restroom. Oddly, I didn't see another soul the entire time. When I returned to the truck, I began to think I had wandered across a tidy little ghost town.

Then out of nowhere, a short elfish man with black-dyed hair that matched his mustache came traipsing across the parking lot carrying two large buckets. Seeing me, he set the buckets down and jogged on over.

"Howdy," he said pleasantly, brushing his hands together and then wiping them on his light blue tank top. "All the way from Michigan, I see." He pointed to the truck's license plate.

"Yeah," I said, "all the way from Michigan."

He ran his fingers through his thick mustache. He looked as though he wanted to ask me something but wasn't quite sure how to do it. Instead, he stood squinting at me with one eye while continuing to stroke his mustache, his sun-worn face scheming.

"You a veteran?" he asked finally. Taking a step backward, he waited for my reply.

"Yeah, a long time ago," I said. "Why, does it show?"

"Nah," he snarled, "I can just tell." His hand moved from his mustache to his shoulder, and he began scratching vigorously until white marks appeared on his skin.

"Oh yeah," I said. "How can you tell?"

A crooked smile crawled up one side of his face to his squinting eye where, together, they merged into a villainous sneer.

"Oh, you know—the short hair, dog tags. But mostly, I can just tell. Vietnam, I bet. There's been a resurgence of you boys since Reagan got elected. Makes me think that we're headed for World War III."

I didn't want to argue with the little guy, but I couldn't help but be defensive. I wasn't into politics, nor had I any real opinion regarding the current administration's policies. Hell, I hadn't voted in the last three elections. But he didn't even know me, and I hated being pigeonholed like that.

"Yeah, I was in Vietnam, so what?" I snapped. "What's it got to do with Reagan or World War III?"

"Everything," he said, taking a step back. "The man's a genuine warmonger. He's going to make Vietnam look like thumb wrestling. You mark my words," he added.

"I don't know about that," I said. "Listen, I—"

"Oh, you'll see," he said, cutting me off. "He's a goddamned fascist!" There was real venom in his words, and it made me want to lash out at him. Not because of what he'd said but the way he'd said it.

For the better part of fifteen years, I had done a brilliant job of avoiding these types of conversations. He might be right. I had no idea, but I resented him accosting me.

"What do you know about it," I said, more statement than question.

He took another step back and slid his hands into his pockets as though my words had moved him. He gave me a passive smile and then shook his head.

"I'm sorry," he said with a forced smile. And then, pulling his hands from his pockets, he showed me his palms in a sort of truce. "Sometimes I get a little carried away. The name's Chuck." He offered me his small hand, which I shook. Strangely, I thought he looked more like a *Sebastian* or a *Sasha* than a Chuck, with his tiny tank top and short cutoff jeans.

"Name's Henry," I said cordially.

"Pleased to meet you," he said. "I suppose it's not your fault you were over there. Hell, the government lies to all of us. How were you to know? You were probably only following orders, anyway. Most of the vets I know don't blame themselves anymore, but blame the government for its lies. Let me tell you something about Reagan I bet you didn't—"

"Please don't," I said, waving a hand dismissively. "I'm sure it's important and all, but I'm really not interested. I could care less if Reagan is the reincarnation of Adolf Hitler. It wouldn't make a damn bit of difference to me. I went to Vietnam. I did my bit over there and then some. I don't know if it was right or wrong, it was a long time ago. And if World War III is coming, I guess I don't want to know about it. Nothing personal, I just don't give a shit."

Chuck gave me a contemptuous look and then glanced back at his two buckets.

"I'm sorry you feel that way," he said.

"Me too," I said.

Chuck gave me a departing nod and then headed back toward his buckets. I climbed into the truck, started it up, and waited for the air conditioner to kick in. I watched Chuck carry the buckets over to the near part of the lawn and begin sprinkling their contents.

Fertilizer—ole Chuck spreads shit for a living. The man behind the tidy little park. It made perfect sense.

I backed the truck out of the parking lot and drove down a quiet city street west toward the interstate. The short chat with Chuck had rejuvenated me some, although I wasn't sure why. Perhaps the idea of World War III or the end of the world in some way appealed to me.

Now I wished I had voted in the last election. I would've voted for Ronald Reagan.

Chapter Five

July 1961

"Damn it, Helen!" yelled Tom, slamming his fist down on the table. "Don't you start that shit with me again!"

The slam was hard enough to cause milk glasses to topple, plates and silverware to bounce into the air, and steamed corn to scatter across the table. A once heaping pile of fried chicken lay strewn around its plate. My younger sister Maggie immediately began to cry while, without a sound, my youngest sister Gwen excused herself and made for her bedroom. My mother sat quietly staring down at the kernels of corn and the white gravy splattered along the front of her pale-yellow blouse. A stream of milk trickled from the corner of the table. I thought about that thing they say about spilt milk.

Tom glared furiously at my mother, his red eyes squinting, his mouth half open, and his hammer of a fist tightly clenched at the ready for another pound.

"You always start this shit, Helen, just when I'm sitting down to enjoy my dinner, goddamn it! You're just like your damned mother! You think you're so damned superior. Jab, jab, jab—always jabbing at me! You can never leave well enough alone! You just have to keep on needling me, goddamn it! I'm tired of it, and I'm not going to take it tonight!"

My mother was a small woman, but sitting in silence with her shoulders slumped and her hands lying prayerfully in her lap, she seemed even smaller still. Maggie had pushed her plate forward, sobbing into her arms; the pink bow in her hair dipped limply in the gravy on her plate.

"Get to your goddamned room," Tom shouted at her.

Maggie sat up, let out a short high-pitched wail, and then scurried away. I knew I was next, but I didn't move. I had been here before, countless times, and I would never abandon my mother—not when he was like this.

Tom gave me a fierce look, but then his eyes went back to my mother. "I suppose I'm the bad guy now, is that it? Goddamn it! You're going to sit there and cry, is that it? I've ruined dinner, I've ruined everything, is that it? For Christ sake, you just had to push it, didn't you, Helen? You had to jab, jab, jab at me—didn't you? For Christ sake, I'm so sick of *this shit!*"

But *this* was always the *shit* around here. It would start with a little argument about nothing at all, really. A dirty ashtray or a late dinner and then, without warning, it would escalate to this—*this shit.* I too was sick of *this shit.* But with Tom glowering over the dinner table, his nostrils flaring red, white, red, and then white again, the sleeves of his faded blue coveralls rolled up tight to the elbows in his *I-mean-business* way, I could tell that on this evening Tom was wanting of a fight.

It's a sickness, Henry, my mother would say. *When he gets like this, don't say a word and go to your room until it all blows over. Remember, you can't argue with the sick.*

That was always her way. I hated her way.

I defiantly picked up a chicken wing and placed it onto my plate. With my fork, I began separating corn from mashed potatoes. I poured some gravy and then took a rebellious bite.

"I suppose you're on her side," Tom barked at me. "Well? You got something to say, smart guy?"

I didn't say a word but picked at the chicken wing with my fork, the whole time staring at Tom.

"What the hell do you think you're doing?" shouted Tom. "Your mother and I are talking here. Now get out of here!"

The *or else* in his tone frightened me, but it was my own anger that compelled me to take another bite.

"Do you hear me? I said get out of here, your mother and I are discussing things, goddamn it!"

I reached for my glass of milk, but Tom quickly snatched my arm and slammed it to the table.

"Don't even try it! Take a drink and you're through!" He raised his eyebrows. "You understand me? You're through!" Then he slowly released my arm, his fiery eyes still on me. "You want to play this game?"

Tom was right. I was playing a game—his game, much to the disappointment of my mother. But as scared as I was, I had to play. I reached for my glass again and defiantly took a drink.

At first, there was a short pause, as if the world itself had stopped, but then I saw Tom's arms disappear beneath the table, and all at once, everything that was dinner came crashing down upon me.

Dishes smashed on the floor; the gravy boat shattered, splattering scalding gravy on the knobs of my bare ankles. I thought I heard my mother cry out, but I couldn't be certain over the clatter from the avalanche of food and dishes rushing over me. The edge of the table lay in my lap along with a piece of chicken, my plate, and scattered kernels of corn. Milk and gravy soaked through my jeans while mashed potatoes slopped down the front of my tee shirt.

Tom towered over me, still holding the table, his eyes raging.

"You see what happens when you play games with me," he snarled.

He turned the table back flat onto its legs. The plate fell from my lap, rolling on its rim to the far corner of the room where it kicked off the base of the wall.

"I have to cool off!" Tom shouted before charging out of the room.

A few seconds later, the backdoor slammed. I sat staring at my mother, tightly grasping a half-empty glass of milk. For several minutes, neither of us said a word.

"Couldn't you have just left?" my mother said finally.

There was an anger in her tone that sent a wave of guilt running through me. It was true. I should have left the table. I should have let well enough alone.

"I'm sorry, Mom," I said, picking the pieces of chicken from my lap and then brushing corn and mashed potatoes from my shirt. My ankles still burned from the gravy.

"I've told you what to do when he gets like this. Why don't you listen to me?" she pleaded through puffy bloodshot eyes.

"I'm sorry, Mother," I said again. And I was sorry—very sorry.

My mother began gathering up dishes from the floor, and so started her post-fight routine. There wouldn't be any trace of it by the time Tom returned. In fact, it was remarkable how he knew precisely how long to stay away—enough time for my mother to make it as though it never happened.

"There are biscuits in the kitchen. You kids can eat them with butter and jam later if you're hungry," she said, darting into the kitchen with an armload of dishes.

She returned shortly with a dustpan and broom, and she began sweeping the food and broken dishes into small piles on the floor. I began removing the chairs from beneath the table so that she could sweep. We hadn't been at it long when I heard the backdoor close.

"Hello! Anybody home?" a familiar voice called from the kitchen. "Yoo-hoo! Is anybody here?"

Jessie.

Although I was glad it wasn't Tom, I wasn't sure if I wanted Jessie to see me right now. I glanced over at my mother who was wiping frantically at her eyes.

"In here, Jessie," I called out.

My mother gave me a stern look that asked, *why did you go and do that?* But it was too late; Jessie stood in the doorway.

"Hi, Jessie," my mother said pleasantly, but I knew it was forced.

"Hi, Mrs. Talbot," replied Jessie, "I was . . ." Her voice quieted as she scanned the room. "Gosh, what happened here?" she said, eyeing me.

"Oh, we had an accident, dear," my mother said quickly. "But it's all right now. We're getting it cleaned up."

My mother's reply, although clever, wouldn't be enough for Jessie. She would continue to ask questions.

"I need to show Jessie something," I said to my mother. "I'll be back in a while."

Before my mother could protest, I grabbed Jessie by the arm and pulled her out the doorway and through the kitchen. I heard my mother shout something from behind us, but we were already out the backdoor.

Outside, there was no sign of Tom. The sky was clear of clouds, but the air was heavy with smoke from a far-off forest fire, making the world appear an ill shade of brownish yellow.

Saucy leaped up from her spot at the corner of the small porch with a "let's go" look about her face. She sauntered over and then followed us down the driveway.

"What was *that* all about back there?" asked Jessie when we reached the dirt road in front of the house.

"What was *what* all about back there?" I said, playing dumb in the off chance she might let it go.

"You know, the mess and the broken dishes," she said and then, stopping suddenly, she spun me around, giving me the once-over. "Look at you, you're a mess. You're covered with . . ." She picked a piece of something off the front of my tee shirt and examined it closely. "*Corn*," she said, flicking it away.

"My parents were fighting," I said, walking by her.

"Hey, wait up!" she yelled. "Your parents were fighting and you get covered in food? How does that happen? Was it a food fight?" She laughed.

"It's not funny, Jess!" I snapped.

"I'm sorry," she said, still laughing, then said calmly, "I guess I don't understand."

"No, you don't understand! Tom got all pissed off and dumped the table on me!"

"Again, I'm sorry, but why did he dump it on you? I thought you said it was your parents who were fighting."

"I don't know," I said, frustrated. "Tom wanted me to leave, and I wouldn't, and then he got all pissed off and dumped the table on me!"

"I see," she said, nodding. "But why didn't you just leave?"

"I don't know why. I probably should've. Tom wanted me to, my mother wanted me to. I just didn't want to. I don't know why. I didn't want to give in to the *bastard!*"

My mother had often referred to Tom as a *bastard* when he got angry; it was the only semi-swear word I'd ever heard her use.

"It was stupid, okay. So instead of eating my dinner, I'm wearing it!"

She giggled.

"It's a little funny though."

I glanced down at the front of my shirt. It was sort of funny, and I grinned at her.

"I suppose," I said.

"So are you hungry?" she said.

"Not really, why?"

"Well, if you are, you can always lick the front of your shirt," she said, laughing.

"You know, Jess? You really should go into comedy. Maybe you could be the next Lucille Ball?"

"Maybe, but I'm not as funny as you . . . look!" she said with another burst of laughter.

"Funny! I see you think a lot of yourself!"

"So what did you want to show me?" she asked.

"I didn't really have anything to show you. I just wanted to get out of there."

"Well then, what do you want to do?"

"I was thinking that we could go take a look at your grandfather's gold mine. It's up the highway about a mile or so. There's still some old equipment around there, not too far off the highway, a quarter mile or so. I couldn't tell you what it all is, but there's a lot of it"

"Neat," she said.

The three of us went marching up the highway, Saucy leading the way. The thick smoke seized my lungs, and I felt a light wheeze in my chest and then coughed.

"You all right?" asked Jessie.

"I'm fine, why?"

"You sound awful," she said, making a face.

"It's just a little asthma. I'll be okay."

"A *little* asthma?" she said. "My cousin has asthma pretty bad, and he can't do anything outside without wheezing. He almost died a couple of times. I've never heard of a *little* asthma."

"Yeah, well I don't have it like that. It was a lot worse when I was a kid, but now it's not so bad. Just a little wheeze, that's all. On account of the smoke."

"Okay, as long as you don't die on me," she said.

I jogged ahead of her a little ways and then began walking backward. "You know something?"

Jessie sent me a curious look.

"Did you know that I am the fastest *backwards walker* in the country?" I said.

"The country, huh?" she said, letting out a little laugh.

"Maybe the fastest in the world," I said. "In fact, it's a new sport. They call it *backwards racing*."

"I've never heard of it," Jessie said, scowling.

I picked up my pace and created some distance between us.

"That's because you can't do it!" I shouted back at her.

"Bullshit!" she yelled, and then she ran after me.

"Backwards!" I shouted at her.

Turning around, Jessie nearly tripped, but she managed to regain her balance and walk backward a little ways. But every time she tried to gain a little speed, she'd stumble until, finally, she fell backward, nearly doing a reverse somersault in the middle of the highway. She got to her feet quickly and began dusting herself off.

I stopped and ran back to her.

"You okay?" I asked.

"I'm fine!" she said, wiping dirt from the backside of her jeans. "You're not so fast!"

"I know I'm faster than you," I said smugly.

She sent me a vicious look.

"Well, it's stupid anyway," she said, crinkling up her face. "Who has ever heard of *backwards racing*?"

"It's all right. I'll give you another crack at me later," I said reassuringly.

We continued our march up the highway in quiet formation. This time I led the way, with Jessie and Saucy trailing close behind. The only sound was that of our footsteps on the pavement and my rhythmic wheezing. We weren't far from the trailhead when, suddenly, I stumbled over something and found myself falling fast to the ground. I landed hard on my hands, nearly cracking my head on the highway.

"Taking a *trip, rube*?" said Jessie standing over me, a shameless grin on her face.

She offered me a hand. I waved it off and quickly got back to my feet. Without looking at her, I brushed myself off.

"Nice," I said. "How long have you been waiting to do that?"

"Since about the first time I saw you!" She laughed.

I forced a smile because I knew, in her mind, we were now even.

"We're getting close," I said. "Look for a trail that leads into the brush. Sometimes it's hard to see from the road."

Lining the highway was a wall of thick birch saplings separating the highway from a creek, which we could hear burbling on the other side. I spied Saucy dash into the brush not far ahead of us.

"There it is!" I shouted.

Jessie followed me down the tricky embankment, and we both jogged over to the spot where I had seen Saucy go in. I pushed my way through the small indentation in the brush, taking the time to settle the whipping branches so they wouldn't slap at Jessie. It wasn't long before we stepped out onto the narrow bank of a small but spirited creek.

"*Rocks*," said Jessie, peering across the creek at an enormous rock-strewn ridge. "I've never seen so many rocks and rock piles in my life. Everywhere you look around here, more rocks. Don't they have dirt in Alaska?"

"Sure we do," I said, shifting sideways to give her a little more room on the tight bank. "But the miners came through here with the gold dredge and sluices and scooped it all up."

"*Sluices?*"

"Yeah, sluices. That's what separates the gold from the dirt," I said. "After the gold's taken out, everything else is spit back out, which is mostly just rocks like the ones you see all over. That's what made all the rock piles," I said, pointing at a gigantic pile of rocks sticking out from the trees. "They're called *tailing piles*."

"*Tailing piles?*"

"Yeah, the rocks left behind by the dredge are called *tailings,* and the big piles of rock are called *tailing piles*. Haven't you ever seen the big old dredge in Fox?" I asked.

"Oh yeah," she said, nodding. "That's what that big thingy is? Sure, I've seen it."

"That's the old Number 8 Gold Dredge. It's the one that spit out most the tailing around here."

"Where do we cross?" asked Jessie, glancing up and down the creek.

"Right here," I replied. "Now, you can either take your shoes off and wade across, or you can try and jump it. It's your choice, but I don't think you'll make it since you can't get a running start."

I was sure she'd take this as a kind of veiled challenge, but I knew I was right about the running start. The creek was over six feet wide and at least two feet deep at the center. The consequences of not making it would be extremely wet.

Jessie studied the creek.

"We should probably wade across," she said finally before kneeling down to unlace her sneakers. "I could definitely make it, though, if I got a running start," she added.

"No doubt," I said beneath my breath.

After successfully wading the creek, we stopped to put our shoes back on. Jessie finished first and sat on her knees with her arms folded, staring at me.

"What?" I asked.

"Your parents fight a lot, don't they?" she said.

"All the time," I said. "So what?"

"I can tell it really it bothers you," she said.

"Of course it bothers me. Before they divorced, didn't your parents ever fight?"

"I don't know," she said, shrugging. "If they did, I never saw them. I never really saw them do anything together. They both kind of did their own thing. Sure, they'd fight, I suppose. Not the way your parents do."

When I had finished tying my shoes, I leaned back on my elbows eyeing Jessie.

"Then how'd they do it?"

"My mom calls it the *silent treatment*. My folks wouldn't speak to one another for days, weeks even. They'd do all sorts of things to piss each other off, though. Mom might not come home or she'd sleep in bed with me for days. Then Daddy would have all his buddies over, and they'd get drunk and mess up the house. The entire time neither one said a word to the other about any of it. They just wouldn't talk to each other. Believe me, it could get bad," Jessie said, nodding. "There was always this *thing* between them. I can't really explain it, but when they were together, you could feel it. I hated it. But since the divorce, it's not there anymore. Actually, they probably speak to each other more now than they ever did when they were married."

No one would ever accuse Tom of giving my mother the silent treatment. It was a good thing that we didn't have any close neighbors, or surely they would be complaining about the noise.

"Sometimes, I wish my parents would divorce," I said, standing. "But I don't think my mother will ever leave Tom, no matter how much of a *bastard* he is."

"Why's that?"

"Because if she hasn't left him by now, she probably never will," I said. "She says he's sick and can't help himself."

"What's he sick from?"

"Tom used to drink a lot," I said, "but I've never seen him take a drop. My mother says it doesn't matter, though. It's a sickness some folks get, and once you have the sickness, you always have it. That's why he's still a bastard sometimes. She says Tom drank for so long that, after a while, it doesn't take much for him get drunk and lose control. I guess Tom was a pretty mean drunk too—meaner than when I've ever seen him, my mother says. She says it's because Tom lost his *tolerance* for it. Once you lose your *tolerance* to it, that's when it's real bad, I guess. I'm not so sure if I know what she means by it."

"I think I do," said Jessie. "There's no one more ornery than my granddaddy when he's been drinking. But sometimes when he gets real drunk . . ." She hesitated, staring off into the distance. "God help us if he ever loses his *tolerance*," she said, shaking her head.

We headed up the ridge. It was a lot steeper than I remembered. When we reached the top, I was wheezing again. Jessie, too, looked winded.

"We need to rest for a minute," I said. I squatted down, trying to catch my breath.

"All right," she said. "It is smoky up here."

"Tom says there's a fire . . . about seventy miles to the north . . . up toward Circle," I gasped.

"So how far away is the mine?" Jessie asked.

"Actually, it's just down . . . the other side of the ridge. Go ahead . . . take a look . . . you can see it from there," I said.

"You going to be all right?" asked Jessie.

"Fine," I said, waving her on.

Jessie walked the twenty or so feet to the crest of the ridge and peered over.

"I can see it!" she exclaimed, glancing back at me. "And it doesn't seem so smoky down there. What are those thingies?"

I liked the way Jessie called anything she couldn't readily identify a *thingy*. The excitement in her voice compelled me to stand and walk over to where she was standing.

The valley below looked like a massive grave left uncovered, as if it had been specifically excavated to enshrine the dozen or so oddly shaped pieces of machinery that lay like rusted iron skeletons waiting to be interred.

"Gosh, this is Granddaddy's mine?"

"Part of it . . . at least it used to be," I said, still winded.

Jessie had been right, the valley did appear clear of smoke.

It might have been the smoke wrenching at my chest, denying my brain oxygen, but on a whim, I reached over and placed my arm around Jessie. Never in my life had I been so bold, but surprisingly, she didn't push away or protest. After a few moments, I pulled her closer, and she leaned her head into mine and slid her arm behind my back. We stood silently, looking out over the valley, holding each other for several long minutes before I released her. Not because I had to or I wanted to, but because I didn't want her to be the first to let go.

I did take her hand, however, and lead her down the backside of the ridge where we stood beneath the faint shadows of the mysterious-looking contraptions.

Saucy moved from piece to piece, sniffing.

"What are they?" asked Jessie.

"Not sure, really. They were just here. I'm sure your grandfather knows. The gold dredge could have left them behind, or maybe they're part of something bigger. I don't know. I only came across them last summer. Your guess is as good as mine."

"They look like big rusty bugs."

There were about a dozen or so of the big rusty bugs, all made of iron rods, plates, and cable, but no two appeared alike. Mostly, they were the same size (roughly ten feet tall and ten feet in diameter), and they were either set vertically on giant corrugated wheels like those on a locomotive or laid sideways on elongated tracks like those on a bulldozer. Yet all were engineless.

One that appeared the most buglike was set on several pairs of enormous jointed legs that jutted out from its sides and arched steadily downward into the rocky earth. It was slightly taller than the rest and vaunted two large rusty antennae-like poles extending upward from its base. The poles stood parallel to each other and were connected at the top by a smaller bar that wasn't rusted at all. Beneath the bar and affixed at the base of the two poles was a partially perforated chute, which descended from the base of the two poles almost to the ground, making the big rusty bug appear to have a long obtruding tongue.

"Check it out," I said, leading Jessie to it.

Releasing her hand, I charged up the front of the tongue to where the large poles connected to the base. Swinging around one of the poles, I stepped out onto the top of one of the jointed legs. Taking a hold of the gray bar, still a little out of breath, I dangled there for a few seconds. Then, lifting my legs up and down and back and forth, I gained enough momentum to coerce my body into a swing.

"You can really get going!" I shouted down to her.

"That's neat," she shouted back up at me. "It's like a gymnastics bar!"

"I suppose," I gasped. I was moving well now, my shoulders nearly parallel with the bar on my backswing.

After a few more moments, I stopped myself by kicking out my legs and catching the vertical poles. Then sliding my hands along the bar, I maneuvered my feet back onto the shoulder of the jointed leg and then, exhausted, skipped down the chute back to where Jessie was standing.

"Cool, huh," I said in a pronounced wheezing. "You can do . . . other things . . . like hang from your legs and . . . and do chin-ups," I said.

"You must have spent hours doing chin-ups with your massive arms," she laughed while pinching at my biceps. "What a *rube!* Now let me try, I had a year of gymnastics."

Jessie ran up the chute and climbed onto the bar similar to the way I had, only much faster. Once on the bar, she slowly began swinging herself back and forth, always keeping her legs together and bending only at the waist. Higher and higher, she soared upward until, at times, her body was parallel with the bar. Then in one fluent motion, she thrust her legs straight upward into the air and pulled her entire body over the bar until, finally, she came to a stop with her hands holding the bar at her waist.

"It's like the uneven bars, except with only one bar, of course," she said, smiling down at me.

"Wow!" I shouted. It was all I could think to say.

After holding herself above the bar for a few more seconds, I watched as she swayed slightly forward and then, hesitating, dove back down below the bar where she swiftly regained enough momentum to thrust herself back up and over it again. Her movements were mesmerizing, as she went twirling gracefully around the bar.

It was so amazing to me that it wasn't until I saw Jessie lying flat on her back on the ground beneath the front of the chute with blood running from her chin that I realized that something had gone terribly wrong. At first, it had appeared that she had purposely let go of the bar during the high point of her backswing, but then she plunged headfirst onto the top of the chute, somersaulting violently down to the ground.

"Jess!" I shouted, horrified by the reality of the scene. I quickly ran over to her. She lay on her back, her left leg twisted awkwardly behind her body. Blood covered her neck and shoulders, oozing from an open gash beneath her chin. Tears and terror filled her eyes. She put a finger to her chin cringing at the sight of her own blood.

"Don't move, Jess. Whatever you do, don't move!" I shouted. I removed my tee shirt and held it up under her chin. I took her hand and placed it on the tee shirt with mine.

"Hold on to this," I said, "and don't move. I'm going to get help!"

"No," she said gasping, her front teeth blackened with blood. "Don't go. Don't leave me alone." She tried to sit up but couldn't. "My leg, my leg. It hurts, Hen!"

"Okay, Jess, don't move!

"Everything is going to be all right," I said, trying to convince the both of us. "I'm going to get help!"

"No . . . please," she said. "Don't leave me, I can go with you."

She tried sitting up again, but again she couldn't. "Don't leave me, please, Hen! Don't leave me here!" she cried.

"I have to go, Jess. I'll be right back with help, I promise. Hold the shirt on it, and I'll be back as soon as I can," I said, pressing her hand tightly against the tee shirt and her chin. Already the shirt was soaked through with blood.

"You won't come back!" she cried, her tears mixing with the blood. "Please don't leave me here, Hen! I'm so scared!"

"You're going to be all right, I promise you, Jess. I have to go and get help. I'll be right back," I said. And then, glancing at Saucy, I had an idea. "Saucy will stay here with you, okay? And I'll be right back with help!" I removed my necklace and placed it in the palm of her other hand. "Hold onto it for me, okay, Jess? It's lucky, remember?

"Okay," she whispered.

I released my hand from hers and the tee shirt.

"Saucy, stay!" I commanded the dog. "Stay here with Jess!"

Saucy gave me a puzzled look, but didn't move.

Then I ran.

I ran up and over the ridge, back into smoky air and hard down the other side. Already I felt the burn in my chest as I sprinted toward the creek. I wasn't exactly sure what I was going to do, but I knew I was in a hurry to get to the highway. Perhaps a car—surely one would come along. And if I didn't see a car, I could always run to the nearest house. I tried to think of all the places I could go when I got to the highway. My house was probably as close as any, and Tom had a truck.

Despite the smoke and my asthmatic airways, I ran faster than I had ever run. When I reached the creek, I didn't hesitate but leaped over it in full stride, barely clearing it and stumbling headfirst into the brush on the other side. Dozens of spiny branches clawed at my bare chest, back, and stomach. Frantically, I got to my feet and tore through the leafy pathway and up the embankment in a half run, half crawl.

I scanned the highway in both directions. Nothing. I listened intently for the saving sounds of an engine, but my ears only echoed the rhythmic rasps of my insistent wheeze.

So again I ran. I wheezed, coughed, and gagged, but kept on running. Several times, I thought I heard something behind me, but each time I stopped to look, I saw only empty highway. After a half mile or so, I began to feel dizzy and I had to stop. I coughed, threw up, but then was running again.

I prayed to Jesus, to everything I thought sacred that something, anything might happen along.

The answer to my prayers came rumbling at me in the form of a semitruck, its stacks billowing smoke as black as parson robes. I waved and screamed as loud as my winded lungs would allow until the truck slowed and then squealed to a stop a few feet in front of me.

"Help . . . need help!" I gasped, trying to yell above the noise of the diesel engine. "My friend . . . she's hurt . . . back up the road a ways . . . off the road a ways! She's hurt bad . . . need help!"

Immediately, the trucker reached for something, a radio, relaying what I had said.

"It's going to be all right, son. They're on their way," said the trucker in a deep throaty voice.

"Please . . . have them go . . . through the brush back there . . ." I said as my vision began to blur. "Across the creek . . . and up and over the . . ."

"It's going to be all right. They'll find her, son. They've dispatched a helicopter."

All at once, the world around me darkened.

———

I awoke in bed behind a constricting plastic mask that enveloped my entire face. Metal rails ran alongside the bed, surrounded by thick drawn curtains. A hospital. Not sure how I had gotten here or whether I was alone, but then I remembered the one thing I needed to remember.

Jessie.

"Hello!" I cried out, my voice hollow behind the plastic mask.

Talking tickled the back of my throat, and I coughed. Then all at once, the drapery walls around me drew away, and a young woman with a soft round face appeared before me, smiling warmly.

"Hello," the woman said in a tone that matched her smile. "I've been wondering when you were going to wake up. I'm Nurse Ann."

"I need to know—"

"Just a minute, please," she interrupted. "I need to check some things first, dear. And let me get that mask off of you."

Still smiling, she lowered the metal railing at the side of the bed and then removed the mask. Putting the stethoscope to her ears, she placed the other end on my chest, listening attentively, her eyes shifting from the ceiling to me.

"Take a deep breath, please," she said.

I did as told. "Can you tell me—"

"Another," she said, cutting me off and then moving the stethoscope up my chest. "Okay great. Now I need to have you sit up, dear."

I again did as told, but her persistent orders were beginning to frustrate me. She placed the stethoscope in several other spots on my chest and back, each time requiring me to take a deep breath. The entire process annoyed the hell out of me. I only wanted to find out about Jessie.

"Your lungs sound great. How's your breathing, dear?" she said with another smile.

"I'm fine," I shouted. "It's fine, really. How is—"

"You're not experiencing any blockage in your airways?" she said.

"No," I snapped at her.

"I heard you cough earlier. Do you have any shortness of breath, dear?" she said. "Do you feel any—"

"No, for Christ's sake, no! I'm fine!" I screamed at her.

Nurse Ann's eyes widened, the smile quickly melting from her face.

"It's okay dear, really," she said calmly. "I only need—"

"Could you please just tell me about Jessie?" I said. "I need to know about Jessie."

"*Jessie?*" She looked confused.

"Yeah, Jessie," I repeated.

Then instantly, her face brightened, the smile returned, and I thought it must take more than I had to piss this nurse off.

"You mean the young girl that came in with you," she said, nodding. "She's here, dear, and she's going to be fine—thanks to you."

"May I see her?" I asked.

"Oh no, dear, I'm sorry," she said. "She just had surgery on her leg, but she's going to be fine. She's in recovery and needs her rest. And so do you, it seems," she said, glancing at her watch.

"But she's going to be okay, right?"

"I told you, she's going to be fine, dear. Now you need to get some rest."

Reaching beneath the bed, she pulled the metal railing back up into place.

"Oh," she said suddenly, "I almost forgot. I do have something here for you." Rummaging through one of her pockets, she pulled out a small blue envelope and handed it to me.

"For you," she said pleasantly.

Then in an instant, Nurse Ann disappeared behind the curtains. I started to call after her, but she was gone, and I was alone again.

Opening the envelope, I was surprised to find my old moose-bone necklace, now stained with Jessie's blood. There was also a folded-up piece of paper. It was a note. I slipped the necklace over my head and read:

Hen,

I thought you might need this more than me right now.

It is good luck. By the way, you're the best backwards racer

in the world. But you're still a rube!

Jess

P.S. I got to ride in a whirlybird.

I knew I wouldn't sleep. Not until I found out more about Jessie. I wondered about the surgery, her leg, and her chin. I remembered the blood and the terror I had seen in her eyes. I thought about how she begged me not to leave her, and how I had hated to go. Nurse Ann had said she would be fine, and I supposed that would have to be good enough for now, but I had already decided that when it came to Jessie, nothing would ever be good enough.

Chapter Six

September 1968

The camp's makeshift mess hall stunk so bad of mildew and rotting chow that it nearly made me puke every time I entered. Even the sturdy aroma of recently cooked beef stroganoff couldn't conceal the stench. But every day at 1800, it was my belly, not my nose, which begged me to enter. I supposed that's the way it was with any other outfit a million miles from home.

When I had heaped my tray with the rank but bland combination of noodles and beefy-like gravy, I scanned the place searching for a spot to dine. Then I saw Ho eating alone at a nearby table.

It wasn't the usual protocol, as aircraft commanders kept mostly to themselves and rarely mixed with the peter pilots, especially a slope peter like Ho. Ho was good guy, though.

"What do you say, Mr. Ho," I said, shooting him a grin. "Got enough room here for me?"

"Sure, Mr. Allen," Ho said. "Have seat."

"Don't mind if I do. Have you seen Flanny or Broadway around here?"

"No, I don't see them much. The lieutenant is pissed at Flanny. You know, that LZ stuff."

"Yeah, I guess I do," I said, placing my napkin in my lap and then poking at the mound of shit-covered noodles with my fork.

Ho had nearly finished his and was mopping up the remaining gravy with a half-eaten piece of bread.

"The lieutenant," said Ho, shaking his head, "he don't like me too much."

"Yeah, I know. The lieutenant can be abrasive." I couldn't count number of times I had used *abrasive* to describe the Broadway.

"Hey, Bronco!" shouted Flanny from behind me. He nodded at Ho before sitting down next to me. "What the fuck you boy scouts up to?"

"Stroganoff," I said, glad to see Flanny.

"You mean *stroke-me-off*, don't you?" he said. "That's some cement-looking shit, don't you think?"

"Delicious," I said.

"*Flanagan!*" a voice echoed loudly from the far side of the mess hall. "I need a word!" Lieutenant Broadway came hurtling toward us. After shoving aside a broom-pushing private that got in his way, he plopped down next to Ho and stared fiercely across the table at Flanny.

"You trying to get us killed?" Broadway shouted at him. "That's twice in four days, you fucking little shit!"

A bead of sweat rolled down the top of his forehead and in between his crossed eyebrows where it lost momentum at the bottom of his giant porous nose.

"Why is it every time you got lead, we get our asses shot off? Don't you know the book says we're supposed to bug out if it's hot like that?

"*The book?*" said Flanny. "Hell, Lieutenant, I didn't know you could read."

"Fuck you!" snapped Broadway. "You know it's true. You know every goddamned one of these extractions has been hotter than hell! You know you don't have to go in! You know these zipperheads we're taxiing around don't give a shit! Hell, half of them are VC anyways!" he shouted at Ho. "What do they care if we leave them out there in their own fucking jungle! Why risk our asses for them, Flanagan? And don't give me that duty bullshit either. You know we're not required to go in when it's hot like that! Some people around here might think you're some hotshot and all," he said, glancing over at me, "but I'm on to you, Flanagan. Your shit stinks like the rest of them! I'm not going to let my ship get chewed all to hell because of your ass!"

Flanny coolly took a bite of his stroganoff but didn't look up.

"Do you hear me, Flanagan?"

Broadway glanced around the mess hall and saw the numerous eyes upon him. If Flanny couldn't hear him, certainly everyone else did.

"You're going to get us all killed leading us into these hot boxes!"

Flanny took another bite of his stroganoff and a sip of his coffee. Then, he deliberately wiped his mouth with his napkin and attempted to pick at something in his teeth with his thumbnail. Finally, he looked up at Broadway.

"You know, Lieutenant," he said, giving him a little nod, "I'll tell you what. Why don't you go and scream at Major Whipple—see if he'll ever make you lead on one of these missions. Then your pussy ass can take us somewhere safe and quiet. A nice little river or lake where maybe we can all have a picnic."

"I'm not fucking around, Flanagan!" Broadway barked.

Flanny looked over at Ho.

"Mr. Ho, perhaps you could make a salad or something." Then turning to me, "Allen, what kind of salad do you like?"

"I suppose I fancy potato salad," I said with a chuckle.

"That's good," said Flanny, "because I like potato salad too."

Broadway shook his head, and his face reddened.

"I like a nice steak, Lieutenant," said Flanny. "Grilled just right—medium rare with just a hint of Worcester."

Ho snickered.

"Shut up, gook!" Broadway fired at him. "I'll waste you right here, you nip motherfucker, and nobody would give a rat's ass!"

"Now, Lieutenant," said Flanny calmly, "the rats around here are bad enough without you winding them up like that."

I laughed while Ho stared down at his plate, shaking his head, a smile spread across his face.

"Fuck you all!" shouted Broadway. "You're all fucking nuts! I'll have you know, Mr. Flanagan, you're on notice."

"Your notice is duly noted, Lieutenant," replied Flanny.

Broadway got up and headed toward the chow line.

"Thanks a lot, Flanny," I said when Broadway was out of earshot. "I still have to live with him. He's going to be in a mood for a while, I can tell."

"What do you mean? That boy's always in a mood," said Flanny.

I hadn't slept much since arriving in Vietnam nearly eight months ago. I was averaging only a few hours a night, and it was rarely continuous. Rather than lie in my bunk staring blankly at the ceiling of the hooch, I decided to head out to the tarmac where I could stretch out on the deck of the chopper and listen to Armed Forces Radio. Guy, my crew chief, would be here at 0600 for a routine inspection of the ship anyway, but since that was still a couple hours away, I thought I might kick back and maybe catch a baseball score or two.

The small hours of the morning had a solemn effect on me, easing some of the uneasiness of the day before. Still, it wasn't enough to allow me to sleep. It wasn't too long, however, before a sportscaster broadcast the American League scores, and I learned that the Tigers had lost a close one to the Red Sox. But the Tigers were feisty this year and, so far, had been playing great ball and had a real shot at the pennant.

It was nearly five when I heard someone approaching the chopper, but I only saw shadows.

"Who goes there?" I shouted into the darkness.

"It's me, Westin, sir—here for the inspection." Guy's West Texas drawl was as thick as the lenses of his black-rimmed glasses. A good-natured fellow, Guy also had a sharp and logical disposition

67

that worked well in crises or calm. The only thing conflicting about Guy was his uniform, which was always at odds with his tall and lanky frame.

"Good morning, Guy," I said pleasantly. "You're here a little earlier than I expected."

"I know—woke up early and I thought you might be here. I brought you some coffee," he said, handing me a steaming thermos-top cup.

"That's nice of you, Guy. I've got to tell you—sometimes I think you sound like Mickey Mantle with that accent."

"Well, I aint from Oklahoma like The Mick. A lot of West Texas boys might take offense to that," he said with an "aw, shucks" grin.

"Sorry," I said. "I didn't mean to offend your boys—hell, Mick's about the best I've ever seen."

"You didn't offend me none," he said, still grinning. "Ole Mick hits that ball pretty good—for an Okee!"

I laughed. It was still too dark to do an external visual inspection of the chopper, but that was okay, as I didn't mind shooting the shit with Guy for a while.

He sat down next to me on the edge of the deck, neither of us saying anything for several minutes.

"I think our bird is in pretty good shape, sir," he said, finally breaking the silence. "I took a good look at her yesterday."

I nodded. "You're a great crew chief, Westin," I said. "It's nice knowing that the ship will do what it's supposed to do when we're out there in the shit. I want you to know that I've appreciated the cool and collected way you've conducted yourself on these missions . . . at times, it's made all the difference," I added.

"Thank you, sir," said Guy. "Really, thank you . . . it means a lot coming from you, sir," he added awkwardly.

"I'll be glad when we are finished with this ARVN support," I said, changing the subject. "They're a real pain in the ass."

"How much longer do you think will we be flying support for them?"

"God knows," I replied. "Until they make some headway against the NVA, I guess. Supposedly, it's quite a force. If the LZs are any indication, it might be a while before we're all through."

"That's what I figured," said Guy, sounding disheartened. "I don't think them guys even fight."

The first rays of sunshine squeezed over the horizon, striking us directly in the face. Guy put his hand up to shield the sun and then looked over at me.

"I've heard the rumors—I know what you mean," I said. "After the insertion, they hide out in the jungle until it's time for us to pick them up. I hear they sit there getting drunk or high—unless Charlie happens to spot them, and then the cowardly bastards run. They say that's why the LZs have been so damn hot on the extractions—because Charlie knows where to find us. I've heard the stories. God, I hope that's not true. We've already lost a couple of crews to ambushes this week."

Guy pulled down his cap and then snapped his sun visor onto his glasses, flipping it down like a center fielder preparing to shag a fly. "Those were good guys too," said Guy. "A couple of the pilots were on their second tour, and that crash the other day killed Noodles."

"*Noodles?*"

"Yeah, door gunner. They call him Noodles on account he's so skinny. He and Jake used to pal around together. They went to rival high schools in Chicago. They were always talking about the dames they laid." Guy laughed. "It was funny, actually. One time they got to talking about some girl they used to know—turns out they'd both been with her."

"No kidding?"

"Yeah, can you believe that?" Guy chuckled. "It's sure a small world. Anyway, ole Noodles was all pissed off about it and was fixin' to fight." Guy shook his head, laughing. "Damnedest thing. Seems that Noodles really liked the dame—kept a picture of her and all. Said he would have married her too, except he said he couldn't trust her."

"Because she got on with Jake?"

"No, because he says she gave him the clap."

"No way!"

"Yep," said Guy, nodding at me. "And when Noodles tells this to Jake, well . . . ole Jake, he can't help himself—starts laughing and carrying on about it. This makes Noodles mad, boy, and he hauls off and decks Jake—knocks him flat to the floor. But Jake, he just gets up and keeps on laughing. So Noodles squares up and hits him again, but Jake just keeps on laughing—eye swollen, face bleeding, and all. This goes on, but no matter what Noodles does to him, Jake keeps on laughing. Finally, Noodles demands to know what's so goddamned funny." Guy paused to wipe his eye.

"So what *was* so damn funny?"

Guy continued to laugh. "Because," said Guy, "ole Jake, he says he gave that shit to her!"

"No way!" I said.

"Them two been friends ever since."

We both laughed together for several seconds before our laughter faded into the quiet of the early morning. That's the way it was in Vietnam. Nothing was funny for very long. I didn't even know Noodles, but the man was dead—and that certainly wasn't very funny.

"How's Jake taking it?" I asked.

"All right, I guess," said Guy. "He didn't appear too broke up about it. Said the son of a bitch owed him fifty bucks and that he'd never loan money again to anybody in-country without taking proper security."

"I thought you said they were pals?"

"Oh, they were pals all right—death just does that to people sometimes. He's just trying to move on the only way he knows how," said Guy, flipping up his sun visor. "It's just the way some people are, that's all."

We were seventh in a row of eight slicks flying in a diamond formation. Flanny and his boys had the lead, as we were on our way to extract the South Vietnamese soldiers we had dropped off early that morning. Flanny had radioed that he had spied the pop smoke marking the LZ, and the gunships had warned us that it might be hot.

Sunshine blasted through the windshield, making it nearly impossible to see even with my visor down. "Keep an eye on Broadway and Masterson," I said to Ho. "We'll keep pace with them until we can see something. I'm glad we're not up front today."

"We one of the last ones in," said Ho, "so shouldn't be too bad."

"I hope to Christ somebody up front knows where in the hell we're going," I said as I watched a tuft of the hazy red pop smoke go swirling by the windshield.

"This is 105, on short final, over!" I called over the radio. Nosing the chopper down, I suddenly spied dozens of specklike soldiers sprinting from a tattered tree line toward waiting choppers. Bursts of machine-gun fire flashed from the dark forest behind them, causing several of them to stumble and then flop lifelessly to the ground.

"Here they come!" I shouted.

I reduced power and then, flaring the chopper, I set it down a few yards from a cluster of wind-bent elephant grass. Immediately, a half dozen or so of the faster soldiers changed their direction and started racing toward us.

"And here come the shit!" cried Ho.

Machine-gun fire flickered from the tree line directly behind the onrushing soldiers, sparing them but tearing into the side of the chopper. A few seconds later, Jake was pulling the men up onto the deck, their sweat-soaked faces pale and panic-stricken.

Afterward, Jake gave me the thumbs-up signal.

"We're all clear, sir!" he shouted at me.

I hit the power and the chopper lurched forward, dragging ass and slow to lift. We weren't more than a couple of feet off the ground when a thunderous blast rocked us from the left, whipping the tail-boom around and sliding the ship sideways.

"Over there!" Ho shouted pointing over my shoulder, and I turned in time to see a throng of yellow, orange, and red flames blaze up into an enormous billowing cloud of black smoke. "It's one of ours—a gunship!"

"Bug out! The fuckers got rockets! Bug out, over! Bug out!" the call came blaring over the radio.

I hit the power again and nudged the stick. But just as we began to lean forward, another explosion rocked us—this time from the right side, dropping the ship hard to the ground and twisting us clockwise nearly a quarter turn. From our new position, I saw three VC men draped in camouflage roughly a hundred yards away—one of them holding a rocket launcher while the other two manned a heavy machine gun. To the right, I recognized a ship lying on its side engulfed entirely in flames. Its skids pitched upward, and its main rotor blades snapped off at their base.

"It's Masterson!" I yelled.

Suddenly, a wafting cloud of thick black smoke surged from the downed ship, and Ho and I could only watch in horror as a single human arm came flailing from out of the smoky mess, waving frantically at the sky for a few hopeless seconds before being swallowed by another swell of flames.

"Shit!" cried Ho, looking away.

For a minute, I thought I might be sick but, swallowing hard, it passed. I gunned the power and then, increasing the pitch, I pushed hard on the stick. The chopper bucked but then inched forward, the rotors screaming as the low RPM light started to flash.

"Easy!" Ho shouted. "We don't want to stall it!"

"I know, I know, shit!" I shouted. "I can't see a thing in all this smoke. I'm sure the bastards have that rocket launcher pointed right at us!"

I pulled back on the stick while adjusting the pitch to bring up the RPMs.

"We're too heavy," said Ho.

"How many do we have back there?"

Ho shrugged.

"Dump everything that's not a gun or a human being!" I yelled into the intercom. A few seconds later, we were climbing through a pocket of pitch-black smoke. "I can't see the tree line! I can't see the ground either. Give me a goddamned visual!" I screamed at Ho.

"We're heading straight for the trees, we need to get up!" he replied.

The truth was we were also heading directly toward the ambushers. The smoke was solid in every direction, and I could suddenly feel my chest tightening.

"We're going to hit them or the trees!" I cried out.

We needed altitude fast—lots of it.

"There!" shouted Ho, this time pointing out his side window.

The smoke had cleared enough to see the three ambushers almost directly below us. Fortunately, their weapons were pointing in different directions.

"To hell with them! We've got to clear the trees!"

"The problem is," said Ho with panic in his tone, "no altitude . . . it's going be close."

Ho tapped the altimeter, which only confirmed our fate, and then shaking his head, he stared at me nervously. The radio started to screech the chaos—two, maybe three maydays—and another earful of alarms and warnings. All I could think to do was switch it off and increase the pitch and power. But Ho was right; we weren't gaining altitude fast enough. We were going to be shot down or fed to the trees—or maybe both. There was nothing left to do but pray. I reached for my old necklace, and then closing my eyes, I prayed to God that we would clear the trees.

For several long seconds, I could hear only the straining sound of the rotors as they struggled to pull us skyward. Then suddenly there was a loud thud, and I opened my eyes in time to see a leafy branch slide off the windshield as the ship began to sway and sputter. But despite the steep pitch and the weight of the ship, we were still moving upward, and after a few more long seconds, I was staring down at the treetops.

"We're over," shouted Ho.

I blinked hard and then, glancing over at Ho, I smiled. I quickly switched on the radio to a clamor of activity regarding the ambush, but all I could see through the windshield was empty blue sky—we were clear. Kicking down on the left pedal, I eased the stick and the chopper to the west, and then back around to the south. There was something about the feeling of a hard descending turn that had a calming effect on me. I wasn't sure why. Maybe it was just the slight change in the rhythm of the rotors or the weightless sensation in my stomach, but it felt good, and I felt good that we had made it.

I set a course for home, which took us back along the southeastern side of the AO. The ship's radio told us that another chopper and crew remained at the LZ with mechanical trouble. The slick pilot was Joe Gorski, a second tour guy that I knew and liked. He had reported that his ship had been all shot to hell by machine-gun fire, and his crew chief had been shot in the chest but was still hanging on. Gorski and his remaining crew were pinned down and desperately trying to stave off the ambushers. Gorski wasn't one to panic, but even over the radio, I sensed the urgency in his voice. They were nearly out of ammunition, and it appeared to Gorski that the ambushers had an endless supply. An air strike had been called in but were still several minutes out, and Gorski wasn't sure how long they could hold on, especially given his crew chief's unstable condition. No plans had been made for an evac, as most of the slicks were full or had already bugged out.

We had a clear view of the LZ now. Although I couldn't see the ambushers, I could see Gorski's ship and the streamers of blue smoke jetting out from both the engine and transmission. Farther off, I saw Masterson's lifeless ship, still emitting the deathly-black smoke.

At first, it didn't seem like anything at all. I barely noticed it. A small dark spot moving steadily across the horizon, but when the spot began to get larger, I saw that it was moving toward us. Curious, I circled the chopper around so that I could get a better look. I thought it might be the promised air strike, but it was a lone ship.

"Why we turn back?" Ho asked.

I pointed toward the mysterious object. Ho leaned forward in his seat and peered intently out the windshield.

"I think it's a chopper," he said.

"Yeah. A slick, I think," I said, as I saw no guns mounted on the skids.

A few seconds later, we could see it more clearly. It appeared to be heading toward us, moving fast, its skids just a few feet off the treetops.

"He's hauling ass," said Ho.

"Sure is," I said, veering the ship eastward. I didn't want to be within range of the ambushers, but I wanted to get a better look at the speeding slick. The mystery ship moved closer and closer to the LZ and then it suddenly made a sharp turn west before reaching the tree line. Something about the maneuver seemed familiar. Then I knew.

"It's Flanny!" I blurted. "What the hell?"

Flanny's ship sped into the sun along the northern tree line just above the treetops and directly behind the ambushers. He then made a hard banking turn to the south with the sun's rays shimmering off the twirling rotors. He continued due south for several seconds before making another hard right turn back to the west and straight at the ambushers.

"He going after them!" shouted Ho. He pushed up his sun visor to get a better look.

"He wants speed," I said.

Flanny's pitch was set so far forward that it appeared as though the chopper was flying on its nose.

"The crazy motherfucker, he knows if he stays low just above the trees, they won't see or hear him coming until he's right on their ass!"

Ho nodded but didn't look away—his eyes glued to Flanny's ship.

"Are we all right, sir?" Westin's voice came blaring into my headset. "Why aren't we heading back?"

"We will," I said. "Hold tight. We're just getting a better look, that's all. We'll be fine. Stand by."

By now, I knew Flanny would be unreachable. I had flown peter to him long enough to know that when he was committed to something, he wouldn't back off. Whatever it was he was trying to do, he'd see it through come hell or high water. I could picture him now, his left hand on the collective—the thumb and index finger of his right hand gently working the stick, the way he always did. Of course, the radio was off. Hell, it was always off when Flanny was flying. His peter pilot—Covey, or whatever his name—was probably shitting in his pants right about now. But Flanny wouldn't care, not when he was the one flying. I could hear him now: *Sit tight, fellas! We're going in!*

Seconds before Flanny reached the LZ, he climbed skyward some fifty feet or so above the treetops where he appeared to hang motionless in midair. For a moment, I thought he might have stalled, but then I saw that the chopper was still creeping forward high above the ground. After a few more seconds, he stopped again. This time I was sure he had stalled, as the chopper began to drop straight downward like a parachute.

"Autorotation!" I said to Ho. "I'll be goddamned!"

Ho shook his head. None of it seemed possible, but once below the tree line, the chopper jumped forward and then dove downward like a hawk on prey, flaring out a few feet from the ground and sliding to a stop directly in front of the ambushers. I saw several flashes coming from inside the deck of Flanny's chopper, undoubtedly the work of his crew and both their .60-caliber machine guns.

I wasn't sure if I actually believed what I had seen. I didn't think a slick was capable of such a maneuver.

"Did that just happen?" I asked Ho. "That's the damnedest thing I've ever seen!"

Ho didn't say anything, but smiled and shook his head in disbelief. We both watched as Flanny's ship sprang up and then spiraled around to where Gorski's wounded bird sat. Just then, the radio relayed the message that Flanny's ship had neutralized the ambushers.

Before bugging out, Ho tapped me on the shoulder and pointed back toward the deck. Guy, Jake, and the packed-in grunts were all cheering and patting each other on the back—all of them marveling at what they had seen.

Hitting the power, I pulled pitch and flew north where I made a hard sloping pedal turn to the port side, about fifty feet above Flanny's ship. Not for any other reason than because it felt good.

Chapter Seven

May 1985

"Hold on, honey," he says, bouncing the truck out of one muddy groove only to slide into another. "I don't know how your mother gets in and out of here every day in her little car."

"She goes the back way, Daddy, where the buses don't go," said Emily as she sat tightly gripping her armrest.

"Why didn't you tell me that before?"

"I thought you knew where you were going, Daddy."

"Well, don't ever make that mistake again. I often don't know where I'm going, honey—always remember that."

"Okay," she says as if she really would make an effort.

They splash through a small pond that was the parking lot at the far end of the school, and he pulls up to the door. "Go and find your mother, and I'll meet you in a few minutes with the treats. I'm going to try and find a dry place to park."

"Okay, Daddy," she says, pulling up the lock and pushing open the truck door. Holding onto the armrest, she climbs down and disappears below the seat.

"Daddy!" Emily hollers the instant he walks through the door. "You have to come see the little puppy—he's so adorable! It's a sled dog, Daddy, and his name is Kobuk! Come see, Daddy!" She tugs at the bottom of his jacket and then begins pulling him down the hallway. "Hurry up, Daddy! He's so cute and little!"

"Okay, okay," he says, letting her lead the way, knowing she won't calm down until he sees the puppy.

She leads him into her classroom, where several parents and children are huddled around a large cardboard box. Kneeling in front of the box and addressing the small crowd is Mrs. Adams—Emily's first grade teacher, a middle-aged woman whose straight black hair is so long that it lightly brushes the floor with every shift or twist of her head.

"The malemute breed originated from a tribe of Inuits called the Mahlemuits," explains Mrs. Adams, peering over her wireless spectacles. "The dog was bred to pull heavy loads and is a lot larger than many of the other breeds of sled dog. Kobuk here will probably grow up to be a fairly big dog and pull a big sled someday." Then taking Kobuk into her arms, she begins stroking the back of his head and neck. The small dog yips and gives her an approving lick on the chin.

"Come, Daddy, look," moans Emily. "It's got one brown eye and one blue eye." She guides them to an open spot into the mix of parents and students at the front of the cardboard box.

"Hello, Mr. Allen," says Mrs. Adams.

"Hi, Mrs. Adams," he replies. "Cute dog, by the way. Is it yours?"

"No, Kobuk's owner is a neighbor of mine," she says. "He's one of six in the litter. But he's such a good boy—aren't you?" she asks the dog, letting him lick her chin again. "We already have two Siberians and we'd love to have Kobuk, but three dogs are a little too much for my husband and me—we're not mushers, you know."

"Really," he says to Mrs. Adams. "You mean the little guy doesn't have a home?" Instantly he can feel the warmth of his daughter's eyes upon him.

"Not yet," she says, smiling at Emily. "But if you're interested, I can check with my—"

"Oh, we're interested!" interrupts Emily.

After a twenty-minute nap at another rest stop, I was back on the road. The heat blurred off the interstate and I was thankful for the air conditioning. I made great time, stopping only to use the head and for gas. I reached Fort Worth, Texas, a little after 8:00 p.m. And by 8:30 p.m., I stood inside a foul-smelling phone booth outside the main entrance to Fort Hood.

"Hello," a young boy's voice answered the telephone.

"Hi," I said, "I was wondering if I could speak to Jeff Broadway."

"He's my dad," said the boy. He didn't sound older than nine or ten.

"That's great, and you are?"

"I'm Ryan," he said.

"Well, Ryan, is your dad home?"

"Sure he is, just a minute." There was a sharp static crack, as he must've set down the phone. Then I heard him yell for his father. Seconds later, a distantly familiar voice said, "Broadway here."

"Jeff . . . Jeff Broadway?" I asked.

"Yeah, this is Broadway. How can I help you?"

"This is Henry Allen," I said.

"*Allen?*" he said, his voice uncertain. Then he shouted, "Henry Allen! For Christ sake, it's *Bronco Allen*! If this isn't a blast from the past! Shit! How the hell are you?"

"I'm fine, Lieutenant—I mean Jeff . . . I'm fine. I'm passing through town and I thought I'd look you up. I got that letter you sent a couple of years back about the reunion. Sorry it's such short notice and—"

"Shit, Bronco, I'm as pleased as punch that you called. Where are you? I can meet you or you can come—forget that, I'll meet you. Where are you?"

I told him where I was, and he gave me directions to some place called *JP's* in Harker Heights, not far from where I was.

It didn't take me long to find the place; I was getting really good at finding obscure bars in strange new towns. The place was huge and busy, but I remembered it was Saturday night. I sat at a table close to the door so that I could see Broadway when he came in. I hoped to Christ that I recognized him—after all, it had only been seventeen years. I ordered a rum and Coke from a chunky blond waitress with big hair and bigger breasts. ESPN's *Sportscenter* blared over the bar, and I watched highlights of the Tigers dropping another close one to the White Sox.

"*Bronco Allen!*" Broadway's voice came roaring from the front door of the barroom. I stood up to greet him, and he hugged me in a close brotherly way. I had never hugged him before, and it felt awkward.

"How the hell are you?" he said, pulling out a chair and sitting down across from me.

"I'm fine," I said.

"Well shit! You look fine. Are you still signed up?" he said, brushing the side of my head. "It's shaved a little close for a civilian."

"I thought that's the way everyone cut their hair down here," I said with a grin—it really was nice to see him. "No, I'm a civilian. I just got it cut short for the summer—with the heat and all."

Broadway smiled. He was heavier than I remembered, but his face was the same. He hadn't aged much and still appeared all army, even without the uniform. I did notice an air of confidence about him that I was sure I had not seen back in Vietnam.

The busty waitress came over, and Broadway ordered a Bud Light and then shot her a wink.

"Thick, but cute," he said when she left. "The more the cushion the better for pushin' is what I always say. So what brings you down here to my part of the country?"

"I don't know if I have a good reason," I said, and I supposed I didn't, "but I'm heading back home to Alaska after being away since before Vietnam. I thought I might make a trip of it and visit some of you fellows along the way. I've been meaning to catch up with you ever since I got that reunion letter. I heard you're still with the First Cav."

"Oh yeah, you know me, I'm a lifer," he said. "That's great you're taking a trip. As you know from the letter, I do the reunions now, and I've been trying to get you to one for years. It's a good time—seeing everyone from the old unit. You should come to the next one—it'll be in March."

"Well, Lieutenant—I mean Jeff—I still want to call you Lieutenant," I said, shaking my head.

"You can, Bronco. Call me Lieutenant Colonel," he said with a lot of pride. "I run a special little chopper outfit here now. It's great. You know that Bush is a friend to Texas and a friend to the army."

I hadn't any idea of what he was talking about, but I was glad he was happy running his *little outfit*.

"I'll do everything I can to make it next time," I lied. "It would be nice to see some of you boys again."

"Yeah, it's great. The last one was in California—San Diego. Who was that little nip you used to fly with?" he asked, waving a finger at me. "You know—"

"You mean Ho?" I said. Obviously, some things about Broadway would never change.

"Yeah, Ho. He was there asking about you. Funny little fucker. I never liked him much in Nam," he said, "but talking to him at the reunion, I found out that he became all right."

"He always was *all right*," I said before taking a sip of my drink.

The waitress set Broadway's beer down on the table, offering with it a smile. Broadway gave her another wink. He took a long drink of his beer, belched loudly, and then pounded on his chest.

"Yeah well, as it turns out that the slope can fly. After the Vietnam, he got a sweet deal flying one of those traffic choppers in San Francisco. He's making a shitload of dough."

"He was always a good pilot," I said.

"You'd know, you taught him everything he knows," he said and then took another drink of the beer.

82

"There was a lot he taught me, that's for sure . . . a lot he taught me," I said, nodding. "I was planning on paying him a visit out there in California. I was hoping you could help me get in touch with him."

"Sure," said Broadway, "I know how to get a hold of the little bastard—I'll set you up. I could probably get you in touch with just about anybody from the old outfit—if they're still alive, that is," he added.

"I'm probably going to head out to El Paso and look up my old CE. You remember, Guy Westin, my crew chief."

"Yeah, tall feller. He was pretty good, from what I remember. He flew with me once or twice. Smart too."

"I've got his address though. His wife called me sometime back and said that he wasn't doing well. She wondered if I'd consider paying him a visit. She said he was always talking about me—said it would be a great surprise. It must have been a couple years now, so I'm not sure about it, but I'll make the trip anyway."

"What's his problem?"

"I'm not sure," I said. "She only said he wasn't doing well—talking Vietnam all the time."

Broadway shook his head and took another drink. "You know some guys. Man, they just can't get past it. I don't know why they can't just move on and be happy that they didn't eat it over there."

"I don't know," I said, trying to be agreeable. "But I never thought of Guy as someone who couldn't get past it. Hell, he was as tough as nails back then. Calmest man I ever saw in a fight."

"That's just it. It's usually the ones that think they're the toughest," he said. "Well, here's to him anyway." He lifted his beer, and we drank to Guy.

"Here's to all those boys back then," I said, and we drank again.

"I never saw you much after you signed up with that spook outfit."

"Yeah, well they were always moving us around," I said.

"That's right, you boys just packed up in the night and were gone. You and that wiseass—what's his name."

"Flanagan," I said. "Danny Flanagan."

"Right, real smart-ass. I never did like the bastard. Everybody made such a big deal about him—as if he was some boy wonder. Frankly, I never thought he was all that," he said, shaking his head. "What was all that spook shit about anyway?"

I hadn't seen Broadway in seventeen years, but it only took a few minutes to remember why it was that nobody liked him much. He couldn't remember anyone's name, yet he was the reunion chairman. In Vietnam, he was always in everybody's shit, and he hadn't changed. But he had his rank now—a career guy. Flanny sure had been right about that. I shook my head and smiled at the old lieutenant.

"Nothing much," I said. "Flanny and I ran ash-and-trash missions for some big shot colonel. You know that protocol-VIP shit," I lied. "We flew him and his boys all over half of Vietnam. It wasn't much of a duty."

"That's about what I figured. I remember being a bit pissed that they didn't take me, but I knew it wasn't much of anything. Didn't matter though, I got transferred stateside a month later. Back to Fort Wolters here in Texas—can you believe that shit? They made me an instructor there until they closed it down in seventy-five, then I came here."

"Fort Wolters, shit," I said, glad he had changed the subject. I suspected Broadway knew more about our operation than he was letting on, but it didn't matter. He had been passed over for the detail and probably didn't want to talk about it, even if I had told him the truth. "I haven't thought about that place in a long time," I said. "Man, that was some time ago—remember that first solo?"

"Yeah, I couldn't wait," he said.

"Well, I was scared shitless," I said, grinning.

"C'mon, you knew how to fly before you got there," he said.

"Yeah, but I was still scared to fly for fear of all those asshole instructors." I grinned.

Broadway laughed.

"You still fly?" he asked.

"No, I haven't flown since I left the army," I said.

"Really?" said Broadway. "I would've never thought that about you. I thought you liked flying those birds."

The waitress came with another round of drinks, and I told Broadway a little about my life back in Lansing, but mostly, I let him tell me about his. He had a wife Kay who was a *fine little homemaker,* and she took great care of their two boys, Ryan and Jason, while he ran his little chopper outfit with an iron fist. It sounded like that's the way he ran his *little outfit* at home. But I could tell he was proud of his boys, as he told me—*they want to be just like their old man.*

I wondered what Flanny would have to say about that.

Broadway went on to tell me everything he had done since Vietnam. It would've all sounded pretty impressive had I not known anything about him. To hear him talk, he was well on his way to becoming a general. Shit, Flanny had been right about that too. I did enjoy seeing him again—not because of what he had become, but because we both had been at the same place at the same time when the world had seemed so much different. Broadway, the lieutenant, the lieutenant colonel, or even the man, had made it out of Vietnam in one piece. He was leading the life he wanted to lead—by his rules. Whatever you wanted to say about him—he appeared to be happy.

We finished a couple more drinks and kept the conversation small. Broadway asked me if I needed a place to stay. He told me he had a big house with lots of room and I could stay as long as I wanted. But I didn't want to be a burden, and I didn't want to have to play guest in a house full of family. I simply told him that I already had a hotel room and that I needed to get an early start tomorrow—and that was true. He said he understood, but if I changed my mind, to give him a call. He also told me to call him when I needed Ho's number.

"Sure was great to see you," he said when we got outside the bar. "I'll keep you posted on the reunion."

"Yeah," I said, smiling at him. "It was great to see you too."

"We can't wait so long next time," he said, shaking my hand. "The world can be a fucked-up place, but that doesn't mean we can't stay in touch."

Offering my hand, he took it and pulled me into a tight embrace—the way he had done when he had first arrived. It still felt awkward. "Take care, Bronco," he said.

"I will, Colonel," I said when he released me. I gave him a respectful nod and then walked toward my truck on the opposite side of the street.

When I reached the truck, I unlocked the door, but just before I got in, Broadway shouted, "Where you headed after El Paso?"

I looked back to see that he was still standing where I had left him. "California and then Boise," I replied.

"Boise, Idaho? Who the hell is in Boise?"

"The best goddamned chopper pilot that ever lived," I shouted back at him.

"Who's that?"

"Flanny!" I yelled at him. "Danny Flanagan! The best there ever was!"

"Oh right!" he shouted back at me. Then he shook his head. "But didn't he—"

"He's there!" I yelled and then got into my truck and drove away.

Chapter Eight

May 1962

James Theodore Mason—or JT as he made everyone call him—was a bulky bear of a man. His biceps were larger than my thighs, and his chest I could only liken to those I had seen in superhero comic books. But for all that mass and muscle, his narrowly set black eyes, chop sideburns, and perpetually goofy grin made him look like a giant gnome.

"Hey," JT grunted at Jessie as she and I stepped off the school bus.

He was leaning back against the grill of his beat-up Chevy truck, his thick arms crossed and grinning wider than usual.

"You two ready to go?"

"Hi, Daddy," replied Jessie.

JT lifted himself off the front of the truck to greet his daughter with a warm hug and kiss. He then said something to me, which was inaudible over the sound of the school bus pulling away.

"How's that, Mr. Mason?" I asked.

"I told you, it's JT, damn it! You save the mister shit for your teachers. I'm a working man."

His grin went to a full-on smile, and he slapped me on the shoulder, nearly knocking me over. "I asked how the hell you are!"

"I'm fine, sir . . . uh . . . JT."

"We're ready, Daddy. Hen says he'll catch more fish than the both of us together," said Jessie.

"I didn't—"

"Is that so," said JT, cutting me off. "I guess we'll just have to show him a thing or two about fishing, won't we?" He gave me a sympathetic wink as we both climbed into the truck. Jessie sat between us.

"Where are we going, Daddy?" asked Jessie.

"We're going to our secret spot on the Chatanika—you know the one. We went there last summer when you had your cast," he said, patting her leg.

"Oh yeah, I remember. That's a good spot," she said, nodding and then glancing at me. "We caught about six grayling if I remember right."

It wasn't much of a secret. I had fished there many times, and I had seen plenty of others fish there as well. In fact, I had taken Jessie there once; she had obviously forgotten.

"Your Granddad will be meeting us later," said JT, rolling up his window. "He had to finish up some things in town."

"Oh," said Jessie, frowning. "I thought it was going to be just the three of us."

"Yeah . . . well, I was telling him about taking you kids fishing, it being the last day of school and all, and he wanted to go." He glanced at Jessie, and his grin disappeared. "That's all right, isn't it?"

"Fine," she said, switching on the radio and twisting the knobs to only static. "This radio is crap!" she said, switching it back off.

"I told you, the antennae's broke," said JT.

"I need a ride into town Friday," said Jessie, leaning back and crossing her arms. "I can ride in with you and Granddaddy in the morning, if it's all right?"

"Sure," said JT. "You know we're working on Saturday. What do you got going on?"

"Nothing much," she replied. "I'm meeting a friend, and we're going to the movies."

"Oh," said JT, looking over at me. "I suppose you need a ride too?"

This was news to me. This was the first I had heard of it. She hadn't mentioned anything about it. And I thought I knew all of her friends.

"Uh . . . no . . . I don't need a ride," I mumbled.

"I'm going with Kenny Brenke. He asked me out on a date, and I said I'd go! It's no big deal!" she shouted at me.

My heart sank. This was unbelievable. Kenny Brenke, the senior? When did this happen? And why hadn't she said anything to me? She didn't know anyone that I didn't know—and I didn't know Kenny Brenke. For the entire school year, I had spent every free moment with Jessie—she went to the movies with me, she did things with me. And why was she yelling?

"Kenny Brenke?" I blurted and then glared at her.

"Yeah, Kenny Brenke," she replied indignantly. "What's wrong with him?"

"Should I be worried?" JT said to me with another goofy grin.

I didn't say anything. What a stupid grin, I thought.

"Well? What's wrong with him?" she shouted again.

"There's nothing wrong with him," I said. "I don't even know him."

Apparently, that was good enough for JT who went about casually lighting a cigarette. Why JT had to be so damn cool about it, I had no idea. Shouldn't he be worried about his fifteen-year-old freshman daughter dating some eighteen-year-old senior he didn't even know? What a goofball!

"That's right! You don't know him! And you're right, there's nothing wrong with him," she said sharply. "He's nice, and I'm going out with him—and he's cute!" she added with a haughty smile.

JT took a long drag of his cigarette and shook his head, still grinning.

Cute, this was crazy. Kenny Brenke—the lanky bug-eyed basketball player? It didn't make any sense. Why was she torturing me like this? In front of her father, for crying out loud! Thoughts went whisking from lobe to lobe in my mind trying to conceive the inconceivable.

"How far to the *secret spot*?" I asked JT, changing the subject, knowing we were less than a half mile from the turnoff.

"Oh, just a little farther," said JT, cracking his window enough to flick ashes from his cigarette.

When we reached the entrance, JT made a wide turn and barreled the truck down off the pavement, causing both Jessie and me to rap our heads lightly against the ceiling of the cab.

"Whoa!" cried Jessie, clutching onto my leg and arm.

I grabbed the armrest to the door and gripped it tightly. The truck rocked and swayed down the embankment and then thrust up and over a slight swell that again caused us to hit our heads on the ceiling. "Whoa!" Jessie cried again, this time gouging her nails into my arm and leg.

"Hold on!" shouted JT as we went tearing through a tangled thicket of black spruce trees, their spiny branches slashing at the sides of the truck.

JT didn't seem to mind that his truck was being scratched to hell, but I supposed what were a few mores scratches on this piece of shit. When we emerged from the thicket, the truck bogged down into a field of spongy moss veined with tree roots that snapped and popped beneath the truck's tires. I worried that we might stall—or worse, get stuck. It was a long walk home from here. I had never seen a truck—or any vehicle, for that matter—take on this trail before, and I hoped that JT knew what in the hell he was doing. Of course, JT never looked like he knew what he was doing.

To JT's credit, however, the truck made it to the dried streambed where the motor revved and the ride smoothed, easing both my anxious mind and Jessie's anxious grip. The streambed snaked through the center of a dense forest where only a couple of years ago Saucy and I used to play among the aspen trees—chasing magical creatures, hunting dragons, and fighting Nazis. However, that seemed like long ago—before Jessie, who didn't play such foolish games. She was into more worldly things like movies and dates with the *cute* Kenny Brenke.

"Almost there!" JT shouted as the truck wielded around a sharp turn.

Jessie squeezed my arm and leg—she had not let go. And even after we had nosed to a stop a few feet in front of the rushing Chatanika River, she still didn't let go entirely, but kept her hand on my arm and began gently massaging the area where she had earlier sunk her nails. After JT cut the engine and got out of the truck, she was still rubbing my arm and staring blankly down at her lap. I didn't move. I thought she might say something, but she didn't; she just kept on rubbing my arm. Finally she turned to me, first with her head and then with her eyes. "You all right?" she whispered.

"Yeah," I said.

"You're my best friend, you know," she said, pulling me close and hugging me. When she released me, I saw that her eyes were heavy and laden with tears. "Now let's go, the fish aren't going to jump into the truck," she said with a little laugh, and then after wiping her eyes, she smiled at me.

I suppose there was more to her tears, and it probably had to do with her telling me about her date with Kenny Brenke. But as bad as I felt about her date with the bug-eyed Brenke, I felt worse that she felt bad about it. Not knowing what else to do, I got out of the truck and went around to the back where I saw two fly poles leaning up against the tailgate—one I recognized immediately as mine. I had left it and my fishing satchel with JT earlier in the week in anticipation of the trip. JT wasn't around. He was probably off somewhere up the creek, his line already in the water. If I didn't hurry, he might stumble across *my* favorite spot, and I couldn't let that happen.

I snatched my pole and then, grabbing my tattered satchel, I kicked off my shoes and tiptoed down to the riverbank. As I went by the cab of the truck, I saw Jessie still sitting inside. I thought about saying something to her, but then decided against it.

I spied JT's colossal form a couple hundred feet upstream spastically whipping at the water with his pole. What a goofball. There sure wasn't a lot of grace to his fishing stroke, but there wasn't a lot of grace to JT, period. At least, the big oaf was well upstream of my spot.

A twisting and swirling river, the Chatanika wound its way through the valley assembling clusters of puzzling little eddies along the way, which entertained some of the largest arctic grayling in Alaska. Their size probably had something to do with the size of the mosquitoes around here, which were fat and ferocious, and I was grateful for the hot sun and slight breeze keeping them at bay.

About fifty yards downstream, I found the kidney-shaped rock that jutted out from the near side bank and marked *my* favorite spot. The stone was flat and large enough to stand on. It made a perfect casting platform, as it was directly across from a pool that played host to dozens of the prized fish. Once atop, I removed a small fly from my satchel resembling a fat juicy mosquito and tied it to the end of my line.

Gripping the rod firmly with my right hand while leading the line with my left, I rhythmically waved the rod over my head and got ready for the first cast of the season. After several seconds airing the fly, I cast it across the river and dropped it softly between two slow churning eddies. Right on target, and it felt good.

I wasn't a serious fisherman, but I knew how to cast a fly and pull a grayling from the Chatanika. I had learned from the best. Spooner had given me the rod and reel several years ago, after I had split and stacked more than a dozen cords of his wood. Spooner was a druggist who spent half of his time at Woolworth's in Fairbanks counting out pills and the other half of his time fishing. Nobody thought much of Spooner as a druggist, probably because he admittedly didn't know a whole lot about the drugs he was dispensing. He had grown up fly-fishing the rivers of Western Oregon until he had come here as a young man to be a pharmacist. He taught me everything there was to know about flies and fishing, specifically how to cast and land grayling.

I pulled the fly from the river, lashing it back skyward, and then set it down again—again, right on target. I wonder if Kenny Brenke knew how to catch a grayling—probably not, the bug-eyed bastard!

A short while later, Jessie came down to the creek cane-pole in hand and walked down to where JT was convulsing wildly with his own pole. From where I stood atop the rock, I could see their silhouettes and watched as they slapped their poles at the sparkling water.

"It's not a damn baseball bat," I heard JT tell Jessie as he guided her pole directly over her head. "Swing it back and forth overhead, not side to side. You're getting the fly wet."

"Yeah, well if I do your way, I can't do this," she said, smacking him upside the head with her pole.

Jessie threw her head back laughing and then playfully pushed JT toward the river.

"You little shit!" he yelled at her and then, scooping a handful of water from the river, he flung it at her.

Jessie screamed and then threw her rod down on the bank and charged at her father. But before I could see what happened next, I felt a sharp tug on my pole. I glanced at the river in time to see a good-sized grayling surface and then flop back beneath the rolling water. In less than a minute, I had landed and bagged the first grayling of the summer. Me one, the Mason family, nothing—and to hell with Brenke!

Looking back upriver, Jessie and her father were still splashing about, unaware that I had caught anything. Jessie had waded into the river a ways and was kicking water at JT who had taken refuge behind a birch sapling just up off the riverbank. Thoroughly doused, he ran after her into the river where he wrestled her down, kicking and screaming, into knee-deep water. He left her sitting in the river, water bubbling over her chest and shoulders, shouting after him. Fishing appeared to be secondary to harassing each other, but clearly, the two were enjoying the outing. No one in my family ever did anything like that—not together, anyway.

After about an hour, the wind picked up, and I found it harder to land the fly between the two eddies. I had pulled in two more grayling to the Masons' *one big one* that got away, but in all fairness, they did little fishing and still appeared to be having as much fun.

"How's your luck?" came a throaty voice from behind me, startling me.

Glancing back, I saw an old man in hip-waders holding a cane pole—Spenser Mason, Jessie's grandfather.

"N-N-Not too bad," I stuttered, still a little shaken. "I pulled out three a bit earlier, but the wind has kicked up some."

The old man peered into my satchel.

"Not bad at all," he said, nodding.

He let out a violent snort and then wiped his nose with the sleeve of his grimy flannel shirt.

"How's my boy doing?"

"JT, you mean?" I asked.

"I only got one boy," he growled and then he let out another loud snort.

Spenser had the largest head that I had ever seen. It looked like a big square knot cinched too tightly around his eyes, nose, and mouth, scrunching them all together at the center of his face. Like JT, he was a big man and probably had been much bigger in his younger days, except nothing about his features seemed to fit right. He hunched badly, and the hip-waders made his arms seem long and lurching like one of those swamp monsters from the picture shows.

"Yeah, well I'm not sure. I think they had one, but I don't know what happened," I said, shrugging. "It must've got away."

"Sounds about right, James was never much of a fisherman," he said, nodding his massive knot of a head. "You look like you're doing all right. I suppose I better go find out what in the hell is going on over there." The old man shot me a scrunched-up smile and then, with a filthy hand, reached into his hip-waders and pulled out a candy mint. "Like one?"

"No thanks," I replied.

The thought of eating anything from the old man's pocket via his dirty hand was revolting. He made a clucking sound as he rolled the mint around in his mouth, mumbling something incoherently before strolling upriver toward Jessie and JT.

I had seen Spenser Mason only one other time, and that was when he had picked Jessie and me up from school. I remembered Spenser didn't say much of anything to either of us, but he did offer up those mints. I watched him greet his son and granddaughter—nodding at JT and hugging Jessie. He was creepy then, and he was creepy now.

A few minutes later, Jessie came splashing up the riverbank.

"Hey, Hen!" she shouted at me. "How's it going?"

"Fine," I said.

"You catch anything?"

"Yeah sure, I caught three."

"Really?" she said, surprised and then looking into my satchel. "Wow! Good job!" She pulled out one of the fish, and then examined it up down before placing it back. She then began fumbling through the satchel.

"You got a knife in here?"

"Should be in one of the pockets. Why?"

"I thought I'd clean your fish for you," she said smiling.

"Knock yourself out." I said.

She found my pocketknife, squatted down in a small pool of river, and began cutting the fish along its belly. She didn't appear to have reservations cleaning fish, and she seemed to know what she was doing.

"You could've told me about your date with Kenny Brenke," I said, a little surprised at myself for saying it. I let out my line and then whipped it crisply back into the air for several seconds before casting it out over the water. The wind caught it, and it landed well off target.

I glanced down at Jessie, but she was too busy ripping out the guts of one of the grayling to notice.

"I know," she said, finally tossing the fish guts into the river. "I didn't think it was a big deal, and I didn't know how you'd be. I had gym with Kenny, and this morning, he asked me out. I didn't think it was any big deal. But you and I do everything together and, well . . ." Still squatting, Jessie duckwalked over to the river's edge and rinsed the fish out in the water just below the rock. Squinting up at me, she shook her head. "I didn't want to hurt your feelings, Hen."

I let the river swallow my fly and gently tug at my pole and at my pride. She was right; my feelings had been hurt. I suppose it was because I had never imagined her spending time with anyone else but me. Kenny was a popular guy—he must have had dozens of friends and dated all kinds of girls. Why did he need to have Jessie too?

"You didn't hurt my feelings!" I blurted.

"Okay, fine!" she snapped back at me.

Jessie shook her head and then grabbed another fish from the satchel. I peered upstream and saw JT and Spenser casting their flies into the wind.

"I see your grandfather made it," I said, deciding to change the subject.

Jessie didn't say a word but went about cleaning the fish. Now I supposed she wouldn't speak to me. Great, I thought as I reeled in my fly. I couldn't help but think about what Jessie had said about the *silent treatment* last summer. It really could be as bad as arguing. I cast the fly out into the wind, but it came swirling back at me and splashed a few feet in front of the rock.

"Shit!" I shouted, gathering in the bunched-up line. "This is hopeless! Can you believe this damn wind?" I glanced down at her again and saw she was cutting open the belly of the last grayling. With her hair swirling around her head with the wind, she gave me a quick look but still didn't say anything.

I was really starting to hate the silent treatment.

The Saturday morning after Jessie's *no-big-deal-date* with Kenny Brenke, I sat at the table inside the small travel trailer listening to the radio. The trailer had adorned the front yard of my house for the better part of a decade and had become my bedroom in the summertime. It was mostly empty, except for a few pieces of barely used camping equipment, some of my clothes, and a stack of heavy wool blankets. It was the perfect place to pass time listening to the radio or reading. It had a small wooden table with built-in bench seating, a full-size bed, and two wall-mounted kerosene lanterns, which not only provided light but some welcomed heat when it got colder.

My family never disturbed me out here, except maybe Tom, and that was only to put kerosene in the lanterns.

Jessie had said she would come by this morning, but yesterday she had gone into town for her date, and now I wondered if she would show at all. At least, she was speaking to me.

Last summer we had spent nearly every day together, except for when she had been in the hospital. Her immobility had caused us to spend a lot of time at Spenser's cabin. The eight weeks she had had her cast, we sat in her yard talking amongst the Shit Towers. Jessie sitting in a lawn chair up in the back of a cabless Ford truck bed with her broken leg propped up on the side of an old Wringer washing machine and me leaning against the ass-end of an engineless Fleetmaster Chevy convertible.

Jessie would want to talk about the Tigers mostly and their pennant race with the Yankees last year, or Tiger Stadium and the games she attended. Listening to her, you'd think Tiger Stadium was heaven itself, and never having been, it just might be. The way she described it, anyway.

Always buy your peanuts outside the stadium, Henry. It's cheaper that way, she had said a hundred times. She would have a copy of the sports page from a day-old *News-Miner* JT had brought home the night before, and he was under strict orders not to reveal to her any scores or any news about the Tigers' games, as she would wait to have me read it to her the following morning.

It had become our thing. I would read aloud the line box score or any other information about the Tigers' games and the games of their league rivals. She would want to know every detail about the game, and before long, I knew exactly how to read to her.

The result of the games would often forge her moods. If the Tigers won, she would cry out, *go Tigers*! But if they lost, she'd snatch the paper from me to see for herself and then she'd sulk. A bad loss, or a loss to the Yankees, and she'd be damn near unapproachable.

When we weren't talking baseball, Jessie would want to discuss her grandfather and the old scandal. Oddly, it had become for her a mild obsession. She had refused to question either Spenser or her father about any of it. Instead, she relied solely on what she could find in the cabin. Fortunately for her, Spenser never threw anything away. But she was a pretty good snoop, even dragging around a bum leg.

Jessie had gotten her hands on an old newspaper clipping and a couple letters.

The newspaper clipping was from the *News-Miner*. It was a short narrative depicting the sale of the partners' claims to the gold dredge company, Spenser's relationship and subsequent fallout with his partners, the O'Brien brothers and his wife Abigail's infidelity and abandonment of her small child JT, Jessie's father.

The letters were both from Charlene, Abigail's sister who made some casual references to one of the O'Brien brothers and the affair.

Nothing she found, however, suggested anything different from the old rumors, but Jessie had her doubts.

I don't think Granddaddy and Grandma got on at all, she had said one day from her perch in the Shit Towers.

I had told her that it didn't surprise me, seeing how she had run off with another man. I remember the comment had warranted me one of her patented icy glares.

Granddaddy didn't treat her all that well, she had said with a hint of sympathy in her tone. *I live with him, and I know how he can be.*

Jessie was convinced that there was more to the stories, and she had a hard time believing that Abigail could just up and leave her father. I had told her that money makes people do a lot of unbelievable things.

Jessie still wasn't persuaded.

Suddenly, last summer already seemed like years ago. I had not seen Jessie since school had let out, and I missed reading the line scores to her. I wondered if Kenny Brenke was a Tigers fan—or even a baseball fan, for that matter. He probably would be, I thought. I got up to switch off the radio when, all at once, the door swung open.

"Rise and shine, *rube!*" shouted Jessie. "Day's a wasting!"

"I'm up. I've been up for a while," I replied. "Where have you been? It's nearly noon."

"Daddy and Granddaddy decided to tie one on last night, and so they got a late start this morning. I had to make breakfast," she said, sliding into the bench seat across the table from me. "I brought the *Miner.*"

She tossed a rolled-up newspaper at me.

"Great," I said, unrolling it. I had to thumb through to the sports section, as she'd brought the entire paper. "Hey, what gives? This is today's paper," I said, noticing the date.

I looked over at Jessie who was smiling.

"How'd you get today's paper?"

"I managed it," she said, still smiling.

"You *managed* it? How did you *manage* it if your dad and grandpa got up so late?"

"Well, let's just say I've got a connection," she said, positively beaming at me now.

"*Kenny Brenke?*" I asked with a look I hoped would display my disgust.

Instantly her smile disappeared.

"Yeah, Kenny Brenke," she said, grabbing the paper from my hands. "And I don't know why I bother with you!" She got up and stood at the door, glaring down at me. "And I already know the score, *rube!* Tigers beat the Orioles five to four on Thursday, and on Friday, they beat the Yankees five to four! Kenny already read it to me an hour ago!"

I could only stare up at her in disbelief.

"That's right," she said, nodding at me. "He drove all the way out here from Fairbanks to bring me the paper. He's romantic that way! What's wrong with that?"

I didn't speak. I could only stare. Never before had she acted this way.

"And you know what else? We're going together now! He's my boyfriend! And if you don't like it, then fuck you, Henry, because he loves me! He said so! He said so, Henry! He said he loves me!"

"He loves you? You only had one date," I said skeptically.

"Yeah, he loves me!" she shouted.

"I don't think anybody can fall in love after one date," I said.

"Yeah, well that shows what you know! You don't know shit—you've never even had a date, *rube!*"

"Maybe so, but he can't possibly be in love with you after one date," I said, shaking my head.

Jessie's glare went cold, and tears rolled down the side of her face.

"And you know what else, Henry?" She didn't wait for an answer. "I let him fuck me last night!" she said viciously and then glanced away.

Her words were unlike anything I had ever heard before—not even from Tom. I had no idea what to do, say, or think. Jessie's teary eyes moved back to mine.

"That's right, *rube!*" she shouted at me, her eyes wild and raging. "I'll let him do it again! He'd never done it before! He said he loves me, Henry! I don't know why I waste my time with you!" She then spun around, kicked open the trailer door, and was gone, leaving me alone, her stinging words still ringing in my ears.

I had a notion to run after her, but that was soon overtaken by another notion—or feeling. This one came from my stomach. I was going to be sick.

Chapter Nine

January 1968

It wasn't more than a whisper, but it woke me.

"What?" I said into the darkness.

"Sir, you're to report to Major Whipple," said the whispering voice.

"Major Whipple?"

"Yes sir. You're to report immediately, sir," said the voice.

"What the hell?" I cried out. "Who's there?"

"It's me, sir. Hedrick . . . Private Hedrick. Major Whipple's clerk, sir," he said, blasting me with the beam from his flashlight.

"All right, all right," I said, shoving the flashlight at him. "I'll be there as soon as I can, goddamn it!" I sat up on the edge of my bunk.

"The major said to tell you *double time,* sir," said Hedrick. His voice sounded uneasy. "He said to be sure and tell you that, sir."

"I got it! I got it! Now leave me alone!"

"Ah . . . yeah . . . sir . . . he said I was to escort you. So if it's all the same to you, I'll just wait, Mr. Allen."

"We'll, if it's all the same to you, Hedrick—I know what *double time* means, and I know where to find the major. So fuck off, if you please!"

"But sir, I—"

"It'll be fine, Hedrick. I'll be there all right, damn it! Go tell the major, I'm on my way! I don't need an escort for Christ sake! I'll be there on the double! Now get lost!"

Hedrick gave me a disconcerting look, shook his head, and then left.

"Was that Whipple's nigger?" Broadway shouted from the darkness.

"That was Private Hedrick," I said, pulling on my tee shirt.

"What in the hell did he want?" asked Broadway.

"I have to report to Whipple for some damn reason," I said, "on the double!"

"It's goddamned two in the morning! What's it all about?"

"How do I know!" I said, lacing up my boot.

"He didn't want to see me?" he asked, as if there may have been an oversight.

"No, Lieutenant, he only wanted me. You can go back to sleep. It doesn't concern you," I said calmly. There was no sense getting him all riled up.

"Well, you tell Whipple he best not be sending his boy around here this time of night! You can't see that big ole coon at all in the dark! I'm liable to blow his head off the next time!"

I grabbed my cap from atop my footlocker and headed for the door.

"I'll be sure to tell him, Lieutenant," I said.

Flanny was the first person I saw when Hedrick led me into the small briefing room. He was sitting across a square table from Major Whipple and some full-bird colonel I had never seen before. Flanny had a tight grin on his face. Then I knew why Whipple had summoned me.

"Mr. Allen," said Major Whipple. "Nice that you could join us. Colonel, this is the slick pilot that Chief Warrant Officer Flanagan has been telling us about."

"Pleased to meet you, son." The colonel stood up and shook my hand. Then staring directly into my eyes said, "Bill Glasson."

Hiding behind wire-rimmed spectacles were eyes the faintest shade of blue. His neatly parted hair was pure white, maybe the whitest I had ever seen.

"They call me Whitey," said the colonel, as if reading my mind.

"But you can still call him *Colonel* or *sir*, Mr. Allen," the major chimed in.

"*Colonel's* fine," said Whitey, flashing me a smile before sitting back down. The colonel gestured for me to sit down in the empty chair next to Flanny.

"You boys are here at the colonel's request," said the major in a tone that said it was not at his.

Major Whipple removed his cap and rubbed the bald part of his sweaty head with his bare hand. He then wiped his hand on his shirt before replacing his cap.

"Actually, Flanagan is here at the colonel's request. You're here, Allen, on Mr. Flanagan's recommendation," said the major. "You should know that Mr. Allen has only logged enough hours—"

"It's all right, John," said the colonel, waving an arm at him dismissively. I'm sure Mr. Allen is a fine pilot. Why don't you let me have a minute alone with these boys?"

Major Whipple let out a protesting sigh and didn't move.

"It's important, John," the colonel said to him solemnly.

The major looked at Flanny and then back to the colonel. Finally, with a defeated tone, he said, "Sure, Colonel. Take all the time you need. It's just important that I be informed about—"

"You'll be informed," said the colonel, again waving his arm at the major. "If you'll excuse us, please."

"Certainly, Colonel," said the major, giving Flanny and me a *we'll-talk-later* nod before leaving the room with Private Hedrick. It was obvious that poor Major Whipple had gotten his feelings hurt.

For several minutes after they had left the room, the colonel sat quietly staring at us, as if he was waiting for us to say something first. But Flanny didn't say a word, and I certainly didn't have anything to say.

The colonel removed his spectacles, pulled a white handkerchief from his breast pocket, and began cleaning the lenses.

"Listen, gentlemen," he said. "I've got a little project, and I need your help. You see, I'm in charge of a special task force that you might say has the thankless job of trying to keep tabs on that North Vietnamese hardware store, otherwise known as Cambodia."

The colonel's eyes shifted back and forth from Flanny to me as he continued to wipe the lenses of his spectacles.

"Cambodia?" said Flanny.

"Right," said the colonel. "Our neutral neighbors to the west. As you know, we're a country that respects the neutrality of a nation, and the sons of bitches in Cambodia are no exception. We've done just about everything to honor that neutrality. And to be frank, gentlemen, it has cost us. It has cost us lives. That son of a bitch Ho Chi Minh has been flanking our ass through Cambodia via Laos the entire war. And for the most part, we've been letting him get away with it because of this neutrality shit. You know it as the *Ho Chi Minh Trail*."

The colonel reached beneath his chair and brought out a rolled up map, which he spread out across the table and then looked up at the both of us. "You recognize this, don't you?"

"Sure, Colonel," said Flanny with a grin. "That's a map of that North Vietnamese hardware store."

The colonel shot Flanny a smile.

"Yes it is," he said, leaning back in his chair. "This is my third fight, gentlemen. I was in World War II and Korea, and now here I am in Vietnam. I've fought in nearly every type of war—fields, deserts, mountains, beaches, and jungles—and in nearly every type of condition. But after all that, I've really learned only one truth about war."

Colonel Glasson looked down at the map and ran his finger along the border between Cambodia and South Vietnam. Then he looked up at Flanny as if he was awaiting a response.

"What's that, sir?" said Flanny finally.

"I've learned that in war there is no such thing as neutral. When there's a war on, gentlemen, everything—and I mean every son-of-a-bitching thing—takes a side. Whether it's ants, animals, people, or countries—they all have a cause, they all have an agenda. And if the sons of bitches aren't with you, they're most surely against you—or, at the very least, they're in your goddamn way. It's as irritating as all hell. And this war is the most irritating war I've ever been a part of."

"What can we do?" asked Flanny.

"Gentlemen, before this war is over, it will be fought in Cambodia. And if we can't get a handle on Cambodia . . ." The colonel paused and then, shaking his head, glanced over at me and then at Flanny. "Well, gentlemen . . . let's just say we have to get a handle on Cambodia. And my job is to make sure we know exactly what it is we're dealing with. And that's where you boys can help."

"How's that, sir?" I asked.

"I run the unofficial task force that is looking into things a few miles across the border. And I need pilots—good pilots to fly my men in and out of that neutral country so that I can figure out just exactly how neutral they are."

"You say this task force is unofficial, Colonel," said Flanny. "How unofficial?"

The colonel smiled and then nodded at Flanny.

"You're about twenty-two years old, aren't you?"

"Yeah," said Flanny, "good guess."

The colonel shook his head.

"Oh it wasn't a guess, son. You see, officially, Mr. Flanagan—or should I say Chief Warrant Officer Daniel E. Flanagan from Boise, Idaho. Husband of Claire Flanagan, father of one boy, a Daniel E. Flanagan Jr. born February 21, 1967, which would make him nearly two years old. And since your first tour officially started in January of '66 and you didn't go back before your second tour, I would surmise that you haven't even met your son yet. And I also know that, officially, you're about seventy-five days short of going home."

"Sixty-five," snapped Flanny, glaring at the colonel. "So what's that have to do with anything?"

"It doesn't, really. But officially, you're a lot of things, son. And so is Cambodia . . . officially. But you see, Danny—may I call you *Danny*?"

"Unofficially," replied Flanny with a grin.

The colonel smiled. "Unofficially, things are the way I see them."

"You mean the way you want to see them, don't you?" said Flanny.

"Perhaps, but officially, what I know about you son is what I read in a file or a report. But is that you? Is who you are in some file or service record?" The colonel shook his head. "I didn't learn about you from any damned file, Danny. I learned about you from those that have flown with you and those that have seen you fly. And I learned you could fly. And I've seen you fly, son. Officially, you're just another son of a bitch that logged a shitload of flight time. But unofficially, I'd say you're probably one of the most talented chopper pilots we have in this man's army, and I want to use some of that talent before you go home. Unofficially, that is," added the colonel.

"But I don't have much time left, Colonel, and I was kind of hoping to spend it on this side of the border doing ash-and-trash missions for the major over there."

Flanny nodded toward the door where Major Whipple could be seen peering in through the window. The colonel shot the major a wicked glare, and he immediately disappeared. Then looking back at Flanny, the colonel nodded.

"As far as Major Whipple is concerned, you *will* be flying ash-and-trash missions—except, you'll be flying them for me."

"You mean the major doesn't know what this is all about?" said Flanny, lowering his voice.

"Unfortunately, Danny," said the colonel, "there is so much that is unofficial about this goddamned war, sometimes I have to call those sons of bitches in Washington just to find out who the hell I am.

But I believe what's going on with those sons of bitches across that goddamned border will be the difference in this war. Officially, we will fight in Cambodia, gentlemen. You can be sure of that. But right now, I can get a lot more done unofficially."

"Do I have any choice?" asked Flanny.

The colonel ran his hand through his pure white hair and then, smiling, he nodded.

"Yeah, you have a choice," he said. "You don't have to come along, but I'll make you a deal. This project will last a couple weeks. So I'll tell you what. You do this for me, and a couple weeks from now, you'll be on your way home to see little Danny Jr." The colonel smiled and then, removing his glasses, he stared at Flanny. "I will confess, I need good pilots, and the sons of bitches in Washington have given me a lot of leeway to get you. We could really use your help. Some of the best men in this army are on this task force, and I need to know they will be flying with the very best. It's the kind of—"

"Excuse me, Colonel," I interrupted. "I can see why Flanny's here. Hell, he's the best I've ever seen. But why am I here? I don't have half the logged hours as he does, and I—"

"I'm sorry, Mr. Allen—or Henry, is it?" The colonel waved his arm to me the way he had done with the major. I could tell he didn't like being interrupted.

"Henry is fine, sir."

"Henry, I need six pilots and their crews, but I also need six more pilots and their crews to be in support. Remember, this is an unofficial project. I prefer to use those trusted by the chosen pilots to act as their support. Obviously, Danny has chosen you, and you should be honored."

The colonel couldn't see Flanny's lewd gesture to me, but it made me want to laugh.

"I see, Colonel," was all I could say.

"Well then," said Flanny, "if support means waiting around for me then it sounds like a cake detail for the ole Bronco here, but what about me? What kind of pucker factor are we talking? You can only make these Huey-birds do so much. We're not talking about anything out of the ordinary, are we?"

"From what I hear, Danny, you can make . . ." said the colonel then pausing, "a *Huey-bird*, as you call it, do just about anything. And from what I've seen, nothing you do is ordinary." The colonel winked at him.

"That's true, Colonel," said Flanny, grinning. "But if it's all the same to you, I'd still like to know what it is I'm getting myself into. After all, Charlie shoots at all of us . . . even in Cambodia."

"You're right," said the colonel, "they shoot at all of us. What I need is insertions and extractions. You will be informed where and when a couple hours before each insertion, and be on alert for the extraction. You'll be alone, and most of the time, it will be between sunset and sunrise. Given the unofficial nature of this project, the less you know about it, the better off you'll be—the better off everyone will be. Get them in and out, gentlemen. That's all I want and expect. I'm hopeful that everything will go smoothly, but I make no promises—not with those VC sons of bitches. That's why you have backup. If something goes wrong and you get yourself in trouble over there . . . Well, let me just say that—"

"You'll cut us loose," said Flanny.

The colonel frowned.

"I was going to say I'll do what I can, but I won't lie to you. There won't be a lot I can do for you."

"So no gunships, no support, no command and control, and no daylight. And if we fuck up, we're on our own. Sounds like a lot of fun to me, Colonel," said Flanny.

"You won't be on your own," said the colonel. "You'll have some of the finest men I know with you."

"With all due respect, Colonel," said Flanny, "none of those sons of bitches knows how to fly a helicopter."

The colonel snickered.

"You're right, I suppose. But that's why you're here—that's why I've dragged your ass out of bed so goddamned early in the morning."

Flanny gave the colonel a stern look. And for a moment, I thought he might just tell the colonel to go fuck himself. Then gradually a smile crawled across his face and he grinned at me.

"Well I guess you better sign us up Colonel," said Flanny slapping me on the shoulder. "Otherwise Allen here will never let me live it down, his part being so tough and all. But a couple weeks from now, Colonel, if I aint bag-dragging it stateside, you won't get me to fly a kite for you."

"Okay," said the colonel returning his smile.

"So when do we start this . . . project?" asked Flanny.

"You'll notify your crews that you will be moving out within forty-eight hours to a camp near An Loc. They don't need to know anymore than that. Until then, you can take some time off and wait for further orders. I'll handle everything else. And remember, everything I've told you and will tell you is classified, gentlemen."

"Don't you mean unofficial, Colonel?" said Flanny.

"That's right Danny," said the colonel smiling. "That's right."

An hour later, we were sitting on the deck of Flanny's ship sipping Jack Daniels from a thermos cap and watching it rain.

"So what do you make of all this shit, Flanny . . . or should I say *Danny*? May I call you *Danny*?" I said mockingly.

Flanny held out the thermos cap and let the rain mix with the bourbon.

"What shit?" asked Flanny.

I shook my head.

"The way I see it, Bronco, it makes me about fifteen days short, and that sure beats the hell out of sixty-five," he said.

"Yeah, well I've never been a part of any spook shit. It gives me the willies—the officially unofficial shit does, anyway. Does that mean if we eat it, it'll be unofficial?"

"If you eat it on this mission, Bronco, it sure as shit better be unofficial, as you'll be sitting on your ass for a couple of weeks while I'm hauling the colonel's *sons of bitches* all over hell and back." He took a long drink of the Jack and water and then handed it to me. "And this spook shit is nothing new. We'll probably know more about the mission running grunts for the colonel than we ever did for Major Whipple. At least, the colonel doesn't give us the pretense that we need to know."

"I suppose," I said. I took a sip of Jack as Flanny put an arm around me.

"What's the matter, Bronco? You got the tastiest detail in the club."

"Nothing, really," I said, shrugging, "but I can't help but wonder why you picked me."

"Man, you're right," he said, pushing me away. "I better go talk to the colonel and you better go wake up Lieutenant Broadway. I just realized I made a mistake and picked a pussy for this mission."

"Come on, Flanny," I said, handing him the cup. "That's not what I'm saying. It's just that there are guys that have been flying a lot longer—like Foley and Hubbard and Gorski. You like those guys, and they're great pilots."

"Listen, puss," he said, his blue eyes fiery, "I'm tired of telling you that you can fly. I'm tired of having to tell you that you're a good pilot. If you don't know it by now, then nothing I say is going to make it true. Goddamn it, Allen! Don't worry about it! Those guys, Foley and all, they're good guys, but I really don't know them. I see them fly and they're all right, but that's it. I don't trust them. I trust you, Bronco. I trust you because I know that come shit or shine you'll do the best you can. And that's really all you can ask for in this shithole. I know you'll have my back in this thing we're doing. And that's all I want—someone to get my back. But to tell you the truth, Allen, this whole thing gives me the willies too." He grabbed the bottle of Jack and refilled the cup.

"How so?"

"I only had sixty-five days, Bronco. I know this outfit. It would've been a cakewalk. I could've done it standing on my head. I just wrote Claire the other day and said that I was home free. I told her I'd see her and the boy in a couple of months. I was certain of it." He shook his head and took another drink. "Now I'm not so sure."

"Why's that?"

Flanny gulped down rest of the Jack, refilled it, and then handed it to me. He spit something out into the rain before leaning back on his elbows.

"You know I love to fly."

"Yeah, I know," I said.

"No," he said, shaking his head. "I mean it, Bronco. I think I'm fucked up that way. It's why I signed on for another tour. Did I ever tell you that Claire nearly left me?"

"No kidding?"

"Yeah, she was so pissed."

"What changed her mind?"

Flanny smiled, leaned forward, and took the cup from me. He filled it again.

"Claire gets it," he said and then laughed. "She knows I love it. I think she's fucked up that way."

Flanny laughed again before gulping down the Jack.

"When I'm up there, Bronco, it's like I know that's where I'm supposed to be. I know it's where I belong. It's what I'm supposed to do. Claire understands that."

"Now you'll be home in a few weeks. That should make her happy."

Flanny forced a smile and then filled the cup again.

"If you're so worried about it, then why didn't you just tell the colonel to forget it—it would've been no skin off my nose," I said, shaking my head. "And don't tell me you did this noble thing for me, Flanny! Oh no, don't go hanging this thing on me!"

"Fuck you!" he said with a smirk and then slapped me on the shoulder. "Hell, I don't like you that much," he said, grinning. He handed me the cup.

I drank it down and then I tossed the empty cup back at him.

"Then why did you accept?" I asked, my voice straining from the burning whiskey.

"There was no way I could've refused," he said.

"What do you mean? That's crazy—you could've told him to go to hell."

"I told you, I'm fucked up that way. I love it too goddamned much. I'll fly for the colonel, all right. I like his style. He's one of the few that seems to know what he's trying to do around here."

"You think so?"

"Yeah, I do," he said with a nod. "Say, Bronco, how many days are you short?"

"Shit," I said, laughing. "I suppose I'll be in double digits in a few months, but right now, as it sits, I've got another shitload of time in-country."

"It'll go by fast, you'll see," he said. "So, I suppose you'll be heading back to Alaska when you get stateside."

"*Alaska?* No, I'll never go back there."

"Really?" he said, looking surprised. "That's some beautiful country. "That's too bad, because I'd sure love to fly my bird over Alaska sometime."

"I'll tell you what, Flanny," I said. "If you ever get a bird in Alaska, I'll go back just to fly with you."

"Deal," he said.

Chapter Ten

May 1985

Emily comes storming through the living room door. "Where's Mom?" she says, her eyes wide and her face flush.

"She's not home yet, honey. I just got here myself. I thought you were with her helping her clean her classroom," he says.

"I was," says Emily, "but Mom had to go somewhere. She dropped me off at Amber's, but she said she'd be home by now. She said she's bringing Kobuk."

The doorbell rings. Opening the door, he is surprised to see Mrs. Adams holding Kobuk in one arm and a blanket in the other.

"Hi!" says Mrs. Adams, handing him the blanket.

Emily rushes to Kobuk.

"Oh, he so cute," she says. "Where's Mom?"

Mrs. Adams glances about the room.

"I thought she'd be here," she says.

"No, she dropped Emily off at Amber's and, I guess, went into town," he says.

"That's odd," she says, lifting her eyebrows. "She asked me to bring Kobuk over since she wasn't going straight home, but she said she'd be here. I don't recall where she said she was going, but maybe—"

Emily shrieks as Kobuk leaps from her arms. Emily runs to him.

"What's the matter, honey?" he says.

"Kobuk isn't very nice, Daddy," she says with a sniffle.

"Why's that, honey?"

"He scratched me," she says, pointing to her chin.

"I'm sorry, honey," he says, examining her chin, "but it doesn't appear to be too bad." He kisses her chin. "You have to be careful, sweetheart. Puppies like to play. Sometimes they get a little rough, but they don't mean to be."

"Really?" she says.

"Of course, honey. You just have to be careful because Kobuk may not know any better. It's going to be your job to teach him," he says, smiling at Mrs. Adams.

Mrs. Adams gives him an approving smile.

"All right," says Emily, and she walks over to Mrs. Adams, who is now holding a squirming Kobuk. "He does like to lick," she says with a giggle.

"He sure does," says Mrs. Adams, handing him to Emily. "Okay, I better be on my way, I have some dogs of my own to take care of. We'll see you, dear." She gives Emily a kiss on the forehead and Kobuk a pat on the head.

"Good-bye, Mrs. Adams," he says.

"Good-bye, Mr. Allen. I'm sorry about the mix-up. I really thought Mrs. Allen would be here. I'm sure she'll be along shortly. I can't believe I don't remember where she said she was going."

"That's okay, it really doesn't—"

"She went to the ranch," says Emily.

"What, honey?" he asks.

"She went to the ranch," Emily says again, "but not the one with horses."

"What ranch, sweetie?" he asks.

"I don't know," says Emily, shrugging. "But I asked Mommy if me and Kobuk could go with her and see the horses at the ranch, but Mr. Marks said that it wasn't the kind of ranch that had horses."

Crashing waves and crying seagulls ousted me from my slumber. But the gusty winds and the warm salt air were soothing. The night before, I had decided not to head west to El Paso right away but, instead, go south. I drove through Austin and San Antonio until I reached the Gulf of Mexico and Corpus Christi where I found the ocean a few hours before dawn. I followed the first sign promising a beach, parked, grabbed my sleeping bag, and followed the sound of the surf. Now, staring out into the darkness that was the ocean, I waited for sunrise.

The morning did much to ease my anxious mind as I found its quiet rays cleansing. I lay there on the beach for a couple hours staring at the horizon, trying everything not to think of anything, but something always came to mind. The sun had done me some good, and back at the truck, I felt eager to hit the highway again.

"This beach is closed," a high-pitched voice came from behind me.

I jerked my head around and saw a small bearded and sun-browned man sitting beneath a *Beach Access* sign staring at me through thick Coke-bottle glasses, which made his black eyes appear enormous.

"This beach is closed," he said again, twisting his face as if he had just tasted something sour. "If *they* catch you, you *will* be prosecuted for *trespass*. Then you *will* be fined, and at their discretion, you may be subject to a short term of *incarceration*," he said, articulating every word.

"Incarceration for trespass . . . on a public beach. You can't be serious." I said, confused.

"At their discretion, you may be subject to a short term of incarceration," he repeated in the same articulated monotone. "And this beach is closed," he added.

"I can't imagine that anybody would incarcerate me for trespassing on a public beach, especially when it's not even posted," I said, shaking my head. "Besides, *they* didn't catch me."

"No *they* did not and probably won't—without my cooperation," he said, smacking his lips together. He then pulled his knees to his chest and began stroking at his matted gray beard.

"Thank you . . . for not cooperating . . . I guess," I said, not sure what to make of the little elflike fellow.

"If you are so obliged, you may offer me a *consideration*," he said.

"A *consideration*?"

"Yes, you may offer me a consideration for keeping you from prosecution, a fine, and a possible term of incarceration."

"You want me to pay you money?"

"Not money," he squeaked, "a consideration."

"What kind of consideration then?" I said.

The little man again smacked his lips together and then got to his feet. He skipped past me wearing nothing but the glasses and a pair of ripped flowered swim trunks that exposed more of his bony ass than I cared to see. He then went over, picked up my sneakers, and dangled them before me by the laces.

"You could offer me these," he said.

"You want my old high-tops?"

"Yes, they would be adequate consideration," he said, flashing me a toothless grin. Then brushing the wild gray tresses from his thick glasses, he said, "Adequate consideration indeed."

Thinking the little guy was probably homeless or crazy, or perhaps both, a pair of blown-out high-tops seemed a small price to avoid any trouble. Besides, I had a pair of old sandals in my duffel bag.

"Sure, take them," I said. "I don't think they'll fit you."

"Thank you," he said, walking back and sitting down beneath the sign. Then slipping on the high-tops, he pulled the laces tight, wrapping the extra around his skinny ankles several times. The shoes were obviously several sizes too big, but he didn't seem to mind as, all at once, he stood up and began dancing around the sign in a sort of Rumplestiltskinian fit, chanting:

"*Tiger, tiger burning bright, in the shadows of the night, what immortal hand or eye, dare frame thy fearful symmetry?*"

He repeated it several times, and I recognized the verse.

"*Blake*, right?" I said.

He didn't answer right away, but instead sat back down and stared at me again with his distortedly big eyes. He scratched his head and then began stroking vigorously at his beard.

"Yes, *William Blake*," he said finally. "The poem is entitled '*The Tyger,*' spelled with a '*y,*' not an '*i*'. And it is taught in most every survey of English literature course in any high school or at any university. But I will not tell you any more without further consideration."

"You're kidding, right?" I said

"Why would you think I was kidding?" he asked me, smacking his lips together again and then twisting his face.

"I don't know," I said, shaking my head and turning away from him. I then walked around to the back of the truck and pulled out my duffel bag. After a few seconds of digging around at the bottom, I managed to find my old sandals. I tossed them to the ground and then stepped into them. When I returned to the front of the truck, I found my curious new friend standing over my sleeping bag.

"It's the only bag I have," I said, "so don't go getting any ideas. I don't care that much about that poetry shit."

"You might be better for it," he said, returning to the sign.

"I doubt it," I said, opening my truck door. "Say . . ." I said, and then hesitating, " . . . I don't think I got your name."

"You never asked me," he said, brushing off a patch of dried sand from his bare chest.

"Well, if it doesn't cost me—or require me to pay or offer you a *consideration*—I wouldn't mind knowing."

"You may call me Eddie," he said, flashing me another toothless smile.

"Pleased to meet you, Eddie," I said politely. "You need a ride somewhere—home maybe?"

"No, I never ride in vehicles," he said, glancing away. He looked back at me, his smile gone.

"I'm sorry about that not-riding," I said, feeling the sudden change in his mood. "I better get moving," I added. "Again, it was nice to meet you." I folded up the sleeping bag, placed it in the back of the truck, and then opened the truck door.

"Very well then," he said, "nice to meet you too . . . *Henry*."

I was somewhat stunned—not because he knew my name or because I now believed that he actually was psychic, but because I knew that he must have gone through my things. And even that wouldn't have been too upsetting, except that I hadn't yet checked for my billfold, and I had a gun in my duffel bag.

"You saw my driver's license, right?" I took a step toward him, slamming the truck door shut. "Listen, I don't want any trouble. Obviously you went through my things to know my name. So what did you take, Eddie?"

At first, I thought maybe he didn't hear me, as he had turned his head away and began stroking at his beard again, but then he turned back and looked at me through the thick glasses.

"I am *not* a thief!" he shouted, his squeaky voice cracking. "I didn't take any of your things, and I only looked at your registration, in case I had to cooperate with the authorities. Go ahead, take a look. If there is anything missing, I assure you, I didn't take it!"

Maybe it was the tone of his squeaky voice, his looks, or his quirky little mannerisms, but I knew right then that he hadn't stolen anything, and I felt a little silly and ashamed.

"I'm sorry, Eddie, I shouldn't have accused you. It wasn't nice," I said, and then I turned back toward the truck.

"Do you have any children?" he asked as I was reaching for the door handle.

"Excuse me?" I said, glancing at him.

"Do you have any children, Henry?" he asked again.

"No," I said. "But why do you ask?"

"No matter," he said, waving his hand at me. "I thought maybe you had, but I am wrong."

"Please tell me," I said, curious.

He went through his series of contortions, facial twists, and head turns. When he finished, he smacked his lips together and then blinked rapidly.

"Two reasons, really," he began. "First, you have a bit of an accusatory air about you—like you have children or deal with them regularly. But perhaps you are a teacher of children, or perhaps a prosecutor. Second, and this is primarily why I asked, you displayed an interest in the *Tyger* poem, and as much as it is a staple in English literature, to me it is still a sort of nursery rhyme, quite rich in rhythm and tone and therefore attractive to children. It made me think that perhaps you had children." He smacked his lips together again and then pulled his knees tight to his chest before continuing. "But I suppose the poem could have interested you for a number of reasons other than its childish appeal—you know, there is the *contrary state of the human* soul. The concept is interesting."

"Contrary state of the human soul," I said. "I'm afraid you got me there. I don't have children, but I am a lawyer. Was—not anymore, but I'm not a prosecutor. I'm only a traveler now."

"No matter," he said glibly. "It is who you are—or were," he added.

"So, Eddie, do you have children?" I asked.

He gave me a wide smile that I was sure would've positively gleamed had he a single tooth. "Two, as a matter of fact," he said, holding up two fingers. "They are back in Alabama. I don't see them as much as I used to. I have a beautiful wife back there too." He let out a squeaky sort of sigh. "And they too enjoy the *Tyger* poem," he added.

To look at him, I never would've taken him for a family man.

"That's great," I said, sitting down across from him. "I thought it was interesting that you should ask me whether I had children or not.

Of course I don't, but lately, I've had these dreams that I do. A child, anyway—a little girl."

Why I chose to discuss my dreams now with this odd little fellow, I hadn't a clue, but I stared at him intently, waiting for his reaction.

"A girl," he said right away without his usual convulsive repertoire. "Splendid! I have two young girls. That is most interesting—most interesting, indeed. Girls are a handful, aren't they?"

"I'm not sure," I said sheepishly. "I don't really have a girl, I only dream that I do. And a wife—I don't have one of those either."

"Yes, yes," he said, waving his hand dismissively, "but I assure you, they are a handful. Always up to something. I miss them very much. But that can't be helped, I suppose—always moving."

I gave him an unconvincing nod. Again, to look at him, I had a hard time believing that he had a family of any kind, but I supposed a part of me wanted to believe that he did.

"What do you do, Eddie?" I asked.

This time, he did a fair amount of twisting and jerking before saying, "I thought you would have figured that out by now, but I'm a teacher."

"A teacher, that makes sense," I said, nodding.

"Now you say you dream about having a family?"

"No, I dream that I actually have a family—a wife and daughter," I explained.

He flashed me another toothless grin. "Girls—they are a handful, aren't they? But I like to say, they are my angels," he said.

"*Angels*?" I said.

"Oh yes, yes, that's right. You do not have any children—only dream that you do. Yes, yes. Well, perhaps I do not understand. I am only a teacher of history and literature . . . not psychology." He cackled.

"Yes, yes. They are everywhere, I guess." He glanced around, twisting and jerking his head then, after cackling loudly, he said, "Yes, yes, they are everywhere."

"Everywhere?" I said.

He nodded and then grinned.

"Sure," he said, "the personification of our thoughts and ideas—some real, others not. I like to think of them as such. *Angels*, yes, yes—so called, sometimes helpful, sometimes not, delivering us from whatever it may be we need delivering—there to guide, to show us the way."

"Like guardian angels?" I said.

He let out a high-pitched laugh, his eyes bouncing behind the thick spectacles.

"If that's how you like to think of them. More to *guide* than to *guard*, however, yes, yes, *guiding angels*," he said.

"And I am to follow these *guiding angels*?" I said.

"Not all of them," he laughed. "Heavens no. They all may have answers, yes, yes, but not all of them are the right ones." He glanced away for a moment, let out a rasping sigh, and his eyes shifted back to mine. "They are there when we need them," he said, suddenly calm. "There are sometimes many, sometimes few, but they are always there—there to guide."

"Guide?" I said.

He stared at me, quiet and motionless for a long while. Then all at once, he burst into laughter and into another twisting and jerking fit, knocking himself backward onto his elbows.

"If we can find the better ones," he cackled. "Yes, yes, the *convenient* ones. Sometimes they are all we see. The *better* angels are sometimes more difficult to discover. You must look for them," he said, leaning forward.

"*Better angels*? I'll keep my eyes open," I said.

"Yes, yes, you must," he said, lowering his voice. "They are there, Henry. Perhaps that is why you dream what you dream. Perhaps you have found them already. It is only a matter of perspective. Blake suggests that there are two contrary states to the human soul in his work *Songs of Innocence* and *Songs of Experience*. That is, the poems contained in *Songs of Innocence* portray an innocence—not to beg the question, mind you," he said, holding up his hand. "They portray a naivety, if you will, as though they were written from the perspective of a child—like the little lamb in the nursery rhyme. When the soul is pure and faith in God is inviolable. While in *Songs of Experience*, the poems portray a corrupt and distorted view of the human condition that is ugly and frightening, and which is born from *experience . . . life experience*. Like the imagery captured in the Tyger poem," he said, then paused reflectively.

"I think I know that condition," I said.

"It's about perspective—fleecy white lambs versus burning tigers."

"I can assure you that there is nothing burning about the Tigers these days," I said sarcastically.

He smiled, as though he had understood the reference.

"It is a fascinating concept, however, one that I have explored myself on occasion. There is an old riddle. You may have heard it before, but I believe it to be an excellent example of Blake's concept. The riddle goes like this: what is greater than God, more evil than the devil? What do the rich need and the poor have?"

My first inkling was that I didn't have any goddamned idea, but I pondered it for a few moments as, admittedly, it intrigued me. And Eddie seemed very interested in my answer, as he repeated it several times, all the while grinning and studying my face with his exaggerated eyes.

"I don't know," I said, finally shaking my head. "Is it a trick question?"

"I suppose, by definition, a riddle is a trick question," he said smiling. "But actually, the answer is fairly straightforward."

"Well, I haven't a clue. What's the answer?"

"*Nothing*," he said, clapping once and then holding out his hands.

"*Nothing* is the answer?"

"Of course it is *nothing*," he said and then he let out a loud squeaky cackle.

"I see," I said, smiling back at him. "Very clever."

"My interest in the riddle is *not* its cleverness," he said before shaking his head rapidly. "Oh no. My interest in it has nothing to do with the truth of the riddle itself, but everything to do with the individual answering it—or the individual who *can* answer it correctly."

"That's obviously not me." I snickered.

"Don't be too hard on yourself," he said. "I use the riddle to illustrate Blake's concept. You see, you are not alone. Most individuals like you do not answer it correctly."

"Like myself?"

"Yes, like you."

"What individuals like me?"

"Adults," he said with half of a squeaky cackle, and he smacked his lips together. "Most adults do not answer correctly."

"Why is that?"

"Because it is, as Blake suggests, *the contrary state of the human soul.*"

"So children answer correctly."

"More often than adults, that is for certain."

"Why is that?"

"Innocence," he said. "Children believe unconditionally that God is almighty and he makes everything right with the world. In fact, the children that answer it correctly do not need to hear the entire riddle. You only need ask them: *What is greater than God?* And they will most emphatically tell you that *nothing* is greater than God. Whereas a grown man like yourself will pass right over the first line of the riddle, thinking as you did, that there must be some kind of trick to it. That is because most adults have *experiences—life experiences* that cause them to question and, in some cases, even reject God as the Almighty. As adults, we've seen the misery, the corruption, and the suffering in this world, and we doubt. You see, it is lambs and tigers!"

"Remarkable," I said. "That does make sense. So I guess I'm a lost cause?"

"Oh, I don't think that. None of us stay lambs forever, although there are those who would try," he said, cackling again. "Blake's concept is interesting, but I am not certain that it does us any good. However, it easy to see our own innocence in our children. I do in mine. They are my *better angels*. Good or bad, it is where we see our innocence again—where we might believe or even hope again. Perhaps it is where you will find *your* angels, Henry," he added with an easy smile. "Perhaps you already have."

I wasn't certain whether it was his words or the sun that suddenly made my face feel warm and its skin feel tight. But I had an urge to move. Eddie was truly a captivating little fellow; even his squeaky nasal voice had grown on me. Looks could be deceiving. He was no doubt one of those eccentric college professors doing one of those lecture circuits, or conducting a summer experiment about perception, or perspectives—probably vagrancy or something. I couldn't be sure, but it was what I wanted to believe.

"Thank you, Eddie," I said, standing up. "I must say that it has been a pleasure. You are a tremendous teacher—I definitely would have signed up for your course. But I've been in the sun too long, and I better be on my way."

"The pleasure is mine," he said, grinning up at me. "Remember, however"—his face and tone became suddenly serious—"if they catch you, you *will* be prosecuted for *trespass*. Then you *will* be fined, and at their discretion, you may be subject to a short term of *incarceration,*" he said.

"I'll be sure to remember," I said, reaching into the back of the truck and taking out the sleeping bag. I walked over and handed it to him.

"Adequate consideration?" I said.

"More than adequate," he said, flashing me one last toothless grin.

Chapter Eleven

June 1962

From high atop one of the enormous tailing piles that loomed bare over the valley, I stood next to Saucy and watched a determined beaver tug a freshly cut log along the near side of the pond toward his dam. Saucy too watched, perched on her hind legs, her ears perked and her eyes fixed on the slogging creature.

"Sauce!" I shouted at her. "Let it alone, girl!"

Seesawing her eyebrows, she let out a defiant groan before obediently laying her head down on her front paws.

"Good girl," I said, reaching down and patting her head. "You don't want to mess with that old beaver anyway."

From where I stood, I could see the evening's sunrays reflecting off the tin roof of my house. Along a thicket of newly sprouting birch and aspen trees, my eyes followed Gilmore's Creek to the dusty road that connected my house to the highway. There, they continued impulsively westward until settling upon the peaks of junk piles that were the Shit Towers and Jessie's home.

It had been nearly two weeks since Jessie's date with Kenny Brenke, and during those weeks, I had not seen or heard from her. I had already cut and stacked Spooner's winter wood. I had fished the shit out of every known river and creek in the valley. Twice, I had gone to Fairbanks to fly the chopper with Tom, and most recently, I had shocked the hell out of myself by volunteering to help my mother do chores around the house. I found that I would do just about anything to keep my mind off Jessie and Kenny. I hadn't been able to sleep or eat, and the only bit of solace I found was here atop the tailing pile, high above everything, gazing vigilantly across the valley at the Shit Towers wishing I could turn back the hands of time to before I had ever heard of Kenny Brenke.

I had had an urge to go see her, or to just happen by her place and try and talk with her, but such urges were soon abandoned when I realized that I wouldn't know what to say to her—or far worse, I imagined what she might say to me. Besides, even if we did talk, how could I ever forget about her and Kenny together? I supposed it didn't matter what I did. She had Kenny now, and I had nothing.

"Screw it," I said. "Come on, Sauce, let's go home."

I awoke to a thumping sound, and at first, I thought someone was knocking at the trailer door. Then I saw a shadow from behind the curtains above the table moving back and forth. Again, I heard thumping—somebody banging on the front widow. I pulled back the curtains and saw a white handkerchief tied to the end of a stick and a hand waving both frantically. I immediately went to the door and pushed it open.

"Jessie!" I yelled, but there was no answer. The air was cool, the midnight sun sunk low in the sky. I glanced at my watch and saw that it was well past 3:00 a.m. "Jessie!" I yelled again, but still no answer.

Stepping outside, I felt a cool breeze across my waist and instantly realized I was standing in my underwear.

"Jessie! Is that—" Then all at once, she stepped out from around the corner of the trailer and stood facing me. Her hair was pulled back into a ponytail, and her dark eyes lay soft on her face. She held the stick with the handkerchief in her right hand and, with her left, she tightly gripped the clasp to her bib overalls. We stood in silence for several seconds.

"*Truce?*" she said, finally waving her flag.

I couldn't think of anything to say and stood staring at her.

"Truce?" she said again.

"Sure," I said.

Jessie lowered the handkerchief and took a step forward and then hesitated. "Can I come in?" she asked, more with her eyes than her voice.

"Sure," I said again, but I didn't move and let her brush against me as she passed. She smelled fresh, like soap.

We both sat silently staring at each other from across the table. I didn't have anything to say, but I knew I wouldn't. Besides, she had been the one to come calling in the middle of the night. She had been the one who had offered the truce. She had been the one to fuck Kenny Brenke, so if she had something to say, she'd better say it.

But Jessie didn't say anything. Instead, she fiddled with the clasp to her overalls and stared blankly out the window. When her eyes did not find anything of interest there, she shifted them to the ceiling and then to walls and several other locations around the inside of the trailer until, inevitably, they shifted to me. When that became unbearable, she pulled the rubber band from her ponytail, shook out her hair, and then placed the rubber band around her wrist.

"Nice tighty-whities," she finally said with a giggle and then brushed a lock of hair from her eyes.

Her tone was sassy and familiar, and at any other time, I probably would've laughed. But my mind was filled with images of her and Kenny together, and that wasn't funny.

"Yeah, well that's what you get when you come calling on folks at this hour," I barked. "Shoot, if I'd known it was you, I'd have *bare-assed it!*"

Jessie's eyes widened.

"What's that supposed to mean?"

I hadn't seen her in two weeks, and I missed her terribly. I missed everything about her—her looks, her voice, her laugh, and even her anger. But I too was angry, and I couldn't let it go.

"I don't know, maybe I should ask Kenny Brenke!" I shouted at her.

The words came out loud and vicious, and by the fierce look on her face, I knew they had stung. She raised her hand and, for a second, I thought she was going to slap me. Then, unexpectedly, she lowered it and leaned back, her face softening.

"You hate me," she said, as tears welled up in her eyes.

I looked away.

"You hate me," she repeated, her voice cracking. "I can't imagine what you think of me. You can't even look at me. You really hate me."

I wasn't sure what to do, but I did look at her. I watched her pull her hair back into a ponytail and fasten it with the rubber band. She slid from behind the table and moved toward the door.

"Wait," I said.

She stopped and then, facing me, she said, "What, Henry?"

"I don't hate you," I said, shaking my head. "I could never hate you, Jess."

"I don't believe you," she said. "You must think I'm a whore—because I am. That's all I am, Henry—nothing but a whore." She fell to her knees, put her hands over her face, and began sobbing loudly into her hands.

"No, I don't, Jess," I said. "I don't hate you, and I don't think you're a whore. I'm not sure what I think, but it's not like that. I only know you're my friend, probably my only friend. And maybe I haven't been such a good friend—maybe I haven't been a friend at all. All I could think about was you and him. But it wasn't on account of what you did, Jess. It was because you didn't do it with me."

I knew it was the truth, but I was surprised that I had said it.

"Please know that I could never hate you, Jess, because I love you."

It was strange to hear myself say the words. Jessie removed her hands from her face and looked up at me through tear-swelled eyes.

"Well don't," she said, shaking her head. "I'm not worth it. And you can ask Kenny Brenke about that."

She wiped her eyes and then her nose on her sleeve.

"What do you mean?"

"The day after our date, Kenny picked me up and we went to his house. He said his parents were at some dinner party and they wouldn't be home until late, so we watched some television—"

"Brenke's got a television?"

"Sure," she said. "A big one, but who cares? Like I said, we were watching television and everything was fine—then it wasn't. He started kissing me all over . . . and, well, he wanted to . . . you know. And I only wanted to watch TV, but he kept on . . . well, you know. So we started necking."

"*Necking?*"

"Yeah, necking—don't be a *rube!*" she fired. "We were *necking*, see, and we were on the sofa when all the sudden his parents walked in and all hell broke loose. His mother started screaming at him and then at me. The whole time, his dad is trying to calm his mother down. I think she called me a tramp, Henry."

"For necking?"

"I might've had my shirt off," she said.

"Your shirt was off?"

"Yes, my shirt was off. I think my pants too."

"Your pants?"

"Yes, Henry, I was in my underwear—kind of like you are now." She giggled, pointing under the table at my tighty-whities. "Anyway, his dad ended up driving me home. Didn't say peep to me the whole way—real asshole. And that was that," she said, shrugging.

"What do you mean, *that was that?* When did you and Kenny break up?"

"The next day," she said.

"I won't say I'm sorry to hear it," I said. "You did well dumping the *bastard.*"

"Oh, I didn't dump him," she said, shaking her head.

"You didn't?"

"No, I didn't. But to tell you the truth, I didn't expect to ever see him again, the way his parents had carried on. I figured after that they wouldn't let him out of the house."

"But you saw him?"

"Yeah, he showed up at my house early the next day. Tells me his parents were still pretty hot about everything and that they wanted him to start focusing on college and his future—you know, since he graduated. They told him he doesn't have time for girls if he's going to become a doctor. They said he had to work and save money for college. He works for his dad at the Food King. His old man is a grocer."

"I didn't know that," I said.

"Yeah, for a long time. They don't want Kenny to end up a grocer like his dad though. That's why they're so set on him going to college and becoming a doctor."

"But they let him come and tell you that?"

"Yeah. He said that since we don't have telephones out here, his parents let him come and see me."

"So he drove all the way out here to break up with you?"

"Yeah, his dad said it was the right thing to do—common courtesy and all."

"He said that?"

"Yeah, can you believe it?"

"What did you say?"

"What do you think I said? I kindly told him that he and his common courtesy could go fuck themselves!"

Jessie laughed, and I did too.

"But get this," she said. "After I told him that, he acted really strange. Told me that he didn't care what his parents thought and that he wanted to see me anyway. Then he up and tries to kiss me."

"No kidding? What did you do?"

"What do you think? I told him to get the hell off my property," she said, leaning back and crossing her arms. "All he wanted was to get down my pants," she added with a smile.

"Did he leave?"

"Not at first, but then I told him that I was going to go and get Daddy, and he hightailed it. I was going to come by here the next day, but I couldn't imagine what you must've thought of me. You know, after the last time we—"

"Doesn't matter," I said, holding up my hand.

"So we can still be friends?" She gave me a half smile and then slapped my knee.

"Best friends," I said.

"Don't be corny," she said, still smiling.

Jessie got up off the floor and sat beside me at the table. She gave me a quick kiss on the lips and then hugged me, and for a long time we held each other. Finally, she stood up, scowling down at me.

"Don't go getting any ideas, rube. We're friends, remember? I'm not sleeping with you, Henry Allen—*ever!*" she said.

"*Ever,*" I said, surprised. "Why not?"

"Because I love you too—more than you'll ever know," she said softly.

She then stood up.

"Get some sleep, rube. I'll be over in the morning with the newspapers. You've got a lot of catching up to do. Also, I found something you might find interesting."

Before I could say anything, she was out the door.

Jessie was true to her word. She showed up early the next morning, her arms full of *News-Miner*s and bottles of Pepsi. She made me read the line scores for the last two weeks. And though I was certain that she'd already read them, I didn't say a word. It had been a rough two weeks for the Tigers, but so had it been for me.

"What do you want to do now?" I asked when I finished reading. There was still a lot of morning left, and I was looking forward to having Jessie back and all to myself.

"Look at this," she said, pulling a pink flowered notebook from beneath the pile of newspapers.

"What is it?" I asked curiously.

"I told you yesterday that I found something that I wanted to show you. It's my grandmother's diary."

"Where did you get that?" I said, curious.

"Now that's funny," she said, flashing me a smile. "Daddy wanted me to hem a pair of his pants the other day, and I found it buried in my grandmother's sewing basket."

"What's so funny about that?" I said.

"I don't sew," she said, laughing.

"I think I figured out who Francis O'Brien is," she said, opening the diary.

"He's one of the partners. I told you that."

"I know," she said, "but he's the O'Brien brother that Abigail was having the affair with."

"How do you know?"

"Because it says right here," she said, running a finger down a page. "It says: *Frankie came by with a drill bit for Spense. Spense was down at the mine, but Frankie stayed and we had coffee and toast and then he fixed the front door. Until today, I did not know anything about him, except he's a little fellow and wears his mustache curled. I told him, next to Spense, he looks like a boy, and he thought that was funny. He said he's from upstate New York. A town called Binghamton. He said he worked in a factory there that made odd machinery. He said he's even been to Flint a time or two. He said he had a girl back home, but isn't sure anymore as he's been gone so long. He said he hasn't heard from her in over a year. When I thanked him for fixing the door, he said I could come up and mend the curtains in his cabin. Gosh, I wonder what Spense would think!*"

Jessie looked up at me with a curious smile.

"So what's the big deal about that?" I said.

"The big deal is," said Jessie, scowling, "Frankie, or Francis—whatever you want to call him—is the man she ran off with."

"What makes you think that?"

"Two things, really," she said, glancing back down at the diary. "See this? The cover of the diary has a flower pattern." She held it up for me. "It matches the lining inside the sewing basket. The diary is a false bottom to the basket. It was well hidden."

"Then how did you find it?"

"I'm a clever woman," she said coolly. "Besides, I've seen one before—back in Michigan.

"What's the other thing?"

"It's fairly obvious from the diary that the two were having an affair. She's always referring to him as *sweet Frankie* and *my darling Frankie*. And they did everything together. Kind of like we do. You know—walks, picnics, that sort of thing."

"We're not having an affair, are we?" I said.

Jessie scowled at me again before her eyes jumped back to the diary.

"Everyone already knows she was having an affair," I said. "She ran off, for crying out loud."

"That's true, but they didn't know who she was having the affair with or where they ran off to," said Jessie. "I thought the diary might give me a clue."

"What's your dad say?"

Jessie shot me another vile look. "Daddy was three when she ran off. He doesn't remember a thing. Granddaddy's sister up in Bay City raised him, remember?"

"Bay City?"

"Bay City, Michigan. That's where he lived, except the summers he spent up here working with Granddaddy. Most think they ended up in New York, since that's where Frankie was from originally. But I did find out that the other partner was Frankie's younger brother, Jules O'Brien. It says in the diary that Jules was a carpenter of sorts."

Jessie flipped through the diary and then, stopping at a particular page, she said, "*Jules up the Fairbanks way again building his cabin for that woman—a Russian—said her father knew Felix Pedro . . .*"

Jessie's voice broke off. "I wonder who that is," she said with another scowl.

"Nobody really—only a legend. First to discover gold in these parts." I laughed.

Jessie shot me a vicious look, but then continued to read. "*Haven't met her yet, but Frankie says she's very pleasant. She had been married before to a prospector from one of the Dakotas. He and two others were killed in some type of mine collapse five years ago. God forgive me, but at times I wish Spense had found his way into a collapsed mine.*"

"Your grandmother sounds wicked," I said.

"Or maybe Spenser was. Believe me, Hen," she said. "He can be a *bastard*. He was mean to her."

"How so?"

Jessie flipped some more pages around in the diary.

"Says here, *was late getting back yesterday. Spense upset about dinner, locked me up in the meat cache. Didn't let me out until James started fussing the next morning. He wouldn't let me eat but told me to feed James. Spense gets so angry sometimes—he would surely kill me if he knew where I was.*"

Then thumbing to a page she had marked with a piece of purple ribbon.

"And listen to this," she said, examining the page. "*Man from the dredge company came to dinner today. Asked Spense if he and his partners had agreed to sell. Spense said they were all in agreement. I let out a laugh because Frankie says he and Spense couldn't agree on anything. Afterwards, Spense was furious. Arm in a cast for next six weeks. Spense told doctor I slipped and fell in the kitchen. Spense not the least bit sorry about it. Said he'd break the other one if I ever embarrassed him again. Made me cook dinner.*"

"You think Spenser broke her arm?"

"Sure I do," she said, her eyes fiery. "You should see how he gets."

"What will you do if you find out where they went?"

"Nothing, I guess. I'm just curious," she said with a sigh. "Besides, I haven't really found out much of anything everybody doesn't already know. She didn't say peep about running off in here," said Jessie, tapping the top of the diary. But she did meet Frankie a lot at some place they called *the rendezvous*."

"The rendezvous?" I said.

"Yeah, it's some spot where they always met," she said, flipping through more pages of the diary. "Right here, it's the last entry. It says, *walked the line to the rendezvous and am waiting on Frankie. I hope he doesn't make me wait too long. I can't wait to give him the news.—April 2, 1938*."

"Why would she write that stuff? It seems that if you were having some scandalous affair, you wouldn't want to write it all down—particularly if Spenser is the bastard you say he is."

"She loved him," said Jessie with a trace of admiration in her voice.

"She says that in there?" I asked, pointing to the diary.

"On just about every other page . . . in so many words," said Jessie. "It's very romantic."

"I thought you said it was a *shit thing* to do?"

"Oh, it is a *shit thing* to do, but that doesn't make it any less romantic. Abandoning her baby is unforgivable, but nonetheless, it's a good read."

"I will have to take your word for it," I said.

"I wonder where their rendezvous place was. Have you ever heard of it?"

"Heard of what?"

"A place where someone could *walk a line*," she said. "Have you ever heard of such a place?"

"What kind of line—a power line, a trout line? What?"

"A power line. Yeah, that could be it," she said, nodding. "Are there any power lines around here?"

"Sure, plenty, but probably not when your grandmother was around. It's probably a cabin or something. I mean it was spring, and still cold around here. I don't think they would rendezvous outside in a snowbank if they *rendezvoused* the way I think they *rendezvoused*."

Jessie didn't see my shameless grin but, instead, continued to peer down at the diary. "I wonder what news she has for him and why it suddenly ends here."

"A lot of reasons—maybe she ran out of pages in the diary?"

"No, can't be," said Jessie, holding up the diary. "Nearly half the pages are still blank."

"I don't know . . . maybe she thought Spenser was on to her. Maybe she didn't have time. Maybe she got bored with it—who knows? There could be a million reasons."

"I suppose," she sighed. "Sure seems odd though."

"What's odd is that she kept a diary in the first place."

"Maybe. That's why I would like to find the rendezvous. Do you know any place like that?"

"Wait," I said. "She doesn't mean a power line. I bet she means a trap line. Remember, her sister said something about a trap line in that letter. There are a half dozen or so known trap lines around here, and several of them have cabins or warming huts along the trail."

"You think so?"

"Definitely, all we have to do is find the right one. I know of two that are within a couple of miles of the *Shit Tow*—I mean your place," I said. "We should check out those first. There are several more within about five miles or so that I haven't been to in a while. It's probably one of them. We could check them out sometime, if you're up for a hike."

"I have two working legs now," she said, smiling. "But it can't be today. I have plans for us today."

"Plans?" I said curiously.

"It will be fun," she said, but her tone suggested otherwise.

"What?" I asked.

"Bootlegging," she said.

"*Bootlegging?* You mean like the mountain boys do on *Andy Griffith*? You know, making moonshine and all."

"For somebody that doesn't have a television, you sure know a lot of TV shows."

"Yeah, well they have one at the hangar in town. You mean like running booze?"

"Sort of," she said. "But we really wouldn't be making booze—we'd just sort of be stealing it."

"Stealing it? I'll have you know there're no distilleries or liquor stores this far out of Fairbanks—and besides, I'm not in the mood for being shot at."

"It's not like that," she said, holding up her hands and making a face. "It's my granddaddy's rum."

"Your grandpa makes rum?"

"No, of course not," she said, shaking her head and waving her arms at me. "Listen to me," she said sharply. "He's got about a case of rum, and sometimes he drinks too much of it. And, well, let's just say he doesn't act right."

"Doesn't act right?"

"He drinks too much, and it's not healthy. He drinks every night, and it's not good for him."

"How will stealing his rum help—won't he just buy more?"

"Not necessarily," she said with a wry grin. "Not if he doesn't think any rum's been stolen."

"I don't understand," I said.

"It's simple," she said, crossing her arms. "He has a case of rum or so. What we do is open every bottle and pour half of it or so out and fill it back up with water. It's called *watering down*—they do it in bars to save money. Daddy always says you can't get a decent drink in town because they're all watered down. But I think it's the perfect idea for Spenser—if he drinks it watered down, maybe he won't get so drunk. And he won't be so much of a *bastard*," she added.

"Why don't you just tell your dad and have him do something about it?"

"I would, but he probably drinks too much himself, and nobody can really tell Granddaddy anything," she said, shaking her head.

"All right. I guess, if you think it best. I'm in," I said, smiling. "I've got nothing better to do."

"It'll be fun," she said, raising her eyebrows. "We can always drink what we steal," she said, winking at me.

"Yeah, well I don't know—"

"What's wrong?" she said, sighing.

"It's just that I've never been drunk before."

"You've never been drunk before?" she said with a wide grin.

"No."

"Well there's a first time for everything," she said.

———

I hadn't been to Jessie's house since she had had her cast removed, but nothing much had changed. The outside was still heaped to the sky with junk, and the inside was the same—except the junk heaps on the inside were reluctantly capped by the ceiling. Amazingly, we found our way to the kitchen without incident (that is, nothing fell on us), and even more amazingly, Jessie was able to discern from several dozen boxes labeled *Meyer's Rum* the one that actually contained the *Meyer's Rum*. Jessie was also able to locate another much smaller box containing a dozen or so *Ball* canning jars and their lids.

"We'll put the rum in these jars and seal them. That way, we can store them somewhere," she said. "It's important that we cut the labels with a knife, so that he won't notice that they've been opened."

I examined the bottles and their caps; a paper label sealed each. "Why can't we just take off the label?" I asked, trying to peel one of them back with my thumbnail.

"You can't," she said, snatching the bottle from my hand, "I've tried—they just tear, and then it looks funny. He might notice."

Obviously, Jessie had done her homework. She had gotten all the jars and lids together. "All right," I said, shrugging, "whatever you think."

Jessie reached beneath the sink and pulled out a small paring knife and cut the label on each side and then slowly unscrewed the top. Then she poured approximately half of its contents into one of the canning jars.

"Here, hold this," she said, handing me a plastic funnel. I placed the funnel into the bottle as Jessie filled a pitcher up from a large five-gallon water jug and began pouring it into the funnel.

"Fox spring water?"

"Only the best for Granddaddy," she said with a giggle.

It must have been hard for Jessie. They didn't have running water here, which meant it had to be hauled from the Fox water hole, and then heated on the stove for cooking and bathing. My family had only had a well a few years, and I remember how difficult it had been without one. But Jessie never complained, and she always appeared fresh and clean.

"Does this mean your grandpa will only be half drunk?" I asked as Jessie screwed down the cap and carefully lined up the cut labels

"I hope so," she said, laughing. "If he's half drunk and I'm half drunk, we should get along just fine."

It took us a little less than an hour to water down all the bottles of rum, fill and seal the canning jars, and then pack them neatly back into the boxes. When Jessie had stowed the box back where she had found it, she handed me the one containing the jars of rum and, obediently, I followed her out of the kitchen.

"Where are we storing these?"

"I figured you would know what to do with them," she said, holding the door open for me.

"Shoot, I don't know. Couldn't we just hide them somewhere around here?" I said, glancing over junk. "You could hide a mountain here."

"Believe it or not, Spenser knows where everything is around here—chances are he'd find it," she said.

I did have a hard time believing that, but I would have to take her word for it. Suddenly, Saucy leaped out from behind what looked to be a stack of rotten box springs.

"Hey girl!" shouted Jessie. "You know," she said, kneeling down to rub Saucy's face, "Saucy came to visit a couple times this past week."

"Damn *traitor* dog," I said to Saucy who was basking in all the sudden attention.

"Hey, I know where we can hide the rum."

"Where?"

"Grab a shovel and follow me," I said.

By the time we trekked through the woods, crossed over the beaver dam, and then climbed to the top of the gigantic tailing pile, I wondered where I ever got the stupid idea to hide them up here. My arms were already sore, and I still had digging to do. Jessie took the box and set it down. We both sat for a few moments to catch our breath.

Jessie removed one of the jars from the box, opened it, and took a large sip of the rum. She made wicked face but swallowed it down nevertheless. "Usually I mix it with Pepsi," she said, coughing. "But this'll do." She handed me the jar, and I held it to my nose, inhaling the pungent aroma. "Go ahead," she said, nodding. "It's no big deal."

I took a tiny sip, but even that went down like molten lava. "Shit!" I said, gagging. "People drink this stuff?"

"Usually not straight like that, but yeah, they do." She nodded. "It's not so bad," she said, grabbing the jar and taking another good-sized sip. This time she barely made a face. "It's not bad at all," she said, handing it to me.

I wasn't at all concerned with the notion of getting drunk, but the thought of swallowing more of that bootlegged gasoline made my insides curl. "I don't think so," I said, shaking my head.

"Oh c'mon, you big baby," she said mockingly.

"Since you put it that way," I said, taking the jar. I held my breath and took a full swallow. Everything inside my body from my tongue down was on fire, making it difficult to breathe. I thought for sure I would puke. Miraculously, I was able to keep my composure, and I was eventually able to breathe again.

"That-a-way!" shouted Jessie, taking the jar from me. "Goes down pretty smooth, doesn't it?"

"I wouldn't go that far." I coughed, pleased that it had gone down at all.

However, I soon learned that the more I drank, the easier it did go down—and the easier it went down, the more I drank. It wasn't long before the hole was dug and the stash buried, and we sat sipping rum and tossing rocks down at the trees below.

"How do you know when you're drunk?" I asked after swallowing down the last bit of rum from the jar. "I don't feel any different, and I drank most of a jar. Are you sure the stuff wasn't already watered down?"

"No, it wasn't watered down," she said. "Maybe you're just tougher than most."

"Maybe," I said. "Do you think we should open another jar?"

"If you like," she said. "But you've had plenty."

"I don't think so," I said. "I'll get another." I went to stand up, and suddenly, the ground beneath me seemed to slip. "Whoa!" I said, grabbing Jessie's shoulder.

"Oh my, you're not drunk at all," she said, holding on to me.

I did feel a little dizzy, but in a good way. The kind of dizzy you get after riding the merry-go-round for too long. Strangely, whenever I went to take a step forward, the ground beneath me seemed to slide backward. It all seemed so silly until I discovered that the ground beneath me was sliding backward a lot faster than I was moving forward. After several shaky steps, I stumbled and then fell, first over myself and then over the hill. Suddenly, my world went tossing painfully about me. At last, it came to a sudden stop at the bottom of the hill.

I lay there, scratched and sore, staring up at a pale blue sky until Jessie's face eclipsed my view.

"You drunken *rube!*" she laughed. "Are you all right?"

"Yes, I think so," I said, but I wasn't all too convinced. "Maybe I could just stay here for a while. Yes, I think that would be best. Maybe I should just sleep here, and you could come fetch me tomorrow."

"C'mon, get up," she said, grabbing my hand and pulling me to my feet. "So how does it feel being drunk?"

"Swell," I said, holding onto her shoulder to keep from teetering. I tried focusing on her face and found it extremely difficult. "I don't see the big deal about getting drunk. You're right, Jess, it is funny—I mean it's fun. Aren't I fun, Jess?"

"Sure you are, Hen," she said, guiding us along the pathway down to the beaver dam.

"Doesn't your grandpa have fun drinking?"

"Oh yeah, he has fun all right," she said. "That's the problem, he has too much fun."

"Well, I'm having fun," I said, finding it suddenly hard to talk. "And you know what?"

"What?" she said, pulling me along.

"You can't have too much fun, Jess," I said. "But you know what else?"

"What?"

"I think you're pretty, Jess," I said as she pushed me across the beaver dam.

"That's nice," she said.

Then all at once, the world began moving around me again—slowly at first, then faster, then very fast—spinning around me. When we reached the other side of the dam, I could no longer hold onto Jessie—the world was spinning too fast. I fell and tried holding onto the ground, but it kept on spinning. I couldn't stop it. "I think I'm going to be sick," I said. Then I was. I threw up on the ground in front of me. I coughed, spit and then threw up again—but still the world kept on spinning. "Why is everything spinning, Jess?"

"You're having too much fun," she said.

Chapter Twelve

October 1968

"The AO will extend farther west, gentlemen. You see this river here," said Captain Griggs, pointing to a spot on the map. Eight of us stood huddled around him during the second of our usually four daily briefings.

"This river here, *Tras-be* something or other—hell, I can't pronounce it. Anyway, when you reach that, you'll know you're close. The LZ will be southwest of there. You'll recognize it because it'll be the only damn place you'll be able to land."

The captain glared over the top of his wire spectacles at Flanny, obviously waiting for a response. Of course, Flanny didn't let him down.

"We'll actually be landing then? That's new," said Flanny, smirking. "I thought these ranger boys were having too much fun swinging their dicks from my skids."

"I'm sure they were, Mr. Flanagan, but they didn't think you were enjoying it, so they found this nice spot for you to land. They said it's *small*, but you could handle it."

The captain removed his spectacles and then smiled subtly at Flanny. The captain was a serious man in his early thirties, with just enough of a sense of humor to appreciate having a guy like Flanny in his outfit. It was easy to tell why Colonel Glasson chose Griggs for the job. The captain had a way of getting the most out of his pilots by allowing them to do what they did best—even when they weren't in a chopper.

"*Small?* That's what they said? Well that concerns me, really, Captain," said Flanny, "because those ranger boys think they have some pretty big dicks!"

We all laughed, including the captain.

"All right, all right, that's enough," said Griggs, replacing his spectacles. "Now, Flanagan, you will insert at twenty-three hundred. And, Walters, you at twenty-three forty-five. As usual, the support crews will be on alert. Any questions?"

He glanced at each one of us individually then looked back to the map. He drew several invisible circles with his index finger around the area of the targeted LZ. "There have been reports of activity in these directions. I know it's been smooth sailing so far, gentlemen, but it's important that you be aware of the latent dangers. The more of these recon missions we run, the more susceptible we become to hot activity—and ambush. Remember, you do not have any support whatsoever. If they are on to you, you are to get out. In other words, gentlemen, if the LZ is at all hot, you're to bug out—no matter what. That's an order. Are we clear?"

There was a collective assent as the captain again glanced at each one of us, staring a good amount of time at Flanny. There was a concern on his face that I hadn't noticed before now, and I could see the beads of sweat materializing around his nose and forehead. The weather was warm, but the captain was tall and exceptionally thin—rarely did he perspire, even on the hottest of days.

"All right then, dismissed," said Griggs, his eyes still moving over us.

When we all had filed out of the bunker, Flanny pulled me aside. "You do your preflight yet?"

"Sure, that's all I do around here. Guy and I have done a pre-pre-preflight at 0600, a pre-preflight at 1100, and a preflight at 1400. Remember, my bird is strictly for show."

"That's right. I'm sorry I forgot," he said, grinning. "Good then. Tell Westin to get with my boy Phillips and have them go over my bird one more time. It will give him something to do, and then we can have some chow."

"I already ate, while you were van-winkling it in the hooch," I said. "And there is no way I can eat another round of that *whatever-it-is* they're dishing out."

"That's okay, I'll get it to go and meet you back at the bunker."

"It's not like I have anything better to do," I said, walking away.

"Hey," Flanny yelled after me, "don't forget to tell Westin about my ship!"

Back at the bunker, I sat on my cot waiting for Flanny. In the week that I had been here, I had flown twice, both just little jaunts to see if my ship was still working and the crew still sharp. The rest of the time, I was in a briefing or waiting on Flanny. I wondered if anyone had been a casualty of boredom in this shitty-ass country. I was really beginning to regret my decision to be a part of this project.

"Hey!" shouted Flanny, stepping through the door, holding what looked to be some type of meat sandwich in one hand and mail in the other. "*Dear John roundup*, Bronco," he said, tossing two letters at me. "Could you please explain to me how it is that a glass-jawed motherfucker like yourself manages to receive two, sometimes three, letters a week from two unrelated chicks in two different parts of the country?"

"You know how it is, Flanny," I said, winking.

"Yeah," he said, plopping down on his cot. "But what I don't understand is—and don't take this the wrong way—how a simple country boy like yourself, from Bear-Shit-In-The-Woods, Alaska, has it going on with a girl in Michigan and another in Washington State. It doesn't seem possible—physically, I mean."

"I told you, I grew up with Jessie in Alaska. She's my friend. She lives in Michigan now, and my fiancée I met when I was in college," I said, opening the letter from Jessie.

146

"Sure, I get it," said Flanny, smirking. He took a bite of his sandwich and then mumbled something through the mouthful of food—probably a smart-ass remark.

The letter from Jessie contained a ticket stub from the World Series game she attended at Tiger Stadium. *Keep it with you—it's good luck,* she had written. Then she went on to tell me again about the game and the series. *You know I've never seen the Tigers lose,* she had reminded me. She closed by telling me she was doing well and that she would write again soon.

I had received more letters from Sara than I had from Jessie, but not as of late. I had purposely saved Sara's letter for last as I had been longing to hear from her and I would probably want to read it a few times. As I opened the letter, I glanced over at Flanny who had finished his sandwich and was now lying on his cot reading a letter—probably from Claire.

Sara's letter started out like any other letter she had ever written me. Penned in her girlish scribble, it contained the perfect amount of opening pleasantries. She hoped that I was well and that I was staying out of harm's way and, more importantly, that I was taking good care of myself. But from that point on, the letter took a dramatically different tone—more informative than pleasant. It wasn't until I read it a second time that I truly understood the nature of its intent. It was words like *difficult, regret, unfortunately, distance,* and *sorry* and then phrases like *I'll always care for you, you have meant so much, I wasn't searching for it, I was drawn to someone else, I don't know what else to do, we both need to move on,* and *I'll never forget our time together* that caused me to check the return address and reexamine the postmark.

The letter was concise and unambiguous, and I could tell that she had put a lot of thought into it. There were enough intimacies to make me think that she had written it believing that no one had ever written such a letter before. Prior to closing the letter with a simple *I'm sorry,* she explained to me that her perceptions and, ultimately, her position regarding the war had materially changed—and that it was her duty and also mine to bring a swift end to all the *wretchedness this war has caused*. She never provided any specifics as to what she was going to do or what I should do, but clearly, she had made up her mind about the war and about me.

"So what says your harem today, Bronco?" asked Flanny, sitting up on his cot and brushing crumbs off his shirt.

"If I had a harem, I'm one short now." I handed him the letter. "Read it," I said.

"What are you talking about?"

"Read it, you'll see."

I sat back on my cot waiting for Flanny to read the letter, my mind hopeful that there had been a mistake. Her letters up until now had been so pleasant and encouraging.

"Shit, Bronco," said Flanny. "That's some cold shit. I've heard about these letters, but I never actually read one. Sorry about that *Dear John roundup* shit—I didn't know."

"Of course not," I said. "Who would ever believe something like that?"

Flanny shook his head and continued reading. When he finished, he reached into his footlocker and pulled out a half-empty bottle of Jack Daniels.

"You look like you could use a drink," he said, handing it to me.

"At least one," I said, taking the bottle and quickly gulping down two giant swallows.

"I'm really sorry, Bronco. From what you told me, she seemed like a really sweet gal. It's hard to believe that she could do something like this—especially to a stand-up fellow like you."

"Thanks," I said, taking another big swallow of the Jack.

"But let me ask you something."

I nodded.

"How long did you know this broad before you got engaged?"

"I told you before, about six months. We hit off right from the start."

"That's not a long time, really," he said, leaning back on his cot. "A lot of these gals can be a bit needy, you see—especially the ones waiting on a war."

"What do you mean?"

"Now don't get me wrong," he said, taking the bottle from me. "It was a really shitty thing for her to do to you. But to understand it—to *move on* as they say. I think you really do have to look at it from another perspective. I mean, you two get together and it's all cherry pie this and cherry pie that. Everything is wonderful and perfect, am I right?" Flanny took a swig and then handed me back the bottle.

"I suppose," I said.

"And tell me something else. You got engaged just after you decided to sign up to fly birds for Uncle Sam?"

"I suppose," I said, taking another drink. "So what does that mean?"

"Now be honest with me here, okay?"

"Sure," I said.

"Would you have gotten engaged if you had stayed in school?"

"What the hell are you talking about?"

"I mean, would you have proposed had you not got the hair up your ass to come over here?"

I took a long, deliberate swig that finished the bottle of Jack. His point was well made, but not well taken—even if he was right, it didn't make it any easier.

"Maybe not, but she wanted to get married. She was the one that brought up marriage, and she was always talking about forever," I said, tossing Flanny the empty bottle. "Damn it! She was always saying that she would wait for me no matter how long I was away! She promised me! She's the one that wanted to get engaged! She said she'd wait for me, Flanny! She did! I even went to see her parents, for Christ sake! Met her old man—had a drink and a cigar with the bastard, asked him for his daughter's hand and all that bullshit! I was a real gentleman about it too! Did you know her old man was in the navy?"

Flanny shook his head.

"I should've known something was up there, for Christ sake—the fucking squid! I should've known, Flanny! You know what that squid bastard told me?"

Flanny shook his head again and then looked down at the floor.

"The bastard told me he'd been in Korea and had seen action on some goddamned battleship—I can't remember which. The *USS Fucking Bullshit* was what it was! He said it changed his life, you know? Made him a man. Told me he'd been assigned to some turret or something—shot the hell out of some North Korean boat! Said it was the best thing that ever happened to him! Said it made a man out of him, but you know what I think?"

Flanny didn't answer.

"I think he was full of it, Flanny! You know the type—like those grunts you see talking all the shit before seeing anything! You know, how they're going shoot themselves a gook—like they've got it all figured out. Kill gooks and then go back home and fuck the shit out of their best girl! Like it's supposed to make you a man! Her old man didn't do shit—I know it! And she's just like him, Flanny—full of fucking shit! She promised me she'd fucking wait! She fucking promised me!"

I laid my head facedown on my pillow and began to cry. I couldn't imagine what Flanny thought of me now. I'm sure I was being a big pussy. But at the moment, nothing seemed to matter. I hated everyone and everything.

I don't know how long I lay there sobbing into my pillow, but at some point, I must have fallen asleep. I awoke with a gentle nudge to my shoulder. It was Flanny.

"Are you all right?"

It was late, the hooch was dark, and I knew Flanny had a mission.

"Yeah," I said, "I'll be okay."

"Good, you lucked out. Missed a couple exciting briefings. Don't worry though, I told them you were feeling sick, but that you were a go tonight. I'm counting on you to be there for me, man," he said, patting me on the shoulder.

"I'll be there for you," I said. "I'm sorry that I—"

"Don't worry about it," said Flanny dismissively. "You've had a day," he said. "Sorry about all that shit I said earlier—about broads being needy and all. I only said that because my wife Claire, well she's just about the neediest dame I know. You know something? Every time I open a letter from Claire, I think that it's going to be just like the one you got today—telling me she's fed up and has had enough. And we're already married. I'll tell you this. If I ever did get a letter like that, I don't know what I'd do. I really don't. That might just be the end for me. You see—as much as I like flying and all, I couldn't do it knowing that I didn't have Claire back home waiting for me. I know it sounds nuts, but the very reason I can stay away from her and that boy for so long is the belief that she so desperately wants me to come back home. I only tell you this because I want you to know that there is no way I could ever know what you're going through right now, and I don't want to give you any pretense that I do. I know I'm being selfish when I say this, but you're the only friend I've got here in canopy jungle, and I don't want you doing anything stupid that will keep you from watching my ass. So if there's anything I can do for you, let me know. I'll do all I can."

"I think I'll be all right," I said, rubbing my eyes. "You're right, I don't think Sara and I ever really knew each other—at least, not the way I thought we did. We both had these ideas, I suppose, about marriage and the future, but I don't think we ever thought them through. Not really. It just happened so fast, like a whirlwind. Did you know that she's the first and only girl I've ever laid?"

"Really?" he said, grinning. "No, I didn't know that. The first and only, huh?"

"Yeah, I was the first for her too . . . but not the only. Not anymore, anyway."

"Well, it's probably all good then," he said.

"What do you mean?"

"It's just that who wants to marry the first piece of ass they ever come across?"

"I suppose," I said, trying not to laugh.

"I've got to go see to my bird," he said. "Thanks for letting me use Westin, that boy really knows his shit. Nothing against Phillips, but it's nice to have somebody look at your ship that knows the difference between a Jesus nut and his own nuts."

"Yeah, he's a wiz. I'm glad I got him," I said.

"As long as we're working together, *we've* got him," he said, grabbing his gear and heading for the door.

"Hey, Flanny," I called after him.

"Yeah," he said, glancing back at me.

"What did you make of all that dove shit Sara wrote about in her letter?"

"You mean the *wretchedness this war has caused?*" he said.

"Yeah," I said, surprised that he remembered the line. "What do you make of it?"

He looked at me thoughtfully for a moment, then smiled.

"It's just an extra *fuck you*," he said.

I didn't have to report for at least another hour, so I pulled out a pen and some stationary from my footlocker. I wasn't sure exactly what I was going to say to her, but I knew I had to write something. There were things I wanted to say—things I needed to get off my chest. She may not understand, but I was sure she would want to know about them. And suddenly, I missed her terribly.

Dear Jessie, I wrote.

Chapter Thirteen

May 1985

I had been to Corpus Christi one time before, in '67 with Sara. It had been between flight school at Fort Wolters, Texas, and advanced helicopter training at Fort Rucker, Alabama. It was the last time we were together.

Sara had never been in the ocean. I remember holding her trembling hand as we walked together out beyond the breakers where heaving waves thrust her into my arms, breathless and afraid. I remember back on the beach where, anxious and fumbling with words and a ring, I had asked her to marry me. She had said yes and that she would wait for me.

It all seemed so silly now.

And although my memories were vibrant, my bearings were vague. I stopped for directions at a little roadside diner called *Betty's Pie House.*

The place was tiny and had only a few tables and a thin Formica bar that ran along the far wall and fronted a long and rectangular pick-up window. On the near end of the bar was a large glass case that contained Betty's pies, and on the other end, next to a cash register, sat a heavyset man drinking coffee. He appeared to be Betty's only customer.

I sat down at the bar, a couple of stools down from the man.

"Betty!" the man hollered.

"What is it?" a woman's voice shouted back from somewhere beyond the pick-up window.

"You have a customer," said the man.

A few moments later, a squatty woman wearing an apron, hairnet, and painted-on eyebrows came out from a door next to the pick-up window.

"Hi, honey," she said with a rich Texas accent. "What can I get you?"

Feeling a bit guilty because I only wanted directions, I ordered a piece of apple pie and a Coke. I asked Betty for directions back to the interstate, which she happily gave me with the assistance of the heavyset man whose name, I learned, was Ben.

"You look like you got a lot of sun today, honey," said Betty when she brought me the pie. "You're face is a bit red—you at the beach?"

"For a little while, mostly just chatting," I said. I took a bite of the pie. "Delicious," I said, nodding at her.

"Good, aint it?" she said, smiling. "So what were you chatting about for so long that gave you such a toasty little sunburn?"

"Oh, nothing much," I said and then took a sip of the Coke. "Talking to some kind of professor I ran into on the beach—real character," I said. "Didn't much look like a professor though. To tell you the truth, he looked more like a bum."

"Professor," she said, lifting her painted-on eyebrows. "You must be talking about old Eddie. He'll talk your ears off!"

"Yes, that's right—he said his name was Eddie. He said he was a teacher or professor of history and literature."

"Oh, did you hear that, Ben? Looks like Eddie's in town! And he's a professor now!" she said laughing. "Well, shoot, Ben. I better bake a banana cream!"

"I suppose it's about the time for him to come wandering through," said Ben.

"Yeah, he said he's here on business—teaching, I guess," I said.

Betty laughed and then shot Ben a wink.

"Oh yeah. He teaches, all right."

"You mean he's not a teacher?" I asked.

Betty laughed again and glanced over at Ben, who chuckled.

"At one time he may have been," she said, "but about the only teaching he does these days is on the beach, pestering the tourists."

"What do you mean?" I said.

"Oh, he's harmless, and we love him to death. I let him come in here and talk up a storm while he eats his banana cream pie—best in three counties!" she added proudly.

"So he's not teaching in a school?" I asked. "What about his wife and kids? I suppose he doesn't have a wife and two little girls?" I said, feeling silly that I had been so gullible.

The smile disappeared from her face, and she leaned in toward me.

"He told you that he had a wife and two little girls?" she said, her painted-on eyebrows crossing.

"Yeah," I said. "He told me that they were back in Alabama."

Betty looked over at Ben who shrugged and then took a sip of his coffee.

"You know that Eddie, he's not right in the head. He hasn't been right for some time," she said, slowly shaking her head. "Eddie *had* a wife and kids back in Alabama, and I think he was some sort of teacher at one time—at the university or someplace. But his wife and those little girls are dead—dead for a long time," she said, nodding at me. "They may well be in *Bama*, but as sure as day, they're six feet under the ground now. They was killed in a car crash a dozen years ago. I don't know much more about it other than he was the one that was driving. But since then, he hasn't done nothing but walk up and down the Gulf talking to folks about this and that. Comes around here a couple times a year—talking all that scholar stuff you was talking."

Betty backed away from the bar and stood staring at me, her painted-on eyebrows pinched.

"Shit," I said softly. I didn't know what else to say. All I could think about were the Blake poems and the riddle he had told me and how he had seemed so happy talking about his girls—his *angels,* he had called them. I sat there for a long time just nibbling at my pie and thinking about him. Neither Betty nor Ben said much of anything to me.

I finished my pie, paid my check, and started for the door, but Betty stopped me.

"Hey, honey," she said, her painted-on eyebrows now seemingly at ease. "Where is it that you saw old Eddie?"

"Not sure," I said. "Hell, I'm not sure if I saw him at all."

Chapter Fourteen

February 1963

Patrick LaCroux and Jessie Mason were as different as right and wrong, but that didn't stop Jessie from agreeing to go with him to the Lathrop Winter Formal. I knew Patrick pretty well, as he and I had Mrs. Anderson for homeroom where we spent a good deal of time playing chess together. Patrick was extremely bright, top of the class, National Honor Society, French club, German club, Latin club, and every other club, association, or organization that required an ounce of academic prowess. He was an excellent chess player too, so I should've known something was up when, during homeroom, he allowed my knight to fork his king and queen.

"You want that bullshit move back?" I asked him.

Patrick brushed his hand over his pomade-slicked hair and then stared at me through his black horn-rimmed glasses, a real dumb-ass look on his face.

"You want that bullshit move back?" I repeated the question.

"No, no, no," he said finally, and then moved his king out of check.

"Then wave good-bye to queeny," I said, moving my knight and taking his queen. I made her give him a cute little wave good-bye.

"Good move," he said, pushing a pawn and allowing my petulant knight to fork his rook and his king.

"Did you forget how to play since yesterday?"

"I guess so," he said, giving me another dumb-ass look and then, again, he moved his king out of check.

"Now you can say good-bye to rooky," I said, taking his rook with my knight. This time I made the rook wave and say "bye, bye" in a high-pitched tone.

"I asked your friend Jessie to the formal," he said unexpectedly, in a tone that carried with it all the confidence of a chess grand master.

"You did what?" I asked, showing him *my* dumb-ass look. "When did you do that?"

"This morning during math," he said. "I was helping her with an algebra problem, and I got the nerve up to ask her."

"What did she say?"

"At first, she said that she had to think about it, but then after class, she all of the sudden said she would. I asked her if she needed a ride, but she told me no, that she and her dad would pick me up."

"Swell," I said, my mind suddenly miles away.

"Are you going?" he asked, capturing my bishop and putting me into check with his knight.

I hadn't been to one dance or a single social gathering in the year and a half I'd been in high school—I didn't know anybody who did. Jessie didn't even like those sorts of things, or at least, she never acted like she did. Or did she?

"I don't know," I said, moving my king. "I haven't really thought about it." That was the God's truth—up until now, anyway.

Patrick moved his only rook all the way across to my side of the board, and then he looked up at me, his eyes sharp and calculating. "Checkmate," he said.

———

I caught up with Jessie outside the lunchroom where she was sitting on a little bench with Carrie Ferguson.

"Hey," she said as I approached. "What's going on?"

"Not much, just left homeroom where I was playing chess with *Patrick LaCroux*," I said to her smugly waiting for a reaction.

"Yeah," she said cheerfully, "he asked me to go to the Winter Formal. He's so sweet, and smart!" she added glancing over at Carrie.

Carrie nodded in agreement.

"Yeah, he seems pretty excited about it," I said.

"You should go too, Hen," she said grabbing my elbow and shaking it. "It'll be fun! You can ask Carrie," she said taking Carrie's elbow and then glancing back and forth between the two of us.

Carrie's blond bobbed hair nearly encircled her entire face, and by her flushed look, I could tell that she was as surprised as I was. Carrie and I had had a few classes together our first year. She was a pretty enough girl, and always very nice to me, but I never imagined us going anywhere together, especially not to a formal dance. Completely stunned, I stared at Carrie who only stared back at me with dark blue expectant eyes.

Did she really want me to ask her to the dance? I wondered.

"So what do you say, Hen?" Jessie shot me her impatient glare, which Carrie couldn't see. Had Carrie not been there, I was sure Jessie would have socked me.

"Yeah, sure," I said hesitantly. "What do you think Carrie?"

"Sure!" she said enthusiastically, "It sounds fun!"

I looked to Jessie for a clue as to what to do next. I didn't know how much longer my patience or pride would permit this exhibition of my dumb-ass look.

"It's settled then!" said Jessie, her cheerfulness restored. "I'll have Daddy drive us all! It'll be fun!"

I politely dismissed myself and went on into the lunchroom—suddenly, not the least bit hungry. I didn't know what to make of any of this but I suspected that I had just gotten myself into something that could only end in embarrassment or frustration, or both. I didn't have any idea as to what I was going to do with Carrie Ferguson at a formal dance. I didn't own anything formal, did Jessie? She would have a lot to answer for.

———————————

On the bus ride home, Jessie had assured me that the dance would be *no big deal,* to use her words. I still had my unremitting doubts.

On Wednesday, Jessie informed my mother of our weekend plans, which suddenly made *no big deal* seem certainly a *much bigger deal.* My mother's elevated level of excitement at the prospect of her *only boy going out on his first date* led to an overwhelming amount of enthusiasm for the preparation.

An enthusiasm which, on Thursday, drove us to a tuxedo shop in Fairbanks where my mother—along with an elderly man with disgustingly rancid breath—aggressively poked, prodded, and pulled at my precarious inseams while repeatedly asking me, *Do you have enough room down there?*

I must have tried on half a dozen pants and a dozen or so jackets until they finally agreed on—as dragon breath put it—*a smart little black-and-white number.*

After the manhandling at the tuxedo shop, my mother then dragged me to a flower shop for the purchase of a corsage. I told her it was unnecessary, as this whole thing was *no big deal,* but my mother insisted. *You can't show up empty-handed. She'll be expecting a corsage, Henry*, my mother had said. *It would be rude otherwise,* she had added.

Finding the right corsage was nearly as trying as the tuxedo rental. The florist—a bony woman with towering hair and freakishly oversized earlobes—interrogated me relentlessly, referring to me as *my dear* and to my date as *the darling.*

"What color dress will *the darling* be wearing Saturday evening, *my dear*?" she asked me.

"I don't have any idea," I said, despondently looking at my mother for some assistance.

My mother only shook her head.

"You will need to learn these things, *my dear*, if you will be entering the social scene," she said, glancing at my mother. My mother nodded in agreement, although I could tell she wasn't sure as to which one of us the comment was directed. I wasn't even aware that Fairbanks had a social scene.

"Does *the darling* have fair features, my dear?"

"I don't know what that means," I said, again looking to my mother.

"It means," said my mother, smiling at the florist, "does she have light hair, skin, and eyes?"

The florist nodded at my mother approvingly.

"She's got blond hair and blue eyes, and her skin is white," I said, frustrated. "I'm not sure if that's *fair* or not!" But I was suddenly certain of what wasn't *fair*.

"It sounds to me like *the darling* is fair then," said the florist, scowling at me.

The questioning went on until, at last, it was decided that *the darling* would probably be keen on a cluster of three white roses entwined with something the florist referred to as *baby's breath*—although Earlobes couldn't be absolutely certain without knowing the color of the dress. But my mother thought it was lovely, and as I was running out of patience, I did too.

The production didn't end at the flower shop. When we got home, my mother made me put on the tuxedo and parade about the living room for Tom and my sisters. Gwen and Maggie marveled at the way I looked in it, but Tom didn't seem too impressed.

"How much did that monkey suit set me back?" he asked, eyeing me skeptically from his customary position at the end of the sofa.

"It didn't cost you a penny," interjected my mother. "Henry used his woodcutting money."

My mother glanced at me, as if to say, *isn't that right?* It was a lie. I had spent that money months ago, but neither of us wanted to get Tom started, so I nodded dutifully.

"He'll need to wear your wool overcoat, Tom," said my mother.

"It'll be too big for him, Helen," said Tom, eyeing me again.

"It might be twenty below Saturday night, Tom. His coat is already too small, and it surely won't fit over the jacket. Your overcoat should do just fine. I'll go and get it so you can try it on, Henry."

"She's fucking nuts," said Tom after my mother left the room. "There's no way that coat will fit you. It's too big for me, for Christ sake. You want this girl to think you're a fool? She will, you know, if you show up swimming in that goddamned coat!"

I didn't know what to say, so I didn't say anything at all. My mother returned with the coat and made me put it on. It smelled musty of mothballs, but surprisingly, it fit pretty well.

"Well, I'll be damned," said Tom. "I never would've guessed it. I could've sworn it was too big for me." His eyes gave me a once-over. "You must be growing."

"Or you are," my mother barked at him. She began tugging and pulling underneath at the armpits of the coat. "I would say it fits just fine, just fine," she said excitedly.

"Who gives a shit what you say!" shouted Tom, leaning forward on the sofa. "It's still my goddamn coat! Get your own goddamned coat—with all that woodcutting money! Just don't take *my* shit!"

"I don't want it!" I shouted back at him, pulling off the coat and tossing it at him. "I never asked for it! I never asked for any of *your* shit!"

Tom had caught the coat with one hand, but immediately threw it to the floor.

"Who do you think you are?" Tom shouted at me.

I started for the door.

"Wait!" my mother shouted. Then in a calming voice, she said, "Now just wait a minute, everyone."

I stopped at the door and looked back.

"Please, Tom, is this really necessary?" My mother glared at him. Tom looked at me and then at Maggie and Gwen, sitting together in silence at the other end of the sofa, as my mother continued glaring at him.

Tom shook his head and then snickered.

"Does he have to have everything of mine? That's my good coat, he'll probably ruin it. That coat was expensive."

"It doesn't even fit you, Tom," my mothered pleaded.

I didn't want to be there. These were the times I wished that I could disappear, or I wished I could make everyone else disappear. It was too cold to go to the trailer and too tense to go anywhere else in the house. Tom couldn't stand it when my mother gave me any attention, and now she was practically rubbing his nose in it.

"How do you know?" Tom glared at my mother and then at me. My mother hung her head, defeated. I knew what would follow, and I could do nothing to stop it. "I'm the bad guy again—aren't I, Helen? That's what you think. I'm the bastard because I don't want him wearing my coat. It's my coat, goddamn it! I say who wears it and who doesn't! It's my goddamned coat!"

I bit my tongue and prayed that he would calm down. Tom glared back and forth between my mother and me.

"You two," he said, shaking his head. "You're always working against me."

He picked up the coat from the floor and stared at me coldly. "You want the goddamned coat? You want the goddamned coat?" he shouted at me.

I shook my head, but didn't say a word.

"Well, you can have it!" he yelled, taking the coat in both hands and ripping off one of its sleeves. He tossed the sleeve at me. It hit me in the stomach and then fell to the floor. "Here, have some more!" He ripped off the other sleeve, again tossing it at me. This time, it hit me in the chest. He got up off the sofa, glaring at both my mother and me.

"Fuck you both!" he said and then, storming out the doorway, he shoved what was left of the coat at me. "It's yours!"

I watched my sisters quietly cry—and I too wanted to cry—over a crappy old coat that I didn't even want to wear! But I couldn't help but feel this was somehow my fault. All because of some bullshit school dance that I didn't even want to go to.

The minute Tom left the room, my mother walked over and picked up the pieces of coat from off the floor.

"What are you doing, Mom?" I asked.

She looked up at me with a wry smile.

"You heard him, it's your coat now. It will be a snap to fix. It's only torn along the seams, and now you have a new coat," my mother said, smiling.

All this over a bullshit school dance, I thought.

Saturday came around faster than any Saturday I could ever remember, and before I knew it, I was sitting alone in the backseat of JT's Oldsmobile as we pulled into Carrie Ferguson's driveway. Carrie lived out of town as well, just off Farmer's Loop Road. The plan was to pick her up first, and now they wanted me to go in and get her.

"What are you waiting for?" Jessie shouted from the front seat, a few seconds after JT had brought the big car to sliding stop.

I shook my head, snatched the corsage, and then begrudgingly got out of the car. Sporting patent-leather dress shoes that had no traction, I tiptoed carefully up the icy walkway to Carrie's front porch. I couldn't help but think how stupid this entire thing was and how, somehow, it was all going to end badly. I pushed the doorbell button, but of course, it didn't work—probably frozen. I know I was, even in my patched-up wool coat.

I gave the door a good rap and then waited, but that only got the attention of the porch light, which flickered and then went out. I banged on the door again—or at least, what I thought was the door. I stood there in complete darkness, knowing for sure that Jessie and JT were having a good laugh at my expense. A few moments later, the front door opened and a short curly haired man dressed in an argyle sweater and dark slacks stood staring out at me.

"Hi, I'm Henry. Is Carrie home?" I said politely. How stupid did that sound. For crying out loud, I sure hoped she was home!

"She certainly is," said the man pleasantly. "I'm Peter Ferguson." He offered me a hand, and I shook what had to be one of the tiniest hands I had ever shaken. "Come on in for a minute," he said, looking up at the porch light. "Did that thing go out again?"

"I guess so," I said, shrugging.

I never actually made it inside the house as we only got as far as the arctic entryway before Carrie and a woman who could only be Carrie's mother—having the same bobbed hair and blue eyes as Carrie—greeted me.

"Honey, let me zip up your coat, it's freezing out there. Oh, hi!" Mrs. Ferguson squealed. "I'm Nancy, and this is my husband Peter, who you've probably already met."

"Hi," I said to everyone. I had no idea what to say or do next, however. My mother had told me to *be charming*, whatever that meant. She had also told me to compliment Carrie on her dress and to make sure I gave her the corsage in front of her parents. *It will show her and her parents that you are a gentleman*, she had said. But since Carrie already had her coat on, I couldn't tell if she was even wearing a dress, and the way her parents were ushering us out the door so fast, I didn't think either were going to be possible.

My salvation came in the form of Mrs. Ferguson's keen eye.

"Did you bring her a corsage? Oh, how sweet," she said.

I quickly handed it to Carrie.

"It's simply gorgeous," said Mrs. Ferguson. "It matches your dress, perfectly! How did you know?" she said, looking at me.

I shook my head and smiled. I could have kissed Ms. Earlobes right now. Instantly, I felt like a prince, and as Mrs. Ferguson pinned the corsage on Carrie, I could see her dress was a dark satin-blue, the color of her eyes.

"Pretty dress," I said, looking at Carrie. "It brings out the color of your eyes," I added, feeling suddenly brave.

"Oh, how sweet," said Mrs. Ferguson again. "I told you," she said to Carrie.

"Thanks," said Carrie, smiling at me.

Shuffling back down the walkway, Carrie took my arm and let me escort her to the car.

"You're such a gentleman, Henry," she said with a little giggle.

I opened the car door allowing her to climb in first, but before she did, she paused long enough to tug at the lapel of my overcoat.

"I like your coat," she said.

"Thanks," I said, grinning. "It's new."

When we were both inside the car, Carrie slid her arm under mine.

"Don't you two look cozy," said Jessie, glancing back at the both of us. "You behave yourself, Henry Allen," she said with a half scowl.

"Don't worry," I said, still grinning. "*It's no big deal!*"

By the time we got into Fairbanks and picked up Patrick, it was a quarter to eight. JT dropped us off at the front entrance and promised to be back to pick us up a little past eleven.

At the coat check, I was wickedly pleased to discover that Patrick had shown up both tuxedoless and corsageless. Instead, he wore a dark gray suit that appeared to be a couple of sizes too small, accented with a grungy black tie and dingy white socks—all of which looked worn and in desperate need of ironing. To make matters worse, he quickly checked his coat and wandered off into the gymnasium, unaware that Jessie had been standing next to him patiently waiting for him to assist her in the removal of her own coat. Both Carrie and I rushed over to help.

Jessie looked stunning. She wore a sleek lavender dress that accentuated her young womanly curves, and she had her hair tied back with a matching lavender band intertwined with what I had only recently learned to be *baby's breath*.

"That's some dress," I said, taking her coat.

"That's some tuxedo," she replied with a grin. Then she whispered to me, "Your mother did well."

Just before I could hand her coat to the gal at the coat check, Jessie snatched it from me.

"Wait, Henry, we have something for you and Patrick," she said and then reached into one of the pockets of her parka and pulled out a little cardboard box.

"*We*," I said.

"Carrie and I ordered them—Daddy picked them up today."

Jessie opened the box, which contained two red rose boutonnieres. She handed one of them to Carrie, who promptly pinned it onto my lapel.

"Thanks," I said to Carrie.

"You look very handsome," she said.

I felt my face warming.

"Yeah, even with the crew cut!" said Jessie, rubbing my head. "Now what happened to my date?"

We caught up with Patrick just inside the gymnasium standing next to the dance floor, his hands behind his back, seemingly taking in the surroundings. He didn't see us coming.

"*Boo!*" shouted Jessie into his ear.

This caused Patrick to stumble and nearly fall.

"Where in the Sam-hell have you been?"

When he regained his balance, he looked at her sheepishly.

"I've been here, waiting for you," he mumbled.

Jessie turned to Carrie and rolled her eyes. She then grabbed Patrick by his wrinkled lapel and stuck the pin of the boutonniere hard into his chest.

"Ow!" he cried out. "You poked me!"

Jessie glanced over at Carrie, again rolling her eyes. I laughed, as the whole thing seemed very funny. Jessie may have been dressed to the nines, but even dolled up like she was, she was still the same ole Jess. It made me feel good to think that I knew her so well. Patrick would be in for a long night if he kept this shit up. I laughed again, and Carrie shot me a contemptuous look, but then she too let out a half chuckle.

"This way," I said confidently. I then led our party through the clusters of dressy tables and dressed-up crowds until I spied an empty table at the far corner of the divided gym. We all sat down as a jazz band began to play a wispy tune. The theme of the dance was *Winter Wonderland*, and the place looked spectacular. Silver and white streamers adorned the walls and then ran to the center of the ceiling, blanketing the entire dance floor. Encircling the floor were numerous tables, each draped in white paper and garlanded with tiny tinfoil snowflakes. It was still early in the evening, but several couples were already dancing.

"Would anybody like some punch?" I asked, seeing that we were relatively close to the refreshment table.

"Not me," said Jessie, grabbing Patrick by the arm. "I want to dance!"

"Sure, some punch would be swell," said Carrie.

Walking over to get the punch bowl, I watched Jessie drag Patrick clumsily around the edge of the dance floor, and I wondered when Carrie would want to do the same. My mother had tried to teach me a few steps this morning, but after a few unhappy minutes, I would have no more of it. Now I wished I had paid more attention or, at the least, been a little more patient. So far, my mother's advice had been right on the money.

The more I watched Jessie and Patrick, the more I thought maybe it wouldn't be so bad. After returning with a couple glasses of punch, I boldly asked Carrie to dance.

Surprisingly, my foray into the world of Dick Clark and the American Bandstand went without incident. The band played a snappy little tune and I did what everybody else did—rock back and forth on the balls of my feet while pretending to snap my fingers to the beat.

It didn't matter. Carrie and I were having fun and danced to several songs, and when at last the band played a slow one, I moved in close and she took my hand. "I'm not very good at this," I said nervously.

"It's not so hard," she said, looking into my eyes. "Simply follow my lead until you get the hang of it."

I did as she directed, and soon we were moving gracefully around the floor—or at least, that is how I saw it. Carrie did most of the leading and I did most of the stumbling, but after a while, I was moving as easily with her as she was with me. Before we knew it, we were *two-stepping* (as she called it), even to the faster tunes.

When the band finally took a break, we went back to the table. Jessie and Patrick were gone, and there was no sign of them on the dance floor.

"I wonder where they are," I said to Carrie as we both sat down.

"They probably went to get some air. It's hot in here," she said.

I supposed it didn't matter where they were; I was having a good time with Carrie. During the band's break, I enjoyed learning more about her. I learned that her family was originally from Madison, Wisconsin, and that her father was a pastor at the local Lutheran church. She had moved here a couple of years ago and was still adjusting to our long and dark winters. I also learned that she was an only child and that her parents *doted on her constantly*, as she put it. I asked her if that meant she was spoiled, and blushing, she admitted it was probably true. We talked until the band started their second set, and then we danced nonstop until the next break where we drank punch and talked some more. The more she told me about herself, the more I liked her. I told her a little about myself too—a little about my family and about how Jessie and I were best friends.

"I really like Jessie," said Carrie. "She so brave, she's not afraid to say anything."

"Yes, she's strong-minded, all right," I admitted. "Those two sure have been gone a long time."

"Yeah, that's odd, isn't it? It's been over an hour. I wonder what they could be doing."

"Knowing Jessie, they're probably hanging out in the hallway," I said. "She's probably reading Patrick the riot act about something."

We both laughed as the band began to play again.

"We can go look for them," she said.

"Or we could go dance," I said, holding out my hand.

Carrie snatched it with a smile, and before long, we were two-stepping to what Carrie informed me was an old Benny Goodman tune. A few dances later, Carrie had to use the ladies room, so I told her I would escort her and then see if I could track down Patrick and Jessie. When I left Carrie at the restroom, I walked by the coat check and down a few of the halls nearest the gymnasium, but all the hallways were dark and empty. On my way back to meet Carrie, I thought I might check the narrow hallway that led to a small stairwell next to the boys' locker room, but again there was no one.

I don't know what it was that compelled me to walk down to the end of that hall or enter the stairwell, but had I known what I would find, I surely would've thought twice. About halfway up the first flight of stairs, I found Jessie, her eyes shut tightly and her arms wrapped firmly around the neck of Patrick LaCroux, his face buried into her half-naked breasts and his hand well up her dress, groping ravenously beneath a pair of white cotton panties.

My first reaction was to run, but my eyes resisted their commands, paralyzing my body and causing me to stare at the two of them in a kind of semi-catatonic trance. Then suddenly, Jessie's eyes opened and she stared back at me, her look indifferent at first and then defiant. She didn't move a muscle but went on allowing Patrick to maul her in front of me. When I could stand no more, I turned and ran away.

I found Carrie sitting at our table drinking a fresh glass of punch—there was also a glass for me.

"Did you find them?" she asked as I sat down.

"No, and I checked everywhere. I don't know where they went," I lied, "but I'm sure they'll turn up sometime."

"That's really odd," said Carrie. "Oh well, I guess maybe they don't like to dance."

"Well I do," I said, forcing a smile. "Would you like to dance?"

"Only if it's with you," she replied.

The band played a slow number, and I held Carrie so close that I could feel her breath upon my neck. And although our bodies moved together around the dance floor, my mind was elsewhere—in the stairwell with Jessie and Patrick, watching him molest her with his mouth and hands, and her consenting. I had the same sick feeling I had when Jessie told me about Kenny Brenke, but this was different—worse, because I had witnessed it.

"Would you like to sit down?" I said to Carrie.

"Okay," she said with enough hesitation that I could tell she didn't.

"Just for a minute," I said reassuringly. "I need to drink something."

"Oh, all right," she said, smiling.

Back at the table, Patrick and Jessie had finally made their long-awaited return. The two sat across from each other gazing off in different directions. Neither looked any different than they had before they had disappeared into the stairwell. Jessie had put herself back together nicely, and Patrick still looked wrinkled.

"There you guys are," said Carrie pleasantly as she sat down next to Jessie. "We thought we had lost you. What have you two been up to?"

"Oh, we were hanging out and . . ." said Jessie, hesitating, " . . . talking," she added.

Taking a sip of punch, I glanced over at Patrick. He was staring across the dance floor, wearing his dumb-ass look, his boutonniere dangling from his jacket.

"Would you like to dance?" I said to Carrie.

"Sure," she said sweetly.

———————————

It was well past midnight when at last I spied JT's Oldsmobile pulling into the school's driveway. Carrie and I had been standing lookout for nearly an hour as Jessie and Patrick sat on the coat-check table ignoring each other.

"There he is!" I shouted, much to the delight of a custodian who stood at the entrance impatiently waiting for us to leave so that he too could go home.

The four of us ran to the car. Hit with the warm smell of cigarettes and sour booze when I opened the backdoor, I was surprised not to find JT's goofy face behind the wheel, but instead the scrunched-up puss of Spenser Mason.

"Who is that?" Carrie whispered to me.

I put my arm around her shoulders and pulled her close.

"It's Jessie grandfather," I said softly.

"Oh," she said, nodding.

As soon as I slammed the backdoor shut, Jessie opened the front door.

"Where have you been? We've been waiting for—" she shouted, pausing the instant she saw her grandfather. "Oh, it's you. What are you doing here? Where's Daddy, and why are you so late?" she asked as both she and Patrick climbed into the front seat.

"Turns out your father had a date himself," Spenser grumbled. "Sent me out here to fetch you kids. Had to switch vehicles and all sorts of shit, but I'm here now by God. So where in the hell am I going?"

Patrick quickly tried to give directions to his house, but clearly Spenser was drunk.

"What the hell's the name of that street you say you want, boy?" Spenser shouted at Patrick in jumbled slur.

"Lacey, it's off of Lacey," Patrick repeated.

The old man suddenly swerved, nearly driving us into the ditch. Carrie let out a sharp squeal.

"Goddamned ice!" Spenser yelled, while glancing back at Carrie and me.

"I wish he would keep his eyes on the road," Carrie whispered to me.

"It's going to be all right," I said, pulling her close.

Truthfully, I wasn't sure that anything was *going to be all right.* Carrie held tight to me as we went weaving our way down the icy streets of Fairbanks and, on more than a few occasions, the icy sidewalks.

Somehow, through grace of God and a couple of conscientious and defensive-minded drivers in the oncoming lanes, we made it to Patrick's house. After a quick round of listless good-byes, we were soon on the road again heading north and out of town.

"Carrie lives just off of Farmer's Loop," I told Spenser. I repeated it a few more times to be sure he understood. My persistence paid off when, miraculously, we made it to Carrie's house, shaken but unscathed. I escorted Carrie up the walkway, happy that the porch light was once again working.

"Thanks, I had a terrific time," she said as we reached her front door.

I couldn't see her face hidden deep inside the hood of her parka.

"My pleasure," I said, smiling. "I had a good time too. I'm sorry we're so late." I pointed at the dull and amber glow coming from one of the front windows. "I think somebody's still awake."

"That would be my mother. She won't go to bed until I get home," said Carrie. "Thanks for asking me. I only hope that you'll be all right," she said, turning toward the idling car. "Driving home," she added.

"I'll be fine," I said. "See you at school on Monday?"

"You bet—"

But before she could finish her sentence, I thrust my face deep inside the hood and kissed her. First on the tip of her nose, as it turned out, but then on her mouth. She kissed me back, and for the first time in my life, I felt a girl's tongue touch mine. It lasted for only a second or two, before the sound of the car horn came blaring through the moment.

"Impatient bastard," I said.

"Impatient *drunk* bastard, you mean," said Carrie, shaking her head.

When I saw to it that Carrie was safely inside, I slid down the walkway, opened the door of the car, and climbed into the front seat next to Jessie. On the final leg of the drive home, Jessie sat silently, her head hung low and her hands folded in her lap. Spenser's driving had not improved, but of course, neither had his sobriety as we sped aimlessly down the highway, drifting from one side to the other as if we were more boat than car. At some point, Jessie reached over and took hold of my hand, placing it in her lap and gripping it tightly. Unlike Carrie, there was no reassuring Jessie; so I remained silent, watching the road and praying that we would make it home alive.

I was greatly relieved when Spenser made a wild but fortunate turn onto the road leading to my house. I thought Jessie would be too, but she continued to sit silently, holding my hand. When the car came to a sudden stop at the end of my driveway, I tried to get out but Jess didn't let go of my hand.

"I can see you tomorrow," I said to her, trying to sound encouraging, but she still wouldn't let me go.

"What the hell you waiting for, boy?" grumbled Spenser, tilting his head back and squinting at me inquisitively. "I'm not sitting here all night!"

"I've got to go, Jess," I said impatiently.

But Jessie's grip only tightened.

"You hear me, boy!" shouted Spenser. "Get the fuck out the car!"

"Really, Jess. I have to go. I'll see you tomorrow, okay?" I said anxiously, glancing at Spenser.

I was just about to rip my hand from her grasp when she looked up at me, her eyelids swollen, her cheeks tracked with tears. She shook her head pleadingly, and I saw the terror in her eyes, the same terror I had seen before when she had fallen off the bar and lay bleeding.

"Please don't leave me," she whispered. "Please don't go."

"Goddamn it, boy!" shouted Spenser. "Move it!"

"It'll be all right, Jess," I said softly into her ear. "You don't have to go far. You're almost home, it'll be fine. You'll see." I looked her in the eyes and hugged her. "I'll see you tomorrow, Jess. I promise."

When I felt her grip loosen, I quickly got out of the car and slammed the door behind me. Without too much difficulty, Spenser backed them out of my driveway, the snow crunching and crackling beneath the tires. I watched their taillights slowly disappear into the darkness, wondering why Jessie was so upset. I didn't get it, even Spenser's drunken ass would get them home safely from here. Yet, staring vacantly off into the night, all I could see was Jessie's face and the terror in her eyes. There must be something else—maybe it had something to do with Patrick? It bothered me, and I stood there until the frosty air bit sharply at my nose and ears. I saw that the kitchen light was on. I guess Carrie's mother wasn't the only one waiting up tonight.

I awoke Sunday morning before everyone, got dressed, and went downstairs. I shoved a couple pieces of firewood into the kitchen stove and then put on my snow-pants, boots, and coat. Outside it was still dark, but the moonlight reflecting off the snow was just bright enough to see by. Saucy spied me and leaped out from inside her doghouse.

"Let's go, girl!" I called to her, and she was instantly at my side.

A half hour later, Saucy and I were walking amongst the Shit Towers just outside the entrance to Jessie's cabin. I banged hard on the heavy wooden door and waited patiently as Saucy sniffed around at what in the moonlight looked to be a stack of empty cigarette cartons. I saw the Oldsmobile, but both trucks were gone. JT and Spenser were not there, and I was glad for it. I banged hard on the door again, but there was still no answer. Finally, I tried the handle, and the door pushed open easily. Welcoming me inside was a gush of warm air that smelled of burning wood. The only light came from the damper of the iron stove in the living room, but it was enough for me to see my way through the piles of junk to where an old Louisville Slugger stood propped against the wall, guarding the entrance to Jessie's room.

Her room was tiny and had no door; only a thin curtain hanging halfway to the floor separated it from the living room.

"Jessie," I said, pulling open the curtain.

There was no reply, but I saw some shadowy movement from the bed on the far side of the room.

"Jessie," I said again.

"Henry?"

"Yeah, it's me," I said.

There was a sudden flare from a struck match, and I could see the orange glow of Jessie's face as she lit a candle on the nightstand next to her bed. She blew out the match and placed it into a small silver ashtray next to the candle.

"What time is it?" she said, rubbing her eyes.

"It's morning, probably around seven-thirty. I'm not really sure," I said shrugging.

"What are you doing here?"

"I came to check on you," I said, walking over and kneeling next to her bed. "I wanted to be sure you got home safe. You had me worried."

"I'm fine," she said, rubbing her eyes again.

I noticed that she was still wearing the lavender dress, and the matching lavender tie hung loosely from her hair.

"Too tired to change last night," I said, picking the tie from her hair and handing it to her.

"Something like that," she said with half a grin.

"At first I thought you were upset about your grandfather's driving, but then I thought it might be something else—maybe something to do with Patrick."

"Patrick?" she said frowning. "What are you talking about?"

"You know, when I ran into you and Patrick in the stairwell. I thought that you might've had a fight afterward or something. You two weren't talking when you came back. Then you were so upset in the car. I didn't know—"

Jessie put her hand to my mouth.

"Shush," she said and then smiled at me. "I'm sorry you worried," she said. "I wish I could tell you why I was so upset last night, but I can't. The truth is, I'm not so sure myself. I can't explain it. It was such a weird night. I'm just glad it's all over with."

I pulled her hand away from my mouth.

"So it had nothing to with you and Patrick?"

"Patrick, that little slimeball?"

"The *slimeball* had his face in your breasts and his hands up your dress," I said.

Jessie sighed. "I know," she said, shaking her head, "but that was sort of your fault."

"My fault, what in the hell do you mean by that? How could it have possibly been my fault?" I said indignantly. "It wasn't my fault that—"

She again put her hand over my mouth.

"Shush," she said again. "I suppose I was a little mad at you. To be honest, more like jealous."

I again pulled her hand from my mouth.

"Jealous, of me?"

"Yes, I was jealous. You and Carrie were so perfect. You with your fancy tuxedo and your flashy corsage—and your manners, Henry. I never knew you had such manners. When I saw you and Carrie dancing around the gym like damned Fred and Ginger." She shook her head again. "I knew you two were hitting it off, and here I'm stuck with *Patrick the Klutz*. I didn't know what to do. Sometimes I don't know why I do half the things I do, Hen. So I let him feel me up. Hell, he wasn't worth a shit on the dance floor."

"You let Patrick put his paws all over you because you were jealous of Carrie and me?"

"I thought if I let ole Patrick cop a feel, he might treat me better."

"God, Jess, you've got to know that it doesn't work that way."

"I know, but sometimes I think it's the only way it works for me."

"No, it doesn't. People *will* treat you right, Jess, not because you let them feel you up or be with you, but because they know you and they like you—and they love you," I added.

"I don't want anybody to love me," she said.

"It's too late," I said smiling. "They already do."

"You don't count, Hen. You're my best friend, remember?"

"I count—of course, I count! I wasn't the one getting all jealous!"

"I had never seen you with another girl," she said grinning at me. "I didn't like seeing you with her, all dressed up and gentlemanly—and her so goody-goody."

"Gee, Jess, I've never seen me with another girl either." I laughed. "And as for gentlemanly—shoot, I was just trying to get a kiss."

"You got your kiss," she said. "I saw that slick move you pulled underneath the porch light."

"It was barely a kiss," I said. "I might've got a real one if your grandfather didn't blast that horn!"

Jessie laughed and then gently brushed my face with her hand.

"What makes you so sure that was my grandfather?"

Chapter Fifteen

December 1968

"Three pretty ladies," said Jake, an unlit cigarette dangling from his lower lip.

"Beauty in eyes of beholder," said Ho, disappointed. He threw down his cards. "They don't look too good to me!"

I was glad I had folded my two kings early; otherwise, Jake would've had my money too. Jake was a man among boys when it came to poker. The only one that he couldn't consistently beat was Westin, but he hadn't joined us yet.

"Where the hell is Westin?" I said, watching Jake rake in a good-sized pot of wadded and wrinkled bills.

"He's replacing some doohickey on the bird," said Jake with a wide grin. "Let's hope it takes the bastard all night."

The army typically frowned upon its officers gambling with enlisted men, but the assignment required everyone not flying to be on the alert, which meant the last two weeks the two backup crews had spent a lot of time being bored together. So, naturally, we played cards. We spent our nights here in the largest bunker that doubled as a mess hall during the daylight hours, orders of Captain Griggs. Cozy, but it served its purpose.

The captain had concerns regarding a VC sniper spotted in the area. Only three weeks ago, the sniper had shot and killed two grunts pulling guard duty. And yesterday, the bastard had taken a shot at one of the rangers on his way to the shower. But I didn't mind the close quarters, and playing cards with the crew seemed much better medicine than sitting around with my thumb up my ass thinking about Sara.

"Okay, fellas," said Jake, glancing around the table over the top of his aviator sunglasses. "The game is *Low Chicago*. It's like seven-card stud, see, except that nothing's wild and low nigger in the hole takes half the pot—no offense to you, Weatherly," Jake said, winking at the large black door gunner sitting directly across the table from him.

"I takes offense to that," said Weatherly, tossing in his ante. "And if you were to talk like that where I come from, you'd get your nigger in the hole all right," he added with a chuckle.

"Now, now," said Jake dealing out the cards. "I'm from ole Chicago, see, and I've played poker with lots of you boys, and every one of them calls it low nigger in the hole."

"Oh, we calls it low nigger in the hole where I come from too," said Weatherly. "But where I comes from, the game's called *Baltimore,* and the boys back home wouldn't take too kindly to a honky like you calling it *Low Chicago.*"

"Well then, Weatherly, where you from?" asked Jake, glancing at his hole cards.

"Where do you think?" said Weatherly, tossing in his cards. *"Baltimore!"*

Everyone had a good laugh. I folded my cards. If Jake was going to get my money, it would be one ante at a time. I took a swig of water from my canteen. It was hotter than hell. Even seven feet beneath the ground, the humidity was torturous. I was looking forward to having a cold one when Flanny got back.

"Hey, Gleason," I said to Jake, "how long have the boys been out?"

Jake looked at his wristwatch. "It's well past five and getting close to dawn, so I'd say nearly two hours. They should be back anytime now."

He then stared curiously at Arty Knutson, the other backup AC. Knutson was glaring back at him hard, stroking his thick black mustache. "That's ten to you, Gleason," he said, taking a second peek at his hole cards.

"Ten, eh," said Jake, nodding, the unlit cigarette still hanging from his mouth. "That's a big bet for someone who's been awful quiet all night. You must think you've got something—maybe the *low nig* or something. I've got to tell you, sir, normally I would let you have this one. Really, I would, but . . ." Jake paused and then started thumbing through his stack of money. He quickly pulled out a ten and tossed it into the pot. "There's your ten," he said and then went about thumbing at his money pile again.

This time, he pulled out a hundred-dollar bill and slid it slowly into the pot.

"Don't get me wrong, sir," said Jake. "I do think you have something, really I do. It's just that I'm feeling sorta lucky tonight, like I'm holding the winning hand, see. Like today's my lucky day."

Knutson peeked again at his hole cards and then went back to glaring at Jake.

"You sure are a smart-ass," he said. "Are you ever going to light that cigarette?"

Jake leaned back in his chair, rolling the unlit cigarette between his lips, but didn't say anything.

"I should call your ass, that's what I should do," said Knutson, shaking his head. "Teach that smart mouth of yours a lesson. But I guess tonight is your lucky night, you lucky little shit."

He took one last look at his cards and then flipped them over. Had he stayed in, he would have had a full house—deuces over threes and the two of spades.

"Shit, you weren't kidding, you did have a good hand. In ole Chicago, we'd call that a monster of a hand," Jake said, snickering.

"Shit, sir, that's a monster hand in Baltimore," agreed Weatherly. Then to Arty, he said, "You know that's a full house, don't you? That's a very good hand wherever you're from, sir."

"I know it's a goddamned full house," fired Knutson, "but he had jacks and queens, right, Jake?"

"I had the winning hand, I know that," said Jake, neatly stacking his new pile of bills.

"With all due respect, sir," said Weatherly, "how could you lay down a full house?"

"I told you, the little bastard had me beat. Isn't that right, Jake?" said Knutson.

"I had you beat, that's for sure," said Jake. He flipped over his cards and tossed them at Knutson.

"Rags," said Weatherly, shaking his head and then smiling at Knutson. "Aint even a *nigger* in the hole."

"You little shit," said Knutson, his eyes now afire. "You little bastard!"

"Man, he played you, sir," said Weatherly. "Played you like a damn fiddle."

Knutson glanced at Weatherly.

"Fuck you, Weatherly. What the hell do you know?" shouted Knutson.

"I know better than to lay down a full house," replied Weatherly.

"Yeah, well fuck you both!"

Knutson continued to lash at Jake with his eyes. "Are you ever going to smoke that damned cigarette?" he said.

Jake took the cigarette from his mouth and tossed it over in front of Knutson.

"You can have it, sir," said Jake. "I don't smoke."

"He sure can play the cards, Jake. I'll give him that," said Weatherly.

"Bullshit," said Jake. "I never play cards, I always play the man—can't lose that way."

It was my deal and I was thinking five-card draw when, suddenly, the bunker door swung open and in walked Captain Griggs.

"Allen, Knutson, come with me!" he shouted.

I gave Arty an inquisitive look, but he just looked away, still smarting over Jake's bluff. We both got up and followed the captain to the bunker's only other room, used primarily as a storeroom. He led us around a stack of empty C-ration crates and then stopped. He looked each of us in the eyes.

"I don't want to alarm your crews, but get them ready to fly. I don't have all the information yet, but we have a ship down," he said, a look of deep concern on his face.

"Who's down?" I asked, a chill running down the length of my spine as both Arty and I waited for the bad news.

"We got a mayday from Abbott," said the captain to Arty with a sympathetic nod. "But we don't know much more than that. Initially, the LZ appeared clear. Abbott spotted the rangers' flare and went in with Flanagan following. A few minutes later, we got Abbott's mayday, and since then, we've heard nothing from either pilot. So I need you and your crews to be on the ready ASAP."

"We can be ready to fly in five," said Arty, nervously stroking his mustache.

"Me too," I said.

"Good, then get to your ships and stand by. I'll keep you posted," said the captain.

Five minutes later, we were in the ship and had the rotors turning. I had Ho go over the briefing notes and chart a flight plan to the LZ. So far, the radio had been silent and we had received nothing from Griggs. I wasn't too concerned about the radio silence, as Flanny probably had switched his off anyway, especially if the situation was hairy. What did concern me was the mayday. It was possible that it could've been mechanical failure, but Abbott was a good pilot with a solid crew, so somehow that didn't seem likely. No, something was up, and I was sure that Flanny was in the middle of it.

Suddenly, a voice came squealing into my headset.

"Foxtrot 222 to Foxtrot 5, copy, over!"

It was Flanny's peter, Covey.

"Roger, Foxtrot 222, this is Foxtrot 5. Go ahead, we copy, over," came Griggs's squelchy voice.

"Roger, Foxtrot 5, Foxtrot 222 is down. I say again, Foxtrot 222 is down. We're scratched and heavy, scratched and heavy. Losing water, losing water. Scratched and heavy, losing water on the run, over!"

"Roger, Foxtrot 222, we copy! Find a roost and wait for Mongoose 51 and 52 on the run. Foxtrot 5, out!"

"Roger, Foxtrot 222 out!"

The message was simple and clear. *Scratched and heavy* meant Flanny had taken a hit while loaded with troops. They were also *losing water*, which meant he was leaking something—fuel or fluid of some kind. Finally, he was *on the run*, which meant he was still on the Cambodian side of the border somewhere on the preset flight path. Command gave instructions to *roost*, which meant that he would set down in a place along the flight path where we could find him—unless, of course, the dinks found him first.

"We're off," I said in the intercom.

"Mongoose 51 to Foxtrot 5, over!" said Ho over the radio.

"Roger, Mongoose 51, over," said Griggs.

"Mongoose 51 running, over," said Ho.

"Mongoose 52 running, over," Arty's voice came over the radio.

By the time we got airborne, I could already see the sun poking up over the horizon. I hoped that Flanny could find somewhere safe to set down, because in the daylight, if they were onto him, he would be a sitting duck.

Pushing it with all the throttle and pitch I could, the chopper charged forward, the jungle blurring green beneath us in the early morning sun. It wasn't long before we had crossed over into Cambodia, the entire crew with our eyes peeled for Flanny's ship.

"There!" shouted Ho, pointing northwest at a column of hazy blue smoke. The smoke appeared to be coming from out of the trees and then bending eastward before scattering with the breeze.

"Are they in the trees?" I asked Ho.

"No, it's a clearing! Looks like big clearing!" shouted Ho excitedly.

I banked the chopper hard right and flew straight for the smoke. Ho was right; it was a clearing. Flanny had found the only place in the damned jungle that you could land a chopper. But as we approached, I soon realized he wasn't the only one.

"Holy shit!" yelled Ho as we flew over the clearing, "this place crawling with Charlie!"

"How do you know they're Charlie?" I asked, looking at Ho. "I thought we were in Cambodia?"

Ho looked at me as if I was an idiot. "They're not us, that's for sure!"

He was right; I just didn't want to believe it. Dozens of soldiers were flooding into the clearing from the northwest. Flanny's ship lay grounded and smoking in the center of it, an easy signal to Charlie. The rangers, along with members of Flanny's crew, had spread out forming a small parameter around the downed chopper. Charlie was still a couple hundred yards away and had fortunately pulled back to the tree line and taken cover, but they wouldn't hold back for long.

"Mongoose 51 to Mongoose 52, copy, over!" I shouted into the radio microphone.

"Roger, Mongoose 51, copy, over!" replied Knutson.

"Going in on short final, 52, we don't have much time. Let's get them out of here. Mongoose 51, out!"

"Roger that," Knutson replied, "52, out!"

Hovering over a patch of short wet grass, I set the chopper down some fifty feet behind Flanny's ship, which lay dead on its tail and skids fuming blue smoke from its main rotor. Knutson landed behind me. The smoke and the slope of Flanny's ship made it difficult to see anything or anyone. No doubt, they were dug in. I just hoped to hell they weren't too dug in, as we didn't have much time before Charlie would be crawling up our ass. I wondered if the rangers knew just how outnumbered they were. Glancing back at the deck, I saw Jake ready with his .60 awaiting orders. But Flanny's ship was between us and Charlie, so there wasn't a whole lot for him to shoot at.

All of a sudden, four rangers along with Flanny's door gunner—Percy, I think, was his name—leaped out from beneath the downed chopper and rushed toward Knutson's ship. Two more rangers immediately followed, dragging a wounded man behind them, and charged toward us. Westin scrambled from the deck and ran to meet them, lifting the wounded ranger up over his shoulder. He carried him back to the chopper and heaved him up onto the deck.

I saw no sign of Flanny.

"Where in the hell is the rest of the crew?" I shouted to one of the rangers as he came aboard.

Then all at once, an enormous gust of wind and dust swirled through the inside of the chopper, and looking up, I saw Knutson's ship spiral upward and out. The ranger, a Hispanic man with a bright pink scar across his nose, gestured that he couldn't hear me.

"The chopper crew—where the hell is the rest of the chopper crew?" I shouted again at him.

This time, the ranger nodded and then pointed through the deck toward the front of the downed chopper. That was when I saw them. Covey and the crew chief, Phillips, crawling out from beneath the nose of the chopper, and between them was Flanny—his feet dragging, his head slunk down, and his chest drenched in blood. Westin ran out to help but immediately had to turn back when bullets strafed the ground between the two choppers. The shots appeared to be coming from a small ridge some fifty yards away.

"Full suppression, Jake," I shouted into the intercom. "Full suppression, damn it!"

Jake swiveled his .60 all the way to the right, aiming at the little ridge before opening fire. It did little. Some twenty feet away, while standing near a patch of sagging elephant grass, a bullet ripped into Phillips from behind, jerking him forward and causing him to stumble and then fall, taking Flanny and Covey down with him. Covey got back on his feet quickly, grabbed Phillips by the collar, and dragged him toward the chopper until Westin could pull them both onto the deck.

"Flanny!" I screamed at Covey.

Covey only stared at me blankly and, for a moment, I thought he too had been hit. But then he blinked and shook his head.

"He's hit bad, sir! Shot in the neck!" replied Covey, pointing to his own neck. "He's lost a lot of blood! We couldn't stop it!"

"He won't make it!" Phillips added. "We have to leave him!"

"No!" I shouted at Phillips. "We're not leaving him! I'd just as soon leave you, you fucking bastard!" I turned to Ho. "You got the ship!"

Within seconds, I had freed myself from the chopper and ran toward Flanny who lay between the choppers facedown in a pool of blood. I had no idea what I was doing, except that I had to bring him back. As I approached him, the world around me suddenly slowed and fell silent. All I could hear was the faint sound of my own heart beating. When at last I reached him, I thought for sure he was dead, but when I rolled him over onto his back, his sea-blue eyes stared up at me, blinking—sharp and alive.

"Flanny!" I shouted. "Let's get you out of here!" I tried to take hold of his shoulders and lift him up, but he pushed me away. He put his right hand to his throat and, with his left, he grabbed hold of my arm.

"No!" he cried out, his voice gurgled and sounding hollow.

Then he coughed, spurting blood through his fingers, spraying my face. I tried to lift him, but again he shoved me away. He looked up at me coldly.

"No," he groaned, his chest heaving hard and fast. "I need you to . . . do something for me."

"What can I do?"

Then a sudden burst of machine gun struck the ground gravely close to our heads.

"Tell Claire . . ." he said, swallowing hard as more blood seeped through his fingers. "Tell her . . . that . . . this whole time. Tell her . . . I was thinking . . . I was thinking about . . . her and Zion. Tell Claire for me, Bronco. Promise me you'll tell her that . . . I was thinking of . . . her and Zion. Tell her for me. Tell her . . . I'm so sorry . . ."

Flanny's eyes closed, and then he coughed again as more blood spurted from his throat.

"No, damn it!" I shouted at him. "No, fuck you, I won't do it! You can tell her for yourself! You're not getting off so easy! I'm not doing your dirty work, you son of a bitch!" I slapped the side of his helmet, and he opened his eyes. "You hear me, damn it? I won't do it! I'm going to get you out of here!"

My eyes blurred with tears as I again slid my arms beneath his shoulders, but Flanny grabbed me by the nape of my neck and pulled me down to him. Helmet to helmet, it was as close as I had ever been to him. I could feel his blood-spattered breath on my face. He stared at me intently at first, but then his eyes fell and he smiled at me mockingly. The way he'd done a hundred times before.

"Don't you do it," he said, slightly shaking his head. "Don't you do it."

"Do what?"

"Go off and be a *pussy* your whole life," he said. He let out a little laugh followed by a cough as the last bit of blood and life echoed from his throat. He blinked once before the blue in his eyes faded to a cold and deathly gray.

He was gone.

I pulled him to my chest and then, struggling to my feet, I lifted him up with me and dragged him toward the chopper.

I hadn't taken more than a few steps when I noticed Westin beside me holding Flanny's legs and pushing us quickly along. When we reached the deck, Covey and the Hispanic ranger pulled Flanny's lifeless body on board as bullets exploded all around us, slamming first into the side of the chopper and then into Westin, cutting into him below the waist and dropping him to the ground.

I reached down for him, but before I could get to him, I was yanked up and shoved onto the deck by the powerful hands of the Hispanic ranger.

"Wait!" I said. But before I could speak another word, Westin's long body came sliding in beside me, and I felt the floor beneath us suddenly lift.

From the blood-smeared deck of the chopper, I watched as Jake and the other ranger fired hopelessly down at the VC soldiers, now swarming like incessant ants to Flanny's abandoned ship.

I glanced over at Phillips who was nursing a bloody shoulder that didn't seem too serious. Westin, though, lay beside me, his eyes clenched shut with pain as Covey administered morphine while the Hispanic ranger devised a tourniquet from what looked to be a pair of socks and a screwdriver.

"It's real bad, aint it?" said Westin, grimacing.

"It's not so bad," said Jake, giving Westin's leg the once-over and shaking his head. He gave Westin a forced smile and then looked over at me. "I've seen worse. Looks like a ticket home to me," he said, letting his eyes wander out the door and over the horizon.

My own eyes were drawn to Flanny's lifeless body lying beneath the other sixty on the opposite side of the ship. The back of his helmeted head rocked rhythmically with the whirling of the rotors. I couldn't see his face, and I was glad for it.

Back at camp, I watched them unload Flanny's body from the chopper and place it inside a black body bag.

"It never gets any easier," said a voice from behind me. "Three wars, hundreds of deaths, and it doesn't ever get any easier."

I turned to see Colonel Glasson staring at me.

"I don't know if you're aware of this or not, but Abbott's ship was shot down just before landing at the LZ. They didn't know what hit 'em—the entire crew was killed. We'll probably never get those bodies back, the sons of bitches!" he added angrily.

"I didn't know that. I only knew they went down, Colonel."

"I didn't mean to be the bearer of any more bad news, son, and it's not why I mentioned it," he said, running a hand through his snow-white hair.

"Then why did you mention it, Colonel?"

"I want you to know that my rangers sniffed out the ambush and put up one hell of a fight trying to neutralize it. But as you know, they were greatly outnumbered—lost three good men and wounded another. He's one of the men you brought back," he said, nodding at the chopper. "But seeing the ambush, our man Flanagan didn't bug out, but instead began circling the LZ—disobeying a direct order, mind you," the colonel added.

Then a subtle smile formed on his face.

"That crazy son of a bitch starts dropping flares all over a spot several hundred feet from the ambush site, in the opposite direction of our boys—even flew over the flares a few times getting off a few rounds." The colonel shook his head and gave me a look of pure admiration. "And as sure as shit, those dumb VC sons of bitches bought it and went charging for the flares. That's when he circled around and landed blind—a few hundred feet behind our boys."

"Blind?"

"That's the way Covey tells it. Said Danny had the entire LZ memorized. I guess from the insertion notes or a previous mission—who knows, maybe the crazy son of a bitch was a bat. All I know is that the rangers heard him coming down and ran toward him. They probably would've gotten out, but his goddamned door gunner lit a flare for the rangers—probably the last one."

"And Charlie spotted it," I said.

"Yeah, they sure as hell did," said the colonel, removing his glasses and rubbing the bridge of his nose. "They had to dump everything to get that ship airborne, including both .60s. I guess it was slow moving, and they took a beating before they even got airborne. That's when it happened." The colonel paused to replace his glasses.

"What happened?"

"That's when Flanagan was shot."

"He was shot back at the LZ?"

"Yeah. Covey said it was a one-in-a-million shot—a shot in the dark, literally. It came directly up through the nose of the chopper and hit him in the neck, between his helmet and his chicken-plate. Said Danny didn't think anything of it, thought it only nicked him. 'Just a scratch,' he said, although Covey did say that it was bleeding pretty badly. The son of a bitch kept on flying, but they were leaking fuel. Covey said they were going to have to set it down, which they did. That's where you found them."

"And they couldn't stop the bleeding."

"No, it looks as though the bullet clipped the jugular—Covey was surprised he stayed conscious as long as he did. Said Flanagan landed the goddamn chopper. Tough little son of a bitch, that's for sure," said the colonel, shaking his head admiringly. "I'd have that son of a bitch up for the Medal of Honor, if I could," he added.

"Why can't you?"

"Everything's confidential—you know that. It's all unofficial."

I nodded, remembering that first meeting Flanny and I had with the colonel.

"If everything's so goddamned *unofficial,* Colonel," I said angrily, "then why are you telling me this?"

The colonel patted me on the shoulder again, and then looked me straight in the eye.

"Don't you worry about it. He may not get the Medal of Honor, but he'll be properly decorated. And I promise you, I will personally visit that wife and son of his."

"What are you going to tell them, Colonel? What can you possibly tell them about what happened today? You didn't even know him! You didn't know shit about Flanny!"

"You're right," he said. "There isn't much I can tell them other than he was an excellent pilot that did his duty for his country. Officially, I can't tell them anything about today, and maybe that's why I'm telling you, because you're one of the few I can tell—and maybe I think that it's important that somebody know something about Daniel Flanagan that isn't in the *official* record."

"I'm not sure if I understand any of that, Colonel. But you're wrong if you tell them that he was an excellent pilot," I said, tears filling my eyes.

"Then what *should* I tell them, son?"

"Tell them that he was the *best*, Colonel. Because that's what he was—*officially* and *unofficially.*"

Chapter Sixteen

May 1985

He is greatly encouraged at the hardware store when a scrawny young salesman with frizzy yellow hair and self-tinting glasses tells him that building a doghouse will be "no problem," and all he really needs is a couple of two-by-fours, a piece of plywood, and some sawdust.

"Really, sawdust?" he asks the young man.

"Sure, you use the sawdust to insulate the walls and cover the floor. You also might want to cover the roof with tar paper—you know, to keep it from leaking."

"That makes sense," he says.

"Make sure that you don't slope the roof too much either. You want it to hold the snow—to insulate the ceiling."

"That makes sense," he says again.

On the way home, he rolls down the window to the first nice day of spring as Kobuk chews on the passenger-side safety belt. He tries to think about insulated walls and a non-sloping roof, but instead, his mind wanders suspiciously as he thinks about his wife and Marks.

Pulling into the driveway, he sees Emily hanging upside down from a tree branch. Spying him, she rights herself, climbs down, and sprints across the yard to greet him.

"There you are!" she shouts at him as he rolls to a stop in front of the garage. He has to restrain Kobuk before he leaps out the window at her.

"Kobuk and I went shopping this morning," he says, opening the door and releasing the frenzied little dog.

"Where'd you go?" Kobuk jumps up at her and begins frantically licking her face.

"We went to the hardware store to get stuff to make a doghouse," he says.

"Really?" she says excitedly.

"You bet," he says with a wink for her.

"Can I help?"

"Of course you can—remember, he's your dog."

"Hurray!" she yells and then darts around to the back of the truck, Kobuk bouncing after her heels. She climbs up onto the bumper and peers over the tailgate. "Do I get to hammer?"

"Of course," he says. "We can't build a doghouse without some hammering."

"Hurray!" she yells again.

"What are you two up to?" comes a descending voice.

"Hi, Mommy," Emily shouts up at her. "We're going to build Kobuk a doghouse!"

"You are? That's terrific!" she shouts back.

"You want to help us?" asks Emily.

"Oh, I'd loved to, honey, but I have to go to the school. Maybe when I get back."

"What's at the school?" he says coldly.

"I never finished cleaning my classroom yesterday—because I had that doctor's appointment."

"Yeah right, I guess I wasn't clear on that," he says crossly. "Nobody knew where you were, and I didn't think the doctor's office ran so late."

"I'm sorry, honey. I forgot about the appointment."

He holds up his hand to shade his eyes from the sun. "I have to tell you, I was worried."

"I'm sorry, I didn't mean for you to worry. I didn't think it was a big deal," she says, glancing at her watch. "But I better get going."

"What's the hurry?" he shouts up to her. "You can help us with the doghouse and then we'll all go and help you with your classroom. We'll even take Kobuk with us."

He glances over at Emily.

"Hurray!" she yells.

She glances again at her watch. "Well, Keith is going to be there in about fifteen minutes to let me into the building, and I don't want to hold up construction," she says, nodding toward the truck.

He glances again at Emily and then back up at the deck, but she is gone. A few moments later, he hears her car start, and they watch her back out of the driveway.

Sunrays creeping over jagged mountains to the east brought with them a couple of startling West Texas revelations. First, I discovered that I had set up camp only thirty feet away from the interstate, even though last night I had driven for what seemed like miles off the exit. It wasn't a big concern, except that in the heat of the night, I had stripped off all my clothes and lain atop my collapsed tent, thus giving the early morning commuters an eyeful of my beaconing white ass. More alarming, however, was the discovery of a small army of red ants occupying my naked body. This sent me hopping amongst the spiny frontier bushes, slapping and swatting at the tiny bastards like a lunatic.

When finally I was insect-free, I dressed, packed up the truck, and headed back toward the interstate, slowed only by a determined little armadillo poking his way along the road (if he was looking for a big breakfast, he was going the wrong way).

The terrain was dry and barren and reminded me of those old spaghetti westerns that Clint Eastwood did—real cowboy country. I knew that somewhere close, the *Rio Grande* ran through here, but I didn't see it or there wasn't much to see. My head was clear as I hadn't had a drink since seeing Broadway, but my back was killing me, so I stopped for gas at a service station a few miles outside of Fort Hancock, Texas. I stretched my back and legs and then searched my wallet for the address and phone number for Guy and Luisa Westin. From a phone booth, I tried calling, but all I got was a recording informing me that the number I had dialed was no longer in service. It had been nearly two years since I had received the call from Luisa asking if I would come for a visit. I didn't know Luisa, and between her broken English and my lack of interest, all I got was that Guy wasn't doing very well and wanted to see me. Although I kept the information, I never gave it a second thought. Now there was a good chance that Guy didn't even live there anymore.

The address I had did contain the name *Rancho del Sol* and included a lot number, which could only mean trailer park. Fortunately, the gentlemanly attendant told me that I could find *Rancho del Sol* just north of El Paso on Highway 54. Before long, I was inching my way between the rows of mobile homes looking for lot number 318.

To my surprise, Lot 318 was still inhabited by the Westins—or persons referring to themselves as the Westins as that's what the scripted sign in the front window read. From the look of the place, it didn't appear that there had been any recent change in residency. Attached to the doublewide trailer was the traditional redwood deck, except that this one was strewn with garbage, a washer and dryer (which I couldn't tell whether were on their way in or out), and a rusted-out old barbecue grill that looked as though it hadn't seen a cookout in years.

Most of the trailer's skirting lay in timeless piles around the deck. However, partially covering the stairway to the door was a makeshift wheelchair ramp that appeared recently trodden.

I gave the door a gentle but firm rap and waited for any sign of life.

"What?" a muffled voice came from inside.

"Guy!" I shouted back. "Guy, is that you?"

"I aint interested in anything you might be selling," said the muffled voice. "So scram!"

"Guy!" I immediately shouted back at the door. "It's Henry Allen from First Cav!"

There was a short pause, and then I heard a faint clicking at the door handle. When the door opened, I was shocked at what I saw. Standing before me on an artificial leg with the assistance of a wooden cane was a much larger man than the one I remembered. He had to be at least three hundred pounds and wore a filthy OD tee shirt with matching filthy sweat shorts. Little of him resembled the man I had once known in Vietnam. His hair was long, gray and greasy and he looked and smelled as though he hadn't bathed in days. Squinting at me through puffy eyes, I wasn't sure if he could even see to recognize me.

"Allen?" he said, his squinty eyes widening as a tight little grin began forming across the diameter of his swelled face. "Shoot, Henry Allen. I'll be a son of a gun!"

"It's me," I confirmed, smiling back at him.

He shook his head, and then my hand, gripping it tightly, pulling me to his breast and into a bear hug. I nearly gagged but was now certain that it had been more than just a few days since his last bath.

"I'll be a son-of-a-gun," he said beckoning me inside, "I never thought I'd ever see you again," he said in that same old slow-awe-shucks-Mickey Mantle drawl I remembered.

He sat down in an old lounge chair swathed by a Mexican blanket. He pointed to a torn leather sofa across from it and I sat down. The place smelled of body odor and stale cigarettes, but was surprisingly clean and well decorated. Adorning the wood paneled walls were various black and white photographs of what I assumed to be the West Texas landscape. An enormous console television sat along the far wall and was quietly airing Bob Barker and *The Price Is Right*. Atop the television were a half dozen or so smaller framed photographs—one I recognized immediately as our old bird in Vietnam.

"I sure remember that," I said pointing to the photograph.

He smiled at me and I noticed he had put on glasses—the same old thick horned-rimmed specs he had worn in Vietnam.

"Yeah, she was a good ole ship," he said nodding. "Damn good ship." He scratched his stomach and then, reaching beneath his chair, he pulled out a half-empty bottle of *Rebel Yell*. He took a long swig and then, offering me the bottle, said, "You want a snort?"

"No thanks," I said, but a part of me did want the drink. "You made it the ship it was, Westin," I said sincerely. "There wasn't a better-maintained bird in Vietnam."

"I don't know about that, Mr. Allen," he said squinting behind the lenses of his glasses.

"Don't give me that *Mr. Allen* shit, Westin. It's *Henry*. We're not in Nam anymore, and I'd like it if you called me *Henry*."

"Okay, Henry," he said grinning. "So what brings you clear out here to El Paso? It's got to be a long way from Alaska. You certainly didn't come out here to see little ole me."

I thought about the irony in his *little ole me* comment, and it caused me to chuckle. "I haven't been back to Alaska since I left Vietnam," I said. "But I'm on my way there now, and I thought I would see a few folks along the way. I got a call from your wife Luisa a couple of years ago." I paused a moment for his reaction, but he gave none. "She wanted to know if I would be coming out this way, and I told her I didn't know, but here I am."

"She tracked you down, eh?" he said, but still there was no real reaction.

"Yes, she did. I figured you were trying to put together a reunion or something," I lied. I didn't have any idea what she was trying to do, but I knew it wasn't a reunion.

"Shoot!" he said, taking another swig of the whiskey and then exhaling forcefully. "Luisa is a good woman. I just wish I was a better man, and she might still be here." He shook his head and stared down at his prosthetic leg. "She done went back to Monclova in Mexico nearly eight months ago. She's back home with her momma now—haven't seen her since. Don't suspect I will. I'm surprised she stayed as long as she did with my drinking and carrying on."

"Carrying on?" I asked curiously. I never knew Westin to be the *carrying on* type.

"She says I spend too much time in the past, too much time at the tavern reliving those days in Nam." He paused, squinting at me again. "And I suspect I do. I suppose it's easier to just do what I do than to change. You think about them days, Mr. Allen—Henry, I mean?"

"I've thought about some of those things lately."

I wasn't certain if it was good idea for us to be having this conversation, but Guy had such an honest nature. He knew he had problems, but still didn't want to do anything about them. It made you wonder whether it was his vice or his virtue.

"I went and saw Broadway the other day, back there in Fort Hood. He's a lieutenant colonel now."

"I heard that about him," said Guy grinning. "Hell, probably be a general someday."

"Yeah, he's doing what he wants, running some special helicopter outfit or something. He's got a couple of kids and like I said, he appears to be doing what he wants. Seeing him, and I suppose you now, made me think some about Vietnam. I thought a bit about that day you got hit—the day Flanny died."

Westin didn't reply but continued squinting at me. He seemed content to hear me out, whatever it was I was trying to say.

"I probably should've left him there, Guy. If I had, you wouldn't have been hit. I should've stayed with the chopper like I was supposed to do—got us the hell out of there. I know that's what I should've done but I didn't. And you got shot up and lost your leg. You know I should've been the one that got hit. Maybe that's why I wanted to come down here after all these years—to tell you I'm sorry."

A long awkward silence lingered about the room before Guy leaned forward in his chair.

"I don't believe it would've made a damn bit of difference," he said waving the bottle at me. "Nobody knows what's going to happen or how the shit's going to come down as they say. Mr. Flanagan was your friend and one hell of a good pilot. Of course, I've thought a lot about that day myself, but I see it differently. Hell, Henry, if you hadn't gone back for him, I would've. I knew he was alive when you reached him. We could all see you talking. That's why I came after you."

Although his words were comforting and somewhat relieving, I had decided long ago that it was my fault that Guy got hit. But I also had decided long ago that if I had to do it again, I wouldn't have done it any differently.

"I am sorry, Guy. I can't imagine what it's been like for you with . . ." Impulsively, I glanced at his leg. "With your injury," I said, nodding at it. "And I'm sorry to hear about Luisa. I really am, Guy. But I'm glad to see you. I've wanted to see you for quite some time. It's just . . ." I said, hesitating because I didn't know what else to say.

"It's good to see you too, Mr. Allen," he said, taking a large swig. "But there's no need to be sorry, I mean it. I have no one to blame for me, but me. Luisa used to tell me that I lost more than just a leg in Nam. She says I lost part of my *alma,* which is Spanish for soul. Maybe she's right—maybe I did lose more than just my leg, I don't know. She'd know though, she knew me before. We'll have been married for twenty years this August," he said proudly. "I wish you could've of met her. She's the sweetest thing. Put up with me all these years until there just wasn't any good reason to stay. Hell, I sure didn't give her one—not a one," he added, shaking his head.

"But I know it wasn't because of this," he said, tapping his artificial leg. "No sir. Hell, my problems are my problems. Many boys never made it back—like ole Flanagan. I suspect what gets me is that no one gives a shit about that war anymore. People are ashamed of it, and they want to forget all about it—make like it never happened. They don't want to remember. It's embarrassing to them. They've explained all they can explain, and they've blamed everybody they're going to blame. Now they just want to move on, I suppose, and forget about it. I reckon I don't blame them none. But the problem for me is, I can't forget. Every time I look at my leg or think about the ones that didn't make it—Flanagan and the others," he said with a nod, "I know it was real, and I know it did happen. I reckon that there are some folks—some folks like myself that are put on this earth to remember the ones that didn't make it. Even if it's embarrassing and aint nobody want to talk about it no more. Even if it means I can't do nothing else."

Guy finished the rest of the bottle and set it on the floor next to his chair. He leaned forward, reached for his cane, and then stood up.

"What you say Henry, why don't we go and find us a drink," he said grinning.

"It's a little early don't you think?" I said glancing at my watch.

"Ah hell," he said with a sort of grunt. "I know a place. You'll have to drive though. My regular ride don't come till 'bout eleven thirty. Lost my license about a year ago, see—drunk driving, so I don't drive no more. But we'll catch ole Marty down there. You'll like Marty. He did his tour in '69," he added and then limped toward the door.

Sure enough, Guy found a place that was open at a quarter to eleven in the morning.

Decorated in old western cavalry motif, I followed Guy as he hobbled his way across the hardwood floor to the bar.

"Howdy, Guy!" exclaimed the bartender as we were climbing onto the barstools.

He had short sandy brown hair and wore an orange UTEP polo shirt with the collar turned up. He looked remarkably young for a bartender, particularly for this type of bar.

"Hello, Carl," said Guy, nodding. "I'll have whiskey and water. What'll you have?" he said, turning to me.

"Rum and Coke," I said.

Carl smiled pleasantly and then went about preparing our drinks.

"You seen Marty?" Guy asked.

"Haven't seen him," said Carl. "I don't think he's been in yet."

He set our drinks in front of us and gave us each a pleasant little nod. I paid him for the drinks before Guy could reach for his wallet. "No," I said, waving him off. "The drinks are on me today. It's the least I can do."

"Shoot, you don't have to do that," said Guy in his slow way. "I told you, you don't owe me a thing. You were a fine chopper pilot—you always done right by me."

"I wish I felt that way, Guy. I really do, because you always did right by me—Flanny too. You know, he told me once that you were the best chopper mechanic he ever saw, and I didn't disagree."

"Ole Flanny was one hell of a pilot, spent a lot of time on his bird those last weeks. That's was nice of him to say."

"What was the name of that crew chief of his?"

"Phillips," said Guy, staring down into his drink.

"Yeah, well Flanny wasn't too keen on Phillips. That's why he was always borrowing you."

"I knew Phillips pretty well," he said thoughtfully, "but I suppose I knew most of the other CEs in the outfit. He was just scared shitless. Didn't know whether he was coming or going, most of the time. The son of a gun was always asking me questions about one thing or the other, scared all the time he was going to mess something up. And hell, he had Mr. Flanagan's ship—I know he didn't want to make a mistake there. Oddly, he met a similar fate," he said, pausing before taking a sip of his drink.

"What do you mean by that?" I asked.

"Ole Phillips was reassigned and then killed in a crash—shot down. Everyone was killed."

"I'll be damned," I said and then took a drink myself. "How did you find out?"

"I keep in contact with a few guys from the old unit, and a bunch of us still chat down at the VA. But I found out about Phillips because of that mobile memorial they have going around the country. I saw his name on the wall when it came through here a couple of years back.

Then I went to the library and looked him up—found out his bird was shot down." He chuckled and then took another drink.

"What?"

"I looked for your name on that damn wall," he said, grinning. "I was sure glad when I didn't find it."

"I'm sure you thought it might be," I said, laughing. "I did get us into a few spots, didn't I?"

"Oh no, not like that," he said, looking over his shoulder at me. "I looked for any name I could think of. It's just a sad way to find out about people, that's all. I always thought you were a fine pilot, and I was proud to serve with you." He patted my hand. "You always done right by me," he added.

"I'm not sure," I said, shaking my head.

"Well, you did," he said, patting my hand again.

"So what the hell have you been doing with yourself these past seventeen years or so?"

"I was hoping you wouldn't ask," I said, grinning at him. "A little of this, a little of that. I went back to school and then to law school—been practicing around Lansing, Michigan, ever since. Recently, I had enough of that, and now I'm doing a little traveling and making my way back up to Alaska."

"What kind of law?"

"Divorce, mostly."

Guy laughed.

"I'll never need a divorce lawyer, that's for sure. I may never see Luisa again, but she'll never divorce me. She gets the little I have when I kick off."

"Hey, Guy!" said an extremely thin man slapping his back and then hopping on the barstool on the other side of him.

"Hey, Marty," said Guy. "We've been waiting for you."

"Yeah," said Marty, glancing over at me. "I went by your place, but you weren't there. You must've gotten another ride."

"Sure did," said Guy, backing away from the bar so that Marty and I could get a better look at each other. "This is my buddy, Henry

Allen from the First Cav. He was my slick pilot, the one I'm always talking about."

Marty shook my hand and said he was glad to meet me. I did the same. Carl came around, and we ordered another round. Marty wasn't much older than me and had soft brown eyes that appeared exceptionally large for his small round balding head. He wore a long-sleeve denim shirt buttoned all the way up and baggy jeans cinched tightly around his waist by a thick black belt and confederate buckle.

"So you flew a slick in Nam, huh?" he said, piercing his lips and then sniffing into his thick brown mustache.

"That's right," I said. "In '68 I was with Guy here, but I did another tour in '69."

"Did you fly a slick in '69 as well?"

"Yeah, I did, but mostly dust-offs then," I said.

"I did my tour in '69," said Marty, "but I wasn't in the shit or anything. I spent most of the time around Chu Lai area with the Twenty-Third Supply and Transportation Battalion of the American Division. I had to deal with several slicks, however."

"Sure," I said, trying to sound interested.

I would've bet he had too—loading and unloading or refueling them. I was getting a bit tired of all the Vietnam talk, especially the lingo. I could always tell the grunts that never saw a lick of action—they had the lingo down and always referred to any hot activity in terms of *the shit*. It wasn't that I didn't think that what he had done wasn't important—everybody over there had an important job and was exposed to all sorts of dangers. But I had talked a lot of Vietnam lately, and I really just wanted to hear about Guy and his life now.

"Yeah, I spent a lot of time stocking convoys, that sort of thing," he said. Marty then proceeded to tell me every mildly interesting anecdote of his entire tour. I listened intently along with Guy, who sat drinking his whiskey and nodding affirmatively, as though he were making sure that Marty was telling his stories correctly.

We were into about our fourth or fifth round, I had lost track, but the booze and Marty's stories were going down a lot more smoothly when, suddenly, Guy turned to me and put a hand on my shoulder, silencing Marty who was in the middle of some story involving a water buffalo and a truck full of rations.

"Tell me something," he said, his squinting eyes giving me the once-over. "You married, or do you just deal in divorce?"

He let out a little chuckle.

"No," I said, grinning back at him. "I've never been married. Tried to be a few times, but it never seemed to work out. And I really don't know why. Maybe that's what I'm trying to find out."

Guy nodded his head, and his squinting eyes went suddenly serious.

"I thought as much," he said, nodding again. "I suppose a fellow like you, a lawyer and all—he's either got it all figured out, or he's still searching for an answer. And I don't suspect that you need any more answers from Nam or those that have been there. No, I'd say you got something else in mind, something else entirely."

"What do you mean?"

"A fellow like you wouldn't be alone if they could help it. Remember, I knew you back then. Don't take this the wrong way, but I always figured you for sensitive type."

"You mean soft?"

"No—not at all, you weren't soft. You were well liked and well respected, as a pilot and a man. And that was important to you. You always took the time to get to know your crew and the people you served with, and I always thought that once you got stateside, you'd find somebody and settle down."

"Like I said, I tried to do that, but it never worked out."

"I know," he said, squeezing my shoulder. "That's why I know that you didn't just come through El Paso to talk about good ole days. You came here because you truly want to see me, and find out how I'm doing. Hell, you may've even been a little worried about me. I'm just sorry that I'm such a piece of shit, and that I'm unable to provide you with any answers."

I knew Guy—at least, I did back then. I had known him to be calm, steady, and sure of himself, even in the most difficult situations. And he was right. I had wanted to see him and to see how he was doing, especially after I had blown off the call from Luisa. I was curious to know how a man so calm, steady, and sure of himself could fall down. But despite all his physical changes, he was still the same person that he was back then.

"I did want to see how you were," I admitted and then smiled. "And I can see you're doing fine."

"All things considered," he said, grinning at me and then over at Marty, "I am."

We all had a good laugh, and then Marty went back to telling his stories. After a while, even Guy chimed in with a few of his own. Before long, I was completely drunk but thoroughly enjoying listening to Guy talk with his deliberate drawl—still sounding like The Mick.

"Shoot," Guy said. "You remember ole Jake, don't you?"

"Of course," I replied.

"Remember the time he and that other door gunner, Noodles, made it with the same gal?"

"I remember you telling me about it," I said with an intoxicated grin.

Guy told the story the same way he had all those years ago in Vietnam, and afterward, we had a good laugh.

Chapter Seventeen

July 1963

Splitting four cords of dry pine for old man Spooner was a hell of a lot easier than splitting the two cords of the wet and knotty shit that Tom had purchased yesterday. But as part of his new work for flying lessons program, I was happy to oblige. I could handle it. I had a damn good swing, but as Jessie kept reminding me, it did little to improve my batting average.

Quit chopping at the ball, it's not a goddamned piece of wood! she had hollered at me the other day when we had been hitting the ball around. *You need to level out your swing or you'll never hit it!*

She was right about that. I hadn't hit anything she'd thrown at me, partially because she threw the ball so damn hard.

I hadn't seen too much of Jessie since school let out a couple of weeks ago. She had been attending a summer basketball camp at the university, and I had been cutting wood and taking flying lessons from Tom.

The high school had sponsored Jessie in the basketball camp. They were fast learning what I already knew: that Jessie was an amazing athlete. Baseball, basketball, volleyball, track—you name it, she was good at it, as good or better than some of the boys. But that didn't stop her from dating them. She went out with anybody and never gave a reason why—but the guys she went out with sure had one. And people had taken notice—even Carrie. We had been *kinda-sorta* dating since the Winter Formal but we hadn't given our relationship an official title. However, we had gone to several movies and had spent nearly every lunch together.

Jessie goes all the way, Carrie informed me one day in the cafeteria. Carrie wasn't one for spreading gossip, but as Jessie's friend, she seemed genuinely concerned. She had apparently learned this from Victor Andrews that morning in English class.

Of course, I knew it to be true. Victor was another basketball player that had dated Jessie a few weeks after the Winter Formal. It didn't last long, but she had told me that she had had sex with him. She now confided in me often. And as uncomfortable and as painful as it sometimes was to hear, I listened attentively, most of the time without speaking and always without judgment.

Have you and Carrie done it yet? Jessie had asked me one afternoon on the bus ride home, the same day she had told me about Victor.

With my face burning red, I told her no and that we had only kissed a few times.

I wanted to say that Carrie wasn't that type of girl, but I wasn't sure how Jessie might take it. *You know, her father is a preacher and all*, I had said instead.

That's when Jessie told me that it didn't make a lick of difference. *You know what they say about preachers' kids, don't you?*

I said no I hadn't and that I had no idea what she was talking about.

Preacher's kids are the worst, she had said.

I didn't understand that at all, because I couldn't imagine anyone worse than Jessie when it came to having sex—even her reputation as an athlete was being overshadowed by a far less flattering one.

I had told her that Carrie was moving, that her father was starting a new parish somewhere near Anchorage, and that although Carrie and I had agreed to see each other over the summer, the likelihood of us ever having sex was small—partly because of her, but mostly because, despite my unrelenting internal desires, I was secretly terrified at the idea of having sex. Of course, I had never mentioned that to Jessie.

Rather than wrestling the maul from a particularly twisted piece of pine, I instead lifted it and the wood high into the air and thrust them both down hard, maul-first onto the chopping block—halving it cleanly.

"Such a waste of so much power!" said Jessie from just beyond the woodpile, Saucy sitting by her side panting.

"Hey, Jess!" I said, driving the maul into the chopping block and wiping the sweat from my forehead. "What are you doing here? Didn't you have basketball today?"

"Yeah, but we finished up this morning, so I thought I'd come and see what you're up to. I've missed you," she added with a short but sincere little smile.

"I see Saucy found you. I wondered where she went. I guess she gets so bored when I'm cutting wood, but as you can see, I'm up to my ears in it. And not just any wood either," I said, making a face. "But Tom said if I split and stack it, he'll give me flying lessons, so it's worth it."

"Gee," said Jessie, her eyebrows pinched, "I didn't know you actually like doing things with him."

"He's a hell of a chopper pilot, and he's actually a great teacher. He doesn't get pissed at me at all when we're flying—it's sort of strange, but I'm not complaining. He's been letting me fly too, really fly," I said excitedly. "I'm not supposed to tell anyone though—on account of it's supposed to be a maintenance flight or something. Last week, he let my fly this one copter called a Sikorsky. It was the biggest goddamned copter I've ever seen—a huge mother. And he let me fly it! We even flew it over the house, the beaver pond—and your house too, Jess. I looked for you, but I knew you were at your camp and all."

"You mean you flew a whirlybird over my house?" she asked, looking skyward.

"Sure did. Damned near blew your roof off!" I said with a wide grin.

"Wow," she said, grinning back at me. "I would've loved to have seen that."

"You will, that's why I've got to get this wood cut. By the way, how was the camp?"

"Swell. My team won the tournament, and you're looking at the *most valuable player*," she said proudly.

"That's great, Jess, but I have to say, I'm not surprised. The rest of those girls don't have much on you, unless it's cheerleading or hair style or something."

"I can cheer," she snapped. "And what's wrong with my hair?"

"Nothing at all," I said, backpedaling. "I was only kidding."

"I know," she said, giggling. She walked up to the chopping block and wiggled out the maul.

"You want some help?" she asked, weighing the maul in her hands. "Say, this ax is awful heavy."

"That's because it's not an ax, it's a wood splitter's maul," I said, placing a piece of wood on the chopping block. "You want to try it?"

"Sure," she said enthusiastically and then stepped up to the block. "It looks like fun."

"Be careful," I cautioned her, "it can get away from you sometimes."

I stepped back a bit as she staggered bringing the maul up over her shoulder. For a moment, I thought she might fall, but she somehow managed to balance it by its handle straight over her head.

"Wait!" I shouted, and before she could bring it down, I grabbed hold of the handle. "You'll cut your foot off doing it like that!"

"I can do it," she said and then tried to pull the maul from me. We were standing so close together that her lips were nearly touching my chin. I could feel the moistness of her breath on my skin and, for the first time, I could sense there were limits to her strength and size, and I felt her succumb to me—her body relenting, and she let go.

"Show me," she said in an almost whisper.

Taking the maul into my hands, I heaved it up from below my waist, hurling it around my shoulders and high above my head where, extending my arms, I brought it back downward with all my might—slamming it violently into the block. With a crisp sharp *crack*, like the sound of a well-struck baseball, the wood split in two and fell haplessly to the ground.

"You got all of that one," she said with a kind of quiet admiration—a tone that I had never heard her use before with me.

For the next couple of hours we worked, neither one of us speaking, but each enjoying the other's silent company. I split the wood while Jessie collected it from beneath the block and stacked it neatly on the woodpiles. Although we didn't talk, I was astutely aware of Jessie's eyes upon me, following me, watching me cut the wood. It made me feel good, powerful—as though we were together, as though she were *my girl*. And for those couple hours, I believed it was true, and I forgot about everybody else and everything else.

Finally, Jessie broke the wistful silence when she cried out that she had gotten a sliver on her thumb. After a fair amount of fussing, a few quick pinches, and one long squeeze, I was able to get it out without the need for further medical attention—for either of us.

"It still hurts," she said, holding her thumb out to me.

I gently cupped it in the palm of my hand and kissed it.

"There, all better!" I announced.

"I don't think so," she said skeptically. "Let's go to the hill and get a drink. That'll make it feel better," she said playfully.

"It's okay with me. I'll go with you, but I'm not drinking that shit again," I said, shaking my head. My head ached and my stomach churned just thinking about it.

"You don't have to drink it straight, you know. It tastes better when you mix with soda, and it's not as potent that way. Actually, it's the way I prefer it. I've got a couple of pops at home we can go and get," she added.

"No, that's okay, we have some in the icebox," I said. "I'll go grab a couple, but I'm not drinking a lot. I'm hoping to fly tomorrow."

"You're such a rube!" she said as playfully as I had ever heard her say it.

"I don't think my grandmother ran off with anyone," Jessie announced high atop the tailing pile as we were sipping our rum and Pepsi. "I'm not sure what might've happened to her, but I don't think she and Frankie ran off anywhere together."

"What are you talking about?"

"None of it makes any sense," she said, frowning. "What my grandmother wrote in the diary. I must've read it a hundred times. She loved Daddy too much. She would've never left without taking her baby. I'm telling you, it doesn't make any sense. She took her baby everywhere—even when she was with Frankie. Why would she all the sudden decide to leave him behind—her only child? I'm telling you, it doesn't make any sense."

"What do you think happened then?"

"I don't know, but I'm sure Spenser's not telling the truth. There's something he's not saying—I know it!" she said adamantly.

She sat beside me staring intently across at the ridge on the other side of the beaver pond until a kind breeze bustling up from the side of the hill swirled between us catching her hair and her attention. She was so beautiful when she was like this, all wound up and resolute.

"I'll tell you something else," she fired. "I'd go so far to say that the bastard done something to her, and him!" she added.

"What?"

"You heard me."

"Are you saying—"

"The bastard killed her," she said firmly. "I wouldn't put it by him! He would've never let her go. Even if she had run off, which I doubt!, he would've hunted her down and killed her, and him—the bastard!"

"You can't be serious, he's your grandfather," I said.

"And I hate him, Hen!"

"How can you be so sure?"

"I told you, it doesn't make any sense," she said. "It's pretty clear from the diary that my grandmother and Frankie were having an affair. But I found the diary, Hen. Spenser never did. Why wouldn't she take the damn thing with her? It doesn't make any sense to leave it. You've heard all the rumors, everyone knew they were having an affair. Why do you think that is? Because *he* told them, that's why! Which means he must've caught them, or found out some other way—probably around the time she stopped writing in the diary. Then he killed them both and told everybody she was having an affair and ran off."

"That's crazy, Jess. You think he killed them both? What about the brother, *Julius*, or whatever his name is?"

"Jules, you mean, he killed him too," she said. Jessie stood up and pulled something from the front pocket of her jeans and handed it to me. "It's a timepiece," she said.

I took a good look at it. It was a pocket watch—gold, the type a conductor might carry. But it was unlike any I had ever seen before. At first glance, it appeared old and cracked, but after a closer examination, I discovered the entire watch was adorned with small gold nuggets. The front cover plate opened easily, revealing a pristine crystal behind with ornately decorated hands fronting a pearly-white face set with sharp black roman numerals. Connected to the watch was a chain made completely of larger gold nuggets, which ended with a gold medallion with a three-dimensional view of a log cabin on one side and the initial *V* on the other. The watch was stopped precisely at three o'clock.

"Fancy," I said. "Where did you get it?"

"Look!" she shouted, taking the watch from me. "It's engraved!"

Fiddling with it, she somehow managed to open the reverse side of the watch, exposing a shiny gold inner plate with words etched on it. She handed it back to me.

"Read it!" she commanded.

"*E. Mathey*," I said with a shrug. "Who's he?"

Jessie shot me a vicious glare.

"No, not that," she said, her tone frustrated. She directed me toward the bottom of the plate. "*Mathey* is the watchmaker, I think. Read what's written below it."

There appeared to be a serial number and then—in smaller, finer print—another set of words that I had a hard time reading. I held it up to the light.

"*J . . . something . . . so . . . you . . . won't be late . . . yours . . .* I can't make out the rest," I said. "It looks like . . . *O-K . . . something.*"

"Look here!" she said, snatching the watch from me. "It's says right there: *J-U-L-E-S. Jules!*" she shouted. "The watch belongs to Frankie's brother, *Jules*, you rube! She then paused, rubbing and scratching at it. "And see here: *O-K-S-A-N-A. Oksana!* Whoever Oksana is, she gave this watch to Jules O'Brien."

"*Oksana?*" I said, confused. "What kind of name is that?"

"Not sure," she said, tapping the back of the watch, "but that's what it says right here!"

"So what's the big deal?" I said. "So the watch belonged to Jules O'Brien. How did you come across it?"

Jessie smiled wickedly. From the resolve in her eyes, I suddenly knew what her answer would be. It sent a chill down through me.

"I found it among some of Grandaddy's things," she said.

I swallowed hard. "It doesn't prove anything," I said, but my own resolve was as weak as my words.

It was over an hour's hike to the top of a large hill they called Pedro's Dome and down the other side through a grove of blackened spruce trees, the victim of a forest fire several years back. But Jessie had to see them. By the time we reached the dried creek-bed that led to the O'Brien cabins, I thought perhaps the forest fire had destroyed them too, but a half mile later, the trees turned green again.

I had only been there one time before, several years ago with old man Spooner. He had wanted to fish the creek back when there was water. We didn't see so much as a tadpole in the creek and after a couple casts, we decided to head elsewhere. Spooner had taken the time to show me the cabins however, and pass on a few of the stories.

"It's through here," I hollered back at Jessie just before ducking through a grove of cottonwood trees. On the other side, a trace of a trail led up to a small clearing where there stood a fire-blackened log cabin skewed and slightly sunk into the mossy ground. Next to it, a mound of wood and weeds marked the remains of another.

The cabins were as I remembered.

"This is it," I said as Jessie stepped through the trees. "Not much left."

Jessie pushed past me and on over to the upright cabin. It had no door, and Jessie stepped inside. I followed.

Dusty beams of sunshine shone down through holes in the rusting tin ceiling. For the most part, the cabin was empty, except several corroding metal rasps and an old iron vise, which lay on the center of the rotting floor.

"I'm no Sherlock Holmes, but I can't imagine—"

"Hush," said Jessie, raising a hand to me as she scanned the room. She went over, picked up one of the rasps, and began examining it closely. "Frankie and his brother didn't live here," she said, tossing the file to the ground.

"So what? What does that prove? So they lived in the other one. I don't think you'll find anything there. It's a pile of moss."

"Maybe not," she said, "but it's curious that this one is still standing and the other is not."

I didn't see the correlation. Jessie walked past me and out the doorway. I kicked around inside the cabin for a little while to make her think I was searching for something. After a few long minutes, I found her over at the collapsed cabin. She was picking through the remains of an old mattress, which now was nothing more than a bundle of rusted springs. Saucy had reappeared and was nosing around the partially buried potbellied stove. I caught the reflection from what looked to be the remnants of an old-time hand mirror. I picked it up and lobbed it toward Jessie.

"What's that?" she said.

"It's a broken mirror. You think it might be a clue, or perhaps just bad luck?" I said and then prepared for a look.

Jessie didn't disappoint.

"You could be more helpful," she said, glaring at me.

"Well, maybe if I knew what it was we're supposed to be looking for," I replied.

"I'm not sure either, but I'll know when I see it."

"That's helpful," I said. "I just hope we see it soon, it's a long walk back."

Jessie rolled her eyes and then went back to rummaging through the wreckage. I wanted to be helpful, but it all seemed so pointless. But I went on pretending to search. After twenty more minutes, however, I was completely bored. Even Saucy had given up the investigation and had found herself a warm patch of sunshine to sprawl out in. I envied her.

"Hey, Hen," Jessie suddenly called from the woods beyond the cabin.

I walked over to where she was standing.

"I can't find anything," she said, her tone defeated.

"What did you expect to find?"

"Not sure, but something more, I guess. Something to help prove that Granddaddy killed them folks."

"That's crazy," I said. "You find a few things lying around and suddenly your grandfather killed three people."

"They're personal things, Henry. Why in the Sam-hell would a woman run off without her personal diary and a man leave without his gold pocket watch—engraved to boot, Hen. Nobody leaves these kinds of things behind. And why did I find Jules's watch in Granddaddy's things?"

She made sense, but it was difficult to believe that old man Spenser was a triple murderer. There had to be a better explanation.

"He probably burned these cabins," she said.

"Why would Spenser burn the cabins?"

"To destroy evidence," she said firmly. "I looked it up. The fire was reported the day after they supposedly ran off. The rumor was that the three of them set the fire to cover their tracks, but I don't buy it. It doesn't make any sense. What reason would they have to burn down their own cabins? And another thing. Do you know when that big mining deal with the dredge company went down—the one where supposedly Spenser got *swindled* by his partners?"

"No idea," I said.

"March 30, 1938."

"So what?"

"So what!" she exclaimed. "So that's three days before Grandma's last entry in the diary!"

"I don't think that proves anything," I said.

"You can think what you want, but I'll prove it."

"I don't know, Jess," I said skeptically. "I don't see how you can get all this from a diary and a pocket watch. Maybe your grandmother left the diary and who's to say Spenser didn't find the watch somewhere. And what about the money? Rumor has it, his partners ran off with all the money from the sale of their claims. Ole Spenser isn't a rich man, is he? Maybe your grandmother ran off with the man *and* the money—maybe she thought the money was *worth* leaving your father for."

"I don't believe it," she said shaking her head. "You don't know my granddaddy. No way she would've left her only son alone with that drunk. No, I'm sure he had something to do with it—something he's not saying. And as for as the money goes—hell, he could've hidden it anywhere. Granddaddy's full of secrets."

"So was your grandmother it seems," I said.

Suddenly, I was the recipient of an another icy glare. "Maybe she was entitled to have a few secrets!" snapped Jessie. "I know Spenser didn't know about the diary. If he had, he would've destroyed it."

"Then why would he keep the watch? Seems to me, he'd want to destroy that too."

"Not necessarily," she said shaking her head. "Spenser doesn't like to part with anything. Besides, I know for sure he didn't want to part with the watch."

"How do you know that?"

"Because he's been missing it," she said. She then charged past me and headed back down the trail.

"What are you talking about?" I said following her. "Wait up!" I called, but she kept on walking. I ran after her. "Jessie!" I shouted.

She stopped suddenly and spun around. To my surprise, her eyes held tears.

"What?" she said sharply.

"What's the matter?"

"Nothing," she said and wiping her eyes with the back of her wrist.

"Something's wrong," I said. "What is it, Jess?"

"I swiped it," she said.

"What?"

"The watch, I swiped it from Spenser," she said.

"What do you mean?"

"He carried it around with him all the time. He seemed so fond of it. Then he left it . . ." She paused and wiped her eyes again. "He left it lying around one time . . . and I swiped it. Not sure why—maybe just to piss him off. But I got a good look at it and noticed the inscription. I knew right then and there he had done something to Grandma and them boys. I could feel it, Hen. I hid the watch up on the tailing pile in an empty jar until today. You didn't even notice."

"Did he ever suspect you?"

"Sure he did, and Daddy too. He was sure sore about it. Made a big fuss—threatened to throw us both out. He went through our rooms and tore apart everything. But after a while, he calmed down some, and Daddy convinced him he must've lost it somewhere. Not sure if he really believes that, but he hasn't mentioned it in a while."

"If he doesn't suspect you anymore, then why are you so upset?"

"Because you don't believe it, and I want you to believe *me*."

"I want to believe you," I said weakly. I did too. It just seemed so incredible.

Jessie looked away, her eyes seemed to affix to something high in the cottonwood trees. Then, clasping her hands together, she looked back over to me.

"I know it's hard for you to understand. I know that you think like everyone else around here, that my grandmother ran out on Spenser. Hen, I *know* he had something to do with their disappearance. I just *know* he did. I'll prove it, but I need your help. I need you to help me prove it. If you could just *trust* me, if you would just *believe* me when I say . . ." She hesitated and, again, began to cry.

"Of course, I'll help you, Jess," I said, hating to see her like this. "What do you want me to do?"

For a long while, Jessie didn't say anything but only stared up into the trees. Then she wiped her eyes.

"Help me find the bodies."

The tone in her voice sent a sharp chill down through me. She was stone cold serious. Not only did she truly believe that her grandfather was a killer, but she believed that there were *bodies—bodies* for me to help her find.

I swallowed hard trying to hold back the nauseating swells from my stomach.

"*Bodies,*" I whispered.

"Yes, *bodies,*" she said, "*skeletons* more likely. It has been well over thirty years now, probably not much left of them. I bet they're not far from here though." Her eyes scanned the nearby trees. "It's been a long time, but they say they disappeared in June. They say, she left during the day, caught a train and took all her personal things—never to be seen again."

"She left her diary," I said.

"That's right, but you can't have it both ways, Hen," she said sharply. "Spenser has always maintained that she ran out on him in the summer, taking all her personal things. So why would she leave her diary? A diary that ends at the beginning of April, not June. Besides, I think you've forgotten where we live. It takes time to get anywhere around here, even if you have a car. This is over thirty years ago. If you, your brother, and his mistress were planning to swindle someone and then hightail it out of Alaska, wouldn't you at the very least have had a *plan?* And you surely would've taken your personal diary and your gold engraved watch. No, I'm not buying any of it."

"Well, everyone else did," I said.

"Yes, I suppose they did. But how is it that Spenser had the watch?"

"Like I said before, maybe he found it," I said.

Jessie rolled her eyes.

"Where? The cabins are burned? I suppose next you'll say he could've found it just lying around?"

"It's possible," I said.

"Not likely!" snapped Jessie.

"How do you know that?"

Jessie gave me grave look.

"Because my grandaddy killed them boys, and that's how he got a hold of the watch."

Suddenly, there came a sharp snapping sound from just beyond the trees behind us. Saucy's ears perked and then, springing from her spot in the sun, she rushed past us and on into the woods barking after whatever it was. Jessie and I followed anxiously, our eyes stressing to see anything through the dense forest. We hadn't followed too far before we spied the hindquarters of a giant mother moose go loping through a thick wall of brush. Saucy made a cursory charge and then a triumphant retreat after realizing the enormous creature had fled. For several seconds we could hear the dull thuds and cracks of the moose's plodding exodus.

"That scared the shit out of me," said Jessie placing a hand to her chest. "Damned moose sneaking up on you like that. Little slow there Sauce," Jessie said to the dog. Saucy skipped up to her and awaited her congratulatory rub. Jessie obliged but continued to scold the dog about her timing.

"We should go now," I said impatiently. "It's a long walk home. Is there anything more we need to do here?"

Jessie glanced back at the burned cabins and then with a sigh, she said, "I guess not."

"I still don't know what any of this proves," I said.

"Maybe nothing," said Jessie. "Not right now anyway."

"I just don't see what good any of this will do, Jess. If everything you say is true, what's to say Spenser won't go after you . . . or me even?" I said, feeling my stomach turn. "You live with him, for crying out loud!"

Jessie smiled at me warmly and then put a hand on my shoulder.

"It's sweet of you to worry," she said, "but don't. I know exactly how to handle Granddaddy. I think the bootlegging is working some. Besides, we'll need a lot more before we can nail the bastard. But we have a big clue now."

"Yeah, what clue?"

"*Oksana*," she said. "The woman who gave Jules the watch."

Chapter Eighteen

May 1969

My decision to sign on for a second tour was threefold really.

First, Sara had left me. And although there was a large part of me that wanted to charge home and try and iron everything out, I hadn't seen her in over a year and I hadn't heard from her since my now infamous *Dear John* letter, so a surprise reunion might not be the best way to win her back. Besides, another stretch in this bloody war might be just the thing to piss her and her new peace-loving beau off.

Secondly, the army was giving me a choice of duty, and it was an opportunity to transfer out of Major Whipple's *asinine* outfit and finally do something useful. The army agreed to transfer me to the Fifteenth Medical Battalion of the First Cav, which meant I would be moving south to Third Core. And instead of being a taxi, I would be an ambulance. The missions would be no less dangerous but should be a lot more rewarding. I liked the idea of flying dustoffs, mostly because you were flying boys out rather than into combat, and after the FUBAR shit that I had seen this past year, it appealed to me.

Finally, after my tour, the army had agreed to substantially reduce my obligations stateside and, prior to the transfer, send me to Hawaii for some long overdue *R & R*.

The loss of Guy had been devastating. They had assigned my ship a new crew chief, a tiny little fellow by the name of Grey from Knoxville, Tennessee, who was just short of worthless. He had been in-country for about three minutes before we got him, and I had already spent a good deal of time double checking his work and holding his hand during inspections. To make matters worse, Ho had made AC and was being reassigned at the end of the month. I was happy for him, but if I was going to have to babysit a new crew chief and break in a cherry peter, then I might as well do it in a different outfit.

I had just come from signing the papers when I nearly ran into Jake tearing out from behind my hooch, his shirt off and dog tags bouncing against his sweat-covered chest. Stopping suddenly, he leaned forward, resting his hands above his knees, breathing hard and fast.

"There you are . . . sir," he said breathlessly. "We've got to go . . . the ship's set. You're to report to the flight line . . . immediately. We have to assist with some big lift with the birds at Pleiku. Part of their strip was hit or something, but they're calling in practically every chopper in Two-Core."

"Aw shit!" I hollered at him. "I had the day off!"

"I know, it's fucked up, sir," he said sympathetically. He had recovered enough of his wind to stand straight up. "I hear them flyboys at Pleiku got hit pretty bad leaving a shitload of marines in the field, and they need us to help get them out ASAP."

"And I suppose the LZ's hot," I said.

"Scorching," said Jake.

It was worse than scorching. Apparently, our boys were in a retreat and pinned down along the perimeter. And because it wasn't our AO, the flight was long and our arrival was well overdue.

We were second to last in a formation of ten ships and were hit in the ass the minute we made visual.

"What's the damage?" I shouted into the intercom and waited for Grey to reply. When he didn't, I repeated the question then glanced over at Ho who shrugged. "Did he fall out of the damn ship?" I yelled in frustration. "Where the hell are you, Grey?"

"Here, sir," he finally replied.

"Where have you been? I need a damage report, damn it!"

"Sorry, didn't know you were talking to me," he said, way too coolly for my liking. "We're okay, though," he added.

"When I ask about the ship, I'm only talking to you, Grey, goddamn it!" I screamed. "You're the crew chief here, for crying out loud!"

"Yes, sir," came the weak reply.

But I had bigger things to worry about—namely landing the damned ship. We were heading into a serious firefight that was quickly turning into a rout. The LZ was a rough and sloping piece of real estate rising up to a tattered jungle. Grunts were pouring out of the forest, while behind them came explosions and flashes of fire. A handful of swarming Cobra gunships hovering over the treetops pounded the earth with their rockets as dozens of slicks, nudging up to the tree line, were loading onrushing soldiers—some wounded, some dragging the wounded or the dead, but all of them moving faster than hell.

I swung the ship down a few feet from the ground, well back and below the tree line and then hitting the throttle. I slowly skipped it forward, keeping it low until setting it down some forty or fifty feet behind a ship that was just bugging out. Flanny had called the move *creeping*, and he used it primarily when maneuvering around a sloping LZ—*it gives them less time to get a bead on you*, he had told me.

It appeared to have worked too, as we weren't taking any fire. At first, I didn't think we were going to have any passengers, since I couldn't see shit through the smolder and the trees, and as much as I wanted to let Jake spray bullets into the jungle, I couldn't be sure he wouldn't hit one of our own. Then all at once, a marine sergeant emerged from the smoke, a wounded man slung over his shoulder. Behind him, another marine came sprinting from the fray.

I watched Jake and Grey pull the wounded man on board and the marine sergeant climb onto the deck after him and squat right behind me.

"Let's move!" he shouted, barely audible above the sound of the rotors. "Charlie's all over us—if we don't move now, we're dead!"

I nodded toward Jake who was pulling the other marine onto the deck.

"All clear, Jake?" I said into the intercom. I could see he was engaged in a close conversation with the marine he'd just pulled aboard.

"Wait!" came Jake's reply. "There are two more behind him, one has a chest wound but is still breathing. They sent this guy ahead to have us wait."

"What the fuck you waiting for?" the sergeant yelled at me. "Let's move!"

I shook my head. "We got two more!" I shouted at the sergeant, "We're going to wait!"

"Horse shit!" he hollered at me. "I got a boy who's lost a lot of blood, and he can't wait any longer! We got the entire North Vietnamese Army a hundred feet beyond them trees! If we don't get out now, we never will!"

I glanced at Jake who shook his head.

"We wait!" I shouted to the sergeant.

I thought for a moment that the sergeant was battle shocked or something, because we didn't appear to be in any immediate peril—at least none intended for us—when suddenly a shell exploded behind us, rocking the ship slightly forward. Then another, this time whipping the tail around and hopscotching us sideways, the main rotor coming dangerously close to catching the ground before we slammed hard back down onto the skids. The jolt tossed the sergeant to the floor between Ho and me.

"Now let's move, goddamn it!" cried the sergeant, picking himself up off the floor and grabbing me by my chicken-plate.

I pushed him off, and Ho assisted me in shoving him back to the deck. In seconds, he was back in my face.

"You're going to get us all killed, motherfucker!" he screamed into my ear. "Now move this bird!"

I didn't have time to react as an array of bullets came piercing through the Plexiglas windshield, one of them ricocheting off the doorpost behind me. An instant later, I was again staring into the red eyes and rotting teeth of the seething sergeant—except this time, he shoved a .45-caliber pistol into my cheek.

"Now move, fuckhead!" he screamed as spittle flying from his decaying mouth hit me in the face.

"Fucker pulled gun!" Ho's voice screeched into the intercom.

"Holy shit!" shouted Jake. "We're being hijacked! Can you believe this shit?"

In another time, I might've reacted differently. I might've freaked out and then bugged out. But this wasn't another time. This was now, and time—seemingly slower—made the world before me more lucid and sharp.

"Any sign of them, Jake?" I said calmly into the intercom, glancing past the sergeant at him.

"There they are!" Jake's voice came blaring into my ears, and then I too saw them. They were about a hundred feet away—an enormous black man limping toward the chopper, cradled in his arms was the blood-soaked body of another marine.

"You hear me, motherfucker!" blurted the sergeant pressing the barrel of the pistol hard into my cheek.

"We wait!" I said to the sergeant and then nodding toward the two marines just as a couple more bullets crashed through Ho's side window and on through mine. The sergeant ducked behind the seat as I glimpsed Jake and the other marine leaping from the deck. "Covering fire, Grey!" I shouted into the intercom. Moments later, I felt the .60 awaken.

"Move it, by god, or I swear I will!" shouted the sergeant, cocking the pistol and shoving it back into my face. "Now go!"

Long pools of sweat ran along the crest of the sergeant's thick black eyebrows while rivers of it poured down the crevasses of his matured face. As I watched him grit and grind his yellow teeth, I knew he wasn't used to having his orders ignored. I fixated only on his wide eyes, paying no attention to the gun.

You may not be a goddamned general, but you're the swingin'est dick on your ship. So act like it, I could hear Flanny's voice echoing.

"No, we wait!" I said firmly, glancing out through the deck. Jake and the marines were not so far away. "So if you're going to shoot me, you might as well get to it!" I nodded toward Ho. "He'll get you home once I'm out of the way, but not before then," I added.

The sergeant glanced over at Ho who only glared back at him, face stern, eyebrows crossed, and shaking his head.

"You kill me too, son-bitch!" shouted Ho.

Then another shell rocked the side of the ship, knocking the sergeant to the floor. A barrage of bullets followed the blast, scattering all through the ship—several ripped through the windshield while others skipped off the deck. My ears rang shrilly after another grazed the side of my helmet. Out of the corner of my eye, I saw Jake and the marines lifting the wounded soldier onto the deck an instant before a second barrage slammed into the side of us. The bullets missed their mark, if their mark was men and crew, but the chopper had taken a dreadful beating.

"We're out of here!" I yelled into the intercom with a prayer that the ship would believe me. "Full suppression, boys," I ordered.

The ship pissed and moaned, but slowly and steadily, we climbed out of the jungle. Then, I felt something nudge the back of my seat. I turned just in time to see Jake on top of the sergeant, his fist in full flurry.

"What the hell?" I shouted into the intercom.

It took two marines to pull Jake off the sergeant and a third to pin him back against the back wall. All the while, the sergeant lay on his elbows, shouting at Jake words inaudible over the sound of the rotors. Blood trickled from the side of the sergeant's face.

Jake glared back at him, his eyes wide and wild. He twisted and squirmed but couldn't escape the grasp of the marines. One of the them said something to him and then patted him on the shoulder.

It seemed to calm Jake some as he looked away from the sergeant and nodded several times at the marines. Finally, the marines released him and he slid weakly down on the deck.

"Is everything under control back there?" I said into the intercom.

There was no reply, but something in Jake's eyes told me that this wasn't the end of it.

I set a course for home, westward and into the sun, trying to keep one eye out for Charlie and one on Jake. A deathly stillness fell over the chopper and that is when I saw it all play out—the instant before it happened, and I could do nothing to stop it.

Jake sprang from the back wall, leaping just beyond the reach of the marines and then dove straight at the sergeant. He managed two vicious blows to the side of the sergeant's head before the marines finally caught him. A vicious scrum then broke out at the center of the deck, with fists flying in every direction. Finally, the marines were able to get a hold of Jake as he twisted and squirmed, trying desperately to resist their holds. But eventually the marines proved too much, forcing him to relent.

With a marine securing each of his arms and one holding his legs, Jake resembled a rabid dog at the end of his rope.

"You motherfucker!" he shouted at the sergeant, but the words would be his last.

It happened so fast and was so in line with my premonition that I was sure I had imagined it. It was no more than a flicker of light accompanied by a dull popping sound, but it sent Jake exploding backward into the arms of the stunned marines who impulsively let him slip from their bloody grasps and slide lifelessly down onto the deck.

Seconds later, the sergeant, without remorse or emotion, surrendered his weapon to the marines over Jake's dead body, as if he had performed for them some unpleasant task.

Before I looked away, I saw Grey cowering in the corner, fear paling his face.

Ho notified command and control that we had two wounded soldiers on board and one casualty and that we had set a course for the nearest MASH unit. Ho also requested that the MPs be on alert as one of our crew members was dead—shot and killed by a sergeant in the United States Marine Corps.

In case you haven't noticed, people die around here. Not just on some crazy night mission or on account of some hot LZ, but all the time and because of the strangest shit, Flanny's voice resonated through my mind.

I never play the cards, I always play the man—can't lose that way, I remembered Jake saying. He was right, of course, but I couldn't help but think that it wasn't the cards that had killed him.

Chapter Nineteen

May 1985

Pulling into the parking lot to the heliport, he sees Ray's truck and that the hangar door is propped open with a broken cinderblock. He walks past reception and down the paneled hallway to Ray's office, where he can hear the quiet hum of an electric fan and two familiar voices. One is Ray's, but the other he cannot quite place.

In the little office, Ray is leaning back in his chair, his feet up and hands behind his head.

"It's a lot of area to cover—" Ray says and then, seeing him, shouts, "Henry! I was just telling Joe here about our little operation."

"Joe Callahan," says the man and offers his hand.

He is ghostly familiar—older, heavier, his hair longer and nearly all gray—but the eyes and voice are the same. Without speaking, he takes the hand.

Joe looks at him curiously and then says to Ray, "You didn't tell me he was a mute."

Ray laughs.

"I'm sorry," he says. "It's very nice to meet you. It's just that you remind me of someone."

"I know, I get that all the time," he says. "Apparently, I look exactly like that fat middle-aged guy everybody knows."

Ray laughs again. "Joe here," says Ray, "works for Bell out of Fort Worth. He wants to fly one of our Rangers, and do some performance tests."

"What kind of performance test?"

"Oh, nothing much, really," says Joe. "This is just a program that Bell's got going to allow me to see Alaska. They won't give me a vacation, see, so they send me on these little outings." He chuckles. "Next, I go to Hawaii to fly around with Magnum and TC."

They all laugh.

"You're funny," Ray says to Joe.

"Yeah, well, this is still my day job, so we'd better get going," says Joe, glancing at his watch. "Are you coming with us, Ray?"

"Oh no," Ray says, shaking his head. "I don't fly."

"Really?" says Joe.

"Nope. I never have, not even as a passenger. It's a phobia."

"Now who's funny?" Joe smirks.

Joe pulls pitch and pushes power—they are only a few feet off the ground. A hard bank right and then east into the morning sun.

"I grew up right up here," he says, pointing to the ground below. "My hometown."

Joe smiles at him. They near the old house—he can see the Shit Towers over the horizon.

"Now that's what I call a junk pile," Joe says when they are directly overhead.

"Who are you?" he says, suspicious. "I mean who are you, really? Why are you here?"

Shaking his head, Joe smiles again.

"I already told you. Name's Joe, and I came here in a big jet plane all the way from Dallas."

Joe spirals the chopper downward and then banks another hard right, following the highway.

He shakes his head, his eyes fixed on the ground below—he stares hypnotically at the old beaver pond and then his old house.

"I know a place where we can land," he says.

"Land? Oh no, we can't do that," says Joe, shaking his head. "We've got a schedule to keep."

"It's not far from here. It'll only take a few minutes, I promise."

"Sorry, can't do it!" Joe says, and then he hits the throttle and the pitch. And suddenly they are hurtling through air, the chopper on its nose and the earth below melting into a hazy green. His stomach churns, and he begins to feel dizzy. He looks over at Joe, but his figure blurs into a mass of suffocating colors. He cannot breathe.

"You all right, Henry?"

"Henry, are you all right?"

Opening my eyes, I see Guy squinting at me.

"Guy?"

"Yeah, Henry, it's me," he said, squeezing my shoulder. "You were shouting in your sleep. It sounded like you were having a nightmare or something."

"Yeah, maybe," I said, blinking hard.

"You have them a lot?"

"What?"

"Nightmares—you have them a lot?"

"I suppose. Lately, I've been having dreams. I wouldn't call them nightmares though," I said.

"It must've been quite a dream. You're shaking like a leaf," he said, squeezing my shoulder again.

"Yeah, this one was a strange one," I said, sitting up.

Guy had been kneeling beside me free of his prosthesis.

"I hope I didn't wake you?"

"No bother at all. I was up getting a drink, anyway. Do you remember what you dreamed?"

"No," I lied. I didn't feel much like talking, especially through a hangover. I tried piecing together lasts night's events and remembered the bar, Marty, and most of the conversation, but had no clue as to when I had gotten here, or how.

"I used to get nightmares," said Guy, pulling his huge mass across the floor and into the recliner, "when I first got back from Vietnam. Drove Luisa loco. But after a while, they passed."

"I've never had dreams about Vietnam. A lot of other shit, but not about Vietnam," I said.

"I'll dream about it sometimes," he said, "but not like when I first came back. Probably from the painkillers they gave me for my leg."

I glanced at my watch, 6:30 a.m.

"Like I was telling you, I really haven't thought about Vietnam much. Mostly just recently, since I've been visiting with some of you boys. I think about ole Flanny once in a while—don't think I'll ever forget him though."

"No, I reckon you won't," said Guy, putting on his glasses and shaking his head. "You two were pretty tight."

Guy brushed something that looked to be food from his tee shirt onto the chair, and then brushed it from the chair to the floor.

"It sure was nice seeing you, Henry. It has been a long time. I've often wondered what you've been doing. I always pictured you up in Alaska somewhere, flying some type of bird over all that beautiful country."

I thought about the dream.

"I sure wish you could've met Luisa," he said, smiling at me.

"Me too," I said. "But it's been great seeing you, Guy. You were the best damn crew chief in the whole damn unit—maybe the whole damn army."

Guy smiled and reached for his prosthetic leg. Without much effort, he strapped it on.

"I'm going to make us some breakfast. What do you say?"

"Sounds good," I replied.

I wasn't hungry, but I didn't want to be rude. Guy had been a gracious host who had somehow managed to find our way home last night. Guy stood up and limped on into the kitchen. Before long, the trailer smelled of fried bacon.

I ate all that he gave me. It was the first semiregular meal I'd had in a long time, and after a couple bites, I discovered that I was, in fact, hungry.

Guy talked more about Luisa and their two decades of troubles, and I soon understood that next to Vietnam, she was his favorite conversation.

"Don't know what you got until it's gone," he said through a mouthful of pancakes.

"You never know, Guy," I said reassuringly. "She may come back—after all, you were together a long time."

"It was a long time," he agreed. "She's stubborn that way, I reckon. You know she was dead-set on sticking with me to the end—leaving must have been a hell of a thing for her. But once she gets fixin' to do something—shoot, there aint no stopping that woman," he added proudly.

"You would know better than me, I guess," I said. "What do I know about anything when it comes to women—remember the *Dear John?*"

"I do," he said.

"Sometimes I think my life has been one long *Dear John* letter."

"I worried sometimes that I would get one from Luisa, but I never did. We were married just a year before I went in. Shoot, all I cared about back then was Luisa, fast cars, and the rodeo—and not necessarily in that order," he added with a grin.

"Rodeo, eh? I didn't know that about you."

"Sure, I rode the bulls," he said with a quick nod and then got up and started clearing the plates. "They said I was too big, but I took home a buckle or two. I supported myself for nearly six months riding rodeo. God, Luisa hated it—or hated me doing it. Shoot, she told me she'd leave me if I ever got hurt." He paused, staring blankly at the wall behind the sink. "So I never did, never had worse than a scratch—believe that?" he said glancing back at me.

"Amazing," I said. "Sometimes that's the way I feel about Vietnam. You know, I did two tours and not as much as a scratch myself, but I saw my share of dead and wounded. I suppose flying those ships, you see more than most. I'll tell you this much, though, I don't know what good it did me."

"What good?" asked Guy sitting back down at the table.

"Surviving," I said.

Guy folded his arms atop his large belly.

"What do you mean by that?" he said.

"Sometimes I'm not sure I should've made it out of there. So many good guys didn't. I don't know why I had to be so lucky, that's all. Seems to me there were a lot more deserving. I can't help but think that I messed my life up pretty good. I know this sounds strange, but sometimes I think life in Vietnam wasn't so bad."

Guy gave me a look that said he didn't understand.

"It's strange that you'd say something like that, because you know what your boy Flanagan told me?"

"No," I said.

"It wasn't too long before he died. We'd been assigned to that spook operation with Colonel Glasson. Me and Phillips was working on something on Mr. Flanagan's bird, I can't remember exactly, but Mr. Flanagan was hanging around us the way he did. You know, checking out everything and busting our balls. I don't know why we was talking about it, but we got on the subject of hounds."

"*Hounds?*" I said.

"Yeah—hounds, dogs, and such. Mr. Flanagan's telling us about this dog he had back home in Iowa or someplace."

"Idaho," I said.

"That's right, Idaho," he said, nodding. "He was telling us about this old redbone hound he'd had. Had him since he was a pup, said he'd trained him to hunt—rabbits, coons, and such. I don't quite recall, and shoot—I don't know nothing about no hound. But he's telling us about it anyway, about all the time he'd spent training the damn thing. Said he had him good and trained too. Said another year and he'd have that dog doing his taxes." Guy chuckled, causing his belly to jiggle. "Then he tells how he moved in with this gal—not the one he'd married, mind you. But he said back then he was driving truck and was gone all the time—had to leave the dog with this gal, sometimes for a week at a time with the runs he was doing. And every time he left, she'd let that dog get away with everything. Never ran him, fed him all the time—scraps direct from the table, which I suppose is a no-no. Hell, the dog even slept with her. Mr. Flanagan said that after a while the dog got so lazy he'd have to put him through a kind of boot camp every other week, just so he wouldn't forget who's the boss. Well, he said this went on for some time, until he came home one day and discovered that damn gal had gone out and got the hound neutered."

"No kidding?"

"Yeah, and after that, he said the hound had completely changed—wouldn't do nothing he was trained to do, even when he'd try and work with him. Said he didn't know whether it was because he'd been neutered or whether the hound was just pissed off about it. Either way, he said, the hound was useless."

"What'd he do?"

"He said he left the gal and the dog. Said if he'd stayed much longer, she'd a had his balls too." Guy chuckled again. "But that's not why I'm telling you this. I recall him saying something else that day. Said that the chopper was like his balls, and he didn't want anyone cutting them out from under him when he wasn't looking—that's why he was always on us like he was. I reckon I didn't think anything about it at the time. I was just playing, but I asked him what's he going to do when he gets stateside without his balls. And this I remember well, because it surprised me the way he said it all serious like. He says he didn't know what he was going to do. Said the thought of going home scared the hell out of him sometimes. That he thought life in Nam was hell of a lot easier than going home. I asked him why he thought that, and he just said he didn't want to go anywhere and be useless."

"I hadn't heard that story," I said, surprised.

"Yeah, well it stuck with me, especially after what happened to him and all. And hell, maybe you're right. Life is tougher. Maybe he's the one that got off easy."

We went on talking for the better part of the morning, mostly about Luisa and Vietnam. The conversation was pleasant, but shortly before noon, I told Guy that I had to be moving on as I had many miles ahead of me. I thanked him for his hospitality and for breakfast and then gave him a weak promise that I'd try and keep in touch.

"You're welcome down here anytime," he said as I was getting into the truck. "Next time, maybe we can head on into Mexico."

"Sounds like a good time," I said.

I started the truck and the air conditioning and watched as Guy slid his way down the ramp and limped over to me.

"Before you go," he said with a troubled look about him. His giant body leaned heavy into the side of the truck. "I've been meaning to ask you something. It's about ole Jake," he said and then hesitated.

For two days, we both had danced around the subject, neither one of us wanting to bring it up. At least, that's how I saw it. Not that I was intentionally avoiding it, I just thought it had been avoided.

"You know, I think about him a lot," he said, rubbing his hand along the open truck window. "I heard what happened with that marine sergeant and all." He shook his head. "I really liked that kid, but he was sort of a firecracker. Of course, you knew that. Sometimes I think that if I'd still been around, I could've somehow prevented it. Believe it or not, he listened to me."

"I know he did, Guy," I said, turning off the engine. Instantly, I felt the sweat bead up on my forehead. It had to be over a hundred degrees. "We all listened to you, Guy, but I don't know if anything could've . . ." I said, then paused. "It was just the way he was, Guy. He was young and full of beans. We all were."

"I reckon so, but do you think I could've made any difference?"

"I don't know, Guy. Maybe, but there's really no point to it."

Guy nodded, but I could tell he wasn't convinced. Again, I felt the sway as he leaned back away from the truck.

"Damn shame what that sergeant got away with."

"For crying out loud, I did all I could do," I said defensively. Sweat trickled from all parts of my body. "I really don't know what more I could've done!" I shouted at him.

"That's not what I mean," said Guy, raising his palms to me. "Please don't think that I'm blaming you. I'm just saying that it was an injustice, that's all. Really, Henry." Guy patted my shoulder. "I don't blame anyone except that godforsaken sergeant."

I took a long breath of hot air. I didn't know why I had reacted that way. Maybe it was because I did feel responsible. I had never really questioned anything regarding the investigation. In fact, I'd probably done the minimum required of me. I remember being so damn tired of the formal inquiries, the questions with their hidden accusations, and all the damned innuendo. Maybe I could've done more—I certainly couldn't have done less.

"I didn't mean to shout at you," I said calmly. "I suppose maybe there was more that I could've done, but it just seemed so pointless at the time. You can't imagine how the whole thing played out, Guy. I just got so tired of it all. You should've seen all the marines that went to bat for that son of a bitch. They painted Jake as some kind of crazed lunatic, claiming that the sergeant acted in self-defense. A couple of the other marines on board testified to that too. It was a damned circus. Nobody wanted to talk about him hijacking the ship—like he was justified or something. But they didn't even pin that on him, not really, unless that's what you call the conduct unbecoming—for hijacking a ship for crying out loud, Guy!"

I stared up at him, searching his eyes for something, perhaps forgiveness.

"All he had to do was stay put! Why couldn't he have just stayed put? I had everything under control, for crying out loud!"

Suddenly it didn't seem so long ago, and I was angry. I wasn't sure whether my anger was directed toward the injustice of it all, or my role in it. Maybe it was both. For years, I had done a pretty good job of not thinking about it.

"You know you did," said Guy, patting my shoulder again. "You know Jake, he was a regular firecracker. I doubt if I could've stopped him even if I had been there."

I knew Guy had only said that for my sake, but coming from him, it made me feel better. For whatever reason, Guy always seemed to make me feel better. He had that way about him.

"You know, I was in Chicago a few years back, on a divorce case," I said. "And the entire time I was there, I couldn't help but think about Jake—him being from Chicago and all. Finally, I did a little research and located his mother. I'm not sure why, but I did. You know, she still lived in the house he grew up in," I added, looking down at the steering wheel. "Anyway, I called her. I remember her name was Pam, and I told her I had known Jake in the war. She seemed very pleased that I had called and invited me over. I went and ended up staying for dinner. She talked nonstop about Jake, told me all about him growing up, about his friends and his girlfriends." I glanced back up at Guy and smiled. "You name it, she talked about it, but she never brought up the war. I thought maybe she was waiting for me to bring it up, but when I did, she quickly changed the subject. I remember wanting to tell her how much of a shame I thought it was and that I'd witnessed everything and that her son was one of the toughest and bravest I'd seen, but she'd have nothing of it. She just went on with another story about Jake's time in the boy scouts or something. I mean, I still wonder if she knew what really happened."

"She knows," said Guy assuredly.

"How can you be certain?" I said.

"She knows, because I told her," he said.

The revelation surprised me, but suddenly I knew what he meant when he told me that it was some people's job just to remember.

"What did you tell her?"

"The truth," he said. "Actually, I've known Pam Gleason for years now. Not too long after I got home, I heard about what happened with Jake, except the army wouldn't tell me anything about it. They were conducting their investigation and I didn't pursue it—I was still in a bad way myself back then. But a couple years went by and I inquired again, and this time the army gave me that cock-and-bull story, but I wasn't buying any of it. I knew Jake and I knew he could get a little hot under the collar, but I also knew there had to be more to it."

Guy's tee shirt was already soaked clear through with sweat, and his wide forehead looked like a waterfall. He removed his glasses and wiped some of the sweat from his eyes.

"So what did you do?"

"Actually, nothing at first," he said. "I kind of just let it go until Pam contacted me. She'd said that Jake had written to her about me, and he'd told her that if anything happened, she should get a hold of me. I'll tell you what, she'd had about enough of the army by the time she got a hold of me," he said, wiping his forehead again. "They were messing with her good, about his body, his pay, his death benefit and all—she didn't know what to do. I reckon the army was having their way with her too. Hell, they had her all worked up in a fit. I was still having some trouble at the time, but I told her not to worry, that I'd find some way to get to the bottom of it. In the meantime, she'd need to get herself a good lawyer."

"Did she?"

"Sure did, and that's the great thing about all this. I told her that I'd been keeping money for Jake the whole time he'd been in. See, ole Jake, he didn't trust nobody, and he was always worried somebody was going to *rook* him, as he called it. He'd collected quite a bit of gambling money, and he was also holding several IOUs. So one day, he asked me to hold it for him."

"Hold it for him? I thought he didn't trust anybody?"

"Me too," said Guy, grinning. "I asked him why he was trusting me, and he said that I was too big, too slow, and too backwards to try anything with his money. And, he says, because I was so big, so slow, and so backwards—nobody ever messed with me. Said it was like having his own bank." Guy laughed.

"Sounds like something he'd say," I said.

"Yeah, I didn't take offense to it none. You know Jake. Anyway, he just kept giving me money—mostly once a week. A lot of money too. Pretty soon, it was taking up a good portion of my footlocker, and then I started to get nervous with all that money lying around. I asked him if I could send some of it home and keep it there for him, and he said it'd be fine—whatever I wanted to do with it, as long as he could get it when he needed it. So that's when I started sending some of it home to Luisa. She set up an account and everything. I'd even show him the statements and such. Every now and then, he'd give me a couple hundred dollars for holding it for him."

"Well, I'll be damned," I laughed. "Sounds to me like you were laundering money for him."

"If I was, nothing was ever said about it," he said, shaking his head. "Anyway, it's what we used to get Pam a lawyer, and there was even some left over."

"So what happened?"

"The lawyer she got took care of everything, and she got the body and the benefits and, well, I suppose it all worked out. But I still didn't know what had happened, at least not from anyone other than the army. I tried to get a hold of you and some of the others, but the only contact I made was Mr. Ho. You know he's up the San Francisco way," said Guy, pointing at what I could only assume to be toward San Francisco. "Mr. Ho explained everything. Told us about the hijacking and everything else—said that Jake had every right. Told how the sergeant had that gun to your head and all and how you weren't leaving anybody behind. To tell you the truth, I was glad to hear all of it and was damn proud of Jake. And damn proud of you too," he added.

Suddenly, images of that day went swirling through my mind—the smothering heat, the ever-present sound of the rotors, and the smell of smoke and cordite. First, I saw the sergeant, his eyes raging, his breath heavy and his yellow stained teeth just inches from my face, the gun pressed hard against my cheek. Then I saw Jake, his eyes fierce and calculating, and then the struggle, the sharp snapping of the pistol and Jake's dead body. I had never been closer to anything in my past than I was right then. But as fast as it came, it was gone, and I found myself staring blankly up at Guy.

"You all right, Henry?"

"I'm fine," I said, blinking rapidly. "It's pretty hot out here. You better get inside before you melt away."

"Hell, I could stand to melt away a little," he said with a slow chuckle.

"Thanks, Guy," I said, starting the truck. "Thanks for everything. It's been too long."

Guy didn't say anything, but nodded passively.

I hadn't got as far as the entrance to the trailer park when, suddenly, I realized that I missed him terribly. I missed all of them—alive and dead.

Chapter Twenty

July 1964

The last days of summer always meant blueberries. Throughout the summer, my mother would meticulously monitor the berry-rich fields that ran along the lower ridge behind our house. And like a fine wine maker, she would pluck, poke, squeeze and taste until she was satisfied that they were ready to pick. So when she walked into the kitchen carrying a shirt-full of ripe blueberries, I knew it was harvest time.

"We're going to pick blueberries this afternoon," said my mother as she dumped berries from her shirt into a salad bowl.

Scooping out a handful, she sprinkled a few on my half-built peanut butter sandwich.

"It's picking time," she said. "The berries are nearly falling off the bushes."

"Not this afternoon," I said. "I was going to go fishing with Jess."

"Well you can't," said my mother matter-of-factly. "I need your help."

"Fine," I said dejected and then slapping the bread together, I took a big bite of the sandwich. "Can Jessie come?" I mumbled through a mouthful of bread, peanut butter and berries.

"Of course," she said and then scowling, "but what did I tell you about talking with your mouth full?"

"Sorry," I said swallowing hard.

"Which field are we picking?"

"The far one," said my mother. "The blueberries seem to do so much better over there. I think they get more sun—not as many shading trees. The path is clear and there are no signs of bears, but we'll be sure to bring Saucy with us."

"I don't think she'd let us go without her," I said, taking another bite of my sandwich.

My mother was extremely cautious when it came to bears. Last summer, Saucy discovered a fresh pile of bear shit—or at least, what my mother thought was bear shit—and she made us all run home screaming and yelling because she said dogs and loud noises ward off bears. Now she wouldn't go anywhere outside without Saucy.

"I suppose not," she said with a soft smile. "I want you and your sisters to do more picking and less eating this time. Last year, I barely had enough berries for a pie. We're bringing the big pails and I want them full."

I nodded, keeping my mouth shut. Gwen came strolling into the kitchen, dragging her Polly Patches doll behind her.

"Mommy," she said.

She was wearing her Sunday dress—the one I'd only seen her wear at Easter. My mother was too busy rinsing berries to notice.

"What, honey?"

"Can I go to school yet?" said Gwen.

My mother glanced back at her.

"Oh, honey," she said. "That's your Sunday dress, you can't wear that now."

"But I want to go to school like Hen and Maggie," she whined.

"You start kindergarten next month, but there are still a few weeks before school starts," my mother explained sweetly. "And you don't wear that dress to school, that's only for church and other special occasions."

"But I want to go now," she pouted.

"You can go with me now," I said to her. Then to my mother, I said, "I'm going to go down to Jessie's to see if she wants to go blueberry picking. I'll take Gwen with me."

Gwen's eyes widened and then bounced from me to my mother pleadingly.

"I guess that's okay," my mother said, "but, Gwen, you need to change first."

Gwen glanced at me.

"I'll wait," I said. Her sharp blue eyes beamed at me before she darted from the kitchen. A few minutes later, she returned wearing pants and a tee shirt and carrying a pair of sneakers.

"Gwen, honey, let me fix your hair," said my mother.

"I already brushed it!" protested Gwen.

"I know, but I just want to fix it," said my mother.

Kneeling down behind her and pulling her long red hair back into a ponytail, my mother fastened it with a barrette from her own hair. Meanwhile, I helped Gwen tie her shoes.

"Don't take too long," said my mother when we finally had Gwen ready to go. "I want to be picking before noon."

"No problem," I assured her.

Gwen's short strides made the trip take longer than usual, but rarely did I get to spend time alone with her, so I didn't mind at all. Most of the way, Gwen talked about going to school and riding the bus. It surprised me how much she already knew about kindergarten. She seemed much more sophisticated than I was at her age.

When we reached the entrance to Jessie's house, I was startled to see Spenser's truck parked halfway up the drive. In light of Jessie's recent murder story, bringing Gwen may have been a mistake

"There's a lot of stuff here," Gwen said when we passed the first of the Shit Towers.

She stopped for a moment, her eyes scaling up and down the tall mounds of junk.

"Is that a car?" she said, pointing to the back end of the old Fleetmaster.

"Sure is," I said. "I don't think there's much the Masons throw away."

When we got to the little entryway, I noticed Jessie's bat and glove lying on the little bench next to the door. It was a good sign that she might be alone and able to get away. I pounded on the door and was surprised when it cracked open a few inches. I then tried peering through, but it was too dark.

"Jess!" I shouted, banging on the door.

At first, I heard nothing, but after banging a second time, I thought I heard some reluctant movement. I was just about to bang a third time when the door suddenly swung open.

"What's all the clamor for Christ sake?"

Spenser Mason stood in the doorway, his scrunched-up face twisted, his grizzled and greasy hair plastered over his giant misshapen head. He wore nothing but a pair of threadbare boxer shorts, which I suddenly realized weren't hiding anything. I quickly covered Gwen's eyes before the scene could cause any permanent damage to her psyche, knowing that mine was forever scarred.

"What in hell do you want, boy?" he hollered, his black eyes glaring.

His breath and body stunk sour of booze.

"We're here to see Jessie," I replied anxiously.

"She aint here," he growled. "I don't know where she is—she done run off this morning. I figured she was with you for Christ sake."

"No, she's not with me," I said, trying hard to keep Gwen from beholding the more intimate component of Spenser Mason.

"If you see her, tell her to get her ass home, pronto, goddamn it! JT's bringing the tiller around anytime now," he said before slamming the door shut.

I was thankful for it, as I'd seen enough of Grandpa Spenser for one lifetime. For several moments, Gwen and I stood in silence in the entryway, neither one of us in a hurry to say anything. Finally, Gwen grabbed hold of my wrist and pulled me away from the door.

"Let's get out of here, Hen," she said in a determined voice.

"I'm coming, I'm coming," I said.

Gwen marched us past the Shit Towers and down the driveway by Spenser's old truck.

"I wonder where Jessie could be," I said, glancing back up the driveway.

"I don't know, Hen," Gwen said. "But you got to get me back home."

"Don't worry, I'll get you home."

"No, Hen, you got get me home in a hurry," she said, stopping and looking up at me, her eyes wide and her face pale.

"Why?"

"So you can go find Jessie," she said in a tone that sounded much older and wiser than her six years. "You got to find her, Hen, and tell her don't go home right now. That man's scary, and mean," she added.

"I'm not sure if anyone can find Jessie if she doesn't want to be found," I said. "Besides, Jessie's real good at handling her grandpa."

Gwen's eyes sank into a look of deep concern.

"I suppose I can check a few places after we get home," I said, more out of guilt than anything else.

"Good idea," she said with a nod. Her face appeared to soften some, and we started walking down the driveway.

Gwen picked up her pace, and twenty minutes later, we were rushing up the trail to the blueberry fields. I could see my mother and Maggie off in the distance.

"You go ahead," I whispered to Gwen. "Tell Mother I'll be along soon. Tell her I forgot something."

"Okay," she said.

I really only had one place in mind, and that was the beaver pond. It was our place, and there was rum there. I figured if Jessie was upset, she might want a drink, especially if she'd had it out with old Spenser. I only hoped that it hadn't been about the past.

The creek behind my house was nearly a half mile downstream from the beaver pond. A tree-shrouded trail wound along the near bank through a thicket of tangled brush and came out just below the lower dam. The path was clear and easy to negotiate. Soon, I was tiptoeing across the dam. There was no sign of Jessie anywhere, so I scaled up the side of giant tailing pile to have a better look around. I was hopeful when I saw that the rum stash had been recently uncovered, which meant that Jessie couldn't be too far away.

Walking around the crest of the hill, I scanned the pond and the surrounding woods below but still didn't see Jessie. I was just about to head back when I heard a sharp knocking sound, like that of a bat hitting a baseball. It appeared to come from beneath a thick grove of birch trees at the base of the far side of the hill. I had gone about halfway down the hill when I spied Jessie barely visible amidst the trees, standing with her back to me, her hair in a ponytail and wearing a tee shirt and shorts that appeared to be wet. I slid the rest of the way down, but Jessie still didn't see me. I watched her pitch a few more rocks at a wide-based birch tree, hitting it nearly every time.

"Hey!" I called down to her.

Jessie was in the middle of her pitching stretch but, hearing me, she stopped suddenly and glanced back. Her eyes were red, swollen, and sad. She didn't reply but turned away quickly, wiping her eyes.

"You okay, Jess?"

Again, she didn't reply, although she did turn around, but kept her head down.

"I've been looking for you," I said. "I went to your house, and Spenser said you ran off, but I thought I might find you here."

"I didn't run off," she said finally, her voice cracking. "He's drunk, and besides, I told him where I was going . . . sort of."

She glanced up at me but then quickly looked away, the entire time fiddling with the rock in her hand. A half-empty canning jar sat next to a tree, and I instantly understood.

"Having a drink?" I said, shifting my eyes to the jar.

"I told you," she barked, "when he's drunk, its better when I am too." She lifted her head up long enough for a glare.

"Okay," I said calmly. "You didn't say anything about anything, did you?"

"Hell no!" she blurted. "You know I wouldn't say anything about that!"

"All right, all right. Then what's the matter?"

"Nothing, I suppose. It's my problem."

"What problem?"

"Nothing, really. You said you just came from my house?"

"Yeah . . . well, a little bit ago. Gwen and I went by to see if you wanted to go berry picking. My mother, my sisters, and I will be picking all afternoon. My mother says *it's time.*"

"So my Granddaddy was there?"

"Yeah. I must say I saw more of him than I cared to see."

Jessie gave me a sharp look, but then said, "Daddy wasn't there?"

"Not that I could tell. Why, Jess? What's going on?"

I knew she had something to say, but I'd have to wait until she was ready to say it. I sat down on the ground and watched her throw several more rocks at the base of the tree, hitting it squarely each time. Finally she stopped, plopped down beside me, and took a large sip from the Ball jar. Afterward, she set it down on the mossy ground between us.

"I'm going to hell, Hen, I know it!" she announced, shaking her head. "I'm going to burn for all the bad things I've done!" She wiped her eyes with her hands and then took another drink from the jar. Again, she glanced away.

"What happened, Jess?" I said softly. "Tell me."

After a long silence, she finally looked back at me, a lone tear scurrying down the side of her face. She shook her head. "

"Nothing," she said.

"What happened?" I asked again. "Was it Spenser?"

When she didn't answer, I set a hand on her shoulder. "It doesn't work that way, Jess."

"How do you know how it works!" she shouted defiantly and then brushed my hand away.

"You're not going to hell," I said, trying to sound reassuring. "If anyone's going to hell, it's Spenser. I know I'm not the sophisticated type. I'm certainly not all that smart when it comes to religion, but I've been to church a time or two—been preached at about God and all his disciples. Believe it or not, I own a Bible, a big fat one—has all the testaments and everything."

Jessie laughed, her dark eyes brightened some.

"I was even been baptized in holy water—blessed and everything. And when I was eight years old at one of those summer Bible camps, I recall asking the Lord Jesus Christ himself to come into my heart and be my everlasting savior. I pray every night before I go to bed for my soul—my family's and yours too, Jess. I may not know everything about God, but what I do know is that He's pretty reasonable and forgiving, so I'm pretty sure He'd never forsake you.

"No?" she said with half a smile.

"No way, Jess," I said. "But I'll tell you what, if He does, and for whatever reason you're all damned to hell—I'll go with you.

"You will?" she said weakly.

"Sure. Not that I've got anything against God, but I don't want to go anyplace where you're not, Jess."

Jessie wiped her eyes, but still, tears came. She put her arm around my neck and pulled me to her.

"You're the sweetest person I've ever known," she said, "but I'd never want you to go to hell on my account."

"I mean it, Jess."

"I know you do," she said, forcing a smile. "When you learn to fly them whirlybirds, I want you to promise me something."

"What's that?"

"I want you to promise me that you'll fly me away somewhere far from here, far from Spenser . . . and the rest of them. Anywhere but here—just you and me, Hen," she said. Then cupping her hands around my face, she kissed me softly on the lips.

"I promise," I said.

Jessie stood up and wiped her eyes.

"Let's go berry picking," she said.

———————————

Thirty minutes later, we were walking up the trail to the blueberry field. We had nearly reached the field when Saucy leaped out from behind a heavy thicket of tall grass, startling Jessie.

"Saucy!" scolded Jessie.

But Saucy wasn't the wiser, and hearing her name, she affectionately nudged her nose between Jessie and me.

"About time!" my mother hollered. "What took you so long?"

"I don't know," I said, not wanting to get into it.

Jessie didn't offer up any further explanation, and my mother appeared to let it go.

For the better part of three hours, Jessie, Gwen, and I picked blueberries together in a large patch at the opposite end of the field from my mother and Maggie. Gwen wanted to talk about starting school and riding the bus, and Jessie gladly obliged, telling a few amusing stories about both, several of which were at my expense. But I didn't mind, and the three of us spent a good deal of the time laughing.

"Your grandpa scares me," Gwen said to Jessie unexpectedly, her soft red eyebrows pinching, a gritty look on her face. "We went to your house today," said Gwen, "and he said bad words and wanted you to come home."

Jessie gave me a passive glance and then to Gwen said, "It's just as well. Make sure you stay away from him. He can be scary—even to me," Jessie said to her. "It's just the way he—"

"We're heading back!" shouted my mother. "Gwen, you come with me, dear!"

251

The three of us walked over to where my mother was standing. After a close examination of our pails, my mother smiled and emptied each of our pails into her own.

"Well done, everyone," she said, delighted. Then to me, she said, "Are you coming home with us?"

I glanced at Jessie who looked as though she wanted to wait.

"No, you go on ahead," I said to my mother. "I promised Mr. Spooner I would help him move a smoker this evening."

"Okay, but don't be too late, dear."

"All right," I said.

———————

"Who do you think Oksana is?" asked Jesse on the trail to Spooner's cabin.

"*Oksana?*" I said, confused.

"Remember the gold watch?" said Jessie, pulling it from the front pocket of her jeans. Then handing it to me, she said, "See how it says, *Jules, So you will never be late. Yours,* and then it's says, *Oksana.*"

Examining it closely, I could easily make out the inscription. Jessie had cleaned it up quite a bit. As old as it was, it still glistened in the sunlight.

"Yeah, I see it. So what?"

"Remember the diary said something about Jules building a house for a Russian woman in Fairbanks?"

"Yeah, right," I said weakly, trying hard to remember.

"I thought Oksana and the Russian woman might be the same person. Maybe she's still around—maybe she knows something about what really happened to Jules," she added excitedly.

"Maybe," I shrugged. I wasn't as convinced. "You can ask Spooner, he was around back then."

"That's my plan," she said smugly.

———————————

When we arrived at Spooner's, the old man was standing in front of his cabin busy brushing ashes from the homemade smoker he had fabricated from an old refrigerator.

"Mr. Spooner!" I called out when he was in earshot.

He greeted us with a slight nod. "Just in time," he said. "I think it's ready to go."

"Hey, Mr. Spooner!" said Jessie enthusiastically.

"Hey!" I said again, surprised by Jessie's sudden enthusiasm. "Where are we moving it to?"

Jessie had met Spooner only one time before when she had helped me stack his wood after school. I remember at the time she acted shy and didn't say more than a couple words to him, and afterward had confided in me that he seemed like an *odd duck*.

"Not far," he said. "Around the other side of the cabin closer to the meat cache. I'm tired of hauling fish back and forth."

Spooner's cabin had been around as long as he had. Built from mud and rough-cut logs well over three decades ago, its walls had now faded to an ancient gray. Surprisingly, however, it still supported an earth-laden roof, which at this time of year yielded at least two feet of grass and weeds.

Over the years, the tiny windowless cabin had sunk some three feet into the ground, requiring him to dig out his front door every spring. I would joke with him that in another few years, his basement would finally be ready.

It only took the three of us a few minutes to move the smoker, and after a couple more minutes spent balancing it on its legs, Spooner began preparing it for the next batch of fish. Jessie and I gave him a hand filling the hotbox with what looked to be pine needles.

"Pine needles?" I asked.

"Yeah, I thought I would try it," he said, scratching his forehead. "An Athabaskan fellow came into the store the other day—said it beat the heck out of hickory chips—said it was tasty. I've had some good luck so far this season, so figured I'd try it," he said with another slight nod.

The small picnic table next to the cabin held three large trays of freshly filleted fish. Spooner caught me eyeing them.

"Grayling," he said, "and a couple of pike from a buddy that was up the Lake Minchumina way."

We helped Spooner load the fish from the trays onto the racks of the smoker. He then closed the long door on the front and adjusted the vents and valves. He ran a hand over his balding head and gazed off in the distance, mumbling something inaudible as if he were going through a checklist in his mind.

To look at him, you wouldn't think he was more than sixty years old, but he was late into his seventies. Trim and fit, he had faded blue eyes and tightly cropped white hair, which formed a semicircle around the sides and back of his balding head. I'd never seen him wear anything other than a button-down flannel shirt, even on the hottest days.

"You know a woman named *Oksana*?" Jessie asked Spooner when he had finished lighting the smoker.

"What?" he said, glancing at her sharply, his white eyebrows crossed.

"Did you ever hear of a woman named *Oksana*?" repeated Jessie. "She knew Jules O'Brien."

Spooner shot Jessie an anxious look. Then he nodded slowly. "I know her."

"You do?" said Jessie, her eyes widening.

Spooner appeared shaken.

"She's trying find some information about her grandmother," I said. "She's looking into some particulars about the old story."

Jessie nodded, seemingly satisfied with my explanation. "So then, you know where we could find Oksana."

"Yeah," he sighed. "I know where you can find her." He paused and then ran his hand over his balding head. He looked over at me. "But some stones are best left unturned."

"What's that supposed to mean?" snapped Jessie.

"It means some things are better left alone," said Spooner, his expression anxious. "It was a long time ago, but for some, the old stories never did settle right."

"Why's that?" asked Jessie.

"Oksana Vorden *believes* that she was *engaged* to Jules O'Brien," said Spooner, running his hand over his head again. "Nobody knows for sure, but it's what she *believed*. When word got back to her that Jules ran off . . . well . . . she didn't take it well. Supposedly, she had a breakdown of sorts. Couldn't get over the fact that Jules left her."

Jessie's face flushed in excitement.

"Where can we find her?" she blurted.

Spooner shook his head. "It's not a good idea," he said. "She was terribly upset about it—they said she tried to take her own life."

"That was a long time ago, Mr. Spooner," said Jessie. "Besides, I don't believe Jules left anybody. So if it's all the same to you, I'd like to know where to find her."

Spooner shook his head again, and then his sharp stare softened some.

"With all her troubles, her son moved her to Fairbanks."

Jessie looked at me and then to Spooner, her eyes wanting for an explanation.

"Her son?" she said finally.

"Yes, she has a son," said Spooner. "Her son is from a previous marriage she had to a gold miner. He and another fellow were killed when their shaft collapsed. Vladimir was about six or seven when his father died."

I thought Jessie might jump out of her shoes.

"She's Russian, isn't she?"

"Yes, she's Russian," said Spooner, sounding surprised. "For years, she had an embroidery and quilt shop off of Third Avenue until Vladimir got the gold fever several years ago and moved her back out to their old mine on Fairbanks Creek. Henry knows where it is," Spooner said, nodding at me. "Oksana and her son live in that large cabin over the other side of the dome—about fifteen miles up Fairbanks Creek, just past the dredge there."

Spooner and I had fished the slews there a couple of times for some elusive Arctic char a customer of his had *supposedly* transplanted there from the coast. We caught nothing, but I did recall the enormous cabin there.

"I do know it," I said to Jessie. "Too far to walk though," I added.

Jessie stared vacantly at Spooner for several long seconds, then finally, she said, "You think Vladimir knows anything about my grandmother and the O'Brien brothers?"

"I don't know," he said. "He was only a boy back then."

"Will you take us there?" Jessie asked.

"Tonight?" said Spooner, glancing at his wristwatch. "It's nearly eight o'clock."

"Will you take us?" she asked him again. This time, her look was solemn.

The old man shook his head skeptically, but then his eyebrows lifted.

"Hop in the truck," he said.

———————————

Comprised of tightly packed tailings, the less than winding route shadowing Fairbanks Creek was smooth and easy to follow. About a mile before the Verden cabin, the tailings ended abruptly and mammoth heaves, twisting the suddenly tight roadway twice, threatened to overturn Spooner's pickup, each time sending Jessie and me tossing about the cab.

We were both quite relieved when Spooner stopped the truck at the bottom of a narrow path. The path led up a small rise to a wall of high brush where we could see white smoke spitting from a tin chimney.

The three of us walked up the slight hill to what had to be the largest cabin I had ever seen. Its freshly lacquered logs stretched back at least a hundred feet behind a broad summer deck that nosed out over the valley. Jessie and I followed Spooner along a boarded walkway lined with miniature white picket fences behind which grew bright flower gardens.

"Hello!" Spooner shouted into a screened doorway at the back of the cabin.

A few seconds later, the door opened and a tall thin man with a dark bushy face stepped out.

"Hello," he said in a deep bellowing voice that resonated from behind a thick black beard and mustache. He slowly let the screen door shut behind him.

"Vladimir!" said Spooner enthusiastically.

Vladimir's eyes widened with surprise. "What brings you out here, doc?"

Vladimir extended to Spooner his hand as his dark eyes caught a glimpse of Jessie and me.

"Who are your friends?" he said to Spooner.

"This is Mr. Henry Allen and Ms. Jessie Mason," Spooner said. I was taken by the formal introduction. I had never heard him use my last name before, and I didn't think he knew Jessie's. "They're friends of mine," Spooner continued. "They were hoping to have a word with you and your mother."

Vladimir glanced at Spooner suspiciously.

"A *word*?" he said.

"Yes, they want to talk some history," said Spooner, his tone reassuring. He placed a hand on Vladimir's shoulder and patted his back. "Ms. Mason is the granddaughter of Abigail Mason. She had some questions about the past."

Vladimir nodded at Spooner cynically before his suspicious eyes perched on Jessie.

"My mother is sick, you know," he said to Jessie.

"Yes," said Spooner. "Ms. Mason thought perhaps *you* might be of some help to her."

Vladimir shook his head.

"How could I help?" he said sharply.

"It's a beautiful home you have here," Jessie said suddenly while squinting past him at the cabin. "You build it?"

Spooner gave her a curious look, and I too wondered what she was up to.

"No," he said, shaking his head. "I was only a boy when it was built."

Jessie's eyes shifted back to Vladimir, and then she nodded toward the cabin.

"Jules O'Brien built this place, didn't he?"

Vladimir threw his head back, surprised. He glanced back through the screen door and then, scowling back at Jessie, he said softly, "That's right. It's no secret. But please, keep your voice down. I don't want to upset Mother."

"*No secret?*" said Jessie, raising her voice. "If it's no secret, why should I keep my voice down. *Jules O'Brien* built a *fine* cabin!" Jessie shouted at the screen door. "*Jules O'Brien* was a fine builder! *Jules O'Brien*—"

"Okay, okay, quiet please!" cried Vladimir. There was a sudden terror in his eyes. He glanced back at the screen door again. Then lowering his voice, he said to Jessie, "You mustn't mention that name. It will upset her, miss. I told you, Mother is very sick."

"I'm sorry if a name of a man some thirty years *dead* upsets you . . . or your mother," said Jessie sternly. "I only want to know—"

"You say Jules O'Brien is dead?" interrupted Vladimir.

Jessie glanced over at me and then sighed.

"It's my theory," she said. "I was hoping that you or your mother might help me—"

"So you believe that Jules O'Brien has died?" he interrupted her again.

"Not *died—murdered*," she said. "I believe he was murdered all those years ago." Jessie hesitated and then sighed again. "I think he was murdered by my own granddaddy."

Vladimir raised his eyebrows and then ran his fingers through his thick black beard.

"I see," he said, nodding at Jessie. For several seconds, he appeared to ponder the information. Finally, he said, "Come with me."

Vladimir led us through the screen door and down a narrow hallway to a large open living area where giant ridgepoles, stripped and stained, hung high over our heads. The room's intricately decorated furniture was positioned tastefully on Persian rugs, while portraits of Russian aristocrats stared pretentiously down on us. Three arched windows revealed a handsome view of the valley. Off in the distance, I could make out the gold dredge.

"Have a seat," said Vladimir.

Both Jessie and I sat down on the edge of a burgundy velvet sofa while Spooner sat across from us in similarly designed chair.

"Would you care for some tea?" asked Vladimir from the doorway, his tone was welcoming, warm even, but his eyes were neither. Instead, they shifted uneasily about the three of us.

When we politely declined, an awkward quiet fell over the room while Vladimir stood motionless, a look of indifference in his face, as if awaiting something or someone—perhaps one of us to speak.

"How have you been, Vladimir?" Spooner said finally.

The question appeared to animate Vladimir.

"Good, good," he said glancing back down the hallway behind him. "Make yourselves comfortable," he said and then excusing himself, he rushed from the room.

Hunched over in a tall wooden wheelchair, Oksana Verden looked tired and frail. Pushing her slowly around the outside of the room, Vladimir rolled her up to the edge of a dark polished oval-shaped coffee table across from us. He then locked the chair's wheels and sat down on a small ottoman beside her.

"Welcome to our home," the old woman said, her words strong and accented. She then strained her head back so she could see everyone. She had a deeply lined face with long grey-black hair that dangled heavy over her lap. For as fragile as she appeared, her voice was as rich and as bellowing as her son's.

"I told Mother the reason for your visit—that you had questions," Vladimir said to Jessie. Then glancing at his mother, he said, "You know, if you're tired, Mother—"

Oksana waved at him dismissively.

"No, no, I am fine," she said, straining her head to see Jessie. "Tell me, dear. What questions?"

Jessie appeared uncomfortable with the sudden attention.

"I suppose it's not a big deal," said Jessie, shifting uneasily on the sofa. "I was hoping you could tell me something about Jules O'Brien."

At the mention of the name, the old woman bowed her head where she remained motionless for several long seconds.

"Oh my," she said finally, then released a heavy sigh. "Jules was the love of my life. Yes, I can tell you something about him. And you are?" she said, raising a trembling hand to Jessie.

"Jessie Mason," she said. "I'm the granddaughter of Abigail Mason."

"Oh yes," she said. "That makes you the granddaughter of Spenser Mason."

"Yes it does," said Jessie in an apologetic tone.

"What do you think of your grandfather?" said Oksana.

Jessie hesitated and then shifted some more. "The truth?" said Jessie.

"Of course, my dear." The old woman dropped her trembling hand. "We only speak the truth here."

"I hate him," said Jessie flatly.

Vladimir's look was one of confusion, Spooner's held mild surprise, while the old woman smiled.

"I see," she said with a difficult nod. She again raised her hand. "He killed my Jules," she said.

Jessie's eyes widened, and she bounced up to the edge of the sofa. "So it's true?"

Vladimir looked at his mother and then at Spooner.

"She's been talking this way for the past several months," he said. He turned toward his mother again. "Before that, nothing, not a word about it—only that Jules had left her years ago. Now, she won't stop talking about how Spenser killed her Jules." He scowled at Jessie. "Now you show up saying it too."

"Vladimir!" protested Oksana. "Don't talk like I am not sitting right here!"

"I'm sorry, Mother," he said to her. "But it's true, you know it is."

"I know what I said! But you know nothing of it," she scolded him. "I go along with the story about the three of them running off together—if I don't, Spenser would have killed me." Then eyeing Jessie, she said, "Jules was to be my husband. We were lovers. I knew him better than I know myself." She looked over at Vladimir. "And he is surely dead, killed by the man, Spenser. I know this. But I never forget!" She jerked her head back as tears fell from her eyes. Then to Jessie, in an elevated voice she said, "Jules told me this! He told me that lady Abigail go missing. He said Spenser did something to her. He said that he and Francis will go find her. He said that Spenser knew that Francis and she are lovers. In his own words, he told me this!"

"Mother, please!" cried Vladimir. "You are getting too worked up. You are very tired, Mother." Vladimir stood and unlocked the wheels to the chair.

"Leave me alone!" she demanded, violently slapping the armrest. Her eyes then set again on Jessie. "It was the last time I saw him! I know Jules would never leave me," she said in sobs. "But he went to

261

help his brother. I begged him not to go, but he went anyway. It was the last time I ever saw him! I went to find Jules at his cabin. I went to see for myself. But he was not there." She jerked her head back, her eyes wide. "I know he is dead," she said, her tone defeated.

Vladimir rolled her backward.

"Stop!" she screamed at him, her eyes fiery. "You stop at once!"

Vladimir stopped, his dark face nervous.

"Years ago, Spenser Mason came into the store. He looked at me up and down. I knew why he came. He wanted to know if I knew. He asked me if I was a friend of Jules O'Brien," she said, shaking her head. "I told him, I don't know the name." Her eyes filled with tears. "I wanted to be strong—strong for Jules . . . but I was so scared." Her voice trembled and then broke. "But now—now I would spit on him!" she cried.

All at once, Jessie stood up and rushed over to the woman. Kneeling down in front of her, she reached into the front pocket of her blue jeans and pulled out the gold pocket watch. Jessie placed it in the old woman's trembling hands.

"I found this," she said.

Oksana stared down at it for several minutes and then held it to her chest.

"I gave it to Jules. It was my father's watch. I gave it to him," she said. "On his birthday—so he would never be late." She held it up to Vladimir. "You see!" she shouted. "I did not forget! Jules would never run away! He would never leave me . . ." The fire in her eyes turned to gentle tears. Jessie put her arms around the old woman who wept in her arms.

"Did you know my grandmother?" Jessie said softly after several long minutes.

Oksana nodded slowly.

"Yes," she whispered. "I knew the lady Abigail. She loved Francis—she told me many times. That is why Spenser killed them . . . and Jules also."

Jessie hugged Oksana and then stood up and looked over at Vladimir. "I'm sorry," she said.

Vladimir nodded sympathetically and then wheeled his mother back around to the outside of the room.

"Ms. Verden," Jessie called to her just before they reached the hallway.

Oksana slapped the armrest of the wheelchair again, causing Vladimir to stop. He spun her around to face Jessie who was still standing where they had left her.

"By any chance, did you know the place where Abigail and Francis used to meet?"

Oksana lifted her head and then shook it.

"No," she said. "I never knew much about it, except what Jules told me, which was not much."

"Thank you," Jessie said.

The old woman nodded.

"You're beautiful, much like your grandmother. She was a most beautiful woman."

Jessie smiled.

"Thank you," she said again.

Twenty minutes later," Vladimir returned. "She's finally asleep," he said. "It's not good for her to get all worked up like that."

Spooner nodded in agreement. "I'm sorry, Vladimir," he said. "I didn't realize that it would upset her so."

Vladimir nodded.

"It'll be all right." He turned to Jessie who had returned to the sofa next to me. "That watch you gave her . . . it meant a lot to her. Thank you for that."

"It belongs to her," said Jessie.

Vladimir nodded again.

"I really don't know how much she remembers. Some days she does very well. But other days . . ." he said, his voice breaking. "Some days she doesn't remember." He sighed and then wiped his eyes. He walked over and sat down in the chair next to Spooner.

Vladimir sighed, and then turning to Jessie, he said, "I may know something about that place you were looking for."

He had Jessie's instant attention, as she scooted along the edge of the sofa toward him, here eyes fastened to his.

"I was only a boy, ten or eleven years old," he said. "But Jules took me everywhere then. We ran a trap line together, marten mostly, on your side of the hill," he said, pointing at Spooner. It was damn cold. *Colder than a well-digger's ass*, Jules would say." Vladimir laughed. "I remember thinking I might actually freeze to death. Then Jules said he knew of a place not far off the line where we could get warm. He said Frank used it all the time and that had a stove and all the amenities, which meant it had an outhouse." He added and then laughed again.

"You think it's the place where Frankie and my grandmother got together? said Jessie.

"I don't know for sure, but I think so," he said, nodding convincingly. "It had to be. For all its rusticity, the place had a woman's touch about it."

"A woman's touch?" said Jessie.

"Yes—flowery things, yellows, pinks, and baby blues. It even had a little paned window in the front next to the door. Jules told me that he had built the place for Frank. I remember the window having a flowery little curtain that matched the flowery quilt on the bed and the flowery little rug on the floor." He chuckled. "Had things you would likely find in a parlor, not a log cabin. The whole place smelled of lavender." Vladimir ran his fingers through his beard, and I could see his grin. "I think Frank owned the property, perhaps he had a claim there. I remember it faced a little pond or creek," said Vladimir. "I remember crossing ice to get to it anyway."

"Fine place to get warm though, far enough off the trap line that nobody knew about it. Perfect place to have an affair. Sure glad Jules knew about it, might of froze to death otherwise." He laughed again.

"Do you know where we could find it?" asked Jessie.

Vladimir shook his head.

"I doubt it's around anymore, and to tell you the truth, I wouldn't know where to find it if it was. Remember, I was only a boy."

Jessie looked to Spooner, searching his face for an answer.

Spooner shook his head. "I don't know it," he said.

"Could be anywhere, Jess," I said.

"Probably caved in on itself," said Spooner. "If it wasn't properly maintained, it likely collapsed under the snow-load." Spooner stood up. "It's getting late," he said to Jessie and me. Then to Vladimir, "Thank you for your time."

Vladimir nodded at Spooner and then turned his attentions to Jessie.

"Your grandfather is a dangerous man," he said in a grave tone. "I know you are searching for answers, but please—for your sake, be very careful."

"I will," said Jessie, but nothing in her tone suggested fear.

———————————————

The ride home was slow and quiet. Spooner never had much to say, and clearly, Jessie didn't feel like talking. My mind was at home with my mother—I knew she'd be worried.

Spooner dropped us off at my house, and Jessie and I walked begrudgingly up the short steps to the deck.

My mother met us at the door with a look that I wasn't sure was rage or relief.

"Thank heaven!" she shouted, hugging the both of us. "Where have you been? *We* have been worried sick!"

I understood *we* to mean my mother and sisters, as Tom sat at the kitchen table peering over a flight magazine with a look of indifference across his face.

"We ran late at Spooner's," I lied, glancing over at Jessie for some help.

"That's true, Ms. Talbot. We were helping Mr. Spooner," Jessie assured her.

"Good heavens, it's nearly eleven," said my mother. "What on God's green earth were you doing?"

Jessie's look told me it was my turn again.

"Smoking fish," I said.

My mother shook her head but appeared satisfied with the answer. She liked Mr. Spooner, and the fact that we were doing something that she considered constructive went a long way too.

"I'm going to walk Jessie home," I said. "And then I'm going straight to bed."

"Okay," said my mother. "I'll see you in the morning. Jessie, you have a good night. I'm sure your father's worried sick."

"He's not even home," said Jessie.

We walked back down the steps and then on down the small rocky hill in front of the house, but instead of heading down the driveway, Jessie headed for the trailer.

"Where are you going?" I asked her.

"To bed," she said.

"But I thought—"

"No way am I going home tonight," she said emphatically. "Daddy's gone to Anchorage, and I'm in no mood to deal with my murdering granddaddy."

I followed Jessie into the trailer and sat down at the little table where I watched her strip down to her underwear and slide beneath the covers of my bed. Jessie closed her eyes and mumbled something I couldn't understand.

"Praying?" I said.

"More like wishing," she said. Opening her eyes, she smiled at me. "I'm not sure praying would do a gal like me any good. Wishing might be the better play."

I laughed.

"You think that's funny?"

"Not at all," I said. "It made think about something Tom said once about wishes."

"What's that?"

"He said to put wishes in one hand, shit in the other, and see which one fills first."

Jessie laughed. "I like it," she said.

"Don't worry, Jess," I said. "I'll keep praying for the both of us."

"I'm counting on it." She laughed again. "Are you coming?" she said, patting the bed next to her. "Don't go getting any ideas," she added with a playful scowl.

"I wouldn't think of it," I said grinning.

I quickly undressed and crawled into bed beside her. I lay there staring at the ceiling for the longest time, thinking that the girl of my dreams was in bed right beside me. I had an urge to roll over and kiss her or wrap her up in my arms and tell her how much I loved her. I thought about what she had said about flying her away somewhere she'd never been before. The thought excited me, and soon I started thinking about where we might go—Hawaii, Mexico, or Florida maybe. I had heard some great things about Florida—definitely someplace warm that had a beach, and an ocean, I thought.

"If I could fly you somewhere," I said. "Where would you want to go?"

When there was no answer, I knew she had fallen asleep.

———————

I awoke to the loud blare of a horn—a car horn. Jessie was already awake.

"What the hell!" I shouted.

Jessie shrugged at me nervously.

The horn continued to blare in short intermittent blasts. I got up and pulled on my jeans while Jessie did the same. We then peered out the front window.

"Oh shit!" cried Jessie as we both watched Spenser Mason stumble out of his car. "It's Granddaddy . . . and he's drunk."

"Jessie!" the old man shouted at the house. "Jessie, you get your ass out here, goddamn it!"

Spenser staggered around to the front of the car and then pounded several times on the hood.

"Goddamn it, Jessie, get out here!" He continued shouting and slamming his hand on the hood of the car.

"What are we going to do?" Jessie whispered to me.

"One thing's for sure, you're not going out there."

A few moments later, Tom came storming out of the house wearing only a frayed pair of paisley pajama bottoms and a pair of moccasin-type slippers. He looked altogether harmless, but he was holding his shotgun.

"What in the hell do you want?" Tom shouted at the old man.

The old man grunted and then squinted into the midnight sun behind Tom.

"I don't . . . want no trouble. I only want Jessie," he said. His statement appeared directed more at the shotgun than at Tom.

"She isn't here," said Tom. "Henry took her home hours ago."

"Well, she aint at home, believe you me. You know . . . I'm in charge of her ass until my boy gets home."

It was then my mother came rushing out of the house wearing a mint flannel nightgown and her hair rolled up in pink-colored curlers.

"What's the matter, Tom?" said my mother. She too appeared to be talking more to the shotgun.

"Oh, he's looking for Jessie. Says she didn't come home. Says he's watching her until JT gets back."

"Where on earth could she be? It's nearly three-thirty in the morning for crying out loud," my mother said.

"The little bitch has done run off. When I get my hands on her, you better believe me!"

Although his words seemed to run together, my mother got the gist of them immediately and let out another gasp.

"Oh my!" she cried out.

"Go get Henry, Helen, and we'll get to the bottom of this," ordered Tom.

My mother glanced over at the trailer where Jessie and I ducked out of sight.

"Oh shit, oh shit, oh shit," said Jessie. "What are we going to do?"

Jessie ran over to the bed and buried herself beneath the covers. I wasn't sure what she was trying to accomplish, but she wasn't fooling anyone. I went over sat down on the edge of the bed in front of her. Seconds later, there was a clicking at the door and then it swung open.

"Henry!" my mother called out before stepping inside.

There was no escaping it, so I didn't try to hide anything. Instead, I sat patiently waiting for my mother to find me.

"Henry," she said when she saw me. "What's going on? Didn't you say you were walking Jessie home? Do you know where she is?"

I was going to tell her that I had no idea, when Jessie popped out from beneath the covers.

"It's not what you think, Mrs. Talbot," said Jessie. "I didn't want to go home—we weren't doing anything, if that's what you think. My daddy went out of town tonight, and as you can see—Granddaddy's drunk again. I'm sorry. It's my fault. I just didn't want to go home. Please don't make me go with him."

Despite her intense scowl, she was considering it. She glanced at Jessie, whose eyes were filling with tears, and suddenly, I knew my mother would never let her go with him.

"Okay," said my mother calmingly, "it'll be all right. You two wait here and stay quiet."

My mother and Tom argued endlessly, sometimes about almost nothing at all, but on the rare occasions when they found themselves on the same side of an argument, they could be a formidable force—even for the murderous Spenser Mason.

"So where in the hell is she?" growled Spenser when my mother returned. "I know she's here . . . goddamn it!" The old man took a step toward Tom.

"That's close enough," Tom said, slowly raising the barrel of the shotgun. "What's Henry say, Helen?" He glanced at my mother and then quickly back at Spenser.

"He says he walked her to her driveway and that was the last he saw of her. Henry hasn't seen her, Tom. He has no idea where she could be," said my mother.

"You heard her," barked Tom. "She's not here, so you'd best be on your way. If we hear from her, I'll let you know. Now go on home."

Spenser looked first to my mother and then at Tom.

"If you do see the little tramp, tell her I'm looking for her, and when I find her, I'm going to tan her ass so—ah!" Spenser waved at Tom dismissively before climbing clumsily into his car. He hit the horn several more times before backing out of our driveway. Tom lowered his shotgun, shook his head, and walked over to my mother. They had some words, which I couldn't hear, but I saw Tom nod his head and then shrug. Afterward, Tom went back inside the house, and my mother returned to the trailer.

Sitting at the table, my mother said warmly, "Jessie dear, you will stay with us until your father gets home. I'm sorry you had to witness that. Believe me—I know what liquor can do to folks. I think your grandfather needs to sleep it off."

"Thanks, Mrs. Talbot," said Jessie.

"However, Jessie, I *will not* have you sleeping out here with Henry. You come with me and I'll make a bed for you in Henry's room."

"And Henry," said my mother when she stood up to leave. "Don't you ever do something like this again without telling me. Drinking is a sickness and unpredictable. Be thankful no one got hurt. I want the both of you to stick around here until we can work this out with your father, Jessie. I don't want to have to worry about where you are.

"Sure, Mom," I said.

"All right then," said my mother. "I'll go and get your bed ready, Jessie. Don't be too long now."

"I won't," replied Jessie.

After my mother left, Jessie sat down on the bed next to me.

"We probably better do more bootlegging." She sighed.

"Good idea. Spenser sure looked like a killer today."

"God, I wish he didn't drink so much," she said.

"Yeah, well you know what they say about wishes," I said.

Chapter Twenty-One

October 1969

In addition to the shitload of paperwork, I attended about a dozen debriefings, four depositions, and one formal hearing before I received the official notice of Sergeant Stanley Nathan Richard's court martial. But even that did little to impart from me any confidence in the army's confounding and most lethargic judicial process. I had nearly finished my second tour when I finally learned that Sergeant Richards had accepted a plea bargain, which amounted to nothing more than conduct unbecoming and a dishonorable discharge from the Marine Corps.

"It's a messy affair," said Colonel Glasson, a few days before I was to ship out stateside.

Oddly, since Flanny's death, the colonel had taken a mild interest in my career in Vietnam and wanted to see me off.

"It's hard to imagine that this type of thing could happen in today's army. It doesn't make sense. Maybe I'm just getting too damn old."

"This entire war seems to be one messy affair," I said.

"That's for damn sure," said the colonel, nodding in agreement. "I don't understand it—hijacking your own ship, killing your own men. I'd have had the son of a bitch tried and then shot for treason. I've seen too many good men die for no good reason. There ought to be some accountability."

The colonel reached out and squeezed my shoulder.

"Take care, son," he said.

"Thanks, Colonel," I said. "You too."

It took a good three days of flights and layovers before I finally arrived at Fort Lewis in Washington State. There wasn't much to my homecoming, but that was the way I wanted it. I spent a few days on base recovering from jet-lag and adjusting to life stateside. I had plans to visit my mother and Tom in Seattle and then travel to Michigan to see Jessie. But before that, I had to tend to some unfinished business.

I rented a car, bought a new set of clothes and headed for Pullman. I had neither an address nor a phone number for her, hell I didn't even have a city or a state, but what I did have was a mutual friend.

Lainie Byers was the owner and manager of *The Cubby Hole,* a long-time student watering hole on campus. I had spent a good deal of time there during my nearly two years of college, mostly drinking beer with my fraternity brothers. Occasionally, I would happen by there in the late afternoons to study or to have lunch when there wasn't much of a crowd. That's how I came to know Lainie, and through her, Sara.

Lainie had lived in Pullman her entire life, which by now had to be going on forty years. Although surrounded by academia, she had never set foot in a classroom herself. But that didn't mean she wasn't intelligent, because she was. In fact, few academics had anything on her. Lainie told me she was a sponge for useless information, but it wasn't uncommon for her to be seen assisting an undergraduate in math or proofreading a graduate student's thesis. Many had tried to talk Lainie into going to college. The school had even offered her a scholarship, but she would always refuse, giving them all the same old line, *I don't need a degree to run The Cubby.*

I remembered her to be auburn-haired, green-eyed and beautiful. If it wasn't for Lainie's obvious attraction to women, I'm sure I would've fallen in love with her myself.

After an altogether obligatory visit to the fraternity house, and one endless conversation with a fraternity brother I barely remember, I walked the two blocks to The Cubby, sat down at my favorite table and ordered a beer from none other than Lainie Byers herself. At first, she didn't recognize me, probably because she never got a good look at anybody when she was working. So when she brought me my beer, I took a quick sip and then slamming it down on the table, demanded to see the manager.

"I'm the manager," she said, taking a hard look at me, "and I don't . . ." She hesitated suddenly and then stepped back.

"Henry?"

"It's me!" I said.

"Oh my goodness," she said, launching herself at me.

She hugged me around the neck, kissed me several times on the cheek, and then sat down across from me, taking my hands in hers.

"Oh my god, you're home!" she said, squeezing my hand. "I can't believe it! You're really home! And you're safe and all in one piece," she added.

"How about that, I'm still in one piece," I said.

"Oh my god, Henry, it's been so long. What? Three years? Oh my God! It's been three years, Henry!"

"Yeah, it's been a while."

"I can't believe I didn't recognize you. Your hair is so short, but you look absolutely great, Henry, really great!"

"So do you," I said.

And she did too. Lainie seemed to get better looking with age. She looked the same as she did three years ago, except she had replaced the blouse and blue jeans for a sleeveless cotton sundress speckled with tiny yellow flowers. Her once short auburn hair was now long, braided in several places and held back by a leather barrette.

"Oh, it's so good to see you. You know so many of you boys haven't . . ."

"I know," I said, squeezing her hands.

Lainie got up and gave me another hug and when she released me, she wiped her eyes.

"I'm sorry," she said sitting back down. "Seeing you, it's wonderful."

"It's good to see you too, Lainie," I said.

"So tell me," she said. "Oh wait a minute, don't go anywhere, I'll be right back." Excusing herself, she went to check on other tables. When she returned, she brought me another beer and then sat back down.

"Gosh, when you left you were going off to be a pilot or something, weren't you?"

"That's right," I said nodding. "I *flew* helicopters."

"So what was it like?"

"You mean flying helicopters?"

"Well that, but flying helicopters over there," she said, her voice gradually softening.

I had only been back a week and I found it interesting how so many people didn't even like to say the word Vietnam, like it was a something dirty. It wasn't the first time I'd been asked the question. I never quite knew what to say for fear I might start an argument or incite a small-scaled riot. I suspected that Lainie was probably the peace-loving dove sort, which didn't bother me, I just didn't want to get into it with her or anyone.

"It was a different world," I said trying to be vague.

"That's what I've heard," she said before sending me a look that said, *continue*.

"I flew a lot," I said, "but it's great to be back stateside and in the good ole USA!" I said trying to sound enthusiastic.

"What kind of missions did you fly?"

"Oh, you know . . . at first, troop support and then dustoffs. You know—evacuations, transporting the wounded and all."

"Really, that's incredible! You did two tours, incredible! What made you want to do another tour?"

I dreaded these questions. She was really asking *how* could I have done two tours, and my answer had the potential to ruffle all sorts of politically poignant feathers.

"I suppose it was because I had the opportunity to fly wounded out," I replied.

I had recently learned that the best answer was to make it sound like all I did over there was to help the wounded—so far it had worked on a Dallas shoe salesman and Seattle cabdriver.

"No kidding? That's incredible," she said. "So you flew out the wounded?"

"And the dead," I added.

"Oh," she said her tone suddenly solemn. "Was that difficult to do?"

I thought about being a smart-ass and telling her that the dead were easy to fly out as they never complained. It wasn't far from the truth, but Lainie didn't deserve that. She was only trying to understand.

"It could be," I said, "but there was a lot in Vietnam that was difficult. I suppose it's like anything else—after a while, you get used to it."

"I don't know if I could ever get used to something like that," she said.

"So how have you been, Lain?" I said, changing the subject.

"Oh, me, I've been great. You know how it's football season, so it's been busy. I bought a house. It's not too far from here, and I absolutely love it—much better than living upstairs," she said, pointing to the ceiling.

"I bet it is," I said, "but we sure had some good times up there."

Lainie rolled her eyes and then laughed.

"We sure did, didn't we? Maybe too many good times," she said. "It's only been a few years, but it seems like forever."

"Tell me about it," I said.

Lainie shook her head and then paused. Her face suddenly serious.

"I wanted to ask you, but maybe I shouldn't as it might be a sore subject."

I knew instantly where she was going, and I welcomed it.

"Oh, there's nothing you can't talk to me about," I said shamelessly.

Lainie's green eyes sharpened, and she leaned forward.

"Sara came in not too long ago," she said, almost in a whisper. She leaned back a little, no doubt for a better view of my reaction.

"Oh yeah," I said pleasantly. "How is she?"

Lainie's eyebrows suddenly arched, her back straightened, and she shook her head slightly as if she didn't understand.

It was difficult for Lainie. She had been such a good friend to the both of us. I suppose it had been awkward.

"So what did Sara tell you about us?" I was very curious to hear how Sara had explained it.

"Actually, Sara didn't say anything about it," she said, frowning.

"Really," I said. "How odd."

"Yeah, she didn't say a word about you, or your split."

That was typical Sara, I thought. She would want to avoid the uncomfortable conversation.

"Then who told you we broke up?" I said.

Lainie looked confused.

"I told you, it was obvious," she said.

Now I was confused.

"What do you mean?" I said.

"Sara came in with her husband."

My body understood well before my mind, as something inside of me broke. My face burned, my eyes quivered, and my stomach climbed high up into my throat. For several seconds, I couldn't speak. All I could do was stare blankly at Lainie who, I knew, saw through me.

When I could move again, I reached for my beer, but Lainie grabbed my hand.

"You didn't know, did you?" she said, her tone dripping with sympathy.

I didn't say anything but pulled my hand from her grasp and drank the rest of my beer. I didn't want the glass to be empty—I wanted to keep drinking forever.

"I'm sorry," she said. "I assumed you knew already, Henry. Honestly, she didn't tell me anything about your split. Only that she'd gotten married and was living in Spokane. I'm so sorry. I really thought you knew about it."

"It's no big deal, Lain," I said, although she probably wasn't buying any of it. "We broke up well over a year ago, I should've expected as much. You know how it is . . . I was over there, in . . . *V-Viet* . . . *Vietnam*," I stuttered.

Hell, now I was having trouble saying it.

"If you don't mind me asking, Henry, how did it happen?"

It wasn't that I minded as much as my mind was still trying to process the fact that Sara was married.

"It's the same old story. It's hard when you're apart for so long," I said. I was sure Lainie knew I was talking out my ass, but it was all I could think to say at the moment.

"I suppose," she said, glancing around the bar. "I should really check on my tables. I'll be right back."

I was glad for the time alone. Sara was married. It had never crossed my mind—perhaps because I was still smarting over our breakup. I had never really let go, despite the letter and despite my second tour in Nam.

Lainie came back with another pitcher of beer and a sympathetic smile. Fortunately, I was in need of both.

"How are you doing?" she asked.

"Fine," I said weakly. "Tell me, Lain, how long has Sara been in Spokane?"

Lainie sent me a suspicious look, but then shook her head.

"Not long," she said. "I'm pretty sure they were married in May or June in Seattle. I saw them last month for the Cougs' home opener."

"I see," I said. "So what does he do?"

I knew I was pushing it, but I didn't care. I needed to know.

"I can tell this has been hard on you, Henry. I'm not sure if this conversation will do you any good."

Suddenly, I was angry and I wanted to tell her everything—about the *Dear John* letter, about what Sara had written and the way she had written it, about how I'd never even had a choice. Then, glancing into Lainie's eyes, I saw that it really didn't matter.

"I suppose you're right," I said apologetically. "It probably won't do anybody any good, but it's just that . . ." I paused, shaking my head. "No, I suppose you're right," I said again.

"What, Henry?" she asked.

And I had her. It was a rotten thing to do, but I had her. She'd tell me what I wanted to know, and she wouldn't even have to feel bad about. I wanted to see Sara even more than I had before.

"I would like to send her a few things—her things. Things that I thought she'd might like to have back. You know, personal things. I only want her to be happy," I said shamelessly.

Three hours and three pitchers of beer later, we had talked about everything we both felt comfortable talking about until my conversation became slow and choppy. I told Lainie I should probably head back to the house, as I had lied and said that I was staying the weekend at the fraternity and that I would be attending the homecoming game tomorrow. She told me to make sure to drop by, and I had given her every indication that I would try, even if neither one of us believed it.

I truly enjoyed seeing Lainie, despite her bombshell about Sara. Before I left, I asked Lainie for the check, but she only smiled and shook her head.

"Thanks," I said, "it was sure great seeing you, Lain."

"You too," she said and then kissed and hugged me good-bye. "Don't be a stranger," she added.

"I won't," I said, giving her a hug and a kiss of my own.

Lainie walked me out, but just before we reached the door, she stopped and handed me a little piece of paper.

"Here's her information," she said, staring up at me sympathetically. "I know it's what you came here for. But I think you need to let her go."

"But really, Lainie . . ." I said in mild protest but then stuffed the piece of paper in my pocket.

Outside, the autumn air was crisp and light and filled with the hopeful scents and sounds of homecoming. I watched as the marching band went parading by, playing the fight song. I sang along enthusiastically with the other spirited onlookers. Of course, it reminded me of Sara, but nearly everything around here did. The sentiment was thick enough to make a grown man cry, and I did until I was well out of Pullman heading north on the highway to Spokane and Sara.

It was nearly 10:00 p.m. when I pulled out of the service station onto Division Street with a vague notion of the directions the attendant had given me for the address I'd shown him. *You're not that far away, he had said with a wink.*

Sure enough, a few minutes later, I was parking in front of a modern two-story apartment complex. Perhaps the buzz I had from the beer was beginning to wear off, or perhaps it was nerves, but I sat inside the car for several minutes trying to decide what to say when at last I would confront Sara. For well over a year, I had rehearsed my lines and had had hundreds of make-believe conversations where I'd used just the right amount of reproach and righteousness to compel her to reconsider. Now, however, I was drawing a blank. Maybe Lainie was right. I needed to let go—maybe this was a sign that I should.

Glancing at my watch, I saw that it was well after ten. If I was going to do this, I had better get to it. Screw the signs. I had already come this far.

It didn't take me long to find her apartment. A dim light revealed a doormat that read *Welcome Friends*—the same one I remembered seeing outside Sara's dorm room back at school. A window next to the door had its curtains drawn; however, I could see the faint glow of light coming from inside, which made me hopeful that someone was home.

With all the courage of a church mouse, I tapped lightly on the door and waited. Hearing nothing, I tapped again, this time longer and harder. After several seconds, I heard the clicking of the lock and then, suddenly, the door swung open. Behind it stood a tower of a man at least six and a half feet tall and well over two hundred and fifty pounds. I wondered if I had seen him before in a football program.

At first, the swamp monster stood silently from behind a thick shaggy mop of dark hair and sideburns, but after several awkward moments, he reached up and parted the locks, his dark eyes glaring down at me—lips tight and eyebrows crossed. A cold wave of recognition rippled across his face.

"What do you want?" he grumbled.

"I would like to talk to Sara please," I said politely.

"She doesn't want to talk to you," he said.

"She said that? Really? You haven't even asked who I am," I said.

"I know who you are," he said, nodding smugly, "and I know she doesn't want to see you."

He let out a sort of primitive snort before slamming the door in my face. I don't know what it was that possessed me to start banging on the door again, but I did until the swamp monster returned.

"Is there something you don't understand, fella?" he said, stepping out beneath the door light.

"As a matter of fact, there is. I don't understand why I can't talk to Sara!" I hollered up at him, poking a finger into his massive chest.

"I told you, she doesn't want to talk to you!" he barked, swatting my finger away.

"Sara!" I yelled past him into the dark apartment. "I only want to talk for a minute! You owe me that much!"

"She doesn't owe you anything! Now get the hell out of here, you fucking baby killer," he snarled before shoving me out into the darkness.

I had better and brighter moments, and although I certainly wasn't a baby killer, I wasn't leaving here without a fight. I put my head down and charged the big oaf—after all, who was the damned soldier here?

I let out a wail of a war cry before ramming hard into his torso. The momentum carried us both crashing into the apartment. For a brief moment, I found myself on top of the giant, and that's when I heard a woman scream. Out of the corner of my eye, I got a glimpse of Sara—frightened and crying. After that, I didn't see or hear much of anything, except for the sights and sounds of the swamp monster's fists pounding into my face and body.

At some point prior to losing consciousness, I remember the beast tossing me back out into the night by my shirt collar. When I came to, every part of my face and body was either bleeding or swollen. Struggling to my feet, I noticed a bath towel that lay folded on my chest. Tucked inside was a small plastic bottle of aspirin.

I couldn't be sure as my vision was a bit blurred, but before I turned to head toward my car, I thought I saw some subtle movement from the curtains in the window.

"Good-bye, Sara," I said to the window as I held up the bath towel and bottle of aspirin.

If I hadn't been so sore, I might have taken a bow.

Chapter Twenty-Two

May 1985

It is well past midnight, but he doesn't want to go home. Instead, he orders another round—a Jack Daniels for Joe and a rum and Coke for himself. The Thirsty Fox isn't too crowded for a Saturday night, and they are enjoying the light piano music and the even lighter conversation.

"Some beautiful country you have here," says Joe, nodding, "especially from the sky."

"I'm glad you could see it," he says. "It was a nice day for it."

Joe takes a long drink from his short glass and watches him from across the table.

"Incredible," says Joe.

"You got a family, Joe?" he asks.

"Doesn't everybody?" Joe says, grinning.

"I mean a wife, kids—that sort of thing."

"I know what you mean," he says. "Yeah, I have a wife and a son. Of course, I'm on the road a lot, so I rarely get to see them. My wife hates it—wants me to get a job where I'm home all the time, but I wasn't meant for that type of lifestyle. I couldn't stand being home all the time. What about you? You got a family?"

"Sure, doesn't everybody?" He chuckles. "Yeah, a wife and a daughter."

"Is that right?" says Joe.

"Well, at least, I think I still do," he says, swallowing down the last of his drink.

"What do you mean by that?" says Joe.

"I don't know. Sometimes I think my wife might be having an affair."

"Shit!" exclaims Joe. "That's fucked up! How do you know?"

"There are signs."

"Signs—what signs?" asks Joe.

"You know, the signs," he says. "Comes home late, leaves early—acts like nothing is wrong, but then seems distant."

"Shit, maybe my wife's having an affair!" Joe laughs. "You sound like you've been through this before."

"I know the signs," he says.

"Really?" says Joe. "So she's done this before? I mean you'd know the signs, right?" says Joe with more than a hint of sarcasm.

"I don't know," he says, trying hard to focus. The lights appear to dim, and he can only see the whites of Joe's eyes.

"It's quite a puzzle, isn't it?" says Joe, his voice sounding hollow.

"I don't understand," he says.

Then all at once, he is cold and frightened, and he doesn't know why.

"It's all part of a puzzle," says Joe.

"What's a puzzle?"

"Lambs and tigers," says Joe, his voice now resonating. "It's the damnedest thing."

"What do you mean?" he cries.

There is a sudden flash of light, and for an instant, he sees Joe's entire face—but he is different, much younger.

"Flanny!" he cries out.

The face smiles back at him, and it then begins to laugh.

"Don't be a pussy your whole life, Bronco!" says his echoing voice.

I awoke with my stomach in knots. I had made it into California and was now some fifty or so miles north of San Diego in the town of Encinitas.

Somewhere in Arizona I had called Broadway and had got Ho's address and phone number. Broadway told me that he thought the information was current, but he couldn't be sure and had concluded our conversation by saying: *If you ever catch up with the little nip, tell him I said hello.* But that was Broadway.

With the morning sun behind me, I sat on an empty beach hoping the gentle sound of the breakers might ease my restlessness. For a few short moments, they did, but it wasn't long before the restless world came closing in around me again.

I made my way up the beach and found a pay phone where I dialed Ho's number. I got an answering machine, but I recognized his accented voice instantly. I left a message that I was in Southern California and the number of the phone booth in case he screened his calls.

The warm scent of ground beef from a nearby taco stand reminded me that I was hungry. I hadn't taken more than a couple steps toward the stand when I heard the pay phone ring.

"Hello?" I said.

"Hello . . . Henry?"

Having Ho's static-laden voice in my ear caused my mind to rush back to Vietnam and the chopper.

"Henry, that you?" he said.

"Yeah, it's me, Ho," I said finally. "I know it has been a long time, but I wanted to see you. I'm coming up to San Fran, if it's all right with you?" I added.

"It fine with me," he said excitedly, "but I go to Las Vegas. You come to Vegas and stay with me a few days. We play cards and party! What you say?"

"I'm in, I'm in," I said enthusiastically. "I'll meet you in Vegas. Where do you want to meet?" I asked.

"You stay at the Maxim with me. I be there tomorrow in the afternoon. I wait for you at lobby. We stay a few days and play cards and party. What you say?"

"I told you I'm in, I'm in," I said.

There was something about Las Vegas, something beyond the flash and the flare that had always appealed to me, excited me, no matter what my mood. At least once a year, I'd make the journey west, usually with a number of fellow associates from the firm. The trips were always expensed, as we would sign up for some bullshit legal conference we never intended to attend.

My spirits were high as I pulled into the entrance of the Maxim Hotel and handed my keys to a red-haired valet with a smart-ass look about his face. I slipped him a five-dollar bill that bought me a smile, and I remembered why I loved Vegas so much—money makes the mood. People came and went, and no matter how long you lived or lasted here, money never wore out its welcome. You were never alone in your loneliness, and if you played your cards right, you might just be able to buy a few dollars worth of happiness.

Standing in the long line at the front desk, I glanced around the lobby for Ho. I was early, but I thought I'd find out if he was too. Sure enough, I saw him sitting on a bench next to the door. I was surprised that he'd missed my entrance, but maybe he didn't recognize me. Although he didn't look as though he'd aged at all. I saw him checking out a teenager with shiny blond hair and enormous breasts. Suddenly, I understood how it was that he had missed me.

"A little young, don't you think?" I said, approaching him.

Ho gave me a quick glance, but it took a double take before he recognized me.

"Hey!" he said. "I'm just taking in the scenery."

"I see that," I said, grinning.

We shook hands, and I pulled him into an easy hug.

"God, it's been a long time, man. You haven't changed a bit."

"He reached into his jeans pocket and pulled out a room key. "Room 525, it's all set." He grabbed my backpack, and I followed him to the elevators. I was truly amazed at the way he looked. It was as though not a single day had gone by. His hair was longer, but styled neatly. He wore designer jeans and a chic white tee shirt.

Once in the hotel room, Ho stood at the mirror staring intently at himself, adjusting the subtle particulars of his stylish hairdo while exchanging my ratty jeans and tee shirt for some less ratty ones.

"I thought we meet my friends down in the casino and play some cards. That okay?" asked Ho, still staring into the mirror.

"Sounds good," I said.

In the casino, I found a cashier and wrote a check for five hundred dollars cash. Ho did the same. I suggested we play Blackjack, but Ho shook his head.

"No, Pai Gow poker," he said. "It's better odds, okay?"

"Pai Gow?" I said. I'd heard of it but had never played.

"We can win," said Ho.

I didn't doubt that he could win and, oddly enough, I had an itch to gamble. We met Ho's friends back at the entrance to the casino. Ho did a poor job in the way of introductions, but I did learn their names—a tall and lanky Englishman called Clive and an older much shorter-looking gentleman that went by the name Bull. Like Ho, both were chopper pilots for *Channel 5*. Bull suggested that we have a drink before we hit the tables, and we all readily agreed.

There wasn't much going on at the hotel lounge; in fact, except for a bartender, the place was empty. We sat at a table close to the bar and ordered a round of drinks from the spiky black-haired female bartender. I didn't find her particularly attractive, but both Bull and Ho appeared to be taken by her, or by what was protruding from beneath her tight black *Pretenders* concert tee shirt.

"She's a rocker," said Bull from behind a pair of black *Vaurnet* sunglasses.

The lounge was dark and candlelit, and I wasn't sure why Bull was even wearing sunglasses. Maybe he had a light sensitivity. I remembered Flanny saying, *the sun always shines when you're cool, Bronco*. I chuckled to myself.

"I like that," said Ho, gazing ponderously at the woman before flashing the three of us a smile and a suggestive flick of his brow.

"So you flew with Tuan in Vietnam?" Clive said to me.

"Yeah," I said, making the connection. In Vietnam, nobody had ever referred to Ho as Tuan.

Clive slunk his long body awkwardly back in his chair and then pulled a thin cigar from the breast pocket of his shirt.

"You mind?" he said, holding out the cigar.

"Not at all," I said.

Clive lit the cigar and then blew smoke straight up into the air. He stared at me through dark and sallow eyes. Clive appeared a lot older than he did at first glance. Heavy lines traced his mouth and eyes, indicative of a lifetime of sunshine and smiles.

"Tuan never talks about his time in Vietnam," said Clive, tapping his cigar over an ashtray. "Despite my persistent inquires," he added.

"He was a hell of a pilot," I said.

"And he still is," said Clive, "but the San Francisco skyline is a long way from Vietnam."

"Or Korea," inserted Bull, suddenly shifting his attention from the bartender to our conversation.

"You were in Korea then," I said to Bull.

"Oh yes," said Clive, answering for him, "and he won't let us forget it."

"Really?" I said, attempting to be interested. "Did you fly?"

"No, I didn't get my license until well after the war," said Bull, "but it's the war that made me want to get my license, see. They had choppers everywhere in Korea, and I was good friends with one of them pilots. I may not have flown in a war, but I got a shitload more hours than these guys," Bull said, waving a hand around the table.

"You guys want another drink?" Ho asked.

We gave Ho our drink orders, and now—armed with an excuse to approach the bartender—he took off for the bar.

"He'll be a while," said Clive.

"Let's hope so," Bull said, winking at me.

"You married?" asked Clive.

"Oh no," I said.

"That's fine, just fine," said Clive.

"How about you?" I said.

"Now that's an interesting question—interesting indeed," said Clive, leaning forward to flick his cigar over the ashtray. "It's a vulgar institution, marriage—bloody can't stand it. Neither can Bull here—we're dead set against it. Isn't that right, Bull?"

"Dead set against it," said Bull.

"In fact," Clive continued, "we're thinking about starting our own organization. We'll call it *Men Against Marriage*, or *MAM*."

"Oh yeah, when are the meetings?" I said.

Pointing at me with his cigar, he said, "Meetings, yes, lovely . . . what do you think, Bull? Shall we have meetings?"

"Why not?" said Bull, laughing.

"Yes indeed," said Clive, slapping his hand on the table. "We will have meetings. I have to tell you, Henry, at first, I was thinking only tee shirts, but you've inspired me." He slapped his hand on the table again. "And you, Henry, shall be a member?"

"Me?"

"Of course you," said Clive, slapping my shoulder this time. "You've been married before, haven't you?"

"Married . . . me? Oh no," I said.

Clive looked at me and then at Bull and said, "Oh no, that won't do. What do you think, Bull?"

Bull shrugged and then chuckled.

"But I've never been married," I said. "Wouldn't I make a good member?"

"You see," said Clive. "I mistook you for the *been married* type, or a *BM*."

"*BM*?" I said.

"Yes, a *BM*. Now you see the vulgarity in it." He laughed. "Unfortunately, you and our good friend Tuan over there are the *never been married* type, or an *NBM*, which won't do. Between the two of us," said Clive, waving his cigar in the air. "That is, Bull and myself, we've been married and divorced five times. He," said Clive, pointing at Bull, "one more than me."

Bull nodded in agreement.

"Remarkable," I said.

"I'm sorry to say, my dear man, that you have no frame of reference here. You, I daresay, are a virgin to the . . . shall we say, the objects of matrimony."

"I've been engaged."

Clive's dark eyebrows lifted and then he grinned.

"*Engaged*! Did you hear that, Bull-man? The man says he's been engaged! Oh dear me!" exclaimed Clive with a laugh. "Oh dear, dear me . . . *engaged!*"

He patted me on the shoulder.

"My dear man, if only I could hold my engagements in perpetuity—now that would be something, surely. There is nothing in this world like being *engaged*. I wish I was *engaged* right now. Oh, those expectations—allusions, really. And all that shagging, and all the bloody blow jobs," he added.

"You got blow jobs while you were engaged?" asked Bull.

"Loads of them," replied Clive. "Pending nuptials will do that to a woman—from the proposal to the wedding night, it's all blow jobs. But prepare yourself, because once the honeymoon is over . . . so are the blow jobs. So enjoy it while it lasts because that, gentlemen, is the beginning of the end."

"So what does a man do?" Bull said.

"There are a few options. First, you can follow that path of our friend Tuan over there—a king among men. Never get married and shag everything that comes along—the smart play, really. You may face the occasional drought—not blow jobs, but sex altogether. But face it, that's a problem even for married blokes these days. Next, you can get married, squeeze out an army of kids so that you don't have the time or the quid for a divorce. At least, not until your babes grow up and you realize it is all shit. Or finally, you can do what I do. It's simple, really—bloody long *engagements*." Clive took several long puffs on his cigar.

"That's the stupidest thing I've ever heard," said Bull. "Why don't you shut it and give the guy some peace?"

"I don't mind, really," I said to Bull.

"You will," said Bull, nodding. "Just wait. When you've heard him blather on as much as I have, you soon learn that most of what comes out his mouth is nonsense."

"I've never said that I was an expert," said Clive apologetically, "but I do have a couple of theories."

"Theories?" said Bull, chuckling. "That's a lot of shit, if you ask me," said Bull.

"That's good, Bull-man, because nobody asked you." Then to me he said, "Did you ever hear about the handsome knight who asked the beautiful princess to marry him?"

"I don't think so," I said.

"Well, the beautiful princess refused him . . . and they both lived happily ever after."

We were all laughing when Ho finally came back with the bartender, both of them carrying a tray of drinks.

"Did we order that many?" asked Bull.

"No," replied Ho. "It's two for one, you know. Happy hour—everybody get two."

"I told you," said Clive. "A king among men. Who is your friend, Tuan?"

"This is Virginia. She from Ohio."

"Nice to meet you gentlemen," said Virginia. "Thank you for coming in. My shift was dead until you fellows arrived."

"I sure hope that Tuan took care of you," said Bull.

"Oh yes, I take good care of her," said Ho.

Virginia smiled and then walked back to the bar. Ho's eyes followed her the entire way. He turned back to us.

"They're huge," he said, cupping his hands in front of his chest.

"If you're referring to her exceptionally large tits, I agree," said Clive. "However, she has an exceptionally large *behind* as well."

"But that good too," said Ho.

We all laughed.

It was well past 8:00 p.m. before we even thought about heading to the casino.

"Are we going to gamble or what?" I said as we passed through a formation of chiming slot machines. "What's this Pai Gow poker shit, anyway?" I asked Ho.

"Actually, that's what it is," said Clive. "I believe it means *shit* or something like that in Chinese."

"Right," I said. "That's perfect. I've been dealt a lot of shit lately."

"Well, actually, the object is not to have—"

"I know what you mean," I said, cutting him off.

It didn't take us long to find an empty Pai Gow table, which as Clive said, wasn't that difficult—although what was hard was finding one without an Asian dealer. Clive would have no part of it, as he said the Asian people were inherently lucky by nature when it came to cards. So we finally settled on a wide-eyed Caucasian man that Clive decided looked *dreadfully unlucky*.

As it turned out, Clive was right. We found one of the unluckiest dealers in Las Vegas. In an hour, I had tripled my money. When it was finally time for Steve to take a break, we all hedged our bets until he came back. At one point, Ho was playing five-hundred-dollar hands and raking in black one-hundred-dollar chips hand over fist.

"You are good, man!" Ho said to the dealer after another five-hundred-dollar haul. "Don't worry—I take care of you, Steve." Ho slid a lime-green twenty-five-dollar chip across the table, which was his new custom since staking the big bets. Virginia wasn't playing, but she sat next to Ho, rubbing his back in encouragement. And when he'd win, she'd give him a congratulatory kiss on the neck.

"It's all working for him," said Clive. "Lucky in cards and lucky in love. How often does that bloody happen?"

"It does seem to happen a lot with him," said Bull in a voice that only Clive and I could hear.

"You're quite right," whispered Clive.

Sometime during the night, we arranged for me to bunk with Clive and Bull, as Ho and Virginia wanted to be alone. It was no bother, really, but it gave me a reason to excuse myself from the table so that I could remove my things from the room. I didn't have any intention of staying with Clive or Bull, or anywhere else in Las Vegas. I had an urge to travel, as I had nothing here to give anybody—not even the courtesy of a good-bye.

I scooped up my chips and cashed them out for better than three thousand dollars. It was the most I'd ever won at one table at one time, but the money did nothing for me—I only wanted to move on.

On the way out of the casino, I passed by a small café with a muted television showing the Tigers at Yankee Stadium. I stopped long enough to watch Alan Trammel and Lou Whitaker hook up for an inning-ending double play. It was as pure and as graceful as any I'd seen last season during their World Series run. Still, something didn't seem quite the same.

Chapter Twenty-Three

July 1964

"Have a good time," said Tom before we climbed out of his truck at the bottom of Carrie Ferguson's driveway.

Carrie's going-away party promised to be the social event of the summer. In truth, it was my only summer social event, and I was looking forward to enjoying an elevated social status as her *kinda-sorta* boyfriend.

"I'll pick you up around seven—if that's okay?" said Tom.

"That's great," said Jessie. "We'll see you then."

We both waved as Tom pulled away.

"He sure is in a good mood," said Jessie.

"Yeah, that's the way it is when he gives me flying lessons. He can be a swell guy when he wants to be."

"Do you think it's because of the fuss with my granddaddy the other night?" said Jessie as we walked up the Ferguson driveway.

"I was thinking about that," I said. "I've never seen Tom use the shotgun before. I didn't think it even had shells."

"Maybe it didn't," Jessie smiled. "I don't think Granddaddy knew. It was strange seeing him back down like that. We have to find those bodies, Hen. And Frankie and Grandma's secret cabin," she added.

Since visiting Oksana, Jessie had been affectionately referring to Abigail Mason as *Grandma,* and she was obsessed with finding the rendezvous place that Vladimir had mentioned. As much as I believed Jessie and wanted to help her find the answers, the thought of finding dead bodies and confronting Spenser with any of it scared the bejesus out of me.

"When do you think you'll go back home?"

"Not until Daddy gets back," she said, pushing the doorbell. "He'll come and get me. I might catch some hell, but he'll be cool about it."

The front door opened, and Carrie stood in the arctic entryway wearing Bermuda shorts, a yellow blouse, and a welcoming smile.

"Hi," Carrie said excitedly. "Come on in."

We followed her through the entryway and into the living room where we wound our way through a maze of yellow *Mayflower* moving boxes. We came out of the labyrinth at the kitchen where Carrie's father was busy mixing a salad.

"Hi, Henry," he said when he saw me.

"Hi, Mr. Ferguson," I replied.

"And you must be Jessie," he said, extending her one of his tiny little hands. Mr. Ferguson was in shorts and wearing the same old argyle sweater that I had always seen him in. I reminded myself to ask Jessie about shaking his dinky little hand.

"We've got quite a mob out there," said Mr. Ferguson, pointing to the backyard. "Here, Carrie, take this," he said, handing her the bowl of fruit salad. "I'm going to whip up some more lemonade. Go on out back, make yourself at home," said Mr. Ferguson.

In the backyard, we were greeted by a host of familiar faces—some of whom I wasn't sure whether Jessie cared to see, including Victor Andrews, Patrick LaCroux, Ronnie Finch, and a couple others I had known her to date. If that's what you called it. Also, there were several girls in attendance that I knew didn't care much for Jessie. Her tomboy nature often collided with their prissy personalities, and they were all very aware of Jessie's somewhat *relaxed* reputation with the boys.

The Fergusons had set up several card tables along the outside of the patio area in the backyard and covered them with white paper tablecloths. A picnic table was stacked high with cards and presents for Carrie. Once again, my mother had been right to take us into town yesterday to pick up a card and gift for Carrie. Jessie had picked out a pocketbook, and I a small silver cross attached to a thin silver chain.

"Your mother called that one," said Jessie, nodding at the gift table.

Only a few guests sat at the tables; most milled around the outer edges of the yard awaiting instruction as to the direction of the party. When Mrs. Ferguson came out the backdoor, I nearly didn't recognize her with her bobbed hair pulled back and wearing dark round sunglasses.

"Welcome, everyone," said Mrs. Ferguson. "Welcome to our home . . . well, I guess it's still our home for a little while longer," she said, glancing back at Mr. Ferguson who stood immediately outside the backdoor. "As you are surely aware, we are moving to Anchorage next week and we wanted to give Carrie and you folks a chance to say good-bye."

I had never attended Carrie's church—in fact, rarely had I attended any church—but I could tell instantly that Mrs. Ferguson had mastered her role as preacher's wife. She didn't say more than a couple sentences without looking back at her husband for reassurance. Additionally, she had a voice well-modulated for delivering announcements.

"We will be serving hamburgers and hot dogs," she said, quickly glancing back at Mr. Ferguson again. He gave her a confirming nod.

"We also have salad," she continued. "Both fruit and potato as well as chips, and there is a wonderful—I say it's wonderful because her cakes are *always* so wonderful and brilliantly decorated for the occasion. I'm speaking, of course, of the cake made by Mrs. Willingham."

There was a brief applause as all eyes shifted to a short robust woman with skin and hair so thin that, in the sunlight, she appeared ghostly. Mrs. Willingham's outstanding reputation as a baker and cake decorator were legendary throughout the interior of Alaska.

Her son, Robert Willingham, had been a classmate of mine since the third grade. He was about as popular and as good-looking a boy as I had seen anywhere, including magazines and the movies. He was a starter on the basketball team, he had the leading role in every school play, and he had been elected class president ever since I can remember electing a class president. Unfortunately for Robert, however, he was a dunce. The only reason he was in my class was that he had to repeat third and fourth grade. He probably should've repeated several more grades, but somehow, he'd managed to squeak by—perhaps it had something to do with his mother's delicious cakes.

Of course, Robert was here, sitting next to his ghostly mother and absorbing up the praise as if it were his own.

"Thank you," said Mrs. Willingham meekly as Robert nodded appreciatively.

"We'd like everyone to sign the guestbook located on the gift table," directed Mrs. Ferguson. "This way, Carrie will always remember this day and everyone attending. Also, we've had cards made up with our new address in Anchorage on them. So please take one and enjoy the party," she added.

Jessie and I placed our similarly wrapped gifts on different sides of the table. Then Jessie headed back toward the house, and I—through the shuffling mobs—went to find Carrie.

With the undersized yard and weighty crowd, it took me longer than expected to find her, but eventually I spied Carrie mingling amidst a formation of junior-class girls that she knew from choir.

"Hi, ladies," I said, approaching Carrie who was chatting with Missy Cole and Fawn Voinovich.

I wasn't much of a jet-setter, but because Carrie and I had been kinda-sorta dating, I socialized on occasion with several girls that might not have otherwise entered my friendship circle.

"Hi, Hen," said Carrie. "I was just about to come and find you."

"Right," I said skeptically.

"She really was," Missy said. "She told us."

All my dates with Carrie had a natural progression to them. That is, they always started with a sort of bashful awkwardness whereby every date felt like the first, and we'd spend most of the date trying to regain the comfort level that we'd reached by the end of our last date.

Normally, I wouldn't mind, but this was our last time together and I didn't want to have to start from the beginning again.

So with a little blind courage, I boldly put my arms around Carrie and kissed her quickly on the lips.

"Hi there," I said, releasing her.

I heard Missy and Fawn giggle, but from Carrie's smile, I knew I'd done the right thing.

"Hi there," she said and then, surprisingly, she kissed me back.

"Gosh, you two," said Missy.

"What?" said Carrie, blushing.

Missy didn't reply, and Fawn only giggled again. I liked Missy and Fawn all right; they were *nice*. Carrie was *nice*. Carrie's friends were *nice*. Our entire kinda-sorta relationship was built on *nice*. I'd spent quite an amount of time being *nice* with Carrie and her friends. I didn't want to be *nice* anymore. Not today, anyway—not our last day together.

I kissed her again. This time harder, longer, and with my tongue. I pulled her close, and I felt her surrender to me. I tasted peppermint as her tongue wrestled with mine. Then another giggle from Fawn and Carrie shoved me away.

"Don't!" she cried out.

Then with a fiery look, Carrie slapped me hard across the face. From the look in her eyes, I could tell that she had surprised herself. My face burned red from the slap and the countless eyes I felt upon me.

"I . . . I'm sorry," I said.

I wanted to dissolve into the day. Missy and Fawn looked away, but Carrie's eyes flared.

"That wasn't very *nice!*" she fired.

Before my mind was read further and my pride took another hit, I walked away.

Reeling my way through the crowd, I wandered over to the grill and hid myself beside Robert Willingham, my self-esteem still smarting from Carrie's sharp hand and words. Robert was cramming a hot dog into his mouth while making eyes at a couple of sophomore girls from Carrie's church.

"Hey, Robert," I said.

He mumbled a sort of pleasantry through a mouthful of hot dog.

"Your mom's cake looks terrific," I said, trying to ignite some small talk.

Robert swallowed hard and then nodded.

"She baked it and decorated it herself, you know," he said.

"Yeah, I know. It's remarkable," I said, my patronizing tone wasted on Robert.

"Yeah, my mom's real good at it," he said. "So you and Carrie?"

Fortunately, I spoke Robert's language. It was primitive enough but still a couple steps above grunting.

"Yeah, we went out a couple of times," I said. "I don't think she's speaking to me anymore, though."

"That's too bad," said Robert, "because this is some party."

"Yeah, it's very *nice*," I said.

"Sure is. Maybe she'd throw the graduation party," he said before shoving what was left of the hot dog into his mouth. I scanned his face for even the slightest trace of levity, but there was none.

"Yeah, I'm sure they'd come all the way back from Anchorage just to throw our graduation party," I said, but sarcasm too was wasted on him. Sometimes I wondered whether he was retarded. To his credit, however, he had chased every skirt that ever twirled its way through the halls of Lathrop High, pretty or not. His passions ran high while his standards stayed low, which meant there wasn't a chick in school that he wouldn't track, trace, or trail. I was surprised that he had yet to pursue Jessie, but with his bird-dogging ways and her willing scent, it was only a matter of time.

Searching the premises for an inconspicuous place to hide myself until it was time to leave, I noticed Jessie sitting alone at a far table picking at her fingernails. I slipped on over.

"Why so blue?" I said, sitting down across from her. Jessie didn't look up. Instead, she shook her head dismissively and went back to picking at her nails.

After a several tortuous minutes of her purposely ignoring me, she finally said, "If it isn't the smooching bandit."

"You heard?"

"I saw," she said, glancing up at me.

"It was pretty stupid, I know," I said.

"What are you talking about? She liked it."

"But she slapped me," I said.

"That's only because you did it in front of everybody. Believe me, she liked it. I told you, preachers' kids are the worst."

I never did buy into that "preacher's kid" shit, but I'd believe anything if it meant that there was a possibility that Carrie would speak to me again.

"You really think so?" I said.

"Why not?" said Jessie, shrugging.

"So you think she'll ever speak to me again?" I asked, hopeful.

"I don't know about that," she said, shaking her head. "I know I wouldn't," she added and then, grinning again, she winked at me.

"Great," I said.

"Don't worry about it, rube," she said with a sympathetic sigh. "I'm sure she'll come around before the party's over, or before she leaves for Anchorage. She's a lot *nicer* than I am."

That was for sure, I thought, but I still wasn't convinced. "She's *nice,* all right," I said.

Jessie's eyes shot past me. Glancing back, I saw Carrie coming toward us. Without a word, she sat down next to Jessie. She stared at me coolly, wearing either a sordid smile or a timid frown. I couldn't decide which, but both made me uncomfortable.

"So what do you have to say for yourself, Henry Allen?" said Carrie sharply.

Jessie rolled her eyes in a look of agonizing disgust.

"I am sorry," I said weakly.

Jessie shot me a revolting look before glaring viciously at Carrie. "*Sorry?* You're the one who should be *sorry!* You're the one slapping people around!"

Carrie's jaw began to quiver as she stared blankly back at Jessie. It was strange to hear Jessie come to my defense. She'd never done that before, and I had no idea why she was doing it now, but part of me liked it.

"I-I . . . didn't . . . I-I . . . didn't . . ." Carrie stuttered and then, turning toward me, she shook her head pleadingly.

"Bullshit!" shouted Jessie. "Hen kisses you like that and you haul off and slap him. I thought you were his girlfriend, for Christ-sake!"

While I respected her intentions, the blasphemy was a bit much—after all, she was a preacher's kid.

"It's okay, Jess," I said in a calming tone. "It's all right, really."

"It's not okay," fired Jessie. "She can't treat you that way, Hen!"

Carrie's already fair complexion faded fairer still.

"I-I-I . . . think . . ." Carrie said, still grasping for words.

"I-I-I-I-I!" mocked Jessie. "Listen, Miss Goody-Goody. I know you think you're above everybody else with your father being a preacher, but you don't fool me, Ferguson!" she barked. "Your goody-two-shoes act may dupe the choirgirls, but it doesn't me! You wanted Henry to kiss you! You liked it! What you probably want is—"

"Is there a problem here?" Mr. Ferguson suddenly interrupted.

I was glad he did. As much as I appreciated her allegiance, she had gone too far, as now every eye at the party was cast upon us. Jessie stood up, glancing first at Mr. Ferguson and then the gawking crowd.

"You all think you're so above it all," spat Jessie, her eyes shifting back to Carrie who had her hands over her face, tears streaming through her fingers.

"I'm sorry, Mr. Ferguson. I hope I didn't ruin your party," said Jessie, still staring down at Carrie. "Henry and I were just leaving."

I couldn't think. I could only react and so, obediently, I followed Jessie back through the house and out the front door.

I had no idea what we were doing. Tom wouldn't pick us up for another three hours, and we were ten miles from home.

We had walked nearly a mile before Jessie finally spoke.

"I suppose you're mad at me," she said.

"I'm not mad," I replied.

That much was true. However, I couldn't imagine the party going any worse. Instead of hot dogs and cake, we would be walking for the next three hours. We had just stormed out on the social event of the summer—my only social event of the summer.

"I just don't see where she gets off," said Jessie.

"How so?" I asked.

Jessie stopped us suddenly.

"You see how she is, Hen," she said. "She thinks she's so damn perfect—now you see how she really is. I warned you about these preachers' kids."

I walked quickly past her.

"What's the matter?" she hollered after me.

Without a word, I kept on walking.

"Wait up, Hen!" she yelled.

A couple seconds later, she was walking beside me.

"What's your problem?" she said.

This time, I stopped us.

"I don't have a problem," I said. "I just want to get home. We have a lot of walking to do."

"You want to go back?"

I shook my head in disbelief. "Are you crazy?" I shouted. "I've suffered enough humiliation for one day. Haven't you? For crying out loud, Jess!"

"You can be pissed if you want, but I only told the truth. She slapped you for Christ-sake!"

"I can fight my own battles, thank you!" I said, walking away. "When I want your help, I'll ask for it!"

"I knew you were mad at me!" she replied. Jessie caught up with me again, and for a few minutes, neither of us spoke. Then she stopped us again. "I'm sorry," she said. "I was only trying to help."

"I don't need your help, Jess. I'm a big boy. I don't understand why you had to ride her so hard. I thought she was your friend."

"Oh no, she was never my friend," she said, shaking her head. "No, she's got plenty of friends. Didn't you see them all? Well they can have her. They all love her so much—think she's so damned perfect. For Christ-sake, did you see all her friends? She'll probably make a bunch more friends in Anchorage. Believe me, Hen, I was no friend of hers!"

Then suddenly I understood. This wasn't about Carrie and me, Carrie's prudent nature, or even the slap. It was a lot simpler than that. This was about Carrie's friends. Jessie didn't have any friends, not really. Sure, she knew everyone at the party, and lord knows she had carnal knowledge of a good number of the fellows, but there wasn't a person there that she could really call her friend—except me and, up until a little while ago, Carrie. It explained everything—why she sat alone, why she was in such a mood.

"I suppose it doesn't matter anymore," I said. "You sure let her have it."

"Somebody had to," she said.

We spent the next half mile or so walking in silence, which gave me the opportunity to replay the events in my mind. It didn't seem real. I had eagerly waited for half a summer for this party and saying good-bye to Carrie properly. Why I had to plant one on her in the first five minutes was beyond me. Regardless of what Jessie thought and regardless of my behavior, Carrie was a good person, and I had enjoyed every bit of our *kinda-sorta* relationship.

"You know that Carrie really likes you, Jess," I said.

"What do you mean?"

"I *mean* she really likes you. She liked being your friend. She told me more than once that she thought you were *hip*—that's the way she put it."

"She said I was *hip*?"

"I told you, she likes you. She talked about you all the time. I remember once her telling me that you were the coolest girl in school."

"She said that?"

"Yes, but I'm pretty sure that she doesn't think so anymore."

"What else did she say about me?"

"Oh no," I said, waving her off. "I'm not saying any more about it. You went and bawled her out, remember? Besides, it doesn't matter. No doubt, she hates us now—and can you blame her?"

"I guess not," Jessie muttered.

Although it was late in the evening, the sun still burned high in the sky, making the long walk hot and miserable. Jessie led our forlorn procession up the highway, heads and spirits down, neither one of us talking.

I was about to suggest a shortcut when a green-and-white Buick sedan passed by and then came squealing to a stop some fifty feet or so ahead of us.

"What the hell?" said Jessie, glancing back at me.

I shrugged, but I too was curious. Much to our surprise, sliding out of the passenger side of the Buick was Carrie Ferguson.

"Hey," said Carrie after jogging up to us. She had left the car door open and the driver waiting, as if she might be planning a quick getaway.

"Hi," I said.

Jessie stood in silence. Carrie's face appeared resolute, but I still noticed some pink around the edges. She took a few steps forward while wringing her hands together.

"I just want to say I'm sorry, Henry," she said. "I shouldn't have slapped you. Jessie was right. I liked that you kissed me, but Fawn or somebody laughed and . . . I got embarrassed. I'm sorry. I really like you, Henry, and it's going to be hard for me to move . . . because I'm really going to miss you. I didn't want it to be like this . . . I didn't want you to leave that way."

"I didn't either," I said. "It was a stupid thing to do, kissing you like I did. I'm sorry."

"As long as we're tossing around apologies," Jessie said to Carrie, "then I'm sorry too. I was really hard on you, Carrie, and I didn't have reason to be."

"It's okay," said Carrie, a tear running the length of her cheek. "I had it coming after slapping Henry. You sure are a good friend to him, standing up for him the way you did. I should be so lucky to have a friend like you."

Maybe it was the apology or the earnestness in Carrie's tone, but suddenly, Jessie hugged her.

Afterward Carrie said, "I was hoping that you would both come back to the party, but it's up to you—either that or my dad can drive you home."

Smiling, Jessie looked over at me for the answer.

"Of course we can go back to the party," I said.

It was as fun a party as I had ever remembered attending, although I hadn't attended too many parties. Carrie and I spent nearly every minute of it together and a good part of that time with Jessie. That is, until the bird dog that was Robert Willingham finally caught a whiff of Jessie's scent. I wasn't happy about it, but I had seen it coming for some time, and oddly enough, I was beginning to get used to Jessie and all her beaus. I suppose it didn't matter because I was happy just to spend the time with Carrie, mostly holding hands and talking.

A few minutes before it was time to leave, Carrie kissed me. Not in a way that said good-bye, but one that told me that she was my girlfriend—for a few more days, anyway. When she did finally say good-bye, she began to cry, and from that moment until the moment Jessie and I climbed into Tom's truck, I did too.

I didn't say much on the ride home but listened to Jessie fill Tom in about our time at the party. She conveniently left out the part concerning our first exit. But Tom was still in a good mood and so was Jessie, particularly after Tom informed her that her dad would soon return from Anchorage and she would stay with us until he got back.

"I had a good talk with JT on the telephone, and he said he'd talk to Spenser about the drinking," Tom said to Jessie reassuringly. "I told him that if he is planning any more trips, you are more than welcome to stay with us."

I had always been frightened of Tom and his anger, the times when he lost his temper, but it was his pleasantness that frightened me the most. When he would say or do things that would make me believe that I could trust him, like him, even love him, or that he could love me. But inevitably his mood would change and he would be angry again—at my mother or at me or at the world—and all the pleasantness would disappear and be forgotten.

But for now, it was nice to sit and listen to Tom and Jessie talk while I thought about Carrie and me. I was soon realizing that I was *kinda-sorta* going to miss her a great deal.

Chapter Twenty-Four

January 1970

When Jessie called to tell me she was getting married, I can't say that I was surprised. For nearly three months now, she had been seeing *Winslow "Call me The Win" Marshall*, a hotshot accountant from a big-shot firm in Chicago. Most recently, The Win had earned a promotion to manage the firm's Detroit office, and the two had moved in together.

After completing my stateside army obligation, I had decided to go back to school. Jessie suggested I attend Michigan State University, so I could be closer to her. So on a whim, I made the three-day drive from Fort Lewis, Washington, to East Lansing, Michigan. There, I divided my time between studying and playing third-wheel to Jessie and The Win.

I had gotten to know The Win fairly well since arriving in Michigan some six months ago. The Win was a nice enough fellow and of all Jessie's boyfriends, he was certainly the most successful. In addition to a five figure annual income, he had acquired a shitload of real property, including two or three office buildings in the Chicago area. He owned a small fleet of Corvettes, only two of which he actually drove while the others he kept in storage until, as he put it, *they were worth a mint*. And just before their engagement, he had purchased a big house in one of Detroit's pretentious neighborhoods.

"The wedding is in April," said Jessie over the phone.

"Congratulations!" I said forcing my enthusiasm.

"Thanks," she said. "You're coming tonight, aren't you?"

At Jessie's insistence, I'd been driving from East Lansing to the Detroit suburbs to spend my weekends at *The Win Mansion*, as I christened it.

"I wasn't planning on it. You and Win probably want some alone time with the engagement and all. I'd feel like I would be intruding. You don't—"

"Don't be silly," she said dismissively. "You know we love having you here."

"I don't know Jess, I'm waiting for my new roommate to show and you know I'm carrying a pretty heavy load this semester. I probably should stick around the library this weekend."

"Don't worry about it, you can study here. I'll leave you alone, I promise. I'll cook for you and you can study. I promise. Besides, you'll have plenty of time to break in your new roommate."

"I don't know, Jess," I said.

"Oh come on, Hen, it'll be fun."

It wasn't that I was worried about not having fun, Jessie and I always had fun together, no matter whom she was seeing, or engaged to. I knew Jessie liked having me around, but I wasn't so sure about The Win. He was a gracious enough host and never made me feel uncomfortable, but something told me that my friendship with Jessie annoyed him.

"Are you sure The Win won't mind? After all, Jess, you just got engaged, maybe he'd like one weekend without me hanging around."

"Oh, come on," she whined. "You know Winslow loves having you here. Besides, he won't even be here Saturday. He's got tickets to the hockey game. He and some of his friends are making a day of it. That just leaves you and me, pal."

"I don't know, Jess."

"Come on, please," she pleaded.

"All right, all right," I said. "I'll be there, but not until nine or so. I want to meet my new roommate first."

"Perfect," she said. "I'll see you then."

I set the phone down and then sat down on my bed. I thought about Jessie and The Win getting hitched. I supposed I always knew she'd eventually get married, despite her many declarations otherwise.

Fortunately, I didn't have to think about it long, as the door to my dorm room swung open and in stepped my new roommate.

"Brandon P. Sullivan," he announced, tossing a couple of overstuffed duffel bags onto the naked bed across from me.

Standing, I offered him my hand.

"Nice to meet you, Brandon. I'm Henry Allen," I said as we shook.

"Nice to meet you, Henry," he said cordially, "but please call me Sully."

Sully quickly scanned the room.

"Cozy," he said.

The room was small, but considerably larger than my room at the fraternity, and it was certainly a step up from the barracks or the hooch.

"So they told me you're in the Poly Sci program as well," said Sully as he began unloading items from one of his duffel bags.

"Yeah, that's right," I said. "I took a couple year hiatus, but I'm thinking about law school."

"So am I," said Sully placing a large framed picture of a smiling elderly woman neatly on the corner of his desk.

"That's Grandma Irene," he said pointing at the picture. "She's the only woman in my life. Raised me from a baby by herself." Sully smiled proudly behind bounding locks of curly blond hair. He had an engaging smile featuring a perfect set of pearly white teeth, and I didn't believe for a minute that Old Irene was the only woman in his life.

"Well then, welcome to the room, Grandma Irene," I announced.

Sully smiled again.

"Good ole Grandma Irene," he said.

While Sully unpacked, we had a long and spirited conversation where each of us only imparted our least revealing secrets, but I suppose, we learned enough to conclude that we could be roommates. To my surprise, however, he was a year older than I was.

"But warmongering ages you," said Sully. "You're fortunate you have rugged good looks. It's draft dodging that keeps you young and vibrant," he added.

"Oh, so you're one of them," I said.

"Not really," he said defensively. "I'm on a student deferment."

"I'm only kidding," I said with a laugh. "I don't care if you are a draft dodger. It makes no difference to me. I'm not political."

"You're not political, but yet you went to Vietnam and now you're studying political science?" Sully chuckled. "It makes perfect sense to me. I want to go to law school," he said. "Chicks dig lawyers, you know."

"But I thought Grandma Irene was the only woman in your life."

"Oh, she is," he said, "but the type of chicks I'm talking about, I don't want *in my life*. You know what I mean," he said shooting me a wink.

———

I arrived at The Win Mansion a little after nine. Jessie met me at the door wearing flared jeans adorned with rhinestones, a flashy silver blouse and an enormous diamond ring. All appeared to twinkle with her every move. She gave me a quick kiss on the lips, and then hugged me holding me for an unusually long time.

Afterward, I grabbed her hand and examined the ring there. It was a modern version of the Hope Diamond.

"*Tiny*," I said.

"It's not that big," she giggled.

"You're right," I said. "I'm sure someday they'll dig up a bigger one."

Jessie hit me playfully on the arm and then snatched a full glass of chardonnay from the dining room table before leading me upstairs to the guest room. After helping me unpack, she pulled me down onto the bed and kissed me hard on the lips.

"I love you," she said.

"I love you too," I said taken by the sudden affection. "Where's The Win?"

"He went to get you some rum," she said and then kissed me softly on the cheek. "He'll be right back if you miss him," she added seductively.

I wasn't sure what to make of her playfulness. Perhaps she was drunk or overwhelmed by her recent engagement. Fortunately, I was able to persuade her to go back downstairs. Sitting in the plush leather chairs beneath the high vaulting ceiling in the living room, we awaited The Win's arrival. Jessie poured me a glass of wine from an open bottle of chardonnay.

"Home sweet home," she said.

"Congratulations on the engagement," I said, raising my glass.

"I'm getting married!" she blurted. "Can you believe it?"

I nodded.

"Am I crazy, Hen?" She smiled, but I saw tears welling in her eyes.

"Aren't we all?"

"Not you, Hen. I think you're the sanest person I know."

"That's your problem," I said. "Do you love him?"

Jessie took a sip of her wine and looked over at me thoughtfully. "I love you," she said.

"That's not what I asked."

"I know, but it's the only thing I'm sure about. And it doesn't matter. I'm going to marry him."

"I know," I said.

"Winslow's a good man. He wants children, and so do I."

I nodded, but something in her words stung me. The same way they had when I learned of her and Kenny Brenke all those years ago.

Just then, The Win walked in carrying two bottles of Bacardi Rum.

"*Henry!*" he said loudly. The Win said everything loudly. "You made it, good, good! Jess said you had homework and something about breaking in a new roommate."

He didn't wait for a reply. The Win never waited for a reply. He walked over to Jessie, kissed her cheek, and headed for the bar at the far corner of the room. He began mixing drinks with the rum, his eyes fixed on Jessie.

"How about a man's drink, Hen? Rum and Coke, right?" he said to me, his eyes still on Jessie. "Of course, you've heard the good news. It's a hell of a thing, don't you think? But that's what you do when you finally find your soul mate." He raised his glass to Jessie. "Cheers," he said.

I smiled and raised a glass to the both of them.

The Win sat down next to Jessie, put his arm around her shoulders, and kissed her several times on the cheek. No doubt, the parade of affection was for my benefit.

"Marriage isn't for everyone," he said, "especially when you're surrounded by all those State girls, eh Hen? I know at Michigan, I wouldn't have wanted to be tied down." He winked at me and then kissed Jessie again. "So we're thinking April. Work for you, Hen?"

I nodded.

The Win wasn't a big man, he was just loud. His big head and stocky frame made him appear larger than he actually was. He had patchy gray hair, which he wore cut short, and he had no neck to speak of. He reminded me of a pit bull that was more bark than bite.

"I ran into my army buddy the other day," The Win said to me. "He was over there in '66."

Of course, he meant Vietnam. Interestingly, The Win always ran into one of his military pals a couple days before seeing me. It was surprising how many vets he knew for someone that never done a day for Uncle Sam. *Too young for Korea and too old for Vietnam* is what he told everybody.

"He was telling me that things were a lot different in '66 than they are now and when you were there. He said there's no discipline and a lot of drug use."

I thought about replying, but I wanted to see how long I could go without speaking to him.

"You know what I'm talking about," he said. "As an officer, you probably saw a lot of that. I hear there's hardly a chain of command anymore. No respect for officers, everybody is on drugs. It's the reason we haven't been successful. I'll tell you what, we're in over our heads over there, but I guess that's not your fault. Nothing you could've done about it."

"Gosh, Hen, it's nice to know that you're not the one that fucked things up over there," said Jessie to my rescue.

"I didn't mean it like that," he said. "I'm only saying that things over there are getting out of control. I read the papers. I watch the news. Ask Henry, he'll tell you," he said, pointing at me. "Now there's talk of Cambodia."

My mind raced back to Colonel Glasson. *This war will be fought in Cambodia, gentlemen*, I remembered him saying to Flanny and me.

"Remember, honey, this isn't baseball where you play for nine innings and then it's over. This is for real," said The Win.

With her eyebrows pinched and her nostrils flaring, Jessie sent The Win a biting look.

The Win's eyes widened.

"I didn't mean—"

"Don't be condescending!" she barked at him.

"I'm sorry, honey. I didn't mean it like that. You know I value your opinions. But I know you understand the importance—"

"Now you're patronizing me!" she said, fuming. She crossed her arms and legs. Then looking at me, she said calmly, "I'm sorry, Hen. I didn't know my fiancé was going to turn out to be such an *asshole*."

I did enjoy watching her berate him.

"See, Hen," The Win said, raising his glass to me. "It's like we're married already. Now all we need is the license to fight." Then turning to Jessie, he said sweetly, "I'm sorry, honey. You're right. Let's talk about something else besides the war. I'm sure Henry's had enough of it."

"That's fine," she agreed.

"So what would you like to talk about, sweetheart?"

"I was thinking about getting a job," she said, glancing back and forth between The Win and me. "There's an opening for a teacher's assistant at the high school. You don't have to have a lot of qualifications, and it's only part time. It doesn't pay a lot, but I think I might enjoy it."

"You know you don't have to work, sweetheart," said The Win.

"I know," she said, "but I can only watch so many soaps, honey. It would give me something to do during the day while you're at work."

The Win glanced quickly over at me and then back to Jessie. "I'm not sure if that's the kind of thing you want to be doing," he said skeptically. "But don't you worry, I'll find something for you."

I fully expected her to protest, but she didn't. Instead, she gave him an acquiescent kiss on the cheek.

"Well, I'm glad that's settled," said The Win. "But as I was saying, Hen, I ran into my marine buddy the other day," said The Win, looking at Jessie just long enough to secure a permissive glance. "And he said that he finished his tour with over a hundred CKs—amazing, huh?"

The Win was referring to confirmed kills, probably the least accurate and most overly misused statistic of the entire war.

"Confirmed kills, you mean?" I asked, playing naïve.

"What else?" he said.

"Oh, so your buddy was a sniper," I said, baiting him.

The Win gave me a curious look, which told me he was about to bite.

"No, I don't think so," he said, shaking his head. "I believe he was a company commander in the infantry. But I'm pretty sure he wasn't a sniper. Why?"

And I had him—this might be fun, I thought.

"It's just that a confirmed kill, or a CK as you call it," I explained, "is a record kept by sniper teams when a witness, usually an officer, confirms that the sniper hit his mark. And then it's logged for statistical purposes. I didn't think the infantry logged any of their individual kills, but maybe they do."

"Maybe," said the Win in an uneasy voice. "Or maybe it was because he was a company commander, or did some sniper work over there," he added.

"Or *maybe* your buddy is full of shit," I said, chuckling.

The Win gave me a menacing look. I could tell the remark had caught him off guard. Until now, I had never questioned his or any of his buddies' credibility. I was feeling the rum, and I had the sudden urge to spar with the bastard. He might be able to turn Jessie on and off, but he didn't have any control over me.

"You're not calling my buddy a liar, are you?" he said in a slightly threatening tone.

"Of course not," I said coolly. "That's just the way it is over there, Win. Grunts chat about their kills—how many gooks they knocked off, how many they were going to knock off."

I had serious doubts about any of it.

"I don't think my buddy would make it up," he said.

"Which buddy are you talking about?" Jessie asked him.

The Win's eyes and irritation shifted from me to Jessie. "It's somebody you don't know," he said sharply.

"What's his name?" Jessie pressed.

"I told you, you don't know him." From the annoyed look on his face, I was convinced that his buddy probably didn't exist, but I had decided let to him off the hook. Jessie, however, was looking to finish him off.

"How in the hell do you know? Maybe you've mentioned his name before! Just tell me his damned name for Christ sake!"

"Tim Fitzgerald!" said The Win. "I told you. You don't know him!"

It was as good of a name as any; I certainly didn't have any reason to question it. I suppose The Win didn't get where he was without spreading around a little bullshit once in a while.

"Tim Fitzgerald?" Jessie said to him. "*Tim Fucking Fitzgerald?*"

"Yes, for crying-out-loud! You don't know him!" The Win leaned forward, the frustration rising red from beneath his cheeks.

"Tim Fitzgerald, that's the best you can do. Why not *F. Scott Fitzgerald?*"

"He's reading the goddamned *Great Gatsby,*" she said to me. "He read a little to me last night, for Christ sake!"

Suddenly, The Win no longer looked like the sophisticated accounting executive boasting a huge expense account and a corner office. Instead, he sat staring at the floor, his mouth half open, a blank expression on his face.

"It's really not important," I said.

I finished my drink and tried hard to think of something other than Vietnam to talk about that perhaps The Win might find interesting when, all at once, he snatched the empty glass from my hand.

"I think we could both use another drink," he said.

When he returned, he handed me a fresh drink and sat back down on the sofa next to Jessie.

"You ever kill anyone?" he said.

The question surprised me. I glanced over at Jessie who appeared equally taken aback.

"Pardon me?" I said.

"Did you ever kill anyone," he repeated, "in Vietnam?"

"No," I said, shaking my head. "I never killed anyone in Vietnam."

Chapter Twenty-Five

June 1985

"Daddy," Emily whispers from the doorway, "is it morning yet?"

Glancing at his watch, he smiles at her. "No, honey, it's only five thirty."

"Can I sleep with you until the real morning?"

"If it's all right with your mother," he says, glancing over at the empty side of the bed.

"Where's Mommy?" says Emily as he pulls her up onto the bed.

It's a fair question, he thinks.

"I suppose she left this morning," he says.

"But you said it's not morning yet."

"You got me there," he says, feeling foolish for walking into that one. "Well, it's still morning, but most people are still sleeping in this part of morning."

"But not Mom?" she says, her eyebrows bent curiously.

"Right, but not your mother," he says.

Emily crawls up next to him, laying her head on his chest.

"Good night, honey," he says.

"Don't you mean good morning?" she replies.

The sky outside the hotel room was a sickly gray and threatening rain, but it beat the hell out of the sweltering heat and I welcomed it.

I didn't catch the name of the town I was in, or perhaps I just didn't remember it, but I knew I was less than an hour from Boise.

I had no plans nor any ideas about what I was going to do when I arrived. Since Flanny's death, I had carried with me the memory of his dying wishes. My only thought was to find his widow, Claire, but if she had moved or remarried, it might be impossible to track her down. I had no idea where to look for Claire, but I promised myself that I would make every effort, and who knows, I might get lucky.

Luck didn't come by way of the phonebook, and sadly that was my only idea. There were numerous listing for *Flanagan*, a few for a *C. Flanagan* and one for a *C. L. Flanagan*, but none knew a Daniel or Claire Flanagan.

When at last I ran out of phone numbers, I decided to find the library to see if there were any service records for local boys killed in action—again hoping to get lucky.

It didn't take me long to find the Boise Public Library. Welcomed by the smell of musty old books, I made my way past the circulation desk and through a canyon of ceiling-high shelves lined with books on architecture.

It was eerie the way the microfiche machine stopped precisely on the photograph of Chief Warrant Officer Daniel E. Flanagan dressed to the nines in his Class-A Dress Uniform. For several minutes, I stared down at the picture, trying to reconcile it with the images of Flanny in my mind. Except for maybe the eyes, he only resembled the man I had known. Beneath the photo was a single-column obituary written in blurblike fashion recounting Flanny's life.

Assuming the names and dates were correct, there wasn't much in the obit that said anything about the man I knew, which left me feeling hollow and regretful. Hollow for not knowing him better than I had and regretful for not knowing much about his life outside of Vietnam. Although Flanny never talked about anyone other than his son and Claire, as close as we had been, I couldn't help but think that I should've known more.

I scribbled all the relevant names down on a piece of scratch paper and went to find a phonebook.

If luck be a lady, it wasn't Darlene Loomis. After losing her first husband to some type of surgical botch-up, her son Danny to Vietnam, her second husband to a heart attack, and finally her son Michael to a motorcycle accident, Darlene died of breast cancer in April of last year, Paula Arden—Darlene's sister—informed.

"Sometimes the sun just don't shine for some, if you know what I mean," said Paula after passing on the disheartening family history. "Two husbands and two sons all in a matter of seven years. It's a damn shame is what it is. Now you say you were some kind of friend of Danny's from the war?"

"Yeah," I said. "I was hoping to locate his widow, Claire, and perhaps his gravesite," I said, feeling suddenly uneasy asking about a *gravesite*.

"I'm sorry, Mr.—"

"Allen," I said. "Henry Allen."

"Right, Mr. Allen. I'm sorry, but I just don't remember. I'll tell you what, though. I think I know where you can find her. I know she used to work as a hygienist for a dentist by the name of Blanton."

"You wouldn't happen to have an address?"

"Oh, it's probably easiest if you just call his office. Let me look it up for you," she said.

A few moments later, she returned and gave me the number for Dr. Blanton's office. She told me it wasn't far from downtown, but it would be best to call first. I thanked her for all her help and was about to hang up when she asked me to hold on. "Didn't you want to know about his gravesite?"

"Yes, I almost forgot."

"Well, it's been a while, but I do remember the funeral. It was a lovely service, so patriotic. I remember Claire had a lot to do with that. It was a beautiful day for January, that's when it was. New Year's Day, I think. Anyway, I remember Claire trying to get him a spot at the military reserve, but they wouldn't take any new veterans, so she had him buried up on Morris Hill off of Latah. It's a lovely place and cost Claire a fortune, but she insisted."

"Morris Hill, great," I said.

"If you see Claire, please send her my regards," said Paula.

"I'll be sure to," I said.

The thought of actually speaking to Claire, now that she had become a reality and not just some obscure seventeen-year-old image in my mind, began to generate some anxiety inside me—enough for me to take a few moments to plan what I was going to say.

When I had thought about it long enough, I realized that I didn't have any idea what to say.

"Good afternoon, Dr. Blanton's office," said a young female voice.

"Hello," I said.

"Hello, this is Dr. Blanton's office. May I help you?"

"May-may . . ." I stuttered nervously into the phone. "May I speak to Claire, please?" I said, finally catching my voice.

There was a short pause on the line and then the woman said, "Yeah, just a minute. I think she's available . . . yes, hold please."

I didn't understand my sudden uneasiness, but it was almost overwhelming. My body began shaking uncontrollably as I anxiously waited to hear her voice.

"This is Claire," she said. Her voice came soft and unassuming, calming even, and much like I had imagined it might sound.

"Hello, Claire," I said. "You don't know me, but my name is Henry Allen." Pausing, I hoped for a hint of recognition, but instead there was only silence. Finally, I felt compelled to speak again. "Claire, I was a friend—"

"I know who you are, Henry," she said before I could finish. "I'm very pleased to hear from you. It's just that you've taken me by surprise."

"I'm sorry, that wasn't my intention. For so long I've been meaning to call you, but I . . ." I paused, my words fading along with the sentiment. There was really no point now.

"Actually, for a long time, I thought about getting a hold of you, Henry. It's just that things change so fast and time goes by and you start thinking that you're going to get around to it and—"

"I understand," I interrupted. "Really, I understand. I know you're working now, but I'm in town a couple days, and I wondered if we could meet. I would really like to talk to you."

"Oh, that would be wonderful. Could you come by the house . . ." She hesitated, adding, "yes, that should be fine," as if convincing herself.

"Are you sure?" I asked, sensing the uncertainty.

"Of course, it's fine. It'll be great," she said. She gave me directions to her house, and I agreed to meet her at around six. It would give me plenty of time to check into the motel that Claire had suggested and to clean up a bit. Before pleasantly saying good-bye, she told me that she'd see if Danny Jr. (or DJ as she called him) may be there, but she couldn't make any promises as he was spending the day with friends. "High school seniors," she said. "They're never home."

———

What the *Sleepy Bear Inn* lacked in amenities, it more than made up for in location. Not far from the motel, I found a small but lively mall, featuring a classic *JC Penny* and a swankier *Bon Marche.* I picked up socks and underwear, a polo shirt, a pair of khaki pants, and a new pair of stylish white high-top sneakers that I was certain ole Eddie would envy.

By five o'clock, I had showered, shaved and dressed when the phone rang. I thought it must be the front desk, but to my surprise, it was Claire.

"Hi, Henry," she said. "I'm glad I caught you. Lowell, my husband, just got home—he drives a truck, and has been on the road for the better part of the week. Anyway, I told him you were coming over, and he suggested that I make dinner. So I wanted to find out if there is anything in particular you're partial to."

"Oh, that's kind of you, really. I can eat anything," I said. "I hope I'm not imposing. I don't want to be any trouble, especially since your husband has been away."

"Absolutely not," she said. "It's no trouble at all, I'd, we'd love to have you. I just wanted to make sure it was all right with you if we had dinner. It's nothing fancy, that's for sure—Lowell will tell you that about anything I cook," she laughed.

"That sounds terrific," I said.

"Great, then I'll see you in a little while," she said before hanging up.

As the first drops of rain speckled my windshield, I pulled into the driveway of a small ranch-style house in desperate need of some new siding. I parked behind a blue Ford Escort with a bumper sticker that read: *Proud Mother of a Boise Senior High School Student*. I half expected to see a semitruck parked in the yard or somewhere along the street, but there wasn't one.

Claire met me at the door, greeting me at first with an awkward handshake, but then she hugged me like an old friend. Despite her sharp features, her smile was warm and welcoming. She was thin, but the housedress she wore hid any aspect of her frame. Scattered bobby pins held back lengthy brown hair revealing timeless green eyes. Her beauty was more natural than plain, and I could tell she was a lot prettier than she let herself be.

"It's so nice to finally meet you," she said. "Come on in and have a seat. I'm fixing spaghetti and trying not to make a lot of noise—Lowell's still sleeping. I haven't heard from DJ yet, but I suspect when he gets hungry, he'll stroll on home."

I sat down at the small kitchen table next to a large rain-splashed window that looked out over the driveway. Claire stirred a couple cans of tomato paste into a large pot of simmering sauce while I sipped from a can of Budweiser she had offered me. I made small talk about the weather, my trip, and some simple things about myself.

"So what kind of law did you practice in Michigan?"

"Divorce mostly," I replied.

"I guess that's big business these days," she said.

"Sadly so," I said.

"Danny always was a good judge of people."

"Yeah, well I—"

"Claire!" a man's voice bellowed from another room.

"He sure had Lowell pegged," said Claire, rolling her eyes. She then shouted back at him, "What honey? We have company!"

There was no reply, but a few seconds later, a heavyset man entered the kitchen wearing nothing more than a pair of faded orange Boise Senior High School sweatpants. Without a word, he ambled over to the refrigerator and helped himself to a can of Budweiser.

"Lowell!" said Claire. "We have company!"

"Oh, sorry," Lowell said and then, turning to me, he introduced himself as Lowell Finley, extending a greasy hand to me.

"I meant, put a shirt on," said Claire.

"Oh right," he said, glancing down at his large belly and then he quickly shuffled out of the kitchen.

"I'm sorry about that," said Claire when he had gone.

"So Danny and Lowell knew each other?" I said.

"Oh yes," she said, nodding. "They were in the same class in high school and a couple years ahead of me. I dated Lowell before I ever knew Danny. Lowell was a football player at Boise High. We all went to Boise High."

"God, that was a long time ago," she said. "Lowell and I went together his senior year. Of course, he dumped me just before his graduation. I don't think I was too broken up over it. Lowell was going to play football at Boise State, but that summer, he messed up his knee. He went to work for this trucking outfit the following year. Danny worked there too. That's how we met."

"So you met Danny through Lowell?"

"I suppose," she said, pausing. "It was at their company picnic. Lowell really wanted me back by then. He invited my friend Phyllis and me to the picnic. At that time, I didn't want anything to do with him," she whispered, peering through the kitchen doorway. "And Phyllis knew Danny through the gal he'd been living with. I remember how funny he was, telling Phyllis and me this story about how he became a truck driver." She let out a sudden burst of laughter, causing her to spill some of the sauce she was pouring.

"It's silly, really. Danny said he'd been standing on Front Street in downtown Boise when a big semitruck backed into the side of a building. The driver was trying to back up into a narrow alleyway so he could unload it. He was so upset that he walked right off the job, leaving the truck there blocking traffic. A police officer came along and assumed Danny was driving. He demanded that Danny remove the truck immediately. Danny had never driven a semi before, but that didn't stop him from climbing up inside the cab and moving it out of the way. That's not all, Danny went ahead and backed the trailer into the alley without a hiccup."

"Sounds like Flanny," I said.

"The policeman was very impressed. In fact, he told Danny that he didn't have the heart to write him a ticket, which he said would cost him about a hundred dollars and his license. Danny told the policeman that it was just as well, because he didn't have either one."

We both laughed.

"The way Danny told it, it was much funnier," said Claire.

"It's pretty funny the way you tell it," I said.

"It's what made me fall in love with him . . . right then and there . . . I was . . ." she said, her voice fading. "He'd told me he had broken it off with the girl he'd been living with and moved out. I didn't know him very well, but by the time the picnic was over with, I'd gotten his name, number, and a date for Saturday night."

Claire put a heaping mound of spaghetti on the plate in front of me and then called Lowell for dinner. After setting out a can of Parmesan cheese and a plate of garlic bread, she sat down across from me.

"God, sometimes it seems like only yesterday," she said. "Maybe it's because DJ's becoming more and more like him every day. He's so smart, Henry, and he's always been able to fix things, from his tricycle to his truck. Now he's gotten into racing—cars, that is. I'm sorry he's not here. No telling when he will roll in these days."

"If he rolls in at all," said Lowell from the kitchen doorway.

He was still wearing the same faded sweatpants, but had covered himself with a bright orange Boise State Broncos tee shirt that his gut had long since outgrown. His thick black hair was wet and slicked back from what I suspect was a recent shower.

Lowell plopped himself down in the chair next to Claire and began shoveling in forkfuls of spaghetti.

"Take some time to breathe, honey," she said. "I don't want you to choke."

"Sorry," said Lowell. Then looking at me over his plate of food, he said, "So you're a buddy of Dan Flanagan?"

"Yeah, we flew together in the war."

"Dan was all right, I guess, decent trucker. Of course, I don't know how he was at flying."

"He was the best pilot I ever saw," I said, nodding to Claire.

Lowell looked at Claire and then at me. "I'm sure he was until he went and got himself killed."

"What do you know about it, Lowell?" said Claire.

"I know a lot," said Lowell, shaking a piece of garlic bread at her. "I know he didn't come home when he could have. I know that he left you and the boy in a hell of a way. Remember how tough it was?"

"It was a war, for crying out loud. It was tough on everyone, Lowell. Life's tough."

Lowell spiked his bread down hard onto his plate where it bounced onto the floor.

"Your boy," he said to me, "*chose* to stay away. Then he left everyone else to clean up the mess. I'm sorry, mister, but I don't see how you coming around here stirring up ghosts does any of us any good. Dan Flanagan may have been some kind of hotshot flyboy over there, but he wasn't shit here."

"Lowell, you're out of line," said Claire. "Now just wait—"

"No, you wait!" shouted Lowell, pointing his finger at her. "Who did you come crying to after they brought his dead ass home and you didn't know what to do? Who helped you pick up the pieces and helped you raise *his* kid? You seem to forget that you wouldn't have a pot to piss in if it wasn't for me. What did Dan Flanagan ever do for you?"

Lowell picked up his plate of spaghetti and headed for the doorway, hesitated, and then turned back to look at me.

"Mister," he said, "I don't know you from Adam. You seem like a nice fellow, but I won't sit here and listen to talk about a man that's been nothing but a burden to this family—alive and dead. I don't have anything against that war, even as screwed up as it was," he added, glancing over at Claire. "A lot of good boys fought in that war—hell, I would've gone except for my knee. But war or no war, the fact remains: he was supposed to come home, and he didn't, and then he went and got himself killed."

"You don't know anything about it, Lowell!" said Claire angrily. "It was his job! He was in the army, for crying out loud! It was what he did, Lowell. And he was a good—"

"Ah!" said Lowell, waving at her dismissively. "Remember, I've heard the stories. You forget I was here when that general what's-his-name came around." He glanced back at me. "But all you goddamned army fellows are alike. You never want to admit that anyone fucked up. Anyone that got killed over there is a goddamned hero—that doesn't make them any less dead. He's still dead, right?"

Lowell didn't wait for an answer, but turned and walked out the doorway. A few moments later, I heard a door slam. Outside, raindrops began pelting at the window, adding an awkward rhythm to the already difficult air.

"I'm so sorry," said Claire after several long minutes. "Lowell carries a lot of anger. I suppose, for a while, I was angry too. I was frightened about what I was going to do without Danny. Lowell was a big help back then, and I love him for it, but eventually I understood that Danny was only doing his job, doing what he loved to do."

Claire leaned her head on her hands and stared vacantly out the window. Her sudden distance made me feel even more uncomfortable than I already was.

"So Colonel Glasson came to see you?"

Claire didn't reply but continued to stare out the window. Then, as if something unseen had roused her, she looked over at me.

"Yes, it was about three or four years ago," she said. "I think he's a general now, at the Pentagon. A very nice man, General Glasson. He sat right there where you're sitting now. He said that he'd wanted to see me for some time. He said that there was a lot more to the report we originally received. He said he couldn't go into specifics as a lot of it was still classified at the time, but he said Danny had done real good, saved a lot of lives. He said that no matter what the reports say, Danny died a great hero. I told him I appreciated him coming all the way out here from Washington to tell me that, but somehow I think I already knew it, even before he went off to the war."

Claire stood up and began collecting the dishes. She hadn't touched anything on her plate. I tried to think about what it must have been like for her when she got the news about Flanny's death. It had been hard for me, and I had known the truth.

"I was with him when he died," I said in little more than a whisper.

Claire didn't speak but stopped collecting dishes and stared intently at me.

"Before he . . . died," I said, struggling for the words, "he wanted me to tell you something for him. He wanted to tell you that the whole time he was thinking about you and Zion. I'm not sure what he meant by it, at least the Zion part, but he made me to promise to tell you."

Closing her eyes, Claire smiled, and a few tears slid down the side of her face.

"I'm sorry," I said. "I'm so sorry it took so long. I'm sorry I didn't tell you sooner."

"Don't be. I'm glad it was now—I needed it to be now," she said, wiping her eyes. "It's been hard for me lately. DJ's all but grown up, and he'll be moving out soon—going to college or someplace. He's rarely around as it is. He and Lowell hardly speak to one another anymore, which is only a little less than Lowell and I do. We've been married going on fifteen years now, and we barely know each other. We got married for all the wrong reasons. At the time, it made a lot of sense—being a widow with a baby. I believed it was the right thing to do. Now . . ." She paused, shaking her head. "Now, I'm not so sure. Whatever the reasons were back then, they no longer exist today, and they haven't for some time."

Claire began collecting dishes again.

"Zion National Park was where Danny asked me to marry him," she said. "I didn't suspect a thing. He'd planned this camping trip for weeks. Bought all this equipment and found out the best places to hike. To tell you the truth, I was a little skeptical about my outdoor abilities, but it was perfect. The weather was gorgeous, and so was the scenery. We weren't there more than a few hours when he proposed to me. We'd hiked up the side of this enormous cliff and were looking out over this vast canyon when he popped the question. Said he was going to do it on the last day, but he told me he couldn't wait any longer."

Claire shook her head and giggled.

"Of course I said yes, and it was the best three days of my life," she said, tears spilling from her eyes.

"And they were the best of his, Claire." I said. "Again, I'm sorry that it took me so long."

Claire shook her head again and wiped the tears from her eyes.

"I am so glad it was now," she said.

"I didn't mean to cause any trouble with you and Lowell," I said.

"Don't be ridiculous. Whatever set Lowell off has nothing to do with you and everything to do with me. He'll never understand that I will always love Danny—I won't apologize, and he won't forgive me for it. So the way we live with it is never to talk about it. Whenever it does come up, like with you or with the general, Lowell can't handle it and he pouts, which is what I'm sure he's doing right now. I think DJ reminds him too much of Danny, and that's something Lowell has had a hard time with. I know it's been hard on DJ, who is always asking Lowell and me about his father. That's why I wish DJ could've been here tonight. To meet you, to know someone who knew his father—someone besides Lowell and me."

"I would've liked that," I said.

Chapter Twenty-Six

December 1964

"I can't hear anything," I said to Jessie who was lying next to me in the snow.

"They hum," she replied. "You're not listening hard enough."

"You're crazy, they don't make noise. Who told you that anyway?"

"Nobody, but I can hear it—don't you hear it?" she asked looking over at me, a cloud of breath bursting from the hood of her parka with each word.

"No, I don't hear a thing. They're northern lights, not northern sounds. I really think you're hearing things." For several seconds there was silence, and I stared back up at the dancing green and red lights as they wisped across the starry sky. I didn't hear anything. I never heard anything, and for the past couple of years, I had been listening.

"Maybe you're right," she said finally.

"I really am trying to hear something," I said, glancing over at her.

"No, I don't mean that, I really do hear a hum. I'm talking about me being crazy. I really think I might be crazy—how do you know if you are crazy, Hen?"

"What are you talking about?"

"I mean if you're crazy, how can you *tell* if you're crazy? Do crazy people know if they're crazy, or do they always think they're normal until somebody else tells them they're crazy?"

"What?" I said, sitting up and pulling the ski mask up off my face.

Jessie too sat up.

"You think I'm crazy, Hen?" she said from inside the fur-lined hood of her parka. "I mean really crazy?"

"Crazy on account of what," I said.

"On account of everything," she said.

"Well, if it's on account of you hearing the aurora borealis humming, I'm going to have to go with crazy." I laughed.

"Oh, you!" she said and then playfully shoved me. "I'm telling you, they hum!" We both laughed and then, a few minutes later, we were wrestling around in the snow. I was able to roll on top of her, pinning her arms to the ground. A couple of years ago, I might not have been able to hold her down, but I had grown enough to where I could outmuscle any girl—even a jock-girl like Jessie.

"Chinese spit torture!" I shouted and then let a spitball dangle from my lips a few inches above her face. Jessie closed her eyes, twisting and screaming, trying desperately to free herself.

"That's so gross!" she cried out.

"Let go of me, Hen, that's so gross!" she screamed.

"How can you, of all people, say that's gross?" I said after sucking the spit back into my mouth. "Only last week, I saw you making out with Robert Willingham. You sure didn't seem to mind—"

I heard a quick suck and then a blow just before something warm and wet hit me hard in the right eye. I went to wipe my face and, with her free hand, Jessie hit me fiercely upside the head, knocking me over into the snow.

"Ow!" I cried out, holding my head.

"Don't ever do that again!" she shouted viciously at me.

"I'm sorry," I said. "I was only fooling."

Jessie had walloped me good, enough to make my ears ring. Wiping away the snow and the spit from my face, I stood up over her.

"I'm sorry," I said again. "I didn't mean anything by it."

Jessie pulled back her hood.

"Are you all right?" she asked.

"Yeah, I'm fine," I said, although my ears were still ringing.

"I hate being held down like that."

"I guess so," I said, rubbing my head.

"Don't ever do it again," she said firmly.

"I won't," I said sincerely. "Let's go, we have to be back in a couple hours. It's Christmas, remember?"

It was only four thirty in the afternoon, but it felt more like midnight with the darkness and the northern lights dancing and swirling above us. We had plans to check out a cabin not too far up a nearby trap line while my mother was home preparing a Christmas feast complete with a roasted goose, pumpkin pie, and all the fixings. JT was in Anchorage with his girlfriend, and after Spenser's drunken tirade last summer, he felt it best that Jessie stay with us for the winter school break. Jessie wanted to use our time together tracking down every clue from her grandmother's diary—cold or Christmas be damned.

Jessie now believed adamantly that Spenser had killed her grandmother and the O'Brien bothers all those years ago. Although I readily supported her efforts, I didn't believe that any good could come of it. I constantly worried about Jessie living with Spenser, even when JT was around. However, she was convinced that we would eventually find more evidence against Spenser. We had already trekked nearly every trap line in the valley and had discovered nothing. I wasn't sure what we could possibly find in the cold and dark, but that didn't matter to Jessie. She was determined to *nail Granddaddy*, as she said.

"So where are we going?" asked Jessie, trudging along behind me.

"The other side of the tracking station," I said.

NASA had built a huge facility for tracking satellites and rockets. Tom said that they had built a couple moving dish antennas. He had been hauling pieces of them in a helicopter for the past couple of months, and we had all seen them driving in and out of the site with giant semitrucks. It was the reason I had saved this trip for last, as

I didn't want to draw attention from the tracking station and all the security.

"Cool," said Jessie.

I stopped and glanced back at her. She had buried herself deep inside the hood of her parka and was following the beam from my flashlight, the snow crunching rhythmically beneath our feet.

"What?" she said when she saw that I had stopped.

"Nothing, just checking on you. Where's Saucy?" I knew she had to be around somewhere, and I wanted to find her before she leaped out of the darkness and scared the shit out of us. I shined the flashlight into the shadowy woods on each side of the highway, calling for her.

A few seconds later, the sound of a breaking branch came from just off the roadside ahead of us and then, shortly after that, my flashlight caught the reflection from her eyes.

"Come here, girl!" called Jessie, but Saucy was already bounding toward us. She gave us a welcoming woof before dashing off again.

"Stay close, Sauce," I called after her.

The entrance to *the site*, as Tom called it, was well plowed and made for an easy walk. We crossed over a narrow bridge that both Jessie and I had watched being built last summer, but because of all the activity, we never had the courage to venture across.

On the other side of bridge, the road veered suddenly to the right, and we could see a couple of rectangular buildings brightly illuminated by hundreds of lights.

"Wow!" said Jessie.

"It's huge," I said.

We both stopped, Saucy too, all of us gazing ahead at the dazzling lights. I noticed a couple more smaller light clusters, one farther beyond the main group and another higher up on the ridge to the right of us. Amidst the main group of lights was a row of three giant white dishes, all supported by some type of hydraulic swivel that enabled each one to move in all directions. The three of them were pointing skyward, giving them an imposing grail-like appearance. The largest dish had to be over forty feet high and at least thirty feet in diameter.

It stood between the other two, which were roughly half the size. A triangular scaffolding of sorts protruded skyward out of each dish, and a flashing red light topped each one.

"I've never seen anything like it," I said.

"What are those thingies?" asked Jessie.

"They're antennas, I think for tracking satellites across the sky. I didn't realize that they were so big. They move, you see. I think as satellites orbit the earth. I think they might even track the rockets to the moon. I'm not sure. Tom said he helped move pieces of them around in his chopper."

"Really?" said Jessie, pulling off her hood. "Daddy says all that moon-shot stuff is a spoof."

"Oh yeah, well that doesn't look like a *spoof*," I said, pointing at the monstrous dishes.

"Look, up there," she said, pointing toward the lights on the ridge. "There's another one."

It was different from the others. It wasn't a dish at all, but rather a square consisting of rows of coils making it appear torchlike.

"Wow," I said.

"With all the lights, it looks like a city," said Jessie.

"Yeah, and look," I said, pointing straight up the road.

Directly ahead of us, at what looked to be the entrance to the site, was a small square building with a flat snow-covered roof. A dull glow of amber light came from a giant window at the front.

"It's a guard shack," I said.

"Are we going to be able to get through?" asked Jessie.

"Probably not, but I know what we can do," I said. "Follow me."

I climbed over the waist-high snow berm on the right side of the road and made my way down the sharp embankment. Jessie and Saucy followed. Then I trudged my way through the knee-high snow until I reached the edge of the thick birch forest that lined the roadway. Among the trees, the snow wasn't nearly as deep, and it didn't take long for my flashlight to uncover a narrow but well-packed trail that appeared to be a superhighway for rabbit and other forest critters.

"Where are we going?" asked Jessie with a bit of a whine in her voice.

I stopped and turned back toward her, pointing the beam of light directly inside the hood of her parka.

"Don't!" she snapped, quickly turning her head away.

"Sorry," I said. "I thought we'd head up the ridge a ways. I know a great place where we can get a better look at the whole site. It's on the way."

"How far is it? My feet are getting cold."

I shined the flashlight down at her worn leather boots laced high up her shins. They looked to be a couple sizes too big, and I could clearly see part of a wool sock poking through the toe of her left boot.

"It's not very far," I said. "We can warm your feet when we get there. Keep moving and maybe they'll warm up. You need new boots."

"Yeah, I need a new car too," she said.

"It shouldn't be too much farther."

The trail ran along the same ridge where Jessie had spied the torchlike antennae and was part of one of the many bubbling hills that enclosed the valley and the tracking station. The ridge actually separated the site from the Shit Towers, which got me thinking.

"Are you sure you haven't been here before?" I said, glancing back at Jessie.

"I don't think so," she said, stopping. "Why?"

"It's just that it's awful close to your place. It can't be more than a half mile up the side of the hill."

"Well, good then. If it's that close to a creek, maybe it's the place. How far is it from the O'Brien brothers' cabins?"

"Quite a ways—two to three miles or so on the opposite direction," I said. "And I don't remember a creek."

It had been a couple of years since I'd been up here, but the old cabin I remember was not too far from the top of the hill.

The trail led out of the forest to a small clearing high up on the ridge overlooking the entire valley. We stood for a minute staring silently down at the bright clusters of lights that seemed to mirror the stars high overhead. It looked to me to be what I imagined a moon station might look like.

"My feet aren't getting any warmer," said Jessie.

I shined the flashlight along the base of the far tree line until the spot of light illuminated a dark windowless cabin slunk heavy with snow—a single knotty-pine support pole fronted a rotting wooden door.

"There," I said, waving the light at the cabin and looking back at Jessie. "That's it. That's the cabin."

Jessie didn't say anything at first but instead took a couple steps forward and then, pulling off her hood, she stared intently at it. I could see her face in the glowing light from the valley, her eyes squinting and confused.

"No," she said adamantly. "It's not the place."

"How can you be so sure?" I said, jogging toward the cabin.

The door to the cabin was slightly ajar, and a tiny path leading to it indicated the comings and goings of tiny critters. Trappers and minors alike had used the cabin as a place to get warm on their journeys up and down the hills. I knew there would be matches and wood inside, and I could have a fire burning in a matter of minutes. I shoved the door. It broke loose from the ice and snow with a loud cracking sound, and then I waited for something to stir. I was glad to hear nothing.

Inside, the air was dry and musty, which caused me to sneeze. An old iron potbelly stove stood in one corner and a mattress-less bed leaned up against the wall in the other. The pitched ceiling sagged in the center from the snow load and too many long winters without repair, but the ridgepoles were still holding on, if only barely. I didn't see anything flowery as Vladimir had suggested, and the cabin was windowless. Nevertheless, it was a good place to thaw Jessie's frozen feet.

I found the box of matches in the top drawer of an old dresser next to the door and quickly loaded the stove with some dry kindling and split wood I found stacked neatly against the back wall. It wasn't long before I had a healthy fire. I was surprised that Jessie hadn't yet come inside.

I grabbed the flashlight and headed out the door where I saw both Jessie and Saucy still gazing down at the lights from the tracking station.

"What gives?" I shouted at her. "I got the fire going!"

Jessie didn't move.

"Jessie, come on!" I shouted. "I thought you wanted to warm your feet!"

It was enough for Saucy and she trotted on over, but Jessie still didn't move. I shut the door to the cabin and then walked on over to where they were standing.

"What's wrong, Jess?"

"I'm not going in there," she said. "It's not the place."

"Maybe not, but we can at least warm your feet."

"I'm not going in there," she said flatly.

"What about your feet?"

"They can freeze off, before I'll go in there."

"I don't understand, what's the big deal? I got a nice fire going in there, and we can warm up and then see if we can find any clues. I don't see—"

Jessie turned and then started walking back down the trail.

"Wait!" I said, "I'll go with you, but let me go put the fire out. I don't want to burn the cabin down."

"It'd be the best thing for that shithole," she sneered.

I wasn't sure what her problem was, but I guess she had her reasons. Back inside, the fire was roaring and the cabin was warming. What a waste, I thought. I shut the vent and the fluke then waited a few minutes to make sure the fire was dying. I was tucking the box of matches back into the top drawer of the dresser when I heard something small lightly hit the floor at my feet. A quick examination of the floor with the flashlight revealed nothing. It wasn't until I shined the light on top of the dresser that I made the discovery. There were a half dozen or so of them scattered across the top of the dresser. One must have fallen when I opened the drawer.

I pulled open the door and ran after Jessie. I caught up with her a short distance down the trail. She was sitting with her back against a black spruce tree, her bare foot between her hands.

"I can't feel them anymore," she said when I arrived.

I could tell she had been crying. I took her foot, opened my coat, and placed it beneath my armpit—an old survivor trick I had learned from Tom. Her toes were icy cold and felt a bit swollen, but I was sure she'd keep them. Although they'd be more than little sore once they completely thawed out.

When we were finally on our way again and heading back down the trail to a Christmas dinner, I glanced up and watched the greens, reds, pinks, and purples of the northern lights smudge their way like a dream across the starry night sky. I didn't hear a hum. I didn't hear any sound other than the crunching of the snow beneath our feet. Even so, I didn't believe Jessie was at all crazy, but something was terribly wrong. Something that we had left back there high on the ridge in that old cabin. Something that she didn't want to face, even if it meant losing her toes.

A shiver passed through me as I thought about what I had found back on the dresser. The mints I knew only Spenser to suck down, one after the other. I was beginning to believe that Spenser really was a monster, and I couldn't help but wonder if he had already gotten to Jessie.

Chapter Twenty-Seven

October 1973

Jessie's wedding to The Win finally happened in January of 1972, two weeks before I graduated from Michigan State University with a degree in political science and nearly two years to the day of their original engagement. I didn't know the details of all the delays, but I did know it had to do with Jessie.

When the day did finally arrive, it wasn't exactly the traditional holy affair, but rather a proceeding at the Genesee County Courthouse in downtown Flint, which gave it all the ambiance of a felony sentencing. However, it was followed by a reception dinner at a celebrated little Italian restaurant called *Mario's*—where, of course, the entire night, The Win never let anyone forget that he and the owner were the best of buddies. Not surprisingly, JT couldn't make it, as he was too busy framing an apartment complex in Anchorage for something as trivial as his only daughter's wedding. But Jessie's mother Sharon was there and gave her matriarchal blessing to The Win and the wedding, proclaiming that The Win was a perfect match for her daughter, which meant he was rich. Of course, she should know, as that same Genesee County Courthouse had a well-documented history of her own nuptial and antinuptial dispositions.

Following the wedding festivities, the newlyweds embarked on a three-week honeymoon to the Florida Keys where Jessie returned with a marvelous tan and a Pooka-shell necklace for me. I didn't see a whole lot of Jessie after the honeymoon. No doubt, The Win had something to do with that. I suspect the two were going through a transitional period where each were discovering the certain realities attached to the particular Genesee County Courthouse proceeding.

Sully and I had started law school at Wayne State University. We had been such great roommates at MSU, we decided to share the top floor of an old house outside of Detroit.

I got a job working a few nights a week as an auditor at a local hotel. The hours were shit, but it paid pretty well, and it was a nice supplement to my GI Bill. Sully worked part-time too—for his uncle, doing drywall. Between school and work, there was little time, but we did manage to meet on Friday afternoons at a neighborhood watering hole called *Donna's*. We watched all the ballgames there. The Tigers had lost in five to the A's in the American League Championship Series, so the World Series became more of an afterthought. But Jessie had insisted we watch the first game together, and she'd agreed to meet us there.

The game already started as Sully and I waited for Jessie at our usual corner of the bar drinking beer.

"So where's Mrs. Win?" asked Sully with a dry grin, brushing back his long golden locks from his eyes.

"That's *Mrs. The Win*," I said.

"Right," he chuckled.

Sully had gotten to know Jessie over the past couple of years, and they'd gotten on pretty well. I knew he genuinely liked her, and she him. I supposed that before she had strapped herself to The Win's star, Sully would've been her type. But then again . . .

"You know how she is," I said after taking a sip from my frosty mug of beer. "She's working at some middle school library now. Dedicated, I suppose, although I've never known her to be late for a ballgame."

"Is The Win coming?"

"No, but he's picking her up after, I guess."

"That's a shame," he snickered.

Sully also had the pleasure of spending some time with The Win, and he had found it amusing, to say the least. A political scientist by art, Sully was academically liberal and socially *understanding,* which meant he didn't have a lot of affection for the war or its sympathizers, but he wasn't too in love with war protesters either. Although he had strong opinions, he was rarely judgmental and he always seemed to have respect for me and my time in the service, despite his admissions that he had wished I had joined the Peace Corps rather than the army. In addition to all of that, Sully had a quick wit and a keen sense of humor and found everything about The Win amusing.

"Hasn't your politically scientific mind had about enough of him for one lifetime?" I said.

"Are you kidding me?" he said, rocking back on his barstool. "The man is a dilemma wrapped around an enigma, and as far the political science world goes, the man should be worshipped."

"Worshipped? I don't follow," I said, egging him on.

"The man is a political prism. Ideas go in, but they come out refracted and skewed."

"Wow, a political prism, huh? That's new, or did you say that about Nixon?"

"No, no, I said Nixon was a political predator. You remember it was all part of that predator-prey essay I wrote about the '68 election?"

"Oh, right."

"But he'd make a fine topic for an essay in an advanced political theories class, don't you think?"

"I don't know," I said and then gulped down the rest of my beer. I waved my empty mug at Gina, the busty bartender who was busy chatting up a couple of middle-aged autoworkers camped at the far end of the bar. I had been sweet on her since we had been coming here, and I enjoyed her attention. It was my new favorite pastime, although I had to put up with the shit from Sully.

"Gina!" I finally shouted when I wasn't getting anywhere waving the mug.

"You don't have to yell at her for god-sake," said Sully. "That's a sure way to scare her off."

"Fuck you," I whispered to him as Gina made her way slowly toward us.

"Another one, honey?" she asked sweetly with a pleasant little smile that I was sure was only for me.

"Yeah," I said, trying to sound casual. "You better find one for Sully here as well. You know what he's like when he gets thirsty, Gina."

"I do," she said to Sully with a wink, and then wickedly flashed the bastard *my* smile. All was forgiven when she turned back to me. She gently patted my arm and whispered, "Someone has to take care of the less fortunate."

Both Sully and I watched her walk away, our empty mugs dangling from her fingers, and her perpetual strawberry-blond hair swaying back and forth with every rhythmic step.

Gina was a pretty girl, her gray-blue eyes mischievous, her curves curving in all the right places, her top half just the slightest bit heavier than the bottom half, in the good way. I was sure Sully would agree with me that what made Gina stand out wasn't her good looks, but the way she moved around behind the bar. She was a pacing tiger, never in a hurry, her movements deliberately defined, seductive in nature and seemingly always ready to pounce. Of course, she never actually did pounce, but that's the way I saw it.

"Not bad, Allen, not bad at all," said Sully when Gina was out of earshot. "I mean—sheesh, she was practically groping you."

"You think so?"

Suddenly, someone grabbed me from behind, pulling me backward into a bear hug and showering me with kisses.

"I'll show you *groping*," said Jessie, running her hands along my chest and then sliding them down to my thighs. "So is this the wonder woman whose pants you've been trying to get into, Hen?" she said, nodding at Gina.

I was stunned silent by the remark, but Sully spoke up.

"That's her!" he announced with a smile.

"She's beautiful," said Jessie, nodding again at Gina. "And she was groping you?"

"You missed it," said Sully. "She was practically molesting him."

"Really?" said Jessie, sitting down on the barstool next to me.

"Yes, it's true. She was all over my arm, patted it and everything," I said, holding it up admiringly. "It really is my best arm. You can't blame her for wanting it the way she did. Look at this arm, it's beautiful."

We all laughed as Gina returned with two full mugs of beer.

"Did I miss something?" asked Gina, glancing at Jessie.

"No, no," said Jessie. "Henry here was just telling a joke."

"What's the joke, Henry?" said Gina, smiling at me.

"It's nothing," I said.

"I love a good joke," said Gina, then to Jessie, "Can I get you something, sweetie?"

"Yeah, the house white would be fine," said Jessie.

"I want to hear this joke when I get back," Gina said before slowly backing away.

"There you go. Now's your big chance, Henry," said Sully. "All you need now is a good joke."

"You know what they say, Hen," said Jessie, "laughter is the way to a woman's heart."

"I thought it was diamonds," I said, grabbing her ring finger and shaking it.

Jessie blushed and then, letting out a giggle, she said, "I think they're mutually exclusive."

"Here, here," said Sully, raising his glass to her, and then turning to me, he said, "You still need a joke, my friend. Otherwise, it's over."

"What do you mean by that?"

"I mean," said Sully, "it's like contracts class, you know? You made a promise, and now you must deliver. If you don't, she'll have no respect for you, and you'll be just another boring customer."

"Oh, come on. What kind of contract did I enter into?"

"An implied one, my friend. For god-sake, she fondled your arm," said Sully.

"But what if I don't know any jokes?"

"Everyone knows a joke," said Jessie. "And I know for a fact that you know some jokes—albeit *lame* ones." She glanced over at Sully. "In high school, he was famous for his lame jokes."

"I was not," I said defensively.

"Yes, he was," she said to Sully. "And come to think of it, they were all about poop."

"*Poop?*" inquired Sully, grinning.

"Yeah, poop, crap, shit—you know," said Jessie.

"That's not true," I said, shaking my head.

"It's true. Hen loved telling jokes about poop," she said and then glanced at me. "You know, Hen, I wouldn't go telling her any of your lame poop jokes. I'm not sure if that would win her over."

I did remember a couple of jokes involving *poop,* but they weren't all about poop. For the life of me, I couldn't think of one joke. I glanced down the bar and saw Gina coming toward us, and my mind went completely blank. I suddenly couldn't remember my name, let alone a joke. Gina set a glass of wine in front of Jessie and then looked over at me smiling. I realized she wasn't the only one; they were all looking at me.

"So tell me your joke," Gina said, patting my arm again.

I thought Jessie might blow wine through her nose. She was trying so hard not to laugh, and all I could think about was poop. Then, miraculously, something came to me. I remembered Flanny telling a joke a couple times—it always got a good laugh too. I just hoped I could tell it right.

"It's a little crude," I said to Gina.

"The more crude the better, honey. Look where I work," she said, waving her hand in a circle before resting it on my arm. Then her gray-blue eyes stared at me expectantly.

"There was this old Irishman named *Paddy*, see," I said in my richest Irish brogue. "He was sitting alone on a dock, his head slung low, crying into his beer. Walking by the dock and seeing him, a young boy asks curiously, *'Why do you look so sad, Paddy?'* Paddy wipes his eye and says to the boy, *'You see this dock, lad? I built this dock, post by post and plank by plank, and it's lasted for fifty years, it has. But do they think to call me Paddy the dock-builder?'* I glanced over at Sully and, shaking my head, I said, *'No, lad.'* Then turning to Jessie, I said, *'You see that ship there, lad? I built that ship—built it from aft to stern, I did. Built it with me own two hands, but do they think to call me Paddy the shipbuilder? No, no, lad,'* I said, shaking my head. And then, looking at Gina, I said, *'And you know, lad, I fished these waters for fifty years. For fifty years, I've caught more fish than any man in the village, but do they think to call me Paddy the fisherman? No, lad, they don't.'* Then all at once, Paddy began to cry again, *'But you fuck one goat!'"*

I heard all three of them erupt in laughter, but I saw only Gina. She was laughing hard enough to wipe a tear from her eye before finally having to leave and assist another customer.

"For god-sake, that was classic, my friend," said Sully, trying to cool his own laughter.

"That was hilarious," said Jessie, giggling. "Why couldn't you tell more jokes like that in high school? You might have been more popular," she added.

"I guess I didn't know any of those kinds of jokes in high school," I said. "I heard that one a few times from a good buddy of mine back in Vietnam. So," I said, raising my glass, "the laughs are on Daniel Flanagan—or Flanny, as we called him."

"Cheers, then," said Jessie, lifting her glass. "I've heard that name more than once. Here's to Flanny!"

"*Salut!*" said Sully. "I've heard the name too."

The three of us toasted to Flanny. I was a little sorry that I had brought such a somber note to an otherwise humorous moment, but Jessie put her arm around me and then Sully did too. And a few minutes later, we were all laughing again.

"I think you're in," said Jessie. "I think she really likes you."

"You say that like it surprises you that anyone ever could," I said, scowling at her.

"I didn't mean it like that," she said, slapping me playfully on the shoulder. "I'm just saying whatever you're doing is working, Hen. You know, next to waitresses, bartenders are the hardest game to bag."

"What do you mean by that?" I asked.

"I'm curious too," said Sully.

"Didn't you say that about preachers' kids?" I asked.

"No, I said that preachers' kids are the easiest," she said, grinning, "although you might've been the exception to the rule, Hen." She laughed and then, turning to Sully, she said, "I told Hen once that preachers' kids were the easiest to score, but he never got to second base."

"What's second base again?" I said, and we all laughed.

"So why are waitresses and bartenders so hard?" asked Sully.

"Because they're used to it," said Jessie. "They get hit on all the time, they're practically immune to it. So if you do make any headway, you have to have one hell of a show because they've heard it all before." Jessie's eyes moved to Gina who was making her way toward us. "But amazingly you're doing well, Hen," she whispered.

———

A couple hours later, our party had moved to a small table just off the bar. The conversation did better there against the loud droning sounds of the Series game on the television behind the bar. Through no small miracle, Gina had surprisingly decided to join us at the end of her shift.

"These two are so funny," Gina said to Jessie, casually waving a hand at Sully and me. "They come in here like clockwork every Friday talking about their law professors like they're monsters or something."

"That bad, huh?" said Jessie to Sully and me.

"Oh no, they're not all bad. We just have names for them," said Sully.

Jessie looked at me curiously.

"You know, for our torts professor, Drake, he's *Professor Drakula*," I said.

"And our crimes professor is Jack Thayer, who Henry deemed *Jack Thayer-ipper*," Sully chimed in.

Gina snickered, and Jessie laughed.

"There's also property with Professor Franklin, or I should say *Professor Franklinstein*," Sully continued. "Then, of course, there's my personal favorite, Professor Minton. He teaches contracts, and we affectionately refer to him as Professor *Ho Chi Minton*."

We all laughed.

"Did you come up with that one, Hen?" asked Jessie.

"No," I said. "Actually, Sully was the author of that one."

"Now that surprises me," she said, looking across the table at Sully. "I'd of thought you'd have more sympathy for that man. God, Sully, I thought you were a communist, for crying out loud." Jessie laughed as I watched an agonizing grimace cross Sully's face. I was pretty sure he was thinking that this was something The Win had put in her mind.

"I'm not a communist," he said to Jessie in an obviously defensive tone.

Jessie was still laughing until she realized he had been offended. "I'm sorry," she said. "I didn't mean anything by it. I thought that's what you studied at MSU—I take it that wasn't it?"

Jessie grinned sheepishly and then put her hand over her mouth in surprise.

"Had I known, Sully, I wouldn't have bought you those *red* pajamas for Christmas," she said in a burst of laughter.

Poor Sully hadn't been around Jessie enough to appreciate her vicious humor.

"What makes you think I was a communist?" he said sternly.

"I thought most political scientists were communists," said Jessie. "You don't exactly seem a fan of the war, and you didn't go to Vietnam like Hen, so it made me think you were a commie, that's all."

Jessie truly had a way with words. Her husband was a *political prism*, as Sully had put it, a piece of work certainly in his own right, but Sully was probably the least offensive person at the table.

"You were in Vietnam, Henry?" Gina asked me after quickly glancing at Jessie who was sitting beside her.

From the look on Sully's face, I could tell he had a lot to say, but he would yield to me. Not that I wanted to answer the question, everyone was divided on Vietnam these days. I had hoped that we would have had at least one date under our belt before having to address such a politically loaded question.

"Yeah," I said finally, "a couple years."

I couldn't tell whether her expression was one of sorrow or seriousness, as I knew this would be our moment of truth.

"My little brother is over there now," she said softly, looking at the three of us one at a time. "He joined the marines a while back. I'm not sure why, but he wanted to *get in the fight,* and as luck would have it, he was one of the last ones sent over. It's been nearly a year now, and we haven't heard much. When he first got there, he'd write us all the time. Now, well . . . nothing but a quick note telling us he's okay. My mom is going out of her mind not knowing. He hasn't been in any fighting, as far as we know," she added tearfully.

"Oh, I'm so sorry," said Jessie, reaching over and taking her hand. "I know how hard it is waiting and wondering." Jessie glared at me. "When Hen was over there, sometimes I wouldn't hear from him for months on end, but I didn't stop writing. You have to keep on keeping on, as they say. You'll eventually hear more, trust me." Jessie gave her a sympathetic hug.

"I'm sure he's all right," I said, trying hard to sound reassuring. "They're redeploying troops all the time. Remember, Nixon is promising to get all the troops out of Vietnam—your brother will most likely be one of them. I know it's hard not hearing anything, but there's a lot going on and sometimes you just get caught up in things and it's hard to write home, especially when you miss home so much," I said, glancing at Jessie.

"What do you mean?" asked Gina.

"When you're over there," I said, "you can go out of your mind with homesickness. It's all you think about. You get so lonely sometimes that you don't want to think about it. And that's what writing does—it makes you think about it, and that only makes you lonelier."

Gina gazed intently across the table at me with eyes now more gray than blue. She wiped them and then, leaning forward, she reached out and placed her hands on mine.

"Do you really believe that?" she asked.

"Of course I believe it," I said, but not sure that I really did.

I wanted so much to be comforting and understanding. I wanted to tell her everything she wanted to hear.

"What's your brother's name?" I asked, taking her hands and gently squeezing them between mine.

"Bobby," she said with a half smile.

"Well, Gina," I said. "I promise you that Bobby is going to be just fine. He'll be home before you know it, and you can tell your mother I said so," I added confidently.

My own mother had told me once that what dulls the mind sometimes sharpens the heart. At the time, I didn't know what she'd meant by it, but now—with beer numbing my brain, my soul mate already married to another, and a beautiful girl looking me longingly in the eyes—I understood. It wasn't love, but right now, it was close enough.

"You should meet my mother," Gina said, still holding my hands.

"I will," I said. "I surely will."

Gina smiled at me, and from behind her, I caught Jessie rolling her eyes, but then she too gave me a smile.

"For the record, I'm not—nor have I ever been—a communist," announced Sully. "Or a commie," he added, looking directly at Jessie.

"Yeah," replied Jessie, "but you fuck one goat!"

Chapter Twenty-Eight

June 1985

"Higher, Daddy!" Emily shouts.

He pushes her skyward in the swing. They're alone on the school's playground. Kobuk chases a squirrel around the monkey bars.

"Pump your feet, Em, like I showed you! That way, you can swing yourself!" he hollers after another good push.

He knows she can do it on her own, but she likes him to push her, so he will push for as long as she will ride. The rhythm of the motion frees his mind to think.

The Ranch Motel, the kind of "ranch" that doesn't have horses.

"Higher, Daddy!" Emily shouts.

———————————

The sky still cast a dreary gray, but it wasn't raining when I turned onto the road that led up to the cemetery. At the entrance was a small brownstone cottage manned by a bucktoothed boy with a freckled face.

"Can I assist you in finding a particular plot?" the kid lisped down at me from the drive-up window.

"I'm looking for the site of *Flanagan, Daniel E.*," I said.

The kid squinted into a booklet that I assumed was a logbook of sorts.

"Do you know the year?"

"What year?"

"The year of his birth or his death," said the boy. "Either one is fine."

"He died in 1968," I said.

After all the lefts, rights, and straight-throughs, it didn't take long to find Flanny's stone—a piece of black granite, recently polished. Engraved across the front, in the lightest shade of gray, was his full name and an epitaph that read *Husband, Father, Soldier.* There wasn't a blade of grass out of place—everything had been well scoured and groomed, and a large bouquet of freshly cut red, white, and blue flowers had been set neatly at its base.

Claire had already been here this morning.

I tossed my three-dollar bouquet next to her expensive one and then stared solemnly down at the stone.

Flanny had told me not to be a pussy my whole life. They were his dying words. In the short time I had known him, he had known me better than I had known myself. Flanny never lost confidence in himself or his abilities. He never worried about what anybody else thought. I remember Major Whipple coming down hard on him about something or another, and I had asked Flanny if he was worried about what the major might put in his report.

His report? Flanny had said. *Why should I give a shit about his report? He should be worried about mine! I'm the one flying the damn missions!*

But that was Flanny; that was his way. He had more confidence in himself than anyone else, and if he were going to go down, it would be on his terms—and when he did, it was. And although I was alive today, rarely had I done anything on my own terms. Mostly because I was afraid—afraid of life, death, failure, success, what others thought of me, and what I thought of myself. The only way I could deal with it was to avoid it, as I had done for all the years since Flanny's death. I was a pussy, and Flanny knew it. He had tried so hard to cure me.

I trust you, Bronco. I trust you because I know that come shit or shine you'll do the best you can, I could hear him saying.

351

"You could've done a lot better, Flanny!" I shouted at the stone. "I was a big pussy and you knew it—you knew it, motherfucker! What was your plan, Flanny? Were you going to hold my hand my whole life? Were you? Where are you now, motherfucker? Why didn't you just go home when you had the chance? You did this, Flanny, you did this!"

Don't you do it, I heard him shouting back at me. *Don't you go and do it!* But it was already done. I had been a pussy my whole life. Suddenly, I felt tired and a little bit sick. I sat down, my back to the marker, and stared out across the cemetery. I saw a gray-haired man in the distance kneeling before a white marble cross and, farther on, another man raking leaves. I closed my eyes.

"It should've been me," I whispered to no one.

Flanny was dead; he had been for years, and I wanted so much not to care anymore. I wished I could hate him. I was so tired of loving people who couldn't love me back, but more, I was tired of feeling sorry for myself because of it. Flanny had seen something in me, believed in me, had confidence in me, and I had let him down. Not nearly as much in Vietnam as I had in life. And as time went on and as my life went on, I missed him terribly—probably never more than I did right now.

I opened my eyes and saw that the gray-haired man had moved on, but the person raking leaves was still there. I wondered how many times Claire had come by to rake leaves, cut grass, polish the headstone, and place flowers—probably for all the years Flanny had been dead, and today. I wondered if he was still real to her, and whether she believed that she'd actually be with him again, in heaven or wherever she believed he might be. I wondered just how long you could keep a memory alive with headstones and flowers.

I wasn't sure how long I sat there lost in my thoughts before I realized it was raining and the person raking leaves was gone.

I took a last look at Flanny. I ran a finger inside the carved groove of the first *N* of his last name.

"Take care, buddy," I said finally, patting the top of the marker. "It was a pleasure flying with you. Sorry it took me so long to get here."

I picked up the shitty little bouquet and set it at the base of the shabby old stone next to Flanny. A poor sap named Gilbert Lars who had been dead the better part of a century.

"He needs it more than you do, pal," I said. "You're in good hands."

Leaving the cemetery, I saw a blue Ford Escort parked at a little turnout near the bottom of the hill. It was Claire. I pulled in behind her, and we met between the two cars.

"Hi," she said cheerfully. "I was hoping to catch you on your way out. I've got DJ in the car, and I wonder if you might talk to him."

"Sure," I said.

"Great, do you want to go somewhere and get out of the rain?"

"That's fine," I said.

I followed her to the bottom of the hill and then along several narrow and winding roads that eventually led to a state park. We parked in a lot next to a large grassy field where picnic tables surrounded a large pavilion that contained more picnic tables. A river ran along the far end of the field adjacent the picnic grounds.

Claire got out of her car first and, after removing a large picnic basket from the backseat, motioned for me to meet her up at the pavilion. DJ got out next and flashed me a quick glance before darting up the hill after his mother. I didn't get much of a look at him, but the look I did get was haunting. Except for the long hair, he was the spitting image of Flanny, complete with the ocean-blue eyes and the surly expression.

"I sort of planned a picnic," said Claire when we met beneath the pavilion. "I hope you don't mind, it was a little presumptuous of me, I know. I hope you didn't have plans."

At the nearest picnic table, she removed sandwiches and a variety of oddly shaped Tupperware containers from the basket. DJ sat beside her, his back to me.

"DJ," Claire said to him, "this is Henry Allen, the friend of your father from the war."

I was certain he knew who I was, but the formal introduction was nice, and it caused DJ to scoot around and scowl at me through his father's eyes. He was small like his father and looked closer to twelve than he did seventeen and, like his father, there was a maturity to his expressions.

"You knew my dad?" he asked in a voice deeper than his age suggested.

"Yeah," I replied hesitantly. "You remind me a lot of him."

"I never met him," he said.

"I know," I said. "It's unfortunate because he sure wanted to meet you."

Claire spread a checkered tablecloth over the picnic table and then motioned for me to sit down. I took a spot on the bench seat directly across from DJ.

"So I hear you like to race cars," I said.

"Sure, it's just short track stuff, but it's a lot of fun. Some friends and I formed a racing team, we've even got a couple of sponsors now."

"And you're the driver?"

"Mostly," he said, his tone serious, "but sometimes my buddy and I switch off. He's more of the crew chief than a driver. We've won four races out of five already this season."

"How many of the races were you driving?" I asked, even though I already knew the answer.

"Four out of five," he said with a grin.

"It's uncanny," I said, glancing up at Claire who was still standing over us. Claire nodded and then, smiling down at DJ, she rubbed his hair. "You need a haircut," she said.

DJ shook his head and then laughed.

"It's fine," he said to his mother, and then to me, "So how was it, flying with my dad?"

"I'm sure it was like driving with you," I said, smiling at him.

DJ looked at me curiously and then at Claire.

"There wasn't anything your dad couldn't do with a helicopter," I said. "The problem was that you never knew what he was going to do or when he was going to do it. But whatever your dad did, you can bet it was the right thing to do. He made the rest of us look like bus drivers."

"Are you sure you don't mean truck drivers?" said DJ.

"DJ, that's not necessary," she scolded him, but then she giggled.

"It sounds as though you drive like your dad flew," I said.

"I'm thinking about learning to fly," he said to his mother. "Mom is afraid I'll end up like my dad, that I'll crash or something."

"Your father never crashed," I said. "The laws of gravity didn't apply to him."

"I don't have any problem with you learning to fly," Claire said to DJ. "I just don't want you joining the military. The next thing you know, there will be another war and . . ."

She shook her head and then set a paper plate in front of me with a sandwich and potato salad.

"Its ham and cheese," she said. "I hope that's all right?"

"It's fine," I said.

"How did he die?"

"DJ," said Claire, "you know how—"

"It's all right," I said.

"Mom says you were there when he died." He paused, looking to his mother and then back to me. "I just want to know what happened, that's all. He was my dad, and I never got to meet him. I just want to know how he died from someone who knows, someone who was there."

"I was there," I said, nodding at the boy.

For the next twenty minutes or so, while nibbling at my ham and cheese sandwich, I told him everything I knew about his father's death. I told him every official and unofficial detail, of Colonel Glasson's mission and all about Flanny's heroic last flight. I even told him Flanny's last words to me. I held back nothing. I didn't feel I had a right to—not anymore.

And when I was finished, there were tears in my eyes and Claire's too. I wasn't sure what to make of DJ's expression; it hadn't changed since I had started talking.

"Don't you two go getting all mushy on me," he said, laughing at Claire and me. "What would Dad say about that?"

"He'd probably say what you just did," I said, grinning at him. "Exactly what you just said. Of course, then he'd call me a pussy!"

We all laughed. Then I told a few more stories about Flanny back in Vietnam, and at DJ's request, Claire added a few stories of her own. DJ informed me more about his racing team and then told a few jokes. Like Flanny, he had a knack for telling jokes in such a way that the telling was sometimes funnier than the punch line. It was obvious that Claire and DJ were extremely close. They appeared to understand each other on a level unbeknownst to outsiders. They laughed constantly—at themselves, at others, and me—but it wasn't the kind of laughter that was hurtful or malicious. Rather, it was good-natured and in the best taste. Claire made sure of that.

After lunch, the rain let up, and the three of us took a walk along the river trail. The air was heavy, but the mood was light as DJ kept us entertained with his comments and quips about everything from car racing to high school girls. It was amazing to me how a father and son could be so much alike without ever having known one another. But perhaps Claire had something to do with that too, by keeping Flanny's memory alive in his son.

"I have something I want to share with you guys," said Claire as we all sat on the grassy bank of the Boise River.

"What's that, Mom?" DJ asked.

Claire took a faded envelope from the back pocket of her jeans and, from it, took out a folded piece of paper.

"It's the last letter I received from your father," she said, unfolding it. "I thought I'd read it aloud to you. I'd let you read it yourselves, but your dad wasn't much of a speller, and he promised me never to let anyone know just how bad."

Claire giggled and then glanced at DJ.

"I know that I've already read many of them to you, DJ, but this one I haven't. I wanted to wait until you were older, and since Danny makes reference to you, Henry," she said, glancing over at me, "I thought you might also like to hear it."

"By all means," I said.

"Dear Claire," she read aloud through a pair of rectangular reading glasses. "I hope this letter finds you well. I know it has been a while since I've written, but they've got me running night missions again, and you know how I have a hard time sleeping during the day. It's not all bad. The powers that be have suddenly made me less than two weeks short, so if all goes well, I would like to meet you and the boy in Hawaii around the middle of next month. It's beautiful there, Claire, and we can stay a week or two if you'd like. I'll call with the details when I get the chance. There's really not much to the flying so far, other than it being at night. Bronco's the one that's got it real tough. He sits around all night playing cards and worrying about me, and here I thought you were my wife. Ha ha! Sure am going to miss him when I'm gone—not enough to stay, though. Ha ha! I was thinking that when all this is over we could have him over for a visit. I know you'd really like him. He's one of the few sane ones around here. Ha ha! I know it's been hard on you, Claire, me being away, but it won't be long now. Thanks for sending me the new picture of you and little Danny. I showed it to Bronco yesterday, and he asked how someone as ugly as me could have such a good-looking family. I told him I cut the picture out of a magazine. He said he knew it! Ha ha! Well, I got to go and get some chow and then do another inspection before tonight's run. Give my love to that boy of ours, but save some for yourself too. It won't be long now. Love, Danny. PS, buy yourself a fancy bikini for Hawaii. It's been nearly two years, for crying out loud!"

A mournful silence fell over the three of us, and DJ put an arm around his mother.

"You know, I've read that letter a thousand times, and it still feels like I'm reading it for the first time," Claire said, wiping her eyes. "And every time I read it, I always think just for a moment that, this time, he's really coming home. Do you know how many bikinis I've purchased?" Releasing a giggle, she placed the letter into the envelope and tucked it back into the pocket of her jeans.

"You did a wonderful job on the gravesite," I said.

"Thanks. I don't ever want Danny to think that I've forgotten about him," she said, looking at DJ. "Lowell would just die if he knew how much money I've spent on flowers over the years," she added.

"Yeah, but you'd just die if you knew about all the money he spends on cheeseburgers," DJ said with a grin.

We all laughed.

We said our good-byes on the way to the car, Claire hugging me on three different occasions. DJ shook my hand formally after ribbing his mother for getting all mushy on me. I thanked Claire for lunch and told her that I would try to keep in touch, but as it was with all my good-byes these days, I made no promises.

Chapter Twenty-Nine

July 1965

Buried high atop the giant tailing pile, which stood majestically over the beaver pond, were more Ball canning jars of Meyer's Rum than we could ever hope to drink, but that didn't mean weren't going to bury more. Jessie wouldn't think of throwing any of it out, so I dug deeper.

"How can you be so sure this is working?" I said, pitching a spade-full of rocks out of the hole.

"What do you mean?" said Jessie.

"I mean the more of this shit we bury, the more your grandfather seems to buy. He might not be on to us, but I think his liver is." I laughed.

Jessie laughed too. She was sitting beside the hole sipping rum with her legs crossed, watching me dig, which was her custom whenever we were burying jars.

"You're probably right," she said, "but it's still better than it was before."

"*Before*, before what?"

"Before we started watering down the booze," she said sharply.

She took a long swig of her rum and then grimaced.

"Why don't you mix that?" I said. "I brought Pepsi."

"No, it's fine. I'm getting used to it this way."

"Yeah, I can tell," I said, rolling my eyes. "What are we going to do with all this stuff, anyway?"

"We'll save it for parties."

I knew that would be her answer. We had supplied the liquor for the graduation party at Robert Willingham's parents' cabin on Harding Lake. Since then, Jessie had the idea that we'd be supplying rum to every summer party this side of Mt. McKinley. The problem was that we hadn't been invited to any. Jessie and her on-again, off-again boyfriend Robert were presently off again.

"What parties?" I said, tossing the camp-spade out of the hole.

"There are parties, Hen, there's at least one every weekend. As soon as I get my license, we'll go."

"Right," I said, rolling my eyes again. I had my driver's license but didn't have a car, whereas Jessie had a car but no license. I'd already spent a good part of the summer trying to teach her to drive with little success. JT wouldn't let her drive the Olds until she got her license, so all we had to work with was a beat-up Chevy pickup with a manual transmission, which unfortunately had a serious personality conflict with Jessie.

"You want to go to the field and practice today?" she asked after taking another swig of her rum.

"I suppose you drive better when you're drunk, Jess?" I said, nodding at the jar of rum in her hand.

"I might," she giggled.

"I think it's deep enough now," I said, climbing out of the hole. "We've got about four feet now, so if we stack them neatly, I think it'll be fine."

"I want to go to a party, Hen," she said, her eyes pouty.

"I don't know what to tell you," I said, shaking my head. "Why don't you go and get a hold of *Robert* or *Rob* or *Robbie* or whatever you're calling him these days? Maybe he'll drive you to one."

"We're not dating anymore!" she huffed.

"Boy, if I had a shiny nickel for every time I heard you say that," I said.

I had been waiting to tell her about the letter I had received from Carrie. The letter was the most recent in a dozen I had received over the past year. There wasn't much to them, just what I assumed was typical girl stuff. But she always ended her letters with three large *Xs* and two large *Os* and signed them *with love, Carrie.*

"I'm ready for my driving lesson, Mr. Henry," blurted Jessie with a giggle.

"You're drunk," I said.

"Maybe you should be too. I hear that's all they do in college, college boy!"

I had applied to and been accepted at Washington State College. When Jessie heard about it, she was none too happy and had been jabbing me about it ever since.

"I'm not even sure if I'm going, so why don't you just get off my back!"

"Did I strike a nerve?" she asked, then giggled again. She picked up a small rock and threw it at me. It hit me on the side of the head.

"Ow!" I cried out. "What did you do that for?"

"Somebody's got to knock some sense into you." She laughed.

"You think you're so funny," I said, rubbing my head.

"I am," she said. "Just because you don't see—hey wait!"

Jessie leaped up and snatched a jar of rum from the box I was carrying.

"I'll want you, sir, later," she said to the jar and then, setting it gently on the ground, she wiggled down next to it as if it were an old buddy.

I placed the large piece of plywood over the hole and did my best to cover it with tailings.

"That should do it," I said.

"Don't you want to have a party with me, Hen?" she whined.

"I'm not really in the mood."

"Why not?"

"I don't know, Jess. I've got a lot on my mind, and all you can think about are parties and giving me shit."

"I'm sorry, Hen," she said sweetly. "I just don't want you to leave me."

"You think I want to stay here the rest of my life? I'm going to be eighteen, for crying out loud! And you hate it here!" I said, pointing at her. "I can't believe you're planning on staying! I want to fly helicopters, Jess. You know that. And if I can't fly helicopters, then I'm going to college. That's all there is to it!"

"I don't want to stay here, Hen. I never have. But I don't have anywhere else to go. I've written my mother, and she's not very receptive to the idea of having me live with her. And you know I don't have money for college, let alone go somewhere and live on my own. I thought you'd want to stick around here with me for another year, make some money, then do whatever we want. I can get a job, and you have your job at the hangar, right?"

"Yeah, but I don't know," I said, shaking my head. "What do you think about me joining the army?"

"The army, are you serious?"

"I've been thinking about it. Tom says it's the best way to get experience if I want to fly helicopters."

"Wait a minute," she said, her speech slurred. "You mean to tell me that you're listening to what Tom has to say? You and Tom don't even get along, so why in hell would you listen to what he has to say?"

"When it comes to flying, he's taught me everything I know. And he's a great pilot, Jess. It's the way he did it. Remember, he flew choppers in Korea."

"How could I ever forget," she said, waving her hand at me. "What does your mother say?"

I didn't say anything, knowing she'd figure it out on her own.

"You haven't told her, have you? Hen, you're so damned predictable. How long have you and your buddy *Tom* been planning this?"

"You know my mother, she doesn't like me flying. How do you think she'd feel about me joining the army, especially with all that's going on these days? Besides, I'm just thinking about it. My mother has all my college plans worked out anyway. She's got relatives all over Eastern Washington, and it looks like I'll be able to work my way through college as a wheat farmer or something, I don't know. What I do know is that I haven't had much say in it."

"It's settled then," she said, smiling.

"What's settled?"

"Everything. You can just tell your mother you want to save some money for college, and then you can stay here with me and work until we both decide what it is we want to do."

"So it's that simple?" I said.

"Yep, it's that simple. Don't you feel better now?"

Jessie laughed and then began unscrewing the top to her friendly jar of rum. I sat down next to her and put my arms on my knees. Surprisingly, I did feel better.

"We can have a party now," she said, handing me the open jar.

I took a sip and nearly gagged.

"That's horrible," I said, reaching for the bottle of Pepsi I had in my backpack.

"It'll put hair on your chest," said Jessie. "And I've seen your chest, Hen. You could use some hair." She giggled as I mixed some rum and Pepsi.

"Doesn't your grandfather have loads of money?"

Jessie's face soured and then, glancing over at me. "He does," she replied, "but lord knows I can't find it."

"You've been looking?"

"Only nearly every day for three years," she said.

We both laughed. I took another sip of the rum and Pepsi and then passed it to Jessie.

"Where have you looked?"

"Everywhere," she said with a sigh. "It's probably buried somewhere with Grandma and the O'Brien brothers. All I know is that it's somewhere. I don't think he'd keep it in a bank—not Spenser. Besides, after killing the O'Brien boys, he couldn't very well go around making huge deposits. No, it's somewhere. I bet if we find the bodies, we'll find the money," she added.

"We're running out of places to look," I said. "We've already searched every cabin and cave in the area. I don't think we're going to find anything, Jess."

"We have to!" she blurted. "We have to find them. Spenser can't get away with this!" She shook her head violently. "There's got to be a way to find them. There just has to be. Are you sure there aren't more places to look?"

"Hell, Jess, they could be anywhere. I suppose there are always more places to look, but that still doesn't mean we'll find anything. The only one that knows where they are is Spenser himself, and I can't read minds, can you?"

"No, I guess not. Too bad though."

"Wait a minute," I said suddenly. "Maybe that's it."

"We can't read minds," said Jessie, staring at me curiously, "can we?"

"No, of course not. You're drunk." I laughed. "But maybe we can get Spenser to tell us."

"Oh right," she said. "I'll just ask him. *Hey, Granddaddy, where did you bury Grandma and the O'Brien boys?* I'm sure he'd take me right to them. Then I'll ask him about the money." She shot me a wicked glare. "You're such a *rube!*"

"No, I don't mean ask him about it, but get him to lead us to them. I saw it in a movie once."

"Great, another one of your movie ideas," she said, rolling her eyes.

"I'm serious," I said. "This could work. I watched this movie about this police officer—a detective or something. He sent a letter to the killer, anonymous like. The letter stated that the anonymous person knew where the body was and that if killer didn't pay the money, then the anonymous person was going to go to the police."

"Did the killer pay the money?"

"Of course not. They didn't want him to pay. But the killer went to move the body and led the police right to it. Worked like a charm."

"Well, this isn't the movies," said Jessie. "But supposing we did send an anonymous letter, what would it say?"

"I don't know. Maybe something like, *we know where you hid your wife and the O'Brien brothers, and if you don't send us ten thousand dollars, we'll go to the police . . .* something like that, anyway."

Jessie's brows bent in concentration. She didn't speak for several minutes, then she said, "Okay, let's do it."

"*Really?*"

"Yeah, maybe all that movie watching finally paid off. The letter has to be good, though—typewritten and untraceable. We can't have him send the money to us. Then he could find out it was us."

"No, I think in the movie they had a drop-off site."

"Yeah, that makes sense, a drop-off site. I'll leave that to you. You would know the best place. But what if he pays the money?"

"He won't, but even if he does, he'll still want to move the bodies."

"You're right, he will," said Jessie with a mischievous grin. "He sure will. This might work. He'll lead us right to them. I take it back. You're not such a rube at all." She patted me on the shoulder. "No, you're not a rube at all today."

Pleased with her assessment, I smiled and pretended hard that I didn't have my doubts about this new grand plan. In the movies, it looked easy. Everyone read from a script and played a part. It was all there: a beginning, a middle, and an end. We didn't have a script, and that frightened me. Up until now, we had only been snooping around, following a *maybe* or a *what if*. If we didn't find anything, it was no big deal. Now we were suddenly making things happen, pushing buttons. I wasn't so much afraid of the plan not working, as much as I was if it did.

"What are we going to do?" I asked, hoping she wouldn't have an answer.

"We're going to write an anonymous letter," Jessie said, nodding. "That's what we're going to do. We need a typewriter." She glanced over at me. "You have a typewriter?"

"No. Why would I have a typewriter?"

"Do you know where we can get one?"

"I don't know. What about the *Shit Towers* . . . I mean in all those piles of junk around your cabin."

Jessie frowned and then said, "I don't think so, maybe a piece of one."

"They have one at the hangar," I said, instantly wishing I hadn't.

"Swell," she said excitedly. "We'll work it out with pencil and paper, then you can type it all up at the hangar and mail it from the downtown post office."

I couldn't believe what I had just gotten myself into.

"I don't type," I said, knowing that it wouldn't be enough to get out of it.

"Oh, you can too," she said dismissively, and then pouring the remaining rum from her buddy the jar onto the ground, she said, "We better get going, time's a wasting."

———————

We spent the next couple of hours in my trailer writing and rewriting our version of the Lindbergh letter. Jessie insisted on using the word *we* instead of *I,* thinking that it would be more intimidating if Spenser thought it were from more than one person. Phrases like *we know, you must pay $25,000 or else we will go to the police* were all part of the five short sentences Jessie hoped would compel Spenser to rush out and move the bodies. Her plan was for me to type and then mail the letter downtown the next time I went flying with Tom.

"It's so simple," said Jessie, handing me the pencil-written extortion letter.

I wasn't so certain. She had me doing all the work and taking all the chances. Typing the damn thing without Tom being the wiser would be difficult, if not impossible. The typewriter was in the small office attached to the hangar where Tom was always working unless he was flying with me. It was possible that he might go up without me, but that would be hard to maneuver. My typing was for shit. I was slow and made a million mistakes. Typing the letter would surely take time. Then the letter had to be mailed from the downtown post office, which meant I would have to find a way to get there from the hangar and again hope that Tom wasn't the wiser.

"I don't know," I said. "I'm not sure if I can pull it off, it's going to be tough."

"Are you kidding? It'll be cake. You have nothing to worry about. Your part is easy."

"What do you mean? I'm taking all the risks. Do you know how hard it's going to be to get all this by Tom?"

Her answer came in the form of a fiery glare.

"Don't give me that shit!" she snapped. "You've got the easy part. I'm the one that has to live with the bastard waiting for your letter to arrive and then somehow follow Spenser without getting caught—not an easy task, mind you! Once he realizes that somebody is on to him, he'll be watching his every step. It might be impossible to tail him. All you have to do is mail a goddamned letter!"

I supposed I hadn't thought that far ahead. She had a point, but now I was worried. It was bad enough that she had to live with Spenser, but if he ever got wind of what we were doing, Jessie would be in real danger.

"I'll figure it out," I said.

"Good," she said with quick smile and then said calmly, "I know you can do this, Hen."

I nodded, feeling suddenly foolish. I would have to find a way. There wasn't anything I wouldn't do for Jessie, but part of me couldn't help but think that things were beginning to get out of control.

Jessie had been right about my part of the plan. It was a snap. Tom had to drive somewhere and pick up an airplane part. He left me alone at the hangar for well over an hour, which gave me plenty of time to hunt and peck out the letter. There was even time to address a business-sized envelope.

When Tom did return, we took a short flight in one of the choppers, one that I had flown in many times. Tom let me take off and land, then quizzed me on the various techniques. I made several mistakes, but Tom was more than patient. It always amazed me how different he was when we were flying.

On the way home, I casually asked Tom if we could swing by the post office so that I could mail a letter. "I suppose," he said. "What do you have to mail?"

"A letter to Nana," I said, ready with the answer.

Last night, I had written a letter to Tom's mother solely in anticipation of this question. In addition to insisting that I call her *Nana* (even though she was not, in fact, my grandmother), my mother, on occasion, had asked that I write to her. Since my mother was long overdue with her request, I took it upon myself to draft a dull and disingenuous note to a woman I barely knew as cover for the much more deceitful undertaking of sending the Spenser letter.

"You got a stamp?" asked Tom.

"Yeah," I said, pleased to hear the question. "I got one from Mom this morning."

Thrilled with the idea of me writing to Nana, my mother had given me several stamps as well as a small box of cream-colored stationary, just in case I had an urge to write any of *her* relatives.

Tom pulled the car up alongside the two mailboxes outside the downtown Fairbanks post office. Through the open window of Tom's truck, I easily dropped in Nana's letter along with the one to Spenser Mason. I had done my part, completed what had been my charge, and put the grand plan into motion. The ride home was pleasant. For most of the way, Tom and I talked about flying helicopters. It was not until we passed by the Shit Towers that the slightest bit of queasiness crawled its way up into my stomach. It wiggled and twisted there as I thought about old man Spenser reading the letter. Everything had gone according to plan. Spenser would never be the wiser. Why then was I worried? Then suddenly I knew. Whatever happened from here on out, there was no turning back.

It had been two days since I had mailed the letter to Spenser's post office box. Jessie told me that Spenser checked it regularly, but there was really no way to tell when exactly he would pick it up. Jessie thought it might be today and wanted to be there when her grandfather got home. I had agreed to wait with her.

"When do you think he will be home?" I asked Jessie on the walk to her house.

We had spent the morning helping my mother weed her garden, a tedious task that we were both glad to be done with.

"A couple hours, maybe," she said. "He might stop for a drink after work. He does that sometimes when Daddy's away."

Spenser and JT were both gone. Spenser was working downtown, and JT had taken off to Anchorage to be with his girlfriend. Jessie would be staying with us while JT was away, but we both wanted to be around when Spenser got home.

"What if he doesn't come home first, or what if he takes off in his car and we can't follow him?" I said.

"I know, I thought about that too," she said. "It's a chance we'll have to take. But if he does come home first, I need you to be there, Hen, so you can see which way he goes. You know these parts. Maybe you'll know where he's going."

"What if he doesn't go anywhere?"

"Then I'll stay with him until he does."

The gravity in her tone frightened me. It was obvious to me now that the simple plan had holes—big ones, the kind that you can't just fill on the fly. We really had no idea how Spenser was going to react, if at all. And if he did, God knows what he might do. Who says he would go after the bodies? After all these years, he may not care about the bodies. Instead, he might focus on locating the blackmailers. Suddenly, it felt like we were in way over our heads.

"I don't know if that's a good idea," I said. "We may have this thing all wrong."

"What do you mean?"

"Suppose he knows the bodies can't be found and the letter we wrote is bullshit. How difficult would it be to figure out that we're the ones behind it? For decades, he has gotten away with it, and then all of the sudden he gets the letter. He has to realize that there is a short list of logical suspects, and you and I are on that list. This could be a big mistake, Jess."

"It'll work," she said, but her look said otherwise.

"Maybe we shouldn't be there when he gets home. In case—"

"No!" she snapped and then, stopping, she turned, facing me. "We are going through with it, just like we planned. That's it!"

Jessie started to walk away, but then turned back again.

"You know, Henry, if you're scared, you don't have to be a part of this. I'll do it myself."

"I'm fine," I said, hating the fact that she knew I was afraid.

Walking again, Jessie remained silent until we reached front door of her cabin.

"Maybe you should hide yourself out here," she said, scanning the yard. "That way, you can get a jump on him if he takes off right away."

I was sure there was no way I was going to *get a jump on him* whether I was inside or outside the cabin, and the thought of tailing an angry killer alone terrified me.

"Sure," I said weakly.

After Jessie disappeared into the cabin, I mulled around the Shit Towers searching for a place to hide. It was ridiculous that I couldn't stand up to Jessie; it was ridiculous that I was so afraid. There was a mound of gravel at the far end of the yard just beyond one of the Shit Towers. I knew from there I wouldn't be seen, and I could see both the driveway and the front door of the cabin. So there I waited.

It was an hour before Spenser's truck finally rolled up the driveway. I spent the time working myself into a nervous frenzy thinking of all the possible things that would surely go wrong. So when the old man hopped out of his truck carrying a stack of mail to the front door, I nearly passed out.

Another half hour went by before Jessie came out of the cabin quietly calling for me. I stood up from behind the mound, motioning for her attention. When she saw me, she quickly jogged over and dove behind the mound, pulling me down on the other side with her, an impish grin adorning her face.

"He went for it!" she whispered loudly. "He actually went for it!"

"How do you know?"

"He didn't open the letter until he got home. Then he must have read it over a dozen times. You should have seen him, Hen. He sat there in his chair holding the letter, reading it and reading it. Then he told me to fix him a drink while he read it again. He was as pale as a ghost. Can you believe it?"

"What did you do?"

"I fixed him one," she said, staring at me curiously.

"No, after that. Why are you out here?"

"He got rid of me. Told me to go to your place, on account of Daddy being gone. He's never told me to leave before!" she said excitedly. "I've never seen him act like that, Hen, never! I'm telling you, he went for it!"

"So what do we do now?"

"We wait," she said. "We wait until he leaves and then we follow him, just like we planned."

"How do you know he's going to leave?"

"I just know he is, that's all. He was really upset, but he's not the least bit on to us."

"How do you know that?"

"Because he thinks it's someone else."

"Oksana?" I said.

"No, it's not anyone we know. I didn't recognize the name."

"He said a name?" I said.

"Yes. He kept saying it, but I told you, it's nobody we know. It's surely not somebody from around here. Maybe someone from Fairbanks."

"I don't want anyone to get hurt on our account. What if he goes after this person? We have no way to stop him, especially if they're in Fairbanks. We have to warn them, Jess. What's the name?"

"It's a weird name," she said, peeking over the mound at the front door. "I'd never heard of it before. Something like Gaston, I think."

"*Gaston?*" I said, surprised, my insides suddenly wrenching.

"Yeah, you heard of him?"

I took a quick peek over the mound to be certain Spenser hadn't left yet, and then I stared coldly at Jessie.

"What?" she said.

"Gaston Spooner," I said. "He thinks it's Spooner!"

"That's his first name? I never knew that. You always call him Spooner." Jessie leaned back against the mound, breathing heavily. "Holy shit! What are we going to do now?"

The question hung there for several seconds as we both tried hard to comprehend the significance of the situation.

"After all these years, I wonder why he would think it's Spooner," I said finally.

"Probably because Spooner has been around all these years," said Jessie.

"Maybe, but we have to warn him."

"Too late," said Jessie, pointing to the cabin door.

We both watched as Spenser Mason gimped from the front door, passed his truck, and went on down the driveway. From where we were hiding, he looked more old man than murderer, except in the way he was toting the double-barreled shotgun.

Jessie wanted to go right after him, but I told her to wait.

"We can't go too soon," I said, "or he'll know we're following him. It's better if we stay back and see which way he goes."

Spenser knew every trail in the valley better than I did, but if he was making his way to Spooner's cabin, then he would no longer be on the highway by the time we reached the end of the driveway.

"Let's go," I said to Jessie a few minutes after Spenser had gone.

Scurrying down the driveway, we both had our eyes peeled for any sign of Spenser. We didn't see him, nor did we see him when we reached the highway.

"Looks as though he's headed to Spooner's place," I said dejectedly.

There was no way to stop Spenser now. Not with him so far ahead of us and carrying a gun. Our only choice was to keep on following him, no matter how it played out. Our pace up was slow but steady until we reached the cutoff. There, I paused long enough to give Jessie a ready nod. Then, with my insides in knots, I led us on down the grassy path and on across the rocky heaves to the creek-side trail that led up to Spooner's cabin. I had hiked it a thousand times, and I knew every rock, tree, and bend along the way. Now, the pathway suddenly felt narrow, long, and unfamiliar.

When we finally arrived at the base of the ridge, there was no sign of Spenser, but by now he was probably already at Spooner's place. It was just a jog over a small swell of tailings and up an embankment to the backside of his cabin. Our first bit of luck came when I saw the two cords of wood that I had recently double-stacked along the back edge of Spooner's yard. A good part of my summer's work was now screening our arrival. We tread lightly up to and then alongside the back of the woodpile until we reached its end, careful not to make a lot of noise.

A quick peek around the edge of the woodpile revealed nothing out of the ordinary. There was no sign of Spenser or Spooner, and we had a good view of the front corner of the cabin.

"Do you think we missed him?" whispered Jessie.

"I don't think so. He wasn't that far ahead of us."

"I don't see a soul. Maybe Granddaddy didn't come here."

It was possible. Spenser could've wandered off on some other trail that I wasn't aware of, but it was unlikely, especially given the fact that he had suspected Spooner of writing the letter.

"I don't think—"

"Gaston!" a loud voice echoed through the valley. "Gaston, where are you?"

All of a sudden, the head and shoulders of Spenser Mason appeared from out of the hole that was the entryway to the cabin. The old man was waving his shotgun wildly in the air and scanning the surroundings. Jessie and I instantly ducked back behind the woodpile.

"Damn," whispered Jessie.

"Gaston!" yelled Spenser. "I know it's you! What shit are you trying to pull?" Spenser continued to yell for Spooner. His voice becoming sharper and clearer as if it were getting closer to the woodpile and to us. My heart raced violently.

Then silence.

I'm not sure what compelled me to take a look, but I did. I was surprised to see Spenser, his back to me, only a few feet away. I didn't move a muscle but continued to stare at the old man who appeared to be looking at something beyond the cabin. Finally, he let out a dismissive grunt and then hobbled around to the front and headed on down the driveway. A few minutes later, he was gone.

"Should we follow him?" asked Jessie.

"No," I said. "I think he's going home, probably taking the road back to the highway. I don't think he's going anywhere—not tonight, anyway. I'm sure he planned on making a fuss with Spooner. That's why he didn't take his truck. I'm glad Spooner wasn't home."

"Where do you think he is?"

"Don't know for certain. Probably working late at the drugstore or something—too late to be fishing. Who knows what Spenser would've done had he been here?"

"He'd of killed him," said Jessie plainly. "And he wouldn't have thought twice about it. He's cold that way."

Jessie's words were frightening, but somehow I knew they were true. Spooner would've been no match for Spenser and his shotgun. For as many fishing poles he had lying around, I had never known him to own a gun. But he had survived the last thirty years or so without one. Of course, bears and wolves alike had nothing on the monster that was Spenser Mason.

"What do we do now?" said Jessie as we walked toward the front of the cabin.

"We wait for Spooner to get home, and then we warn him. That's about all we can do."

"What do we tell him?"

"Everything," I said. "It wouldn't be fair to him otherwise. He needs to know just what we're dealing with. I don't know if it will do him any good, but he has a right to know."

We had waited nearly an hour before, finally, there came a rumbling from the road beyond the trees. It was clearly an automobile. Afraid that it might be Spenser making an ill-fated return, Jessie and I hid behind the cabin until we saw Spooner's faded-red International truck making its way up the driveway.

We greeted him at the front of the cabin. If he was surprised to see us, he didn't show it. But Mr. Spooner was never one to get too excited about anything.

"Hello," he said in his typically cool manner. As was his way, he waited for an explanation.

"Hi, Mr. Spooner," I said, nodding at him and then glancing over at Jessie. "We need to talk to you about something. It's important," I added.

"All right," he said. "Come on in."

He led us down the steps and on into the windowless cabin. The cabin was pitch black inside, but even with the bit of light creeping in from the doorway, I could tell that the place had been ransacked.

Spooner glanced back at Jessie and me as if we knew something about it, but all I could do was shake my head in ignorance.

"Spenser did this," said Jessie, supplying the words to my expression. "He was here looking for you, and he was angry."

"I guess so," said Spooner, reaching down for a flashlight next to the door.

He shined it upward at a kerosene lantern hanging from the ceiling. Although it was available to him, Spooner didn't have electricity. It only took him a minute to light the lantern and reveal the full extent of the damage.

"Oh my," he said.

There were three rooms inside the cabin—a living room in the front and a kitchen and bedroom in the back. Although the bedroom had a door, it was open and hanging from only one hinge. Inside the room was a heaping mess of bedding and goose feathers from what looked like a slashed pillow. Strewn across the floor of the kitchen was every pot, pan, and utensil, while Spenser had obviously made a point to upend every piece of furniture in the living room.

"Do you know why?" asked Spooner, setting a small wooden table upright.

"I think so," I said.

Spooner gave me a quick glance and then went about setting chairs around the table.

"Please, have a seat," he said.

Once seated, I began the wearisome task of informing Mr. Spooner of our caper. He remained silent, his expression unchanging when I explained to him in great detail how we had written the letter in hopes that Spenser would lead us to the bodies.

Spooner didn't say a word even after I was finished speaking, but continued to stare at me intently, as if I might have something more to say. Then, without a word, he stood up and walked into the bedroom. A minute later, he returned holding a small wooden box slightly larger than one that might hold cigars.

"I found this some thirty-odd years ago at the bottom of a creek not too far from the O'Brien cabins," he said. Spooner removed the top of the box, revealing a long-barreled wooden-handled pistol. "I'm pretty sure now Spenser used it to kill those folks," he said, running his index finger delicately along the barrel of the gun.

"How do you know?" said Jessie.

Spenser wiped his head again. "I might've been there," he said uneasily.

"I knew it!" said Jessie, slapping her hand on the table, her eyes wide and fiery. "The bastard shot them down in cold blood!"

I was surprised at Spooner's revelation. I had spent days with the man fishing and splitting wood, and he had never so much as mentioned Spenser or the O'Briens, except the one time he showed me the cabins.

"Why didn't you go to the police?" I asked, hopeful that I hadn't crossed a line by asking.

"I probably should've," said Spooner, shaking his head. "Those were different days back then. The rush was pretty much over, and the dredge companies were buying up all the claims. Your grandfather and the O'Brien boys had one of the largest claims left. It was just a matter of time and price before they sold out. I remember shortly before the sale there was some fuss between Spenser and the brothers. The only reason I knew about it was because Abigail had mentioned it to me at the drugstore. I'm not sure why, but I remember her telling me they were squawking about percentages or something."

"So you knew my grandmother?" said Jessie, smiling.

"Sure I did," said Spooner. "She used to come in to the drugstore now and then with your father. Of course, he was just an infant back then. Lovely woman, your grandmother," he said directly to Jessie.

Jessie smiled pleasantly at him.

"It was in the spring, early April I think. I remember it was still cold." He continued, "I had plans to hike on up to the O'Brien place and pick up some fly hooks Frank had shaped for me. He was a crafty fellow, made all my hooks back then. I was wanting to tie some new flies. I was less than a mile away when I heard the shots fired. I didn't know what to make of it, really, but I supposed it had to have come from the O'Brien place. They were good-natured fellows, it might have been anything. I didn't think much of it."

Spooner ran his hand over his head, and I could see the perspiration.

"That's when I saw Spenser," he said. "I saw him toss something toward the frozen creek and then head back up towards the O'Brien place. He never saw me, and I didn't make myself known to him. I thought it all strange at the time."

Even in the dim light of the cabin, Spooner's face looked pale.

"I remember something came over me, not sure what, but a kind of feeling, a fear—something telling me not to bother with the O'Briens that day . . ." He hesitated and then rubbed his face. "Something told me that if I had . . . well . . . I wouldn't have left there alive." Spooner placed the top back on to the box. "The next day, my hooks arrived from Frankie by mail, and I thought I must've overreacted. It wasn't until summer that I heard the rumors that the three of them had run off together, and . . . well, you know the rest," he said, nodding at me. "I hadn't heard from any of them in months, but I suppose that wasn't all that uncommon for these parts. But it got me curious, so I went back to where I had seen Spenser and found this," he said, tapping the box. "By that time, the O'Brien place had already burned down. I still wasn't sure what it all meant, and I suppose it was just easier to believe the rumors. So I let it go."

"You let it go?" fired Jessie. "You knew he killed them, and you let it go?"

"I didn't see anything, and I didn't know anything for sure," said Spooner, showing her the palms of his hands. "It wasn't until our visit to the Verdens that I figured there might be more to it. You've got to remember, those were different times. I didn't have any hard evidence."

"Why would Spenser think it was you that wrote the letter?" I said.

"Most likely because I was around back then," said Spooner. "There aren't too many of us left. I'm not sure he knew anything about Oksana. Not sure why he would think I would wait all these years to start blackmailing him."

"What are you going to do if he comes back?" I said. "He seemed pretty hot."

"I suspect he wants to scare me, but I don't scare that easily. Not anymore."

"He had his shotgun," said Jessie.

"I don't think he would shoot first. I'll just explain to him that I wasn't the one that wrote the letter. I've got a gun too," he said, tapping the box. "I only hope it doesn't come to that."

I was surprised to hear Spooner talk like that. I would've never thought he had it in him. He was always so calm and nonviolent, just your common druggist-fisherman.

"What about the bodies?" Jessie asked. "Do you have any idea what he did with the bodies?"

"I never thought much about it. I suspect, however, if he had burned them up in those cabins, he'd a hauled the remains away and probably buried them somewhere in one of the mine shafts around there."

"I'm sorry we got you into this, Mr. Spooner. We were hoping Spenser would lead us to the bodies," I said, glancing at Jessie.

Jessie sent back the glare.

"You won't tell him about us, will you?" she asked.

"Of course not," said Spooner, shaking his head. "There's no need for that."

It was well past eight when Spooner dropped Jessie and me off at my house. He was pulling out of the driveway when he stopped suddenly and rolled down his window.

"You know something?" he called back to us. "If I had to guess where to find those bodies—not that there is anything left to find, mind you—I would look around the ridgeline shafts near the O'Brien place. It wouldn't make much sense to bury them in the dredge line. They might be discovered. But I think Spenser still owns a good deal of that hillside. It might be worth checking into."

"Thanks," said Jessie. "We'll check it out."

Chapter Thirty

August 1978

"Okay," said Gina.

Her answer was the one I had been hoping for, but I had been expecting more—more excitement, more emotion, more something. Perhaps some of her sentiment had been lost in the wind; after all, it was howling off Lake Michigan pretty good. Standing beneath the pale red lighthouse at the end of the long concrete pier in Grand Haven, my insecurity ran hard against the wind.

"Okay," she said again, this time with an agreeable smile and a slightly reassuring nod.

We hugged awkwardly, but she would marry me, and I was grateful.

We walked back down the pier under gray skies, in silence, holding hands, dreaming of our future life together—or at least, I was.

"Congratulations, buddy," said Sully with a weak pat on the back as I passed him.

I wasn't sure how he knew, but somehow Sully always seemed to be in the know. From the anxious grin on his face, I could tell he'd been waiting for me to arrive. He stood at the entrance to my office, leaning against the doorframe.

"Thanks," I said, blushing.

"So, have you picked a date yet?"

"We're thinking about early spring," I lied, although it sounded right to me.

"That's great," said Sully. "So you're sure that's what you want to do?"

The question caught me off guard, and I quickly turned and faced him.

"What do you mean by that, Sully?"

His smile was gone, and I knew he had felt the defensiveness in my reply.

"No reason, I just want to make sure you're making the right decision. It's a big step, marriage—for Christ-sake, Henry, we're both divorce lawyers," he said and then, letting out a nervous chuckle, stated firmly, "It's my duty to ask the important questions."

"As my lawyer or my friend?" I said.

"Both," he said, grinning again. "Come on, Henry. I'm only busting your balls."

I sat down behind my cluttered desk and shot him a forgiving smile.

"This spring, huh?" he said, shaking his head. "I can't believe you're really going through with it. How long you two been together now?"

"Well over five years," I said. He knew precisely how long Gina and I had been together, so I wasn't sure where he was going with this. Sully and I were close, but it wasn't like him to be so concerned with my personal life. Then again, I suppose I didn't get engaged every day.

"Have you told Jessie?"

"I haven't told anyone!" I snapped. "How you know is beyond me!"

"I figured it out from clues I got from Sue."

On cue, Sue squeezed by Sully at the doorway holding a handful of phone messages.

"What about Sue?" she asked, flashing each of us smile.

"I was just telling Henry here," said Sully with a nod in my direction, "that I knew he was up to something with Gina by the clues I got from you."

"From me, what clues?" Sue said, surprised. She glanced back and forth between Sully and me. "I didn't say a word, honest," she added, placing a hand over her chest.

"I know," I said, eyeing Sully. "Sully's just up to his ole antics."

"He didn't hear it from me," said Sue, handing me the messages. "There's one here from Dolce, she's been calling all morning—says she has to talk to you right away. She says *extremely urgent*," Sue said, rolling her eyes. "I promised her that you'd call her first thing."

Sue had a way of melting me into the daily grind by subtly making me feel more important than I actually was. She was really more of a coach than a secretary, always encouraging, nudging me along as a minor league manager would an anxious prospect.

Before me, Sue had spent twenty-plus years as the secretary to Leland Reese, one of the cofounders of the firm of *Bozeman & Reese*. A feared divorce lawyer in his day, Leland had a reputation for acquiring lofty alimony awards and even loftier attorney fees. His caseload was legendary, handling as many as forty divorce cases at a time without missing a single hearing or deadline. All this, despite an inexorable affection for scotch and women. However, the driving force behind all his success as an attorney was Sue. At ninety-five words per minute, she had drafted his letters and filed his motions and briefs. She had organized his days, his weeks, and his years; kept him on time; scheduled his brunches, lunches, and meetings; planned his vacations; and decided when he came to work in the morning and when he went home at night. This suited him well. A devout bachelor, Leland never considered marriage as he already had a devoted wife in Sue. Besides, to die married—Leland was heard to say—was a waste of a good divorce.

When the time finally came for Leland to retire, in a surprise tribute and in appreciation for all her years of loyal service, he presented Sue with a satisfaction of mortgage to her house.

The one thing Sue couldn't do for Leland, however, was prepare him for retirement. After leaving the firm, he didn't know what to do with himself. In the first couple of months, he travelled. But when that got old, he remodeled his house, then sold it, bought a new one, sold it, and finally purchased a small cottage on Houghton Lake in Northern Michigan.

Four months later, members of Troop Thirty-Five of the Mt. Pleasant Boy Scouts came across a Chris-craft adrift on the lake. Inside, they found the dead body of Leland Reese, a fishing pole in one hand and a half-drank bottle of Glen Fiddich in the other. Not surprisingly, Leland was alone.

In her midfifties and passed down to a young upstart, Sue probably thought that the satisfaction of her mortgage was not nearly enough compensation for what she had to take on. But after three long years of training and instruction, that being mine, she told me often now that I had become as valuable a lawyer to her as Leland. After all, she said, *I raised you myself.*

I was a better lawyer for it, and my loyalties lay with her and hers with me. It was why I knew that she had not disclosed anything to Sully about the proposal.

"Thanks, Sue," I said as she squeezed by Sully at the doorway.

"No problem," she replied from the hallway.

I sent Sully a disapproving glance. He looked unsettled, sipping a cup of coffee and staring at me. I started to wonder how long he was going to stay.

"Don't you have work to do?" I asked him.

"Not much. I thought we'd go have some coffee."

"Sorry, Sully, I have to make some calls. Why don't you go and do whatever it is you do when you're not in *my* office?" I said sharply. And then thinking I was too hard on him, I said, "We'll have lunch."

"Good," he said. And then, after tossing me a nervous smile, he left.

I felt bad for running him off, but I really didn't have time, nor was I in the mood for one of his lengthy lectures on marriage and commitment. Sometimes Sully could be mentally draining. After spending two years as undergraduates together, three years of law school, and now three years at the same law firm, we both knew each other pretty well, and there were times when we simply got tired of each other.

Sully wasn't much of a divorce lawyer. After three years, his caseload wasn't even half mine, and he had hired a team of law clerks to do most of his legal dirty work. Often, he had a case settled before the first scheduling conference. His never-say-no personality, coupled with his extreme fear of confrontation, made him a nice guy but a lousy lawyer. Around town, they called him *No-Bully Sully*, because he usually jumped at the first offer from opposing counsel and would spend the rest of the time trying to convince his client to take it. On the rare occasions when some uncompromising attorney dragged him into the courtroom, it suddenly became *our case,* and I would end up holding his hand through the entire process.

Sully never wanted to be a lawyer—at least, not a divorce lawyer. In law school, he and I had palled around with Matt Bozeman, the only son of Martin Bozeman, the other founding partner of the firm. After Leland's retirement but before his death, Martin had been looking for a couple of low-priced attorneys to try to take up some of the financial burden left behind by Leland's departure. Our friend Matt was destined to follow in his father's footsteps and become a real estate lawyer, and neither he nor his father would touch a divorce case. When Matt made us the initial offer, Sully balked, not wanting to *get his hands dirty*, as he said. But when old man Bozeman sweetened the deal by offering us a percentage of each case we handled in addition to a guaranteed salary, the chance to make some real dough was too tempting for Sully and he caved.

Looking back, it was probably his undoing. The first year, he made it clear that the job was only temporary and that he would like to move on—do some political consulting, perhaps even teach. But recently, he hadn't said a word about it. I supposed being a divorce attorney, even a bad one, suited his lifestyle.

And Sully's lifestyle had changed dramatically since moving from Oak Park to Lansing, Michigan, three years ago. When Gina and I moved in together, Sully rented an apartment in East Lansing near the MSU campus. He said he wanted be closer to the college scene again and hoped to pick up where he'd left off as an undergraduate. Whereby all accounts, he had been a regular *Don Juan*. Recently, I had lost track of his hit parade one-night-stands, partly because we were no longer roommates and partly because he hadn't been talking much about girls lately. It made me wonder if he was getting serious with someone. I made a mental note to bring up the subject at lunch.

I put in a call to Ms. Dolce and did what I could to ease her worrying mind. She was a new client and had yet to receive and review her first bill. When she did and took notice of all of my $25 reassuring phone calls, her anxiety would undoubtedly subside.

I called Jessie who was downright giddy when delivered the news. She insisted that we have a party.

"Friday will be perfect. I'll plan everything," said Jessie over the phone. "We'll do it at your house."

"You'll have to talk to Gina about it, but if it's okay with her, it's okay with me," I said.

"I'll talk to Gina, that shouldn't be a problem. She works Saturday nights, right?"

"Yeah," I said.

"Is she home now?"

"Should be. She didn't work last night, of course," I said, glancing down at my watch. "She may not be awake."

Gina tended bar three nights at a little Italian bistro in East Lansing. She slept in most days, even after the nights she didn't work.

"I'll wait a while then. I don't want to wake her."

"So how goes baby-making?" I asked playfully.

Jessie and The Win had been trying to have a child for a couple of years now. So far, they hadn't had any luck, of course. Jessie had been confiding in me every detail of the effort.

"It's going how it always goes. I keep telling Winslow that to further the species, you must engage in sexual intercourse, which requires that the male insert his—"

"I git it!" I laughed.

"I'm glad somebody gets it. When can you come over?" she said with a giggle.

"That bad, huh?"

"I'm seriously considering a gigolo." She laughed again. "Please tell me that you and Gina do it regularly."

"Like bunnies," I chuckled.

"All right then, Peter Rabbit. I'll call Gina later, but plan on Friday at your place."

"Fine," I said.

I loosened my tie and unbuttoned the collar to my shirt before following Sully into *Murray's Grill*. The walk from the office had been sweltering, and I was looking forward to the air-conditioned atmosphere of the restaurant. It was a favorite lunch spot with those from the office, but surprisingly, after a quick scan of the place, I recognized no one.

We sat at a corner table toward the front, beneath a faded oil painting of a wooden Irish harp. I ordered the fish and chips and an ice water and Sully only a Guinness, which told me I was in for the long lecture I had avoided this morning.

When the drinks came, Sully gave me a quick smile and then raised his glass.

"Here's to your . . ." he said, and then clearing his throat, " . . . your . . . well, how should we say . . . your—"

"You can't even say the word," I said, cutting him short. "What is your problem with commitment? Do you actually believe that if I get married, somehow you will have to get married too?"

Sully sat in silence, staring at me, still holding up his glass of Guinness.

"Don't worry, my friend, it doesn't work that way. You're off the hook," I said, grinning at him. "Now who's the girl? She must be quite a gal if you're worried you might have to settle down." I laughed and then tapped his glass with mine.

Sully took a long drink of the Guinness before setting it down on the table and wiping the froth from his lip.

"You're probably right," he said, smiling. "You know me."

Maybe it was the fact that I had been right, or that I did know him, or maybe it all had to do with the idea that I was going to be married—but for whatever the reason, I felt good. I ordered another Guinness for Sully and one for me as, suddenly, I was enjoying our lunch together.

"Of course, I want you to be my best man," I said. "I'll have to include Gina's brother in the party, but I'm sure it'll mean she'll include Jessie. But like I said, I want you to be the top guy."

Sully brushed a few renegade blond curls from his eyes and then squinted at me. "You and Gina discussed all this?"

"Not yet," I snapped, suddenly irritated. I was expecting a reply, not an interrogation. "But we will. You want to be the best man or not?"

Sully leaned back in his chair and lifted his palms to me.

"Of course, I'll be the best man. I'm sorry. I'm honored that you would ask me, really I am. It sounds to me like you've got it all worked out."

"I do . . . we do," I said. "Anyway, I think Jessie's putting together a party on Friday at our place, so keep it open."

"What kind of party?"

"An engagement party," I said. "What did you think? Man, you got it good."

"What?"

"Broad on the brain," I said, grinning at him. "Why don't you bring the new girlfriend? I'm dying to meet her."

It had cooled off a bit by Friday, enough for Jessie to have an excuse to hold the party outdoors. When I arrived home from work, I found her in the backyard mixing mustard into a large bowl of potato salad. The squelchy voice of Ernie Harwell buzzed from my old transistor radio sitting on a chair next to the backdoor.

"What's the score?"

"Tigers clinging to a one-run lead over the birds in the sixth," she announced. "Willie Horton just struck out . . . again!"

"Like a house by the side of the road," I mimicked the conventional Ernie Harwell call for a batter who struck out looking.

"You got that right. I think even Ernie's getting tired of this season. I'll be glad to be done with it," she said.

The Tigers had been a big disappointment: on pace to finish third in the division but still ahead of the Yankees in the standings, which made it all right with Jessie. Maybe they would pull this one out, and we all might have a pleasant evening.

"Are we having a picnic?" I asked, scooping some of the potato salad onto my finger.

"Not really, but I thought some food would be nice. I got some burgers and hot dogs. I thought we might grill," she said, smiling at me. "I put mustard in the salad the way you like."

I tasted the salad and then smacked my lips.

"Perfect," I said, grinning. "Where's Gina?" I hadn't seen her car.

"She ran to the store to pick up some wine."

"Oh," I said, nodding. "So who's all coming to this shindig?"

"Well," she said, handing me the bowl, "the usual suspects." She sighed. "I invited my mother. I hope you don't mind. She's coming with Winslow later."

I never had a problem with Jessie's mother, although apparently, she had a problem with me. According to Jessie, her mother didn't approve of our relationship. She felt your best friend should be your husband. Of course, only a few months prior, she had pinned down her fifth best friend.

"No, that's fine. It will be good to see her again," I lied. "And The Win will be making an appearance, huh?"

Jessie shot me a sour look and then rolled her eyes.

"Take it easy on him tonight, will you, please?"

"Me? I won't start anything," I protested. "Of course, I can't be responsible for Sully," I added.

"I suppose you guys could get him drunk, and then I can take advantage of him," she said, lifting her eyebrows.

"I'll do my best," I said.

Then, without warning, Jessie hugged me. I didn't know why, but I hoped it wasn't that I had agreed to abet her in the inebriation and fornication of her husband.

"I want you to know that I'm happy for you and Gina. She's a terrific girl, and you know how I feel about you," she said then released me. There were tears in her eyes. "I probably don't say it enough, but I really am happy for you. It's why I wanted to have this party."

It was what I so desperately needed to hear. It was her blessing. Gina was everything I wanted in a woman who wasn't Jessie. I was lucky to have her. She was young and beautiful—*full of beans,* as Jessie might say. There was nothing about her that others wouldn't love, yet still she loved me and I was grateful. She had a way of tempering the right amount of tenderness with tranquility, which at times could be mysteriously exciting. We didn't need to talk all the time, or constantly express our feelings as has been suggested by relationship gurus. Albeit unspoken, the communication was there, the *love* was there, and we were happy together.

"Thanks, Jess," I said. "It means the world to me. So you think I'm doing the right thing?"

"Of course," she said with a warm smile. "Don't you think so?"

"I do," I said, "but I've taken some shit from Sully."

"What does he know? He's never been with a woman long enough to commit to a movie."

"I don't know. He's got a new girlfriend, it might be serious."

"No way," gasped Jessie.

"Yeah, he told me Monday. He's supposed to be bringing her here tonight."

"Wow," said Jessie, "I can't wait to see the type of girl that Sully would get all serious over. You don't know anything about her, huh?"

"Not a thing. He has been pretty tight-lipped about it. But it will make for an interesting evening," I said with a wink.

I went inside to change my clothes, feeling suddenly excited about the evening's festivities. It was nice to have Jessie here. With all that was going on in our lives, I didn't get to see her as much as I would've liked. But she was here now and had given me her approval, and that was important to me.

I pulled on a pair of khaki Bermuda shorts and slipped on my favorite Hawaiian shirt. Sitting on the edge of the made bed, I took a good long look around the room. For as small as it was, it appeared strangely empty. The walls were plain and pictureless and reflected only the dull-gray light from the small shaded window. The furnishings consisted only of the frameless bed and a solitary dresser that Gina and I had purchased at an antique store. Atop of the dresser, where photographs and mementos might be, sat several piles of neatly stacked clothes that wouldn't fit inside the dresser. Overall, the room was cheerless, and it struck me that it lacked a personality—the personality of those that lived there. I no longer wanted the drab bed, drab house, and drab life. I wanted our bed, our house, and our life together to be filled with colorful memories that were *ours*.

I was on the threshold of matrimony and there was still time to make all the difference—in *our* room and in *our* life.

I sat alone in a lawn chair next to the side of the house sipping warm beer and watching anxious moths flitting about a streetlight. The once cool and pleasant evening had turned to a sultry night, the air now weighing heavy on my chest and shoulders. Nearly all the guests had come and gone. The few that remained stood huddling around a far table at the back corner of the yard, occasionally casting a curious eye my way, waiting and wondering whether Gina would ever return and if Sully would ever arrive.

Finally, Jessie came over.

"So, what do you think?" she said, her tone disgustingly sympathetic.

"I don't know," I said.

"What do *you* think happened?"

"I don't know," I said again.

"You don't think they're together, do you?"

That was exactly what I thought. I had only mulled it over in my head a few thousand times.

"Oh, they're together," I said, nodding at her.

"What do you want me to do, Hen?"

I glanced over to the group gathered around the far table. Jessie's eyes followed.

"I'll get rid of them," she said.

Minutes later, Jessie's mother, The Win, a friend of his that I didn't recognize, and one of Sully's law clerks went marching somberly on by, all appearing sympathetic—except for Jessie's mother who shot me a disapproving look. I was sure that she was enjoying this.

From where I sat, I heard a couple of cars start and caught the taillights of The Win's summer Corvette turning around in the neighbor's driveway before speeding off into the night. I was somewhat surprised when, a few seconds later, I saw Jessie suddenly appear from out of the darkness.

"I thought you were leaving?" I said.

"No, I thought I'd keep you company," she said. And then, after a short pause, she added, "Unless you want to be alone."

I shrugged and then took a long sip from my warm beer as Jessie pulled a lawn chair next to mine and slumped down into it.

"We'll wait together," she said. "She can't pull this shit and think she's going to get away with it! I plan to give her a piece of my mind, boy! And as for Sully! By God, if somehow that red bastard is in on this . . ." she said, her voice trailing off.

"They might not show," I said, glancing over at her.

"Oh, they'll show, all right," she said, returning my glance with a fierce one of her own. "My guess is they'll wait until they're sure everyone is gone. It's not right, Hen. It's not right at all. You were so good to her. I can't believe that she'd do this."

Jessie put her hand on my arm.

"I'm sorry, Hen. Really, I am. You deserve better."

She meant the words to be comforting, but they stung, and I hated them. And all the while, aching from deep inside me was an idea that this was no surprise. That somehow it was supposed to happen this way. That I knew it was going to happen. I loved Gina. She knew I loved her. Yet I could never really say that she loved me. She only told me she did. She told me all the time, and I had believed—or I had wanted to believe. I was happy with Gina, but I could never really be sure she was happy with me.

"Well, look at this," said Jessie, nodding toward the darkness.

At first, I didn't see anything there, but then I caught a sparkle from an earring. An earring attached to a familiar face.

Gina stepped out from the darkness, head down, hands in pockets, and with Sully tagging along behind her like a repentant child on the way to a spanking. She looked at me through sorrowful eyes, but ones that had not been crying.

"Hey," she said in the way she always said it.

"Hey," I replied weakly.

Gina pulled her long hair back behind her head and then glanced quickly back at Sully who was staring intently down at his wringing hands.

"It just happened, Hen," she said. And then, releasing a long sigh. "It wasn't planned. We didn't know how to tell you." She glanced around the yard, avoiding any eye contact with me. After a few moments, Jessie leaned forward to speak, but I motioned for her to wait and she slumped back in her chair.

Sully peeked at me remorsefully, but when I glared back at him, he looked away.

Suddenly my heart was at the back of my throat and I could not swallow. The entire event was playing out like a reoccurring nightmare. I knew what was going to happen next. I knew what she was going to say. I knew it right down to the expression on her face.

"We never intended to hurt you, Henry," said Gina. "Like I said, it just happened. I care for you, Henry, I really do. It's just that . . ." She paused long enough to wipe a dry eye. "It's that I don't think I love you . . . at least not in the way I'm supposed to, Hen," she added.

Jessie got out of her chair. There was no way of stopping her this time.

"You never intended to hurt him?" she repeated nastily. "You've got some nerve! And how weren't you hurting him when you were fucking Sully, Gina? You slutty bitch! You're nothing but plain white trash," fired Jessie. And then, slashing a glance at Sully. "And you! I feel sorry for you! You're a pathetic piece of shit, Sully, pretending to be so righteous with your big talk and commie ways! You stand there with your little whore holding your balls! You're such a pussy!"

Jessie shoved Gina out of her way and slapped Sully hard on the back of the head. Sully cowered down like a beaten dog and then stumbled away.

Jessie then turned her attention back to Gina.

"Don't worry, I was told never to hit little girls. Now get the hell out of here—both of you!" Jessie bellowed. "Your shit will be on the front lawn in the morning, Gina. You and the red bastard can pick it up then! Now scat!"

Jessie gestured as if she were shooing chickens, causing Gina to flinch, spin around, and then scurry off into the darkness. Sully followed obediently.

"Cowards," said Jessie when they were gone.

I didn't know what to say or do. It had all happened so fast. Gina was out of my life and without so much as a word from me. I thought for a moment my chest might collapse into my lungs. With all my emotions now jammed up into my throat, breathing was suddenly difficult and speaking next to impossible. It felt as though I had had something ripped from me, or out of me, leaving an empty hole exposed to a merciless world.

"What a bitch, Hen," Jessie said. "I can't imagine how you must be feeling."

Jessie knelt before me, wrapping her arms around my legs and then laying her head down on my lap as the streetlight suddenly flickered and then went out.

"I hate seeing you like this, Hen," she said softly. "She had no right, no right at all. You deserve so much more."

Jessie leaned back, sliding her hands under my shirt and across my chest. Then moving her body up mine, she kissed me eagerly on the lips.

"No," I said, pushing her away. "Go find your husband."

Jessie stood up and, for several seconds, stared at me curiously. Then, without a word, she turned and walked away—leaving me there in the darkness, alone and drowning in the night.

Chapter Thirty-One

June 1985

He does not expect confrontation, but he gets it. It comes at him gently, the way she plans it—there on the sofa, holding his hand, immersed in the soft gray glow from the television.

"I have something to tell you," she says simply and in a tone that, at any other time, might suggest good news.

"Oh yeah, what's that?" he says.

"There is someone else," she says in the same simple tone.

He does not speak. It is what he already knows.

"It just happened. I can't explain it," she says. "There is this attraction . . . I never meant for it to happen, but it did. Please know that I never wanted to hurt you or Emily."

He has heard the words before and expects them. They are biting, yet there is still some relief in them.

"I'm sorry," she says.

"Do you love him?"

"No . . . yes . . . I'm not sure," she says. "It's complicated."

It's always complicated. Next, there will be confusion.

"I am confused," she says.

"Yes," he agrees.

She looks at him curiously and then begins to cry.

"I'm so sorry," she says, shaking her head. "I'm sorry I let this happen. I hate myself for it."

"What do you want to do?" he says calmly.

"There's something I have to tell you. Something you need to know."

"Yes, I know," he says. "You're pregnant."

To my disappointment, the sun was shining again when I awoke. I found myself at another rest area, this time a few miles west of Portland, Oregon, off Interstate 84. Outside, the air was dry and cool. I used the facilities, bought a Coke from the machine, and then took a short stroll along the sidewalk in front of the restrooms thinking about everything I didn't want to think about.

I thought I might pop in on my sister Gwen in Portland. It had been some time since I had last seen her, our mother's funeral. Over the years, we had lost touch, but she was the type that might get a kick out of a surprise visit from her big brother. She was married with a couple of kids, two girls. I pulled out the Christmas card that I had received from her last year. It was a picture of the four of them sitting on a toboggan smiling and waving. On the back was an address, another damned reunion.

The doorbell of the two-story colonial-style house didn't work, so I banged on the door. A few seconds later, my sister stood squinting up at me.

"Yes," she said, not recognizing me. "Can I help you?"

"I'm selling vacuum cleaners," I said.

"I'm not . . ." She paused, still squinting, but this time using her hand as a visor. "Oh my god!" she squealed when at last she recognized me. "I can't believe it!" She pulled me down by the neck and into a hug, holding me for a good while. "It's you, it's really you!"

"It's me," I said.

She led me into a large living room sporting stylish leather furniture but strewn with toys. In the far corner, a curly red-haired little girl of five or six peeked curiously at me from behind a plastic rocking horse.

"This is your uncle," Gwen said to the little girl. "This is Henry. He's come a long way to visit us." Then Gwen glanced at me. "Henry, this is your niece, Lila."

"Pleased to meet you, Lila," I said.

Lila's expression didn't change, but the crinkled nose and pinched eyebrows were Gwen's.

"There's another one around here somewhere," said Gwen. "Stephanie!" Gwen called out.

From a wooden staircase across from the front door came the tapping sound of little feet. A platinum-haired girl I recognized from the Christmas card came skipping up to Gwen, saw me, and then hid timidly behind her mother's legs. Stephanie was a couple years older than Lila was, but every bit as cute.

"Don't be shy," said Gwen. "This is your uncle, Henry." Stephanie glanced up at her mother, then over at me.

"Hi, Uncle Henry," she said coyly.

"Hello there, Stephanie," I said.

"Have a seat, Henry," said Gwen. "Would you like some iced tea?"

"Sure," I said, taking a spot at the end of the sofa. Gwen left to tend to the tea while I entered into a staring contest with my two nieces. When I let out a little belch, at first neither one of them balked. But then Stephanie giggled, causing Lila to laugh, and soon we were all laughing. It was enough of an icebreaker to invoke some enlightening conversation regarding their likes and lives. Stephanie had just finished the first grade, and Lila would be starting kindergarten in the fall. Stephanie told me she liked Barbie dolls and paint by number, for which Lila added a *me too*. Stephanie quickly informed me that Lila did have a Barbie doll or two but was too little to do paint by number, and that Lila's sole artistic medium was the coloring book. Each then presented to me several fine samples of their work. In addition, Lila showed me one of her Barbie dolls—a busty blonde named Hannah that was naked from the waist down.

Gwen returned soon enough with two large glasses of iced tea, each garnished with a half a slice of lemon. She sat down in the chair opposite me and handed me the glass.

"I still can't believe you're here. It's been so long, Henry—too long," she said, shaking her head. Her eyes were older and the years had faded her hair and freckles somewhat, but she still displayed the same concerned expressions that I remembered growing up. "So what brings you out this way? Tell me you've decided to move here," she said.

"Not exactly," I said. "I'm on my way up north, Alaska."

"Really?" she said, sounding surprised. She fiddled with her lemon slice, took a quick sip, and then said, "Lance and I went up a couple years ago. It sure has grown with the pipeline and all. You never did get back there, did you, Hen?"

"No," I said. "Not since I left for school all those years ago."

"I remember," she said with a nod. Then her eyes suddenly widened. "That reminds me, Henry. I have something for you."

She hastily set her drink down on the coffee table and then ran from the room.

"I only just received it myself. I was going to send it along, but . . ." she said, her voice fading from somewhere down the hallway.

A few seconds later, she returned holding an envelope.

"Here," she said, handing it to me.

Gwen smiled warmly and then sat back down.

The envelope was plain white and business sized. Written on the front in all caps was *Henry*. Inside, there was a two-page document. It was a deed.

"It's the property. The house and everything," she said. "Dad wanted you to have it."

I sat staring down at the deed with my name typed at the top, and I recognized Tom's signature at the bottom.

"I have to say, it's not in very good shape, Hen. You know, Mom and Dad had a heck of a time with the renters. It's been closed up for the better part of a decade. I'm not sure if it's even habitable. Your old trailer is still there too."

"Why?" I said, shaking my head.

There was empathy in her smile, and I could tell she knew what I was asking.

"He just wanted you to have it, Hen. He didn't really say why, only asked if I could get it to you. It wasn't very long ago either, and it's amazing you showing up like this."

"How is he?"

"Oh, you know. He's still down the California way, Chico. You know he remarried last year, a real nice gal. They seem to get along very well. I think he's mellowed some in his old age."

I thought back to my mother's funeral. I remember Tom standing in the front row wearing a black suit and tie, his face expressionless. We had barely spoken. My mother had been sick for some time before she passed, and the last time I saw her, she didn't know me. She had called me *Tom*. He had taken care of her through all the years of her sickness, refusing to put her in a home. He was the only one with her when she died.

"That's good," I said. "How is Maggie?"

"I think," said Gwen, "of course, I hear from her about as often as I hear from you." She smirked. "You know she has a houseful, six kids. Can you believe it? She and her husband, Freddie, are still over there in Guam. He's been stationed there, what? Going on seven years, I think. I don't know if they'll ever be back, but like I said, I don't hear much from them."

I nodded, my mind still on the deed and Tom.

"So how long are you going to be here?" Gwen asked.

I nodded again, but then realized that wasn't the answer she was looking for.

"Oh . . . I don't know. I'm just passing through," I said.

"Well then, it's settled. You're going to stay a couple days. Lance will be floored when he finds out you're here."

"I don't know, Gwen. I need to be moving on. How about I stay tonight, and I'll take you all out for dinner?"

Gwen gave me a sour look, but then let out a relenting sigh.

"One night is better than nothing, I suppose, but we don't have to go out. I'm fixing lamb. You do like lamb?"

"Of course," I said. Perhaps it was her tone or the inflection in her voice, but it reminded me of our mother.

The past few years, I had not thought about my family much. But suddenly I missed them and felt guilty that I hadn't missed them before. I glanced over at Stephanie and Lila who were coloring quietly on the floor. For the moment, it felt nice to have a family.

"I make it the way Mother used to," she said.

"Sounds terrific," I said. "It's really good to see you, Gwen."

Before dinner, I spent a good deal of time with my nieces, snapping Legos, stacking blocks, and playing a few dozen games of pick-up-sticks. Their energy was endless and reminded me of what old Eddie had said about daughters.

When Lance arrived home from work, the girls met him at the door, announcing the news of my visit and then showering him with affection.

"Good to see you again," said Lance, shaking my hand while Lila rode piggyback and Stephanie tugged at his leg. "What a surprise. We often wonder what you're up to."

I had met Lance twice before, at his and Gwen's wedding and at my mother's funeral. I didn't spend a lot of time getting to know him. I did remember that he was an electrical engineer who worked for the local power company and that he appeared supportive of my sister.

"Just doing a bit of traveling," I said. "I thought I would pop in on some family."

"Excellent, and we're glad you did," he said, his crescent-shaped eyes and lined forehead adding an air of sincerity to his words. Then greeting my sister with a peck on the cheek in the typically domestic fashion, he made immediate inquiries as to supper.

"I told you this morning, we are having lamb," said Gwen.

"Excellent," he said to me. He then put an arm around my sister and the two of them stood together, smiling at me. I noticed he wasn't much taller than she was, even with the additional two inches or so that his bushy blond hair afforded him. "You'll really enjoy Gwen's lamb," he said.

I did enjoy the lamb, and the dinner itself had that traditional family atmosphere, made even more so by Gwen's insistence on referring to everyone according to their genealogical status.

"Please pass the peas to your *father*, honey. Help your *sister* with her napkin, please. Won't you have more potatoes, *Uncle Henry?*" she would say.

After dinner, we sat in the living room sipping red wine. I listened to a rather lengthy discussion regarding the intricacies of raising two girls in the modern world. Interestingly, both Lance and Gwen had strong positions on the subject—Lance suggesting a reliance on compassion and understanding while my sister preferring the more conventional approach of education and discipline. For the most part, I kept quiet, never offering an opinion, content with just listening and glad not to be the focus of the conversation.

When it was time for Lila and Stephanie to go to bed, at the direction of my sister, I received from them a cursory hug and kiss, followed by a sweet but coached *"I love you, Uncle Henry."*

"So, Henry," said Lance, after Gwen left to put the girls down. "How long do you plan on being away from Michigan?"

I had conveyed very little about my plans, and I supposed certain questions were inevitable.

"I'm not sure, Lance. I took an extended leave of absence," I lied. "I don't have any immediate plans to return."

"Excellent," he said. "Doing a little sightseeing and soul searching, eh?"

"Yeah, something like that," I said. "It's turned into more of a reunion tour. I probably should've done it years ago."

"Well, you're doing it now," said Lance reassuringly. "That's what really matters. I know that Gwen is very glad to see you."

"It's great seeing her again too. Motherhood suits her. The girls are beautiful."

"Yes," he said, smiling proudly, "but they sure can be a handful."

"That's what I hear," I said.

Lance looked at me curiously, but before he could speak, my sister returned.

"They want you to say goodnight to them," she said to Lance. "Lila says she won't close her eyes until you go in there."

"Excuse me," said Lance, getting out of the chair.

When Lance left, my sister returned. She sat down next to me on the sofa, leaned back putting her hands behind her head, and then released a long sigh.

"You're the first uncle they've ever known," she said. "Lance is an only child, and of course, we never see Maggie. Stephanie asked me if an *uncle* was the same as an *angel*." Gwen rolled her eyes and laughed.

"Boy, will she be disappointed," I said, laughing.

"I've really missed you, Hen. With Mother passing and Dad in California, sometimes I feel like an orphan. It's nice for the girls to know some family."

A tremor of guilt passed through me, but it wasn't overwhelming and it didn't last long.

"Better late than never," I said.

"I'm not complaining," said Gwen. "I'm happy to see you. I wish you didn't have to leave so soon. I really hope you'll keep in touch *this time*."

Her tone was harsh, but warranted. It nevertheless annoyed me. I hadn't kept in touch, but I was making an effort now. Except for the occasional holiday card, she hadn't exactly been knocking down my door either.

"I'll try," I said.

As the wine flowed, so did the questions. My answers were short, vague, and ultimately led to more questions. I hated to lie, but the truth would be difficult and certainly misunderstood. Gwen seemed genuinely concerned with my well-being, but not having children, I am sure my life seemed foreign to her.

Around eleven, Gwen started hinting that she was tired. I was also tired of avoiding questions. Before long, they were showing me to the guestroom where Gwen had laid out a set of towels and a new bar of soap.

"The bathroom is just down the hall to your left," said Gwen. "Do you need to get a bag or something from your car?"

"No thanks," I said. "If it's all the same to you, I'll get it in the morning."

"Excellent," said Lance.

Then Gwen gave me a long hug.

"It's been so nice to see you, Hen," she said. "It's so hard to believe that you're really here. I'm so glad you decided to stop by. The girls are so happy to have their uncle . . ." She hesitated. "I think I hear Lila. I suppose she needs more water," she said, moving toward the door.

Lance smiled at me as Gwen passed him at the door.

"Children can be a handful," he said.

"That's what I keep hearing."

Chapter Thirty-Two

July 1965

We reached the ridgeline well before 7:00 a.m. Jessie had insisted we get an early start—Spooner's revelation the day before clearly on her mind.

"If I'm right, there should be a mineshaft somewhere just ahead," I said, pointing up the rocky trail. "It's the only one I know of that's not caved in. If we don't find anything there . . . well, then we're—"

"*Shit out of luck*," said Jessie, who was standing directly behind me.

"I was going to say, we're going to have to come up with another idea. But yeah, I think you're right."

"They've got to be in there," she said. "I told you, Granddaddy's not that clever."

I wasn't as convinced. Spenser had gotten away with it for thirty-some odd years without anyone being the wiser. Even if he had hidden them up here, there couldn't be much left to find.

"I don't know, Jess. It seems to me that he wouldn't go leaving the bodies lying around in an open mine."

"That shows what you don't know," snapped Jessie. "I'm telling you, Spenser's not that clever."

Suddenly I heard what sounded like a cough echo from somewhere up the trail behind me. Judging from her eyes, Jessie had heard it too.

"It's him," she whispered loudly, pulling me down behind a cluster of turned-up spruce trees. "He's just ahead of us."

I poked my head around the tree roots, sure enough, I saw old Spenser trudging up the trail only a couple hundred yards away.

"He must of come from out of the woods," I whispered.

Jessie's eyes widened.

"You know what that means?" She didn't wait for a reply. "It means that they're up there somewhere. It means that Spooner was right. We have to keep an eye on him. This is good, Hen," she said looking beyond me up the trail. "He's going to lead us right to them."

If that was what it meant, no way was I feeling good. My mind began to wonder wildly about the realty of finding bodies.

"Maybe we should come back later," I said.

Jessie's look was fierce.

"What are you talking about? This is what we wanted. He's going to lead us right to the bodies. I can't believe you sometimes, Hen," she said shaking her head. "Don't be a rube!"

Her words came louder than she intended and Spenser glanced back in our direction. We both ducked out of sight. A minute later, Jessie peeked over the fallen trees.

"Look!" she said.

I stood up beside Jessie and saw that Spenser had worked his way up to the plateau where he began hacking at the side of the hill with what looked to be a pickax.

"That's it," I said. "That's the mineshaft."

Jessie glanced at me and smiled.

"Once he goes in, then we hightail it over there," she said.

"I don't know, Jess," I said. "There's only one way in and one way out, and we can't let him see us."

"But then how are we going to know where he hid them?"

"I don't know," I said with a shrug. "Maybe he'll bring them out."

Jessie nodded approvingly as we both watched Spenser disappear into the side of the hill.

In five minutes, we had reached the plateau where we discovered the boarded entrance in shambles. An old rail ran out from the shaft, across the small plateau and down a slight grade disappearing into a thicket of black spruce trees. A heaping pile of rusted mining equipment including what looked to be the remnants of a trackless backhoe surrounded the entrance to the shaft.

"We can hide behind there," I said pointing at the backhoe's giant bucket.

Jessie followed me around the backside of the backhoe between the bucket and its rusted-out engine. She climbed into the bucket while I ducked behind it. Then we waited.

What seemed like hours, according to my old Timex, was about twenty minutes when we saw old Spenser step out from the mineshaft holding a kerosene lantern. He didn't dally, but snatched up the pickax and headed back down the trail.

When Spenser was well out of sight, Jessie jumped out of the bucket and ran to the entrance to the mine. I followed her over and we both stood staring into the darkness of the shaft.

"How are we going to see in there?" asked Jessie. "We should've brought a lantern."

"We don't need a lantern," I said reaching into the back pocket of my jeans and pulling out a penlight. "It's not much, but I thought it might come in handy. I borrowed it from Tom's toolbox this morning." I clicked it on and stepped into the mine with Jessie following close behind.

Inside, the smothering darkness made fast work of the narrow beam from the penlight and I could barely make out the rail, which seemed to run downward through an array of puddles and mud. The air was cold and damp and the ceiling and walls trickled with watery streams. I thought seriously about turning back, but after a few minutes my eyes adjusted and we could see well enough to continue.

For the next several hundred feet we sloshed down through a slippery river of mud until the rail veered off in one direction and the river in another.

"Which way do we go?" said Jessie.

"I'm not sure," I said, running the beam from the penlight along the ground in both directions. I thought we would have to pick a path and hope for the best, but then the penlight caught something.

"Look," I said flashing the light down at the rail. For the most part the ground beneath it was dry except for a couple sets of sloppy footprints that went traipsing in and out of the river of mud. "This way," I said.

The footprints were easy to follow and led us deeper into the mine until the shaft split again. We then followed them down a narrowing channel that ended after a couple hundred feet at a wall of plywood. Behind the plywood, there was nothing but dirt. I didn't see anything that would indicate a portal or a pathway even though the numerous footprints suggested that Spenser had been here.

"Strange," I said. "He was definitely here but I don't see anything."

"Maybe the bodies were here and he moved them," said Jessie.

"It's possible," I said, shaking my head, unconvinced, "but Spenser was only in the shaft for twenty minutes, and the footprints lead from the mud in and out of here. I don't think there would be enough time for him to move anything." I flashed the light down at the ground again but saw nothing new. "I suppose we can check the other tunnels," I said, moving by Jessie and on back up the tunnel.

"Wait!" said Jessie.

I glanced back at her, shining the light at her eyes.

"What?" I said.

"The bodies *are* here," she said, shoving the light away. I know they are."

I shined the light around the entire area but saw nothing. "You're crazy, there's nothing here," I said.

"They're here all right," said Jessie, snatching the penlight from my hand. If the bodies hadn't been touched, he wouldn't have to do anything. He would know the letter was a hoax. Don't you see? This *is* where he buried the bodies all those years ago, and because he found they hadn't been touched, he was convinced the letter was a hoax and left. Of course, he didn't count on us following him," she added with a wry smile. "I told you, Granddaddy's not that clever."

It all made eerie sense, but it was the next step that made me shiver anxiously. Jessie placed the penlight in her mouth and then ran her hand along the back wall of the shaft.

"It's pretty solid," she said.

"It's been over thirty years," I said. "It might be difficult to dig up. We'll have to get some tools. Maybe we can borrow your grandfather's pickax," I said with a nervous laugh.

"Damn right we will," said Jessie, a little too seriously.

On the way back, we agreed that I would go to my house and get a spade, while Jessie went to the Shit Towers to retrieve the pickax. We then agreed to meet at the beaver pond and then trek back up the ridgeline to the mineshaft.

"What do we do with the bodies once we find them?" I said.

"You mean the *bones*, don't you?" she said. "We call the state troopers, and hopefully, they'll arrest him for murder."

"Why don't we just turn him in now and have the police go and dig up the bones?"

Jessie stopped us both, a concerned look in her eyes.

"You know, I thought about that for a long time, but I think it's best that we have them before we go handing the case over to the police. That way, Spenser's least likely to suspect anything before it's too late."

"I suppose," I said, unconvinced.

From atop the giant tailing pile, I spied Jessie. She was at the center of the beaver pond swimming on her back, arms wide, feet together, and her naked skin reflecting a holy white against the black water. I didn't call down to her. Instead, for a long minute, I watched her flutter about the pond, leaving aquatic angels in her wake.

When the sight became more than my adolescence could stand, I announced my presence with an echoing *Hey!* and then went bounding down the side of the hill. By the time I reached the edge of the pond, Jessie was already there. I watched her pulling up her panties. When she saw me, she gave me a fierce glare and I looked away, but not before catching an arousing eyeful of her most private part.

"You're such a rube!" she said, rolling her eyes. "I hope you got a good look."

I shook my head, but stared feverishly at her chest as she put on her blouse. Jessie rolled her eyes again, but then smiled.

"Did you get the pickax?" I said, tossing the spade on the ground.

"Yeah," she said, nodding up the bank behind me.

I glanced back and saw the pickax leaning against the base of a birch tree. It brought a sudden chill to the otherwise warm day.

"I was thinking . . ." I said, and then hesitated.

Jessie shot me a piercing look.

"Maybe we should let someone know about this, like your dad," I added before she could bark out an objection.

She scowled, but then seemed to ponder the idea. After a few moments, however, she shook her head.

"No," she said emphatically, "that won't work."

I wasn't convinced it would either, but my fear of Spenser was enough to welcome even JT's goofy mug.

"This is getting pretty serious," I said.

"We will when we get the evidence," she said sternly. "Besides, he's no help. He spends all his free time with his girlfriend, Janice. I think he's trying to get her to move up here from Anchorage."

"He spends enough time in Anchorage, that's for sure," I said.

"That's on account of Janice wanting to get her claws into him," she said, walking past me.

"Claws?" I said, following her.

"Yeah, she's trying to get her claws into him," she said, making a claw out of her right hand and scratching at the air. "I told you, she wants to marry him. He's a good catch. I can't stand her, Hen. She's so fake, and she's got an ass the size of the federal league."

"Oh," I said, not sure really how big the federal league was. I wasn't exactly sure what typified a "good catch" either, but it couldn't be JT—unless, of course, you were talking about enormous muscle-bound gnomes.

"He is for sure," said Jessie, her dark eyes twinkling. "He's good looking, hardworking, and smart. It's surprising more women haven't tried to latch onto him. Did you know that when he was in high school, he was an all-state ball player and wrestler too? He played catcher a year for the Toledo Mud Hens, you know, before tearing up his shoulder. The ladies all adored him, you know, that's how he met my mother," she added, snatching the pickax and wielding it up to her shoulder.

I had heard the story a hundred times, but I knew she loved to tell it. She always did when she was concerned or nervous about something.

"Daddy dove into the stands after a foul ball," she continued. "Snatched it right out of my mother's lap. It being the third out and all, Daddy tossed her the ball and they hooked up after the game. My mother said he was such a charmer. *All man but with a touch of naughty*, she'd say. He caught it right out of her lap—can you imagine, Hen? What a romantic story. I don't see how fat-assed Janice can compete with that. I mean—"

"Marry me," I said, so suddenly and with such earnestness that I wasn't sure if I had really said it.

"What did you say?" she said. The surprise in her eyes had to match my own.

"Marry me," I said again, this time with a greater conviction and purpose. It was as if I were standing beside myself—listening, not speaking. Perhaps it was seeing her swimming in the pond, or the way she went on about JT and her mother, or maybe it was just a last-ditch effort to avoid digging up bones. Whatever the reason, it had been said, and I had said it.

There was a long silence—not awkward but poignant, the kind of pause that comes right before laughter, or tears. Jessie turned to me and looked into my eyes for a long while. Finally, she set down the pickax and reached out to me, gently taking my head in her hands.

"Oh," she sighed sweetly, her eyes softening.

"I'm serious," I said. "I love you. I'm in love with you."

"I know," she said, smiling.

With the back of her hand, she caressed the side of my face and then, pulling me to her, she kissed me lightly on the lips. When she let me go, I saw the tears and I knew what her answer would be.

"You know I can't," she whispered and then quickly looked away.

"Why?"

"It's not that I don't love you," she said, her eyes returning to mine. "God knows that I love you—more than you'll ever know, Hen. And you'd make a fine husband, really you would," she added with a small burst of a giggle. Then she wiped her eyes and placed a consoling hand on my shoulder. "I'm afraid I wouldn't make you much of a wife, Hen. I'm sure I'd do something to mess it up, and I don't ever want to lose you."

"Why don't you let me worry about that? I don't plan on ever letting you go," I said reassuringly.

"I know you wouldn't, Hen. That's why I can't marry you. I don't want to let you down. I don't ever want to hurt you. You mean too much to me, and if I married you, I would only let you down."

"I don't understand."

"I'm not sure I do either, but that's the way it has to be, Hen. I'm sorry."

Suddenly she wasn't making sense to me, and her tone sounded too dismissive. I brushed her hand off my shoulder.

"Go to hell!" I shouted at her. "You're full of shit, you know that? I mean you're chock-full of it! All I've ever done is love you! And stand by you! And be your damned friend! What did it ever get me? Huh? What? You say you love me—bullshit! It's bullshit! All of it! Don't I do it for you? I bet if any one of the parade of boys that you've been with came a calling, asking you to marry him, you'd run right off in a heartbeat!"

To my surprise, Jessie's expression hadn't changed. Her eyes were still soft and understanding, and she hadn't moved an inch. Instead, she stood quietly, seemingly taking it all in. It made me angrier.

"You can find someone else, another sucker, because it won't be me. I'm through!" I said and then stormed away.

I expected her to stop me right away, but she didn't. It wasn't until I was halfway up the tailing pile and heard the sound of sliding rocks that I knew she was behind me. Fighting the urge to look back, I charged upward, not wanting to give in to her. My mind was torturing me with self-pitying thoughts of rejection, and I wanted to hurry and hide myself before I started to cry.

"They're not the same things, Henry!" Jessie shouted from behind me. "They're not the same at all!"

I spun around and was surprised to find her so close, nearly face-to-face, staring up at me with somber eyes.

"What?"

"Love," she said softly, "and having sex. They're not the same thing, Hen."

I must've given her an odd look, because she frowned as though she'd thought I'd misunderstood her. I didn't, but I remained silent, waiting for her to continue.

"I know it's what you think. You think because I go with all these boys that I love them. It's not true. I've never been in love with any of them, not even a little bit—if there is such a thing as a little bit in love. Some of them I haven't even liked, and maybe that's wrong. Maybe it's wrong to be with someone that way when you don't like them. I'm not even sure why I do it." She paused, shook her head, and then said, "Maybe it's because I know it's what they want, and I know that once they get what they want, maybe I'll mean something to them. Even if they mean nothing to me."

Glancing down, she kicked at the ground, and after a few seconds, she looked back up at me.

"I've even done it with people I hate, Hen," she said with a shameful look. "And it has *never* made me like them, not even a little bit."

This time I thought I had misunderstood, and I was certain my look said so.

"What are you talking about, people you hate?

Jessie shook her head and stormed back down the tailing pile. I followed.

"Wait, Jess!" I hollered after her.

Jessie stopped, spun around just before the near side of the dam. I could see tears in her eyes.

"People you hate, Jess?"

She wiped her eyes to make way for the projecting anger.

"Yes, people I hate!" she spat, and I thought for a moment she was going to say more, but she didn't. Instead, she only stared at me, her dark eyes penetrating until I felt compelled to speak.

"Who do you hate?"

"I hate my granddaddy," she whispered, her eyes searching mine.

"I know," I said flatly. "We're going to get him, Jess. Those bones are buried up there somewhere, and I'm sure—"

"It's not that," she said, shaking her head. "I hate him because . . ." Her voice broke. "I *hate* him," she said, this time so clearly and with such pure disdain that there was no doubting what she meant. The statement was followed by a torrential gush of tears unlike any I had ever seen before from anyone. I wanted to say or do something, but nothing came to mind. All at once, it made horrific sense—the bootlegging and her obsession with the murders. My mind went rolling backward to those times when I had nearly nurtured a suspicion of something, something at the time I couldn't put my finger on.

"Why?" I asked.

From the bent look on her face, I knew I had said the wrong thing. I didn't mean it the way she thought, but before I could get out a conciliatory word, she slapped me so hard I nearly fell over.

"Fuck you, Henry!" she said viciously. "*Why*? Why do you think?" She slapped me again, this time causing me to stumble sideways. I hadn't quite regained my balance when she hit me a third time, which dropped me to my knees. That was all I could remember when I came to. But from my watery eyes and pounding head, I figured she must've kicked me in the face.

"You all right?"

I blinked a couple of times until Jessie's blurry head came into focus.

"I think so," I said weakly.

"Get up then," she ordered.

"Promise you won't hit me again?"

"Yeah," she said, but with no assurance in her tone.

I managed to stagger to my feet and steady myself long enough to get a finger to my lip. It was split, bleeding, and soon would swell. Jessie's expression was a mystery to me. I didn't know whether she wanted consolation or to hit me again. I held up a hand in a type of truce.

"Wait," I said, "just wait a minute."

I took a few deep breaths, then wiping my lip with my shirtsleeve, I glanced past her, searching the world for something to say. When I could find nothing, my eyes fell again upon hers.

"I don't know anything about it, Jess," I said.

Even with the afternoon sun blazing down, I felt darkness surrounding me. I suddenly realized that there wasn't anything I could say or do that wouldn't sound inappropriate or warrant another crack to the face.

"That's right, you don't know anything about it," she fired and then turned away, gazing out across the beaver pond, her eyes still gushing tears. "I'm sorry that I'm not what you want me to be. Believe me, I wish I were different. I wish things were different, Hen." She glanced back at me. "Sometimes it's just easier to . . ." She hesitated and then shook her head sternly as if she'd talked herself out of something. "No, I don't have to explain anything to you. You can think what you want, but I don't owe you anything. Fuck you! I know what you think! You think I *let* that dirty old man put his hands all over me, that I somehow wanted it! That's right, Henry, you don't know a thing about it! You say you love me and want to marry me, but then treat me like some kind of whore when I say *no* to you!"

Jessie raised her hand, causing me to flinch, but she only wiped tears from her eyes.

"You're no different from the rest of them! You're not a bit different! You only want to fuck me! That's all you ever wanted, isn't it?" She gave me a look of disgust, followed by one of resignation. "Fine," she said with a nod. "You want me?" She took a step back and then began unbuttoning her sleeveless white blouse. "Take me then," she said as more tears streamed down her face. "I'll fuck you! You know me, I'll fuck anybody!"

In a few seconds, her clothes lay on the ground in piles around her ankles, and she stood naked before me, vulnerable and beautiful. But this time I felt no excitement, no arousal, no sexual ambition of any kind. All I could do was look away, ashamed of myself for ever having had such feelings.

"No," I said, still looking away. "That's not what I want."

Somewhere beneath my petty desires and below all the layers of my guilt, the seeds of anger had been sown. It stirred in me a quiet rage, one that drove my eyes back to her.

"It has to stop!" I said sternly, expecting her to hit me again.

Jessie looked confused but then began gathering up her clothes.

"I have to find those bodies, Hen," she said tearfully.

"You have to tell JT," I said. "He can put an end to all this right now, Jess."

Her eyes widened and then fell, as if all her hope fell with them.

"No," she said sadly and then looked away.

"You have to, Jess. It's the only way. He'll kill the bastard when he finds out, and I wouldn't blame him if he did!"

"No," she said flatly, pulling on her jeans.

"You have to tell him," I said, "We have to deal with this, now!"

"No, *you* don't have to *deal* with any of it!" she fired.

"You're not making any sense, Jess!"

"It's not your problem, it's mine!" she snapped. "I don't need your help, so don't worry about it. It's not so bad anymore . . . I've gotten used to it," she added weakly.

Jessie fastened the last button to her blouse and then walked toward the dam.

"Do you hear yourself?" I called after her. "This is nuts! If you won't tell him, then I will!"

Jessie stopped in her tracks and then spun around, glaring up at me. Her eyes were a mix of anger and tears.

"Mind your own goddamned business! I should've never told you anything! If you say anything to my daddy, so help me God, I'll—"

"There's nothing you can do about it, Jess," I said. "I'm telling him."

Jessie took a couple of steps toward me, I thought for sure to take a swing, but her arms fell to her sides and she released a defeated sigh.

"Please don't tell him, Hen," she said, her voice pleading.

"I'm sorry, Jess, this has to stop. I'm going to tell him," I said firmly.

"It won't do any good," she said, her eyes red and drifting. "*I already did,*" she whispered.

There was movement amidst the cattail reeds just beyond the dam. A beaver poked his nose out from the high grass and splashed into the pond. Had he heard what I just had there was surely cause for alarm.

Jessie stared across the pond as the anger inside of me burst.

I flew past Jessie, crossed the dam, and ran up the grassy incline on the other side of the pond. Jessie hollered from behind me, pleading for me to wait, but nothing could stop me now. Not sure what to do, I knew precisely where to go. I ripped through a thicket of cottonwood saplings that snapped painfully at my shins and thighs. When finally

I broke free of the brush, I slid straight down into a massive crater left from a collapsed gold mine where I landed awkwardly, rolling my ankle. The crater was the result of an old gold mine that had collapsed in on itself years before, leaving only a deep crater to mark its existence. I limped across the crater's soggy bottom and crawled up the steep embankment on other side, finally pulling myself out by grabbing onto the base of a sappy black spruce tree.

I tore my way through a small spruce forest, letting the sharp branches spur me on. Charging out of the woods and onto the highway, I glanced skyward and saw the tops of the Shit Towers. I lumbered down the highway and then up the long driveway.

"Spenser!" I shouted when I reached the cabin.

Not hearing a sound, I shouted again, and then again.

"Where are you, Spenser? You bastard!" I screamed as loud as I could.

I knew he was there. His shitty truck was parked next to the doorway, and the old Buick had been left halfway up the drive.

"Get your ass out here, you old fuck!" I hollered, my voice cracking. "I'll come in there and get you! I swear to Jesus, I will!"

There was a sharp creak before the cabin door swung open, and out stepped Spenser Mason. He stood hunched over himself, his enormous knot of a head splotched with a few oily strands of yellow hair that gleamed insolently in the late afternoon sun. He wore a dingy white tee shirt and dirty tan pants held high on his chest by a thin set of suspenders.

Spenser's black eyes glared sharply at me while my own settled on the shotgun that dangled menacingly from his arms.

"What you fussing all about, boy?" he snorted with a bit of a nod.

The old man moved slowly from the doorway, slightly raising the rifle with every step. When he finally reached me, he stuck the barrel hard into my chest.

"What you fussing all about, boy?" he said again. "I won't ask you a third time," he added with a twisted little grin.

I hadn't planned for the gun. Hell, I hadn't planned for anything. Fear pounded from inside me, and I nearly choked on my words.

"*Nothing*," I said in not much more than a whisper.

Spenser squinted at me, his eyes shifty. He knew I was scared silly, and he wasn't about to let me get off easy.

"It's what I figured," he said with a nod.

Slowly, he lowered the barrel of the gun, and for a moment, I thought as if he might turn away. But in one sudden motion, he grasped the shotgun by its butt-end and thrust it hard at my head.

There was no time to move, no time to react, and it hit me squarely in the eye.

When I came to, the old man was staring down at me, still grinning. A strand of his greasy hair draped over his left eye.

"That's what you get for carrying on like a lunatic," he said. "Now get on home before you make me real mad!"

Spenser then kicked me so hard in the ribs that I thought I might never breathe again.

"Now get on home before you make me real mad," he said, before shuffling back to the cabin.

Coughing and gasping for air, I managed to roll over onto my hands and knees, climb to my feet, and hobble down the driveway, my head pounding in pain and with hate.

Chapter Thirty-Three

April 1980

Winslow "The Win" Marshall had already missed the birth of his first son eleven months ago. A record spring snowstorm in Cleveland had closed roads and grounded planes, making it impossible for him to be back in Detroit when his eight-pound-fifteen-ounce namesake came barreling into the world.

Not to worry, The Win had assured me over the phone, *I just cut a deal here in Cleveland that will set Junior up for life. You understand, Hen. Take care of my girl for me*, he had said. *I'll be there as soon as I can.*

I had done my best during the over-thirty-hour labor, holding Jessie's hand and feeding her ice chips. For the most part, it had only been the two of us at the hospital, except a sadistic little maternity nurse timing contractions and demanding that Jessie push so violently and frequently that I began to wonder what it was we were actually trying to deliver. Afterward, as baby Junior lay quietly on Jessie's chest, the sadistic nurse required more hard pushing until a mass of blood and afterbirth shot so far out of Jessie it caught the witch squarely in the face, causing me to wince and Jessie to burst out laughing.

Nearly a year later, with the maternity ward filled with friends and well-wishers, Jessie was in labor again, this time awaiting the arrival of expected twins. The Win had been sure to be on hand with his ten-dollar smile and his box of celebratory cigars.

"Show should start anytime now," said The Win, handing Junior to me. "He's a little fussy, Uncle Henry. You know how it is."

Then tossing me the pacifier, he strolled over to Jessie's mother and whispered something in her ear, causing her to laugh hysterically while glancing in my direction.

It was the third time in the past half hour that The Win had passed Junior off to me, and I was beginning to wonder if the show would ever start. I made my way through the crowd consisting mostly of friends and close business associates of The Win and sat down on a metal bench next to the elevators. Junior was pleasant, and once I gave him the pacifier, he sat in my lap quietly observing the commotion.

It was closing in on midnight when a nurse came out and told us that Jessie was ready. The Win smiled but appeared anxious as he followed the nurse through a heavy set of wooden doors.

Surprisingly, The Win returned after only thirty minutes, his face pale and his mouth agape.

"I'm not going back in there," he said to the crowd. "I can't be in there with all that bitching and moaning going on."

"That's all right, buddy," said one of The Win's pals, slapping him on the back. "Your job is to pass out cigars anyway. Let the women stick to the birthing!"

There was some light laughter, which caused The Win to grin.

Then the nurse came out again and, scanning the room, she called out, "Henry Allen! Is there a Henry Allen?"

"Yes, that's me," I said, standing with Junior in my arms.

"Well, Henry, Mrs. Marshall has requested your presence in the delivery room."

I immediately glanced over at the Win who gave me a shrug, then over to Jessie's mother who gave me one of her predictable scowls. I walked over and handed The Win Junior.

"I wonder what's going on," I said to him.

"You know how she is," he said.

"Why does she need me?" I said to the nurse.

"She asked for you. Apparently, you've been through this with her before, and Mr. Marshall wasn't quite working out," said the nurse with a caustic glance at The Win.

I didn't ask any more questions and followed her through the wooden doors and into the all-too-familiar delivery room. They had Jessie's legs in stirrups. A blue sheet partitioned her body at the waist, and fortunately, from my angle, I could only see her from the waist up.

"Hey, Hen," she said, her voice straining.

"Hey," I said.

"I need you to help me push these bastards out!" she groaned.

I looked over at the nurse who was darting about the room, fiddling with various equipment and instruments while a doctor barked out orders to her from behind the blue sheet.

Then I had some of my own.

"Ice chips," I said loudly. "We need some ice chips."

It didn't stop for nearly two hours, and then only long enough for the doctor to display for us a blood-covered baby boy, which the nurse quickly swaddled into a white blanket before taking him out of the room. Another cup of ice chips and fifteen more minutes of hard pushing later, the second twin emerged from behind the blue sheet, screaming at life.

When I got back to the waiting room, The Win had already been to the nursery and seen the boys. Now he was busy glad-handing everyone and passing out cigars.

"Good work in there, Hen," he said, patting me uneasily on the shoulder. "Didn't want to put you on the spot like that, but you've been through all this before, and I think Jess felt a little more comfortable with you."

"No problem," I said, "but I think she'd be a little more comfortable if you were in there with her now. I think they're going to let her see the boys."

"Oh, yeah, good idea," he said, handing me a couple of cigars before heading off in the direction of the large double doors.

A few seconds later, Jessie's mother, Sharon, came into the room, hanging on to a wailing Junior. She had the poor kid around the waist, the way she might carry an overstuffed duffel bag.

"Here, you take him," she said, handing him to me by the armpits. "He's been a brat."

I took Junior who buried his face into my chest, sobbing. It wasn't long before I got him calmed down, but finding his pacifier helped.

A few minutes later, The Win came out of the delivery room wearing a sour look on his face.

"They're moving her," he said to me, but didn't offer to take Junior. Instead, he shook his head and marched down the hallway, leaving Junior and me alone in the waiting room.

Another hour went by and no one had returned. Junior had fallen asleep on my shoulder and I didn't want to move for fear of waking him. Finally, the nurse from the delivery room came out and told me where they had moved Jessie.

"It's not far from here," the nurse said sweetly. It's just down the long hallway and to your left. You can follow the yellow line on the floor."

"Thanks," I said. "Does she have a lot of visitors?"

The nurse smiled sweetly again, and then said, "None at all, but there's quite a little party around the nursery window."

"Thanks," I said, returning her smile.

Junior woke up about halfway down the hallway, opening his eyes and quietly looking around. By the time I reached Jessie's room, he had fallen back asleep. Jessie was sitting up in bed and had a welcoming smile on her face.

"I'm having you do all my deliveries," she said. "I think you have a knack for it. I see Junior has taken to you," she added. "Give him to me, he can sleep with Momma for a while."

I laid Junior down beside her, and he didn't wake.

"He's got to be tired," I said. "It's nearly three in the morning."

"I'm sure," she said. "I wish I could sleep like that. I told Winslow to take him home, but I'm not sure where he went."

"I think he's down at the nursery. I hear that's where it's all happening."

"I don't suspect Winslow will be back anytime soon," she said, frowning. "He was pretty pissed off at me when he left here."

"What's he upset about?"

"Everything," she said, rolling her eyes. "First, I kicked him out of the delivery room, only because he was worthless. All he did was stare at me stupidly, shaking his damn head, telling the nurse she should do something. The asshole wouldn't even stand next to me. He kept saying they have nurses for that. Then when they brought the boys in, he got all bent out of shape because of what I wanted to name them."

"Didn't you two already decide?"

"Hell no!" she shouted. "He told me I should decide. Then when I did, he flipped out."

"So what *did* you name them?"

"*James* and . . ." She hesitated. Then looking at me sheepishly, she said, "And *Henry*."

The days following the birth of the twins, I spent quite a bit of time with Jessie and the kids at their house in Birmingham. The Win had taken a weeklong business trip to California, something he said he couldn't put off any longer and had a difficult time explaining.

"It's his way of escaping," said Jessie from the kitchen where she was warming a bottle on the stove. "It's nothing new, he does it all the time. Every time I need him to be here, he goes running off somewhere on business—but I wonder," she added with a scowl.

"What do you wonder?" I asked.

"Sometimes I wonder what does on during those trips, but then most times I don't care," she said dismissively. "If I didn't need his help with the kids, I wouldn't care if he was around at all. I suppose even when he is around, he's worthless."

Jessie came into the living room and lifted James from one of the bassinets, toted him over to the leather sofa where I was sitting and began feeding him the bottle.

"You'll handle my divorce, right?"

"That's funny," I said.

"I'm serious." Then hesitating, she said, " . . . sort of. I mean, I really thought having children would bring us closer together, but it hasn't at all."

I wasn't sure if she wanted me to respond, but when the silence became awkward, I said, "I'm really sorry to hear that, Jess."

Truthfully, I wasn't, nor was I surprised. I had never been impressed with any of Jessie's beaus. Of course, I hadn't liked any of them, and The Win was no exception. I was surprised that he had lasted this long.

"I really don't have the tolerance for him anymore," she said flatly.

"Yet, he keeps you in the lifestyle you've grown accustomed," I said, glancing around the room.

Jessie shot me a sharp look and then grinned wickedly.

"But with a good *lawyer*," she said, raising her eyebrows.

"Sure, I'll hook you up with ole Sully."

Jessie grimaced.

"Ugh, I can't believe you're still associated with that commie after everything he did."

"And *she* did," I said. "Remember, she did it to him too."

"Still, it doesn't mean you have to be friends with the creep."

"We're not friends—*colleagues* at best. I still have to work with the man."

"Who cares if she also dumped on him? You shouldn't want anything to do with him, Hen. He's a shit. There's no getting around it. You can't trust him, which makes him worthless."

"I don't," I said. "I only work with the guy. I suppose if he wasn't so worthless, I wouldn't have to deal with him at all."

"If he's such a shitty attorney, why do you want him to represent me?"

"I wouldn't feel comfortable representing you directly, and when Sully represents anyone, it's like getting me, because he's—"

"*Worthless*," she said.

Chapter Thirty-Four

June 1985

He has been here a thousand times before, in a courtroom, standing with lawyers as they discern, assign, and divide. This time, however, he is the client, not the lawyer. A pickle-nosed judge resting his head on his hand stares vacantly at a clock on the wall, listening to the same tiresome arguments he has heard a thousand times before.

He glances over at the adjacent table where she stands, expressionless, her eyes as cold as the gray in her pantsuit. Sitting on the bench behind her is Marks, his legs crossed, his head forward, looking repulsively supportive.

In the end, he agrees to her terms, but they will share Emily—the only fight worth fighting. He knows that in the world of child custody, more is still less.

When finally their love has been lost to legalese and their lives left "in summary," his lawyer offers him a consoling hand and leaves him alone to hurt.

He passes her and Marks on the way out of the courtroom. There is a sting in the courtesy of her smile, while Marks looks away. He sits on a bench outside the courtroom. There is a familiarity to the loneliness of this place, as if he has been here a thousand times before.

The guestroom was cool and comfortable, but that didn't quash my urge to get back on the road. Nevertheless, Gwen insisted on washing my clothes and wouldn't let me leave until every stitch I owned was properly pressed and packed.

For the better part of the morning, I sat in a chair in the kitchen dressed in one of Lance's sweat suits while Gwen talked and tended to my laundry.

"Things have changed quite a bit up there," said Gwen, pouring herself a fresh cup of coffee and then sitting down at the kitchen table across from me. "Lance and I have been meaning to get back up there. It's still the only place I will consider home. Don't get me wrong, I love Portland, but I miss it up there sometimes, especially the summers."

"Yes, the summers are great," I said, already growing weary of the conversation. "It's probably why I'm in such a hurry. I want to get there while there's still some summer left."

"The last of your laundry is in the dryer. I know that you want to go, it's just that I don't ever get to see you, Hen. It sure would be nice to see you once in a while, at least to hear from you," she added.

"You will," I assured her, even though I was skeptical. "You know how it is."

Thankfully, that was the beginning of the end of our conversation. Although our good-bye was long and included several hugs and handshakes from Gwen, Lance, and the girls, I was on the road by the early afternoon heading north toward Seattle and Canada.

For miles, my thoughts remained back in Portland with Gwen and her family. I was glad that I had stopped, but still I felt guilty I didn't stay. I also thought a lot about Tom and the deed he had given me. Perhaps he wasn't what I remembered him to be; perhaps I had misjudged him all these years. I hadn't given him much thought after I had left Alaska, and certainly not after my mother passed. Now, suddenly, the memory didn't seem so far away.

Traffic through Seattle was grinding. Fortunately, I dialed in a ballgame on the radio and let the innings ease along with the slow-moving cars, and by the bottom of the ninth, I was passing through the Canadian border.

For hours, I saw only the road, holding tightly onto the wheel as I went on passing truck after truck, searching for the elusive open highway. I made Dawson Creek by sunup, my mind wakeful but my body tired and achy. There wasn't much to the town, but I knew it was the beginning of the Alcan Highway, which would take me home.

The first two hundred miles put me deep in the Canadian wilderness, but nothing interested me beyond the road. I had been driving for well over a day without as much as a wink of sleep, but still I wasn't tired, so I pressed on.

The miles caught me just outside of Watson Lake when sleep, weighing heavy on my eyelids, shut them and the truck drifted off the highway, down a slight embankment toward a cluster of dwarfed trees before I came to and could stop it safely. Although startled, it wasn't enough to wrestle off the sleep, which came suddenly.

For the first time on my journey, I awoke without any recollection of a dream. Strangely, I found their absence unsettling, afraid that I might have permanently lost the visions of Emily with them, and that deeply saddened me.

With a kink in my neck and an achy back, I stepped outside the truck to have a better look around. The truck—positioned perpendicularly some twenty feet from the highway—seemed unharmed, except for a few small scratches from a single grabby tree branch.

The sinking sun confirmed what my watch told me: it was well into the evening, half past eight. I had slept for nearly six hours. The highway cut through a valley of low-rise evergreens. It was straight, long, and empty for as far as the eye could see in either direction, and I had a sudden urge to walk it. I hiked north for nearly a mile but saw no vehicle other than my own. I stopped and waited for a sight, a sound, anything that might perk the senses, but none came. When I couldn't take the nothingness anymore, I headed on back to the truck, wondering if perhaps this was all a dream.

I drove most of the night into a never-setting sun. I reached Whitehorse by late the next morning. The spirited little town had enough of everything to satisfy a need for anything, but as far away from the world as it was, it left me feeling more empty and alone. I strolled aimlessly through its windy streets, finally wandering into a log cabin bar called *The Yukon Saloon*.

"What'll you have?" asked the mammoth of a man behind the bar. He looked the type that belonged swinging a hammer or an ax rather than tending a bar.

"Molson," I said, pointing to the tap.

"Fine," he said and began filling a frosty mug of the stuff. I noticed he was missing a couple fingers on his left hand, so maybe he hadn't been a bartender his whole life.

I couldn't be sure, but I suspected the sawdust floor wasn't level, as I felt constantly pulled toward the back corner of the bar. I was hopeful the beer would help to even me out.

I sat quietly sipping my beer as two men stood next to me at the bar, engaged in a conversation having something to do with ice or ice levels. Another couple sat at a table dressed in similar gray overalls while rock music blared from a small boom box high on a shelf behind the bar, playing something that I had heard before but didn't recognize.

"How far is it to Fairbanks from here?" I finally said to the bartender when starved for conversation.

Busy washing glasses, Paul Bunyan hesitated and then said gruffly, "About three hundred miles from here to the border, and another three and change from there to Fairbanks."

I took a quick sip of my beer and thought about asking another question, but then ultimately decided against it. I never in my life felt more alone. I thought about that lonely stretch of highway slicing its way across a valley of nothingness. Suddenly, it was there that I wanted to be. It was there that I belonged.

I paid for my beer and quietly slipped out of the bar. Back at the truck, I dug out the Colt from my duffel bag, loaded it, and then got into the cab. I sat there for a few minutes, staring down at the shiny pistol in my lap. I could do this, I thought. I could really do this.

This time I heard no voices; this time I couldn't fail. I cocked the gun and held it to my head. Not sure why, really, but I said a short prayer. I asked God for forgiveness, and I decided that my last thoughts would be of Emily.

I shut my eyes and pictured her standing at my bedside, an angel shimmering in and out of moonlight. Perhaps she was real—in another world, in another lifetime.

I squeezed the trigger.

Nothing.

The trigger wouldn't budge because I hadn't released the safety. I set the pistol down on the seat beside me as raindrops began tapping at the windshield.

"You're such a coward!" I shouted at myself. "You're such a pussy!"

Then I laughed aloud as, all at once, it seemed funny. Whatever I thought I was doing, I wouldn't let myself do it. I laughed aloud again.

Stepping from the truck, I leaned my head back and let the cold rain hit my face.

"Three hundred miles to the border. I should be there by midnight," I said to no one.

Chapter Thirty-Five

July 1965

I tumbled through the doorway to the trailer, staggered over to the bed and gently lay down. For a long while, I tried to get comfortable, but there was no position that didn't hurt. My head and jaw ached mercilessly, courtesy of the butt end of old man Spenser's shotgun, but it was Jessie's horrifying revelations that had hit me the hardest and hurt the most. It made sickening sense, in some ways explaining so much. Jessie was scared, terrified even—enough to tell her father, enough to tell me. There had been a lot more to the bootlegging and her fascination with the disappearance of her grandmother and the O'Brien brothers.

A sweaty nausea sucked through me. I stumbled outside and got sick.

I sat on the step to the trailer, bent over staring at the ground and my half-digested breakfast. I felt so helpless. Jessie had needed me, and I had failed her. Now I too was terrified, and I hated myself for it. The fear was petrifying, but the shame torturing.

I stood up, fear nearly knocking me back down. I loved her. I had to do something. With my mind a dizzying cloud of throbs and thoughts, I made the journey back to the beaver dam and up the massive tailing pile. Jessie wasn't there, nor was she at a half dozen other places I searched. I was certain where to find her, but my still-insurgent cowardice would make it the last place I would look.

The walk back up the driveway had never seemed so short. Soon I was standing at nearly the same spot where only a little while ago

Spenser had struck me down. If he saw me this time, he would surely kill me, but that didn't stop me from walking up to the rickety old cabin door.

I went to knock but then hesitated, recognizing its futility. Instead, I stood silently, listening. Hearing nothing at first, but then maybe something—something like the sound of a distant hammering or thumping. It was constant, even rhythmic, but I couldn't tell whether it was coming from inside or from far away. I reached for the knob, turning it slowly before giving the door a gentle nudge. It cracked open, and the sound grew louder. It was like nothing I had ever heard before—a rapping or slapping sound accompanied by something human, like a grunt or a moan.

As I pushed open the door, a revealing light spread slowly across the dark entrails of the windowless cabin. The sounds grew louder still, drawing my eyes across the room to the hemmed curtain and the entrance to Jessie's bedroom.

Many things in this world you need not experience to recognize. They are readily identifiable and inherently familiar, even in all their vulgarity and disgust. Somewhere, after the time when images are born and before they become things remembered, what went on behind that curtain will forever be.

For I have no memory of crossing the room or picking up the baseball bat that stood always so vigilantly outside Jessie's bedroom door. I have no memory of any of the repugnant acts that I am sure I witnessed just beyond that curtain. There, the wickedness in this world would find me, even if I cannot remember it.

However, what I recall most vividly was raising the bat up from below my waist, hurling it around my shoulders high above my head where, extending my arms, I brought it downward with all my might, slamming it violently into the lumpy knob that was the back of Spenser Mason's head. There was a splattering crack as warm blood sprayed my arms and face. He let out a single gurgled gasp before rolling off Jessie and sliding slowly to the floor. He laid there, his black eyes lifeless and staring coldly at the ceiling as blood, dark and colorless in the grave light, pooled beneath his enormous head.

Spenser was dead. I had killed him.

Jessie stared up at me through hollow eyes, her naked and blood-smeared body remarkably still. I glanced again at Spenser. The blood had begun to stream and was now rushing toward my feet accusingly.

Spenser was dead. I had killed him.

Jessie reached out, taking the bat from me.

"You better go," she whispered. "I have a lot to do. I'm going to have to take care of this." Her eyes shifted casually down at Spenser as if he were nothing more than a neglected chore. "You better go."

I did as I was told.

"Hen," she called before I reached the front door.

Glancing back, I saw her standing naked at the small doorway.

"I'll take care of it," she said assuredly. "Don't say a word and everything will work itself out. Go home, clean up, and get rid of those clothes. It's going to be all right."

———

No one was home when I got back to the trailer, and I was grateful. I immediately changed out of the bloody clothes and placed them into a brown paper sack. I tossed in my brand-new Chuck Taylors and squeezed into a worn-out pair of old ones. I grabbed the paper sack and a lantern and set out toward the beaver pond. There was a small clearing a quarter mile or so on the other side of it. At the center of the clearing, Jessie and I had dug out a good-sized fire pit where, a couple times every summer, we roasted hot dogs.

When I arrived at the clearing, I doused the grocery sack and the bundle of bloody clothes with kerosene and then tossed a lit match into the center of the pit. It was fast to flame, and soon everything had burned to a flakey gray ash that I quickly stomped down to a powdery white dust. For a few moments, I felt better, even hopeful—but the feelings were quick to fade, and I was left alone shrouded in the darkness of my deed.

I wandered aimlessly around the beaver pond in a foggy daze with no idea where to go or what to do. Then nausea hit me hard, knocking me to my knees.

I got sick again and then blacked out.

Something warm and wet nudged at my face and woke me. Saucy stood over me, licking my ear. I was never so happy to see my dog. I wrapped my arms around her neck and buried my sore face into her thick black fur. Her presence amassed a strength within me, enough to roust me to my feet and find the trail home.

I took a small hand mirror from a counter drawer in the trailer and examined my face. My jaw was a puffed-up mound of purple, my lips split in two places, and my right eye nearly swollen shut. I locked the door before crawling into bed and hid myself beneath the thick stack of Indian blankets. I lay there trembling, anxiously awaiting my fate.

I would have to believe Jessie and hope that everything would be all right, although I wished that whatever was going to happen would happen soon.

At some point, I fell asleep because I awoke to the sound of a sharp tapping at the trailer door. At first, I was hopeful that it had all been a dream, but my throbbing head and face quickly reminded me otherwise.

The tapping came again, and with it a queasy fear from my stomach.

"Henry, honey," my mother's muffled voice came from the other side of the door. "Are you in there? Open up, I need to speak with you."

I lay there paralyzed by fright, hoping that she would go away but knowing that she wouldn't.

"Henry," my mother persisted. This time louder and with a more furious series of taps. "Please, Henry, open up! It's important that I speak to you!"

There would be no waiting out my mother. She would stay there all night, tapping and calling. Pushing off the heavy blankets, I sat up. My head pounded and I couldn't see out of my left eye. The pain in my chest and ribs made it difficult to breathe. I shuffled to the door, unlocked it, and then sat down at the table.

The door opened, and my mother stood staring in at me, her eyes widening.

"Oh my goodness, Henry!" she exclaimed. "What happened to you?" In seconds, she was standing over me, probing my face with questioning eyes. "Oh, my dear, my dear!"

It was then when I discovered she wasn't alone. Two men stood outside the door with Tom. One was obviously a uniformed state trooper; the other had serious dark eyes and wore a wrinkled gray suit.

"May we come in?" asked the suited man. Stretching his whisker-stubbled face inside the trailer, he took a quick look around. "We need to ask Henry a few questions," he said to my mother.

"Go right ahead," Tom said. "He'll tell you anything you want to know."

Tom gave me a sharp look as both men stepped inside and sat down in the seat across the table from me. My heart raced and, for a moment, I thought I might be sick, but the feeling quickly passed.

"Certainly this can wait," my mother said, scowling at the two men. "Can't you see he's hurt?"

"This will only take a couple of minutes," assured the man, taking out a small black notebook from his breast pocket. He flipped it open and began scribbling.

"I need to get some peroxide," said my mother, pointing to my eye. "This needs to be treated immediately. Oh, my dear," she added before darting out the door.

"Henry," said the suited man, "I'm Detective Percival, and this is Trooper Haggy. You know Ms. Mason, a Jessie Mason, that right?"

A lot of my courage left with my mother, and before I could answer, Tom stepped through the doorway and stood hovering over everyone at the table.

"Yes, I know Jessie," I said weakly, my better eye shifting from Tom to the detective.

"And you're familiar with Spenser Mason . . ." he said, hesitating, and then flipping a few pages back in his notebook, "The child's . . . Jessie's . . . paternal grandfather."

"Yes," I said in an even weaker voice.

The detective set the notebook down on the table in front of him and looked me squarely in the eye.

"Spenser Mason's dead, Henry. He was killed late this afternoon, bludgeoned in the back of the head with a baseball bat—a pretty messy scene."

A shiver of nausea ran through me, nearly knocking me over. My mother returned carrying peroxide and a first-aid kit and immediately began tending to my face. I swallowed hard, barely able to hold back the sickness.

"It appears," said the detective, "that Ms. Mason . . . Jessie . . . killed him. It also appears that—"

Then I got sick. I threw up all over the table and then in my lap and on my mother's hands. Both of the officers tried desperately to avoid the river of puke rushing toward them. The detective snatched his notebook from the table just in time. My mother tried frantically to stop the flow with her apron but was too late, and the detective's wrinkled suit suddenly became soiled too.

"Damn it!" my mother screamed at the officers. "Can't you see he has a concussion! Can't this wait? Oh, honey," my mother said to me, wiping my face with the last clean part of her apron.

"I suppose," said the detective. "If you want, we can take him on into Fairbanks and get him looked at."

"No," I said to my mother. Then to the detective, "I'll answer your questions." I was ready to come clean. No matter how frightened I was, I wouldn't let Jessie take the fall for this.

My mother shook her head adamantly.

"No, no, Henry. You mustn't speak. You need to rest." Then turning to the officers, she said, "Gentlemen, my son needs his rest. He can answer your questions when he's feeling better, but right now, he needs his rest."

"He'll answer the questions," Tom piped in and then, glaring sharply at my mother and me, he said sternly, "Henry, answer the questions."

My mother shook her head again but didn't speak while Tom motioned for the detective to continue.

"Henry," said the detective calmly, "as I was saying, it appears that Jessie Mason killed her grandfather. Although I think I know what happened, it is important that you and I talk. Who did this to you, Henry?" he asked, pointing to my face.

I had no idea what Jessie had told the police, but I had already decided to tell the truth.

"It was Spenser," I said.

The detective nodded and then picked up his notebook and jotted something down, while my mother dabbed and poked at me with peroxide and cotton gauze.

"Why did he do it?" asked the detective.

The answer was there on the tip of my tongue, but I couldn't convince myself to say it. The truth was horrifying.

"We know about the abuse, Henry," said the detective.

"Abuse?" said my mother.

"Yes, I can't go into too many specifics, but there is evidence of long-term physical and sexual abuse by her grandfather," said the detective clumsily.

"Oh my goodness!" my mother exclaimed.

Tom gave the detective a confirming nod, as though he already knew.

"So what happened?" said the detective. "Why did he do this to you?"

"Well, I-I found out," I stuttered nervously.

"About the abuse?" the detective said, nodding.

"That's right," I said. I was angry and went to . . . and he . . . he—"

"Knocked you good," said the detective, nodding again.

He then scribbled some more inside his notebook.

"Is she going to be all right?" my mother asked.

"I think so," said the detective. "She's in Fairbanks right now getting an examination. I can't say any more than that. What I can say is this appears to be a case of self-defense, and from the looks of it, Henry, it appears she's not the only one who's been abused."

"Oh my goodness!" my mother exclaimed again.

"I do have some more questions for Henry," said the detective.

The detective's words eased my anxious mind. Whatever it was that Jessie had told the officers, they had bought it.

"She's staying with us until her father gets back," said my mother. "Do we need to go and get her?"

"Her father, let me see," said the detective, flipping back more pages of his little notebook. "A James Theodore Mason has been notified. He's supposed to be back in town tonight to get her and to identify the body," he added.

My mother nodded slowly, and I knew she was thinking that in some way she was responsible for all this.

"What I need from your son is some information regarding Spenser Mason. We believe that her grandfather may have had something to do with the disappearance of her grandmother, an Abigail Mason, and two brothers named O'Brien some thirty years ago." The detective paused and then, glancing curiously at me, he said, "Ms. Mason said you could tell us where to find the bodies."

The look of bewilderment on my mother's face was something I hadn't seen before, and even Tom seemed mildly amused.

"Do you know where we can find them, son?" asked the detective.

I gave him a weak nod, and then said, "I think so."

———————————

Over the next hour, more questions came from the detective, which brought more bewildered looks from my mother as she tended to my wounds. I told them about the diary, the phony letter, Oksana Verden, and the watch Jessie had found. I also told them about Spooner and the gun. Clearly, the detective seemed more interested in Spenser's past than his recent death, and I was glad for it.

I learned that Jessie had walked nearly five miles toward Fairbanks when she happened across the state trooper and made the report. The trooper took her on into Fairbanks where the detective was called in and Jessie made her statement.

"I had been working this case most of the summer," said the detective. "Kind of a side project."

"Most of the summer?" I said, surprised.

"Yes," he said with a nod. "I have to admit, it all came as quite a surprise. I had been receiving anonymous information regarding Spenser Mason for well over a year now. At first, I didn't think anything of it. A thirty-year-old missing persons case didn't have a lot of appeal. The anonymous source was persistent, however, and the more I looked into it, the more things didn't add up. It came as quite a surprise to learn that it was Ms. Mason that had been sending the information."

It was quite a surprise to me as well. Jessie had never given me any indication that she had been feeding the police information, and even more shocking were the number of things I was now learning Jessie hadn't told me.

"What information?" I asked.

"We received a lot of things from Ms. Mason," said the detective. "We received the diary, among other things, and numerous letters

439

explaining her theories. I checked the records from back then and came across an old file. There wasn't a lot to it, but apparently, a sort of missing persons report was taken from a Charlene Betters, Abigail's sister of Flint, Michigan. Nothing much was done with it as the police department at the time—if you could call it that—assumed as everyone else did that the three had ran off together. But the file contained a letter that Ms. Mason didn't have. A letter Abigail sent Charlene after they left town. At first glance, it summed up the general hypothesis back then: the three of them ran off together with the money from the mine deal, abandoning Spenser and the boy. In it, Abigail states that she has fallen in love with one of the O'Brien brothers and she wants to start fresh somewhere in California. But like I said, a lot of things didn't add up, especially when I got the diary."

The detective shook his head wearily. "There were a lot of little idiosyncrasies. For instance, in the diary and in all previous correspondence provided by Ms. Mason, she refers to her son as *James*, but in the final letter to her sister, she refers to him as *JT* or simply *the boy*. Also, from the diary entries and correspondence, Abigail Mason didn't seem the type that would ever leave her child, even if she were having an affair. The last letter seemed obviously contrived or forced but probably worked well with the state of law enforcement around here in the thirties." The detective shot an apologetic glance at the trooper. "Spenser probably counted on that," he added.

"Why didn't you do anything?" said my mother. "Maybe this could've been prevented!"

The detective waved a conciliatory hand at my mother and then, with a regretful nod, he said to her, "Yes, it is unfortunate, but remember this was a very old case and there was still a lot we didn't know." The detective glanced at me sharply. "We didn't know about the weapon, and Spooner, and we didn't know about the letter the two of you wrote to Spenser. A letter that certainly could've gotten you killed."

My mother released a gasping sigh. "Oh my goodness!" she exclaimed.

"At the request of Ms. Mason, I did question a Ms. Oksana Verden. She confirmed a lot of what Ms. Mason had reported. I was really close to questioning Spenser, then this," said the detective, shaking his head disappointedly. "I only hope we can find some bodies, Henry—bring some real closure to this mess."

My scurrying thoughts moved to Jessie, and I wondered if she would ever find any *closure to this mess*. I was glad I had killed that dirty old man. Still, I felt I had failed her. I should've seen the signs. Hell, she as much as told me. I nearly got sick again, which must've been obvious, as the trooper and the detective quickly jumped away from the table. I swallowed hard and raised a reassuring hand, and they sat back down.

"When do you think you'll be able to show us?" asked the trooper. The detective glanced over at him, as if he wanted to say something, but then he looked quickly back at me.

"He'll show you now," said Tom firmly. "We need to get to the bottom of this."

My mother sent Tom a fiery look.

"If he's up to it, of course," added Tom to my mother.

Then they both looked at me.

"Now is fine," I said.

Twenty minutes later, I stood with Tom and the detective just off the highway before the trailhead to the old mine shaft. We waited there until the state trooper arrived in his shiny black cruiser with a small crew of volunteer excavators, three plainclothesmen carrying flashlights and shovels. I led them through a thicket of saplings and on up the tricky pathway to the entrance of the shaft.

"It's here," I said to the detective.

He gave me a half smile and then nodded at the trooper. "We'll need some light in there." Then to Tom, he said, "You should stay here. We'll send the boy out afterwards."

I saw a look of disappointment cross over Tom's face, but then after releasing a heavy sigh, he nodded agreeably back at the detective.

The men switched on their flashlights and followed me into the mine. The detective stayed close beside me as I led them all splashing through the narrow tunnels and then on down the dry channel that ended abruptly at the sheet of plywood.

"Here," I said to the detective. "I think they're buried somewhere around here." The area wasn't large enough for everyone, but two of the men with shovels moved forward and began to dig.

"You head on out, son," said the detective. "We'll find whatever needs finding."

When I came out, I found Tom leaning against the large bucket of the rusty backhoe where Jessie and I had hidden.

"Well?" he said as I came toward him. "Did you show them?"

I nodded and then gently sat down on the ground in front of him. My mother had made sure my head and body were on the mend, but they still throbbed mercilessly.

"You're lucky you didn't get yourself killed," he said. "That was a hell of a stunt you two pulled. Your mother is pretty bent out of shape over the whole thing. It's lucky for you . . ." He hesitated, shook his head, and then looked away.

He didn't see me, but I smiled because it was Tom's way of letting me know that he cared and was glad I was all right.

For the next hour or so, the two of us waited outside the entrance. Neither one of us spoke, but it was the closest I had ever felt to Tom.

Finally, the detective emerged from the shaft, squinting. He nodded when he spotted us.

"We found three bodies," he said. "Well, just *bones* really."

"Goddamn," said Tom. Then to me, he said, "It's really lucky that old man didn't kill you."

The late evening sun did little to warm the chilling reality of the day. Perhaps it was my achy mind or the gravity I saw in the detective's eyes or the sudden compassion in Tom's voice, but I put my head in my hands and began to cry. The truth in all of it seemed sad and overwhelming. Then I felt a gentle hand on my back and, through teary eyes, I saw Tom crouching beside me. He placed an arm around my shoulders and I lay my head on his, and although it felt strangely awkward, I was glad he was there.

Tom and I watched as the coroner and his crew loaded the covered remains of Abigail Mason and the O'Brien brothers into a black hearse.

"It sure puts a nice lid on things," said the detective after the coroner had gone.

I could see nothing *nice* about any of it, and while walking home with Tom, I couldn't help but think of Jessie and everything she'd been through. I wondered if she would ever be able to put a *nice lid on things*.

My mother met us at the driveway with a flurry of questions and concerns. Tom explained everything to her in deliberate detail, occasionally looking to me for a confirming nod. The detective came by to let us know that Jessie was all right and with her father. She would remain in Fairbanks for the night, but tomorrow, she would be sent back to Michigan to live with her mother.

"Can I see her?" I asked the detective.

"I don't think so, son," he said, brushing at his crinkled tie. "With things the way they are—you know, these sorts of things, with what happened—it's probably better off that she get with her mother right away. She's going to need help, son . . . coping with these sorts of things," he said, stumbling over his words.

I knew nothing of *these sorts of things*, but faced with the real possibility never seeing Jessie again, my mind probed the detective with questions as my mind search for answers.

"She's leaving for good?" I said when my thoughts could manufacture the words.

"Yes, son," said the detective.

"I have to see her. I have to at least say good-bye."

"I'm sorry, son, but that's the way it has to be," said the detective. "She's going to stay at the Riverwood tonight, but she'll be on the first plane out in the morning."

I didn't say anything else. I knew it was pointless, and I left them all standing there in the kitchen. I went out to the trailer, my mind already made up.

I waited for the detective to leave and for my mother to come and check on me, which she did only a few minutes later. After she made her fuss, I set out. It was almost twenty miles to Fairbanks, and another mile or so to the Riverwood Hotel out near the airport. It would take most of the night, but I knew I could be there by morning.

———————

The sun made its sluggish dip below the horizon just long enough to turn a tomorrow into a today. The walk had taken me the better part of six hours. I arrived at the Riverwood shortly after 5:00 a.m., and there was little about me that wasn't tired or didn't hurt.

The Riverwood was a two-story monstrosity made of logs and lumber. I had never stayed there, but radio ads offered a *comfortable room at a comfortable price*. L-shaped and boasting a couple dozen rooms, its best amenity was the short distance from the airport.

Fortunately, few vehicles scattered the parking lot. One of them, I recognized immediately as JT's truck. The office was located at the far end of one of the wings where I found an old man with sticky gray hair and rectangular spectacles asleep in a chair behind the desk.

"Excuse me," I said, loud enough to roust him.

He jerked a couple of times, leaned his head back, and then squinted at me from above his glasses.

"What can I do for you?" he said, standing up and hooking his thumbs around his suspenders.

"Mason," I said. "I need the room number for Jessie or JT Mason," I added.

"I'm sorry," he said, shaking his head and pulling at his suspenders, "I can't give out a room number. That's confidential."

This information did little to discourage me.

"Then how may I get a hold of her?" I said with a forced pleasantness.

The old man kept on smiling at me and then pointed behind me.

"There's a telephone right there," he said. "You can dial the operator, and I'll patch you through."

I grabbed the phone and dialed the operator. I could hear the ring from the switchboard behind the desk.

"Riverwood," the old man answered, as if he didn't know it was me.

"Mason," I said, "patch me through please."

It all seemed silly, but I was in a hurry and didn't care. The old man moved a couple wires around the switchboard, and a few seconds later, the phone began to ring.

"Hello," said a voice I recognized immediately.

"It's Henry," I said.

"Henry," Jessie said excitedly. "Where are—"

"I'm here," I said. "I'm at your hotel, here at the front desk. What room are you in?"

"Fourteen," she said. "But hold on, I'll come down."

I waited at the front desk for a few minutes with the old man who stood smiling and pulling at his suspenders like a circus clown.

"Sorry, but I can't give out room numbers," he explained. "It's confidential."

"I got it," I said dismissively before walking out the door.

I spied Jessie coming out of a covered stairwell from the opposite wing of the building. She wore pajamas and an open bathrobe that streamed behind her in the gentle wind. I watched her tiptoeing across the gravel lot in her bare feet, so I ran to meet her.

"Oh my, Henry," she said when I reached her. "Your face, it's worse than before. Are you all right?" She went to touch it, hesitated, and then hugged me. "I knew I would see you," she said. "I just knew it." She held me for a long time, then after releasing me, she glanced around the parking lot curiously. "How did you get here?"

"You're leaving," I said.

"Yes," she said, "in a jet."

"You're leaving," I said again.

"Yes," she said, her dark eyes intense. "I'm going back to Flint to live with my mother. It's not my choice. They won't let me stay here, and with Daddy gone most of the time, it's probably for the best."

"I don't want you to go," I said, a lump the size of a baseball caught in my throat. "I don't think—"

Jessie hugged me again, so tight I could feel her heart racing.

"It's the way it has to be," she whispered into my ear. "I'll miss you."

"You know, Jess," I said, pushing her away. "I've heard just about enough of the *way it has to be* shit for one day. The old bastard is dead, Jess. He'll never lay another grubby hand on you! I don't know how you could be better off in Flint or anywhere else! The old bastard is dead, for crying out loud! You can't just leave," I said, suddenly realizing I was shouting. I paused, glanced away, and then said softly, "*I love you.*"

Jessie raised her eyebrows and then sighed.

"I know, and I wish that were enough," she said, shaking her head. "But you know it's not. They say I'm pretty messed up, Hen. They say I need help. I have to go and see some doctor when I get back to Flint—don't you understand I might be *crazy!*"

"You don't really believe that, do you?" I said. "And who's *they?*"

"The people in the know," she said. "The detective, the police, the doctors—*they* all think I need help."

I felt the awkwardness between us, something I had never felt before. I was sure that later I would regret the things I had or hadn't said, but right now, I was at a loss for words.

I raised an arm to block the morning sun behind her and squinted to see the details in her silhouette. A gentle breeze lifted the hair from her shoulders, enough that I could see her entire face and the sadness in her eyes.

"I killed him, not you," I said. "I'd do it again. Why you have to own that, I'm not sure. Between us, though—it was me, Jess. I did it."

Perhaps it was only the wind, but I thought she said *okay*.

She hugged me again while placing something in my hand.

"*Find it, and it's all yours*," she whispered before turning and walking away.

I thought I heard her say good-bye, but perhaps that too was only the wind.

Chapter Thirty-Six

June 1984

The best day of my life started with a hangover. The night before, I had lost my sobriety somewhere along Michigan Avenue at a gauntlet of pubs and taverns between Lansing and East Lansing. There had been reason to celebrate. I had finally made partner.

I slid quietly from the bed, careful not to wake Natalie—the half-naked, half-my-age coed who didn't know any better. We had only met the night before, an anthropology or astronomy major or something like that. She'd liked my laugh and I had liked her smile, among other things. Our flirty conversation had eventually led here. It had been nice, but not love or anything like it, and after this morning, I probably wouldn't see her again. It didn't matter though, because today was Friday. I had the day off, and there was baseball at *The Corner.*

The Tigers were rolling, and I was meeting Jessie. We had worked it all out late last night during a drunken call from a phone booth outside *Murphy's Tavern.* The Win was in Chicago and had the boys, but she had his company's season tickets. At 37 and 9, the Tigers were off to their best start ever, and I hadn't been to a single game this year—which Jessie said was simply criminal.

I ate a bowl of cereal, took a quick shower, and had a shave before I returned to the bedroom and found Natalie gone. I planned to drive her home, but she must've called a cab. She did leave a note on my pillow to call her later—a sweet gesture, although I knew I never would.

With morning traffic, it would take nearly two hours to reach *The Compound*, as I now called it. Through the years, The Win and his home had become larger than life. The Win himself was approaching nearly three hundred pounds, while his home an impending six thousand square feet, and this didn't include the recently added swimming pool and four-thousand square-foot pole barn to shell his ever-growing fleet of Corvettes. Jessie had confided to me that she hated the place. She complained it was too big, impossible to clean, and that The Win was never there. *Out on business* was the phrase she used. Jessie did have her mild forms of revenge, however. In addition to her regular threats of divorce, she moved her mother into the house for nearly six months—an act that even afforded The Win my sympathies.

Jessie met me in the driveway wearing khaki shorts, a bright orange tee shirt, and a Tigers cap. Her freshly painted lips were rosy-pink and the only makeup she wore. She gave a little wave and a big smile as I pulled the Ranger up to her.

"Am I late?" I asked as she climbed in beside me.

"No," she said. "I thought I would wait outside with the sunshine. It's a beautiful day—a beautiful day for baseball."

"*Let's play two*," I said.

Jessie shot me a wink.

"Okay, *Ernie*," she said with a grin.

Jessie pulled off her cap and shook loose her hair. Even in the last of her thirties, she was beautiful. There was such a shiny glow about her, an aura that time could not touch, so imposing on me that it still caused my heart to leap, leaving me as breathless and bewildered as it did when I was fifteen years old.

"Look at you," she said, shaking her head. "Some Tiger fan you are. You really must've put one on last night, partner. How do you feel this morning?"

"I'm fine, feel great. Why?"

She gave me the once-over. "Jeans and a sweatshirt? You realize it's going to be nearly ninety degrees and we're going to a baseball game, don't you?"

I nodded and then smiled. "The game's not until tonight, and I have a tee shirt underneath."

"What a *rube!*" she said, shaking her head. "We're going to have to get you a cap."

"I've got a cap," I said.

Rolling her eyes, she slipped off her sandals and put her feet up on the dashboard, stretching out her long and tanned legs. She pulled a stick of Spearmint gum from her small purse, ripped it in half, and handed it to me.

"This is going to be fun, really," she said, rolling down her window.

"Do you think you can let me in on why we're going so early?"

"You'll see," she said playfully. She cracked her gum and then said, "Just take us down around Jefferson and find a place to park."

"Jefferson Street?"

"Yeah," she said, grinning. "I'll take it from there."

———

It was nearly eleven before we found an acceptable place to park somewhere beneath the concrete buildings that comprised downtown Detroit. It was a considerable walk to Tiger Stadium from here, but lord knows we had the time. Without a word, I obediently followed Jessie for numerous blocks through the steamy air of the city until my lungs and my curiosity got the best of me.

"Where are we going?" I asked.

"We're almost there," she said.

She led me halfway down another city block, and then into a cathedral of a skyscraper. I had spent some time in Detroit, but I had never been here before. We walked by the security desk and onto the elevators where I got a peek at the directory.

"*Law firms*," I said to her.

"Yep," she said as we entered the elevator. "I have a ten o'clock with my lawyer."

"Your lawyer? Why do you need . . ." And then I knew.

"Does he know?" I asked.

Jessie only smiled.

"He doesn't know this is coming down, does he?"

Again she didn't answer, but from the wry look on her face, The Win hadn't a clue.

"Why do I have to tag along? You should really do your own dirty work, Jess. I certainly don't want The Win to think that I'm behind this."

"What do you mean you're not doing my dirty work? You're not behind any of this. I am," she said indignantly. "Why do you think I came here and didn't go to your firm, other than the obvious reason that you'd set me up with that shit Sully. I did it so you wouldn't be involved. You're tagging along for moral support. Besides, I'm only here to sign papers."

A sharp ding announcing our arrival to the twenty-seventh floor saved me from further scolding. *Martin, Eyre, & Wise* was the firm she'd hired. I had heard of them—not heavyweights in the divorce field, but worthy advocates nevertheless. Sully had locked horns with them a time or two, but I suppose that wasn't saying much.

Jessie's attorney was a man named Owen Nichols, but for whatever reason, he insisted on being called Jimmy. He was several years older than we were and considerably taller. A University of Michigan man, his office accented in the traditional maize and blue, the centerpiece being a football cased in glass and signed by coach Bo Schembechler.

I was glad when Jessie introduced me as her friend and not a lawyer. There was always a little awkwardness when I knew another attorney had the ear of a client. It was a big enough firm, and I was confident they would handle it all right.

Fortunately, Jimmy wasn't planning on this being a long meeting. I learned that the two of them had already spent a good amount of time hashing out the details in the pleadings. Today, Jessie was simply here to sign papers.

Well before noon, we were standing on the sidewalk outside the building wondering what we were going to do for the next several hours.

"Lunch, maybe?" I said with a shrug.

"Sure," she said.

A few minutes later, we were in a diner ordering food.

"That was easy," said Jessie, after taking a sip of her coffee. "It wasn't that big of a deal."

"What's that? I said.

"Signing the papers," she said. "I thought it would be more emotional. We've been together for a long time, Hen, and now it's over."

"It's not over yet," I said. "In a way, it's only the beginning. There's a lot involved here. You have custody, child support, and a litany of financial issues to resolve. You don't even know how he's going to take it."

Through the years, I had built a wall around my feelings for Jessie, a calloused wall forged from the furnaces of my own insecurities. I loved her. I had since I was fifteen. I would always love her. I knew it. I lived with it and was okay with it. I never cared much for The Win, but I hadn't cared much for any of the men in Jessie's life. I never had.

"Well, I thought this would be the hardest part. The actual doing it," she said with a kind of grimace.

Admittedly, the move surprised me. It would be a drastic change in her lifestyle.

"What about the boys?"

She stared coldly at me.

"They'll be fine," she said sharply. "Did you know this is the first weekend that he's had them by himself? Usually, when he takes them to Chicago, he dumps them on his folks. He can't this weekend because his parents are gone. Get this," she said with a smirk, "they're on one of those cruises in Alaska. So he'll have his hands full, but it'll be good for him."

"Alaska? Really, Alaska? I've heard of those cruises," I said.

"It doesn't matter," she said, setting down her coffee cup. "Today is about the Tigers. I want to have fun and not think about any of this shit. Besides, I'm with my favorite man now." She winked at me. "My next man is going to be a Tigers fan, that's for sure," she added.

"There should be several thousand where we're going," I said. "Maybe you can find one."

"Maybe," she said, much too seriously for my liking.

Lunch was slow to arrive and slower still to digest, but the second Bloody Mary was enough to drown the remnants of my hangover.

"You should've married me when I asked," I said to Jessie as we stepped out the diner and into the sultry city air. "It might've been more fun."

Jessie grabbed me by the shoulder, spinning me around, her eyes wide.

"You're right," she snapped. "You should've made me!" Then her eyes softened and she laughed. "So this is your fault!"

We walked a few blocks toward the stadium and then ducked into a hole-in-the-wall tavern called *The Rail*. The place was empty, worn, decorated almost entirely in ripped vinyl and mirrored glass. We sat down at the bar, waiting for any sign of proprietorship.

Jessie cast her eyes about the stark barroom a couple of times and then, glancing back at me, she shrugged.

"Maybe they're closed," she said.

Before I could agree, the silhouette of a woman appeared from behind a curtain at the far corner of the room. She moved with a catlike quickness and soon was standing in front of us, staring, her eyes a sharp and inquisitive green. Her skin was as bleached as her shoulder-length hair, which hung more like feathers. An already too small tee shirt draped from her bony form, exposing the kind of rickety arms that you see on the sick or elderly.

"What can I get you?" she asked in a rasped smoker's voice.

"Rum," I said firmly. "One with Coke and the other without. Ice with both, please." I glanced at Jessie who gave the woman a confirming smile.

"All right," she said with a slow nod. And then, hesitating, she stared curiously across the bar at us. This went on for several uncomfortable seconds until she finally smiled, revealing a wicked cluster of nicotine-stained teeth—black, broken, and almost too painful to look at. "All right," she said again.

When she left, I shot Jessie a wide-eyed look. "Wow," I whispered, shaking my head.

"Quite the creature," said Jessie softly.

It wasn't too long before the woman returned carrying our drinks, one in each hand. She slammed the first glass down in front of me.

"One with Coke," she barked. Then setting the other glass down in front of Jessie, she said, "And one without."

She again shot us her rotting smile and then stood there staring at us smugly.

"How did you know?" I asked, begging the question.

"I've done this before," she said, smirking. Then she let out a cackle that sounded more like a cough, followed by a definite cough which, somewhere along the way, became a fit.

"Are you okay?" asked Jessie.

With a bony finger, she motioned for us to give her a moment and then coughed viciously into a bar rag. When it finally appeared she had gained control of herself, she took a lit cigarette from an ashtray on the bar and gave it a lengthy pull, blowing smoke at the floor.

"When you've been doing this as long as I have, you just know," she said. "There are only two types of people in this world."

"Only two?" I replied, smiling at Jessie.

After a witchy sort of laugh that nearly turned into another coughing fit, she grinned at me and said, "Yes, there are only two types, smarty! You're one, and she's the other!"

"Yeah," I said. "So what—"

"Apples and onions!" she blurted before I could ask the question. She slapped a hand down hard on the bar in front of me. "You're the onion, honey—lots of layers, but no core. Women have already spent a lifetime *crying* . . . and *trying* to figure you out. I'm right, aren't I?" she said to Jessie.

"Sure," said Jessie, an amused look hanging from her face.

Then all eyes were on me.

"I'm sorry," I said, shaking my head. "No way, can't be. That's not me. I have a core. I do. It's down here somewhere," I said, patting my stomach. I laughed, but no one else did.

"I'm never wrong," said the woman. She placed a bar napkin beneath my glass and nodded to Jessie. "Spent a lifetime trying to figure him out, haven't you?"

Jessie's eyes moved from me to the bartender, then to me again. "No," she said in a whisper, slowly shaking her head as if she had only just made up her mind. "He's got a core, all right. It's right here," she said, placing a gentle hand on my chest. "It has always been right here. I'm sorry, lady, there are no layers to him at all."

Jessie slid her hand slowly down my body and laid it lightly on my thigh, the entire time staring into my eyes.

"Well, you'd be wrong," I heard the woman say, but I didn't take my eyes off Jessie's, nor she mine.

Then, without word or warning, Jessie kissed me. The kind of kiss that starts softly as a gesture with the lips, but then crescendos into a full-on movement by the mouths and tongues, wet and stimulating. Holding my head between her hands, she pulled me to her. I reached for the bar to keep from falling on her, but she held me, suspended somewhere between the two barstools.

When finally she released me, it was with her arms not her eyes. They remained affixed to mine, hopeful and wanting. She kissed me again, this time on the cheek, as if to let me know it wouldn't be her last. I glanced quickly about. The lady was gone, but a man sat at the far end of the bar, his eyes cast in our direction.

"Don't mind me," he said when my eyes caught his. "Carry on, you two look good together," he said with a genuine smile.

The man had Jessie's attention, and she smiled back at him.

"Thanks," she said. "I think so too." Then smiling at me, she said, "What do you say?"

I didn't know what to say. My thoughts were still swirling between the barstools. I nodded at Jessie, who hugged me, and soon we were kissing again.

None of it made any sense, and the timing made even less. A short synopsis of each of the consequences went coursing electrically through my mind—her boys, The Win, and the remains of her marriage. But despite the many consequences, it was what I wanted. It was what I had waited a lifetime for.

The afternoon hurried on into the evening while, oddly, *The Rail* remained empty. I sat on the barstool while Jessie stood between my legs, her hair down and her arms around my waist. We drank rum and held each other closely, wanting always to be closer. I hung on her every word, touch, and kiss—each one seemingly awakening parts inside of me asleep since my adolescence. She fit me so well, in size, in mind, in every way. Seeping from the cracks and rifts of my reticent heart gushed streams of newly liberated emotion. "I want to tell you something," I said after another kiss.

"Yes, I know," she whispered sweetly. She put a finger to my lips. "Hush," she said. "There will be time."

Yes, loads of it, I thought, and then kissed her again.

———————————

From *The Rail,* we went again to the muggy streets of downtown Detroit, this time floating along the half dozen or so blocks to the ballpark. I never was much impressed with Tiger Stadium. Back home, Jessie had made it out to be some grand castle, something you might find somewhere at the end of a yellow brick road. The few times I had gone (all with Jessie), I had been secretly disappointed.

Its warehouselike walls were a pale blue but, in the sunlight, shone a dingy gray, even on the brightest days. Colossal light stands jutting awkwardly from its top loomed overhead like watchtowers casting a colorless gloom about the place.

But something today was different. What seemed more of a prison than a palace had all changed. The oranges and blues appeared to jump from the flags. There was color in everything; even the walls seemed to breathe life.

It was wondrous what a few wins could do.

When we reached the stadium, Jessie spied a street vender, dragged me over, and demanded I buy as many peanuts as I could carry inside. Once my pockets were chock-full of goobers, she tugged me along through the front gate where we received a daunted look from a female ticket-taker getting a glimpse of our choice seats. From there, and with the promise of a shortcut, Jessie led me beneath the high-pitched stands and down into the bowels of the ballpark where there lingered a collection of scents and stenches ranging from roasted hot dogs to dried piss. But before my nose could sort it all out, I was again cast out into the sunlight, amongst an eagerly gathering crowd and standing before a field so green, I thought for sure it had to be a dream.

With all the speed of a funeral procession, we followed an old black usher down to our seats, so close I could spit on home plate.

"Enjoy the game now," said the old man after wiping down our seats with a filthy rag. He then stood waiting for us to sit down.

"Thank you," said Jessie, shooting me a contemptuous look.

"Oh, sorry . . . yeah," I muttered, realizing she wanted me to tip the guy. I quickly stood up and arduously pulled a wad of bills from my pocket, along with a few peanuts. I handed all of it to him. Jessie rolled her eyes and sneered at me, but the old man didn't seem to mind. He tucked it all away in his own pocket, giving me an appreciative little nod as he did. I received another little sneer from Jessie, but the old man's warm smile told me all was forgiven.

"You're such a rube!" said Jessie.

I suppose I still had a lot to learn about ballpark etiquette.

As I sat back down, I put my arm around Jessie, and she leaned back into me, resting her head on mine. Together, we watched the Tigers warm up by tossing baseballs and smiles around the infield. Jessie laid a hand on my knee and, with her index finger, she spelled out my name, drew a heart, and then spelled out hers. I knew then that she too had forgiven me.

Usually, *anticipation* was a word wasted on me. I didn't long for anything. For years, I had learned to wait, be patient, and expect things to take longer than they should. Perhaps it was the army, Vietnam, or being a lawyer. I was never in a rush, and rarely did I ever experience urgency. But for the last seven hours, I was in a great hurry.

From what I remember, the game was a rout. Mostly, I had my attentions and my hands on Jessie. The outs were slow to come, the innings seemed to crawl on into the night, and I began to think the game would never end. The Tigers scored something like fourteen runs and had twice as many hits as the White Sox. Sitting in arguably the best seats in the house with a perfect view of the spectacle, my mind was elsewhere—outside the ballpark and somewhere beyond the eternality of the game.

When the game finally ended, Jessie wanted to stand around and watch the players glad-handing each other in victory. It was about all I could take, and I was happy when she agreed to grab a cab back to the truck.

Jessie didn't say a word during the cab ride, but stayed close to me with a hand either on mine or in my lap. Still, her silence bothered me. She hadn't said as much as a word since before the game, and it made me think that she might be having second thoughts about whatever it was we were doing.

Climbing out of the cab, the night air felt warm and weighty, consuming much of my eagerness from earlier.

"Great game," I said, unlocking and then opening the door for her.

"The best," she said and gave me a quick kiss on the cheek before getting in.

Jessie leaned over and unlocked my door as I walked around. My mind probed itself for answers but found nothing. I wondered if I would have the courage to take it any further.

There was more silence on the drive out of Detroit, and Jessie gave no indication that she wanted to talk, this time keeping to herself and staring vacantly out the window.

"It's all right," I said, finally breaking the silence.

Jessie adjusted the dashboard vent and let the cool air blow in her face. She didn't speak, but took off her cap and shook out her hair.

"I'll forget about all of this tomorrow," I said with a forced grin. I knew I wouldn't ever forget about it, but I wanted to give her a way out.

Jessie moved the vent away and then leaned back and put her feet up on the dashboard.

"You better not," she said.

With my eyes on the road, I couldn't get a good enough read of her to know what she meant. But before I could think on it any further, she put her hands between my legs and made it all suddenly clear. I quickly glanced over at her and the truck swerved slightly.

"Careful," she said with a giggle.

My eyes jumped back to the road, while the rest of me swayed with the gentle movements of Jessie's hand.

"Don't take me home," she said softly. "I don't want to go."

"What do you want to do?" I asked. And then, swallowing hard, I said, "Where do you want to go?"

Jessie ran her hand down the length of my thigh and then back upward again. The truck swerved again.

"Don't crash us," she said, giggling.

I steadied the wheel as Jessie removed her feet from the dash and scooted up next to me. She put an arm around my shoulders and kissed my ear.

"There is a motel just up the way," she whispered.

I wasn't familiar with anything *just up the way*, but my body wanted so badly to believe. I did everything I could to keep my eyes and the truck on the road. I took the next exit and was elated to see a motel with a red sputtering neon sign announcing *vacancy*.

Jessie released me just as I pulled up next to the little office. "I'll be right back," I said.

"Hurry," she said, smiling.

Hurrying was my new specialty. I had a room key, a receipt, and parking instructions from a female desk clerk within five minutes, and yet I still felt I was moving too slow.

"It's 206," I said when I got back into the truck. I handed Jessie the room key and then, jerking the truck into gear, drove it around back to where the clerk had told me to park. Within another five minutes, we were inside a stuffy little room quickly peeling off our clothes.

From that point on, everything seemed to slow. We stood beside the bed facing each other, as blue beams of moonlight bounced from Jessie's hair and bare skin, giving her an effervescent glow that added to the enchantment of the moment. Reality, fantasy, or somewhere in between—it was no longer important. Whatever truths tomorrow might bring, I would have this night.

Taking her into my arms, I held her against me, her lips and her skin on mine. We fell to the bed together as one, our bodies moving and rocking in a single, loving rhythm. She was all I ever wanted. My heart led my body into and out of hers, again and again, wanting more and getting it. We made love well into the night, resting only long enough to love again, until there was nothing more to take and nothing left to give.

Asleep in my arms, breathing soft against my chest, Jessie seemed to me as peaceful as I had ever known her to be. Tomorrow would bring with it uncertainty and confusion; daylight was no friend of mine. But for the time being, the moonbeams still rich and alive and tossing about the room their blues, this moment was ours. I ran a finger along the scar on Jessie's chin, remembering her fall and the look of horror on her face. I thought about how different she looked now. The look was new to me and I was happy to know it, because now, I was sure I knew them all.

I stayed awake long enough to watch the moonlight meld into sunlight, exposing the grungy little room and its threadbare amenities. I spied the room key protruding from one of my sneakers that lay on the floor among the piles of our strewn clothing.

I thought it might all seem sleazy had it not been Jessie and me.

A sharp rapping sound startled me. "It is housekeeping," said a choppy Asian voice from beyond the door.

"Go away!" shouted Jessie. She let out a gasp and then rolled from my chest.

"Okay, I come back later," said the voice.

"What's the time?" groaned Jessie.

I rubbed the blur from my eyes and glanced at my watch.

"Nearly eleven," I said. There was a little movement and then another groan. "You have somewhere to go?"

I pulled her into my arms and let the heat from her naked body overwhelm me. I moved into her, and we made love again.

"Wow," said Jessie. Before rolling off me, she giggled.

"What's so funny?"

Jessie smiled and shook her head.

"Nothing," she said, gently putting a hand to my cheek. "I didn't know it would be like this."

"Like what?" I said.

Her eyes moved to my chest and, taking my dog tags into her hands, she rubbed them between her fingers. Her eyes then moved up to my neck.

"You still have this old thing?" she said.

I reached for my old moose-bone necklace. I pulled it above my chin for a better look.

"Yeah," I said, examining it. "I don't go anywhere without it. It's pretty faded now, probably still has some of your blood on it."

"I remember," she said softly, her eyes focused on the necklace. "Does it still hold all your luck?"

I pulled the necklace over my head and placed it around her neck.

"You wear it, then tell me if it's lucky or not."

"I will," she said, holding the moose bone next to her chest.

I kissed her softly on the lips.

"*Wow*," she said.

Chapter Thirty-Seven

June 1985

Heading west, the morning sun behind me, my mind fresh and stirring with sundry thoughts of home, nothing appeared too familiar, just some vague recollections from my exodus some twenty years prior. I topped off the tank in Tok, bought more Mountain Dew in Delta Junction, and found an oldies radio station from Fairbanks and let the music and the miles roll on by.

My first real taste of a memory came when passing the entrance to Harding Lake, the graduation party at Rob Willingham's cabin the summer before I had left. Jessie in a bikini, attempting to water ski, and all Spenser's rum. It seemed like a lifetime ago, and it was.

Soon I was driving by the Air Force Base at Eielson where the highway surprisingly became a divided four-lane, a small marvel that did not mesh well with a memory preferring semblance to change. It seemed too modern, too extravagant, too different—but then again, perhaps I *had* been away too long.

Even North Pole—a nothing little roadside town seventeen miles from Fairbanks, known for its Santa Clause's House attraction—was now a thriving community. There were streets and avenues, shops and storefronts, and a bustling supermarket drawing tour buses and motor homes. Santa's place was more of a mansion than a house, complete with coursing reindeer, giant candy cane fences and something called an elf's den. A twenty-five-foot effigy of old St. Nick himself waved at me as I went by. The closer I got to Fairbanks, the farther away I felt.

When all the roads in my life had finally brought me back to within a few miles from my home, I found it difficult to go all the way. Instead, I drove around Fairbanks. Much had changed in twenty years: roads were wider, buildings were taller, and there were certainly more of them. There were shopping centers, specialty shops, fast-food restaurants, and at least a dozen new schools. The old high school was still there, but it too had undergone major renovations.

I ran across a self-serve car wash and spent a couple hours cleaning a thousands miles of dirt and grime from the truck. I found a *Quick Lube* and had the oil changed and then a *Laundromat* where I washed my clothes. I knew that I was only toying with myself, longing to head north to Fox, but doing everything to avoid it.

I parked downtown and walked the craggy sidewalks of Fairbanks trying to recall everything and anything I could about a city that had long since forgotten me. But there wasn't much to remember that didn't lead farther north, but that didn't stop me from wandering into the old Food King, trying hard to convince myself that I was hungry.

Surprisingly, the store was much as I remembered it. Although it felt small and tired, its round walls and vintage shelves still stocked to the ceiling with grocery items.

I picked out some peanut butter and bread. Then standing in the only open checkout line, I waited patiently behind a white bearded sourdough with hands full of coupons taking a scrupulous accounting of his bargains some three carts full. All the while, the only checker, a cute young lady name-tagged *Crystal* with a sassy Southern accent did all she could to speed things along.

"That there is a two for one," she explained to the man. "The other's a twenty cent off for the same thing. You can use one or the other, but not both.

"I can help you here," a man said from the next check-stand over. I brought him my things, and he quickly ran me through.

"Your receipt, sir," he said, studying me with a pair of bulging eyes.

He was as tall as I remembered and still as thin, except for a little pouch of belly his apron couldn't hide. He wore a white collared shirt, stained yellow at the pits, and a tattered pink tie knotted in a double Windsor. He kept his neatly feathered hair a frosty shade of gray.

"Have a nice day," said Kenny Brenke.

He handed me my bag before forcing for me a smile.

"You too," I said, wanting to say more. Before I could let loose the words, he turned and ambled off toward the back of the store. I wondered if he had recognized me, but then again, how could he? He never knew me. I couldn't remember a single time we had spoken back in high school. Until today, the man had only been an image from my youth, played and replayed within the walls of my mind's eye. I knew then my reasons for dropping in on the Food King. I had wanted to find him here.

I should've said something, or he should have. I had an idea to go back there and find him among the tired and overstocked shelves, tell him who I was, and make him talk to me. Instead, I left him to forever tend his Food King.

I tossed the bag of bread and peanut butter in the back of my newly cleaned truck and headed for Fox.

Widened, re-directed and labeled an expressway, the road to my past promised to get me there in a hurry. Fortunately, a sign leading me to the *Old Steese Highway* saved me from a fast track down memory lane. What the old route made up for in nostalgia, it lacked in maintenance. The frost heaves alone made it more ride than road and on several occasions, I had to swerve to avoid the carnivorous potholes hopeful to devour the front end of my little truck.

Like Fairbanks, things north had changed too. Dozens of new buildings banked the highway—homes, gas stations, churches, a welding shop, a trap-shooting club, and a couple mysterious structures built entirely of blue tarps and plywood. All appeared to have been there a while. I passed the old number-eight gold dredge, which had become an attraction of sorts with several tour buses crowding the entrance. Just outside of Fox, I caught my first glimpse of the pipeline, a serpentlike creature with sheet metal skin that slithered in and out of the valley.

Only a few miles from my home, even as the tides of rocks and tailings hurried on by, I was reacquainted with the gentle lay of the land, the subtle roll to the hills, and the slight bends in the highway. There were a few houses where I didn't expect them, forests now where saplings once grew, but I was sure I didn't miss a single pathway or trailhead.

An excitement arose within me: my heart raced, my hands shook, my face burned, and my throat went dry. I neared the Shit Towers, but didn't see them. After twenty years of growth, I wondered if the surrounding trees had caught them, or if someone had finally torn them down. I rolled the window down and let the air rush over me. It pricked electrically at my senses, freeing my mind to remember. Faces charged past me—my mother, Tom, my sisters, Spenser, Spooner, JT, Saucy, and of course, Jessie. I was back, but I wanted to go back.

To my surprise, an enormous apartment building now marked the entrance to the road leading to my old house. It fronted a neighborhood of a half dozen or so small porchless homes set back amongst the birches that once ran thick along the roadside. I saw no one, save for a single dog that raised its sleepy head to me as I drove slowly past. I neared the old driveway with an intense anticipation. My eyes eager to catch a welcoming shimmer of sunshine from off the old tin roof. None came.

My childhood home—or the *Big Shitbox,* as Tom had christened it—was now a blackened mound of ash and cinders. Had it not been for the despair already dwelling within me, I might've felt bad. Or sad, even. But as it was, I felt nothing.

The fire had taken with it the toolshed and the pigshed but had missed the old boathouse and my little trailer. Slumped badly and sagging at one end, the boathouse was still standing but appeared to have slid several more feet toward the creek. My old trailer had been moved some forty feet down the driveway, probably to escape the fire. There, it had been left listing haplessly on one tireless rim.

I was surprised to find the inside of my old trailer much like I had left it. The bed was made, the Indian blankets were folded and stacked neatly at its foot. The kerosene lanterns were full and in their proper places. A good layer of dust covered everything, but I knew it wouldn't take long to clean.

With the jack from the truck and the aid of a couple sinter blocks, I found among the cinders, it wasn't long before I had the little trailer straight and level again. I found an old broom in one of the cupboards and gave the floor a good sweeping. I stripped the bed and discovered the freeze-dried carcass and fecal remnants of a mouse that had taken residence. It wasn't a big mess and I was surprised that I didn't find more.

I put together a list of cleaning supplies and loaded the sheets and blankets for the *Laundromat*. Although the trailer was equipped with a stove and refrigerator, I had never known Tom to run either of them. I located the outside hookups for both electricity and propane and thought I would place a call to the power company and purchase a propane tank when I was back in town.

It was late afternoon by the time I arrived back in Fairbanks. There was a pay phone at the Laundromat and while the bedding tumbled dry, I spoke to a croaky-voiced man at the power company who knew more about my parent's house than I expected.

"The power has been shut off for nearly a decade, but the placed burned down just this last winter," said the man. "No fire service that far out."

"There are quite a few houses out there now," I said. "You'd think they'd want to get some."

"Yeah, well since the fire, the tracking station has agreed to cover that area for some sort of fee," he said.

"Is that so," I said. My mind went whirling back to images of the alienlike space station.

I asked the man how was it that he knew so much about it and he informed me he lived even farther out than my place. Somewhere up the Chatanika way, he said. He also told me the address had changed and he gave me a number for what was now the *Old Steese Highway*. He left me with a promise that someone would be out in the next day or two to hookup electricity to the trailer.

I made another call, this one long distance.

"Hello, Sue?" I said. I had called her at home, knowing the office had long since closed for the day.

"Henry, is that you?" came an anxious voice.

"Yeah, it's me Sue. I'm in Alaska."

"Alaska? What are you doing up there? Everyone's been so worried about you."

I knew when she said *everyone*, she meant only herself, but I had left unexpectedly, in a hurry and her holding the bag. I owed her an explanation.

"Yes, Sue, I've come home and I'm going to stay."

It was difficult for her, but she informed me that he firm had bought me out. She would send me a check to my new address.

My liquidated legal career had been worth a little more than $20,000. It was less than I deserved, but a lot more than I expected.

Chapter Thirty-Eight

July 1965

Not quite a half mile from the Riverwood, his arms crossed and leaning back against the tailgate of his old Ford truck, waiting for me was Tom. Without a word, I walked past him and climbed into the passenger side of the cab. A few seconds later, Tom got in beside me and started the engine.

"Did you say what you needed to say?" asked Tom.

I nodded.

Tom slipped the truck in gear and pulled out onto the highway; neither one of us said another word the entire way home.

I slept well into the next evening awakening to the sound of raindrops on the rooftop, so peaceful and soothing that I felt hopeful that it all had been a bad dream. Soon enough, I learned from my mother that Spenser was still dead, Jessie was still gone and I was still left to explain everything.

Nursing me back to health, my mother had me relive every detail of the events at least a dozen more times and each time she would say, *You are so very lucky, Henry, you could've been so easily killed.* I never confessed to her that I had been the one to have killed Spenser Mason, nor would I ever. I was careful and consistent enough in my version of the story that after several days, she finally relented and we stopped discussing it.

It was about that time that I received my first letter from Jessie. She made no mention of any of the events that led to her sudden departure, but did assure me she was doing well and relieved to be back living with her mother. She also inquired as to my plans for college and if I would ever be near enough to come for a visit. In closing, she said she missed me.

My mother was truly delighted when I immediately informed her that I would be attending Washington State College in the fall. She then went about making the arrangements while I mapped out routes from Pullman, Washington to Flint, Michigan.

I lay in bed half awake and thinking of ways to get to Jessie when, suddenly, the door flung open and in came Tom with a tin can of kerosene under his arm.

"Wake up!" he shouted. "I thought you were going to split wood for Spooner today."

I sat up quickly.

"Yeah, I was . . . I mean, I am," I mumbled.

Tom gathered up the lanterns, set them on the little table, sat down, and began his careful process of refilling them.

"What's with the old Chevy door key?" he said, his eyes shifting to a spot on the table.

"Door key?" I said.

"The old Fleetmaster door and trunk key," he said, again his eyes shifting. "You buy a car, Henry?"

I had no idea what he was talking about until I stood up and got a look at the table. The two keys Jessie had given me at the hotel. I had completely forgotten about them.

"Is that what they are?" I said.

"Well, this one is," said Tom, picking up one of the two keys. "My old man had a Chevy. That's what the key looked like, anyway. Why do you have it?"

"Oh, I don't know. I . . . uh . . . found them," I said unconvincingly.

"No kidding?" said Tom, shooting me a suspicious look. He then picked up the other key. "Never seen the likes of this one though," he said after a close examination. "Don't have any idea what it could be to. But the other is a Fleetmaster, sure as shit."

He set them both back down on the table and went about filling the lanterns. My stomach growled impatiently. I quickly dressed and waited for Tom to leave. When he finally did, I snatched up the keys and burst out the door.

I had spent nearly an entire summer across from Jessie and her busted leg there amongst the Shit Towers, leaning against that ass-end of that old Fleetmaster Chevy convertible. I was too immersed in Jessie and her stories of baseball and Tiger Stadium ever to think to open the trunk, a trunk that so perfectly and so conveniently protruded from the largest of the piles of shit.

It frightened me to think where Jessie had come across those keys in the short minutes after I had killed Spenser. Dead only two weeks, his life still haunted me. As I walked up the drive, a chill rustled through me. Before me came broken images of Spenser's gigantic knotty head, the bat, and all that blood. I would never grieve for Spenser Mason, nor would I ever hold a regret.

The key turned effortlessly inside the lock, and the trunk opened with a sharp pop. Inside was a lone rectangular-shaped iron box the size of a footlocker. Two strangely shaped locks secured its front. One, however, already held a key identical to the one in my hand. I placed it into the empty lock, and it moved easily. Lifting the heavy lid, my eyes caught all the luster of the first glimmer.

Gold.

Gold bars, more accurately. Enough to make *a lady cuss and a pirate blush*, my mother used to say. Forty gold bars in all. Two rows of five stacked four high, dazzling bright and in salient contrast to the pale heaps of shit surrounding them. This land's last mother lode bought and paid for in the coldest of blood.

I glanced suspiciously around me but saw no one, only Saucy sniffing about a rusty metal bucket. Still, everything seemed to be watching me and waiting for me to do whatever it was I was supposed to do. I glanced around again before picking up one of the bars and rubbing it between my hands, weighty and as shimmering smooth as bright sun on still water. Not a mar or mark on them, each as unidentifiable as the next.

My heart raced, and I didn't know what to do. I had an idea to close it all back up and wait to hear from Jessie, but that might take weeks. If someone did find it, Jessie might never forgive me. In the end, I decided to hide it. I would replace gold for rum up on the tailing pile at the beaver pond.

I emptied the iron chest, leaving the gold inside the trunk. I didn't count on the chest being so heavy, and it took all I had to drag it out of the trunk. I quickly located an old *Radio Flyer* wagon amongst the piles of shit. It was missing its two front wheels but was otherwise in good condition. I moved it to the back of the Fleetwood and somehow managed to lift the chest into the wagon.

It fit nicely and pulled easily down the driveway. It was another thing dragging it through the thickets of rain-sopped birch brush, low-hanging branches, mud-laden creek beds, and what soon became a torrential downpour. Twice the chest tumbled from the wagon, the second time nearly causing me to leave it where it lay. At last, I heard the sound of raindrops on water and knew that I was close to the beaver pond.

It took me another good hour, but I got the wagon and chest across the beaver dam, over the rocky bank and finally up the forty or so feet to the top of the tailing pile. I was exhausted. I rested for twenty minutes before sliding the lid off the hidden vault.

I poured out every jar of Spenser's rum save one before tossing the empty jars down the side of the hill. There must've been nearly a hundred jars that I watched shatter on the rocks below. Afterward,

I sipped rum from the remaining jar and thought about what Jessie would've done had she seen me do it. I was quite certain that she would've slugged me.

I slid the chest easily down into hole. It fit perfectly. Now all I needed was the gold.

The hike back took less than thirty minutes. I spent the next ten rummaging through the shit piles for something to carry them in. I got lucky, nearly tripping over a leather tool belt that had several large pouches that I was sure would hold the gold. I slung the belt over my shoulder, loaded it with four gold bars, and then set off again.

I spent the rest of the day and part of the next slogging the gold bars through the rain. I was just about to load the last four bricks into the belt when the roar of an engine startled me from behind. I spun around in time to see JT's truck come squealing to a stop at the top of the drive.

JT didn't see me when he first stepped out of the truck, but after the slamming the door, he spied me.

"Henry," he said breathlessly, as if he too had been startled. He then glanced over at the passenger side of his truck where a short squatty woman with bleach-treated hair, and perhaps the widest ass I had ever seen, climbed out the cab and waddled around to the front of the truck.

I swallowed hard trying to hold back the panic crawling up my throat. My face burned, and for a few long seconds, I could only breathe in.

"What the hell are you doing here?" said JT, his goofball face sharp and inquisitive. "Jessie's gone, you know."

"I know," I said. But I couldn't think to say more. Caught red-handed, the game was over. Questions were coming for which I had no ready answers.

JT looked past me at the back of the old Chevy.

"What are you doing in there?"

He took a couple steps forward, his narrow eyes squinting.

I glanced back and down into the open trunk where at the bottom lay the four gold bars neatly aligned and newly spattered with fresh raindrops.

Then, as if the gold bars spoke for me themselves, I decided it was best to come clean—nearly clean anyway.

"I got a letter from Jessie," I explained. "She told me where I could find Spenser's gold."

At my mention of the word *gold*, JT's eyes seemed to instantly sparkle.

"What's that?" he said, a smile inching its way across his face. "Gold, you say?"

JT walked quickly up to the open trunk and, peering inside, let out an excited gasp. He lifted out one of the bars and held it with one of his enormous hands while stroking it with the other.

"This here's my old man's gold, you say?"

I nodded at him.

JT glanced back at the big-assed woman and beckoned her to come on over. Waddling up to us, she had a good look at the gold bar JT was holding and then another good look inside the trunk.

"Oh my," she said with a pitchy little giggle. Then twisting her lips into a sort of suspicious smile, she stared intently at JT.

JT's twinkling eyes skipped from hers to mine and then back to hers again. "It's all mine now," he said to the woman as if he understood what she was thinking.

"Jessie told me I should give it to you if I found anything," I lied. "Here's the key she gave me the night she left."

He handed the bar to the woman who nearly dropped it and then took the key from me. I spied Saucy over near the cabin and called out to her. When they both glanced over at the dog, I tossed the tool belt back amongst the shit piles and began walking toward the driveway.

"I better get going," I said.

JT gave me a quick once-over and then nodded, the excitement still beaming from his eyes.

"Okay," he said. "You take care now."

The fat-assed woman shot me a quick parting smile before I walked away. However this would play out, I knew I was in the clear. Spenser and I were the only two people that knew how much gold was in that trunk. I would have to explain it all to Jessie, but I knew that I had done the right thing.

Walking down the drive, I heard a roar of laughter from behind me. What a goofball, I thought. If he only knew.

Chapter Thirty-Nine

May 1985

Not surprisingly, when served with the divorce papers, The Win came out blasting with both barrels. First, he hired Michael Zuccaro, the biggest cannon at the heavy-artillery law firm of *Farmer, Conrad, & Leads*. A superstar in the Midwest legal community, he was known reverently as *Zuke the Nuke* for the ruthless, unrelenting, and sometimes unscrupulous way he spent defending wealth. Then, The Win underwent a dramatic personality makeover that transformed him from heartless corporate money-grubber to the hardworking never-too-busy-for-my-family father-knows-best type.

The war had begun.

Neither my firm nor I had ever opposed the Nuke in anything, but then again, none of our clients ever had the kind of wealth that would capture the eye of such a star legal eagle. I did know a couple of attorneys that had. Both admitted to me that while they were drowning in the flood of arduous and draconian litigation brought on by his army of associates, a ring of probing private investigators dragged their clients through a gauntlet of surveillance and scrutiny, enough to induce quick and diminutive settlements.

It didn't take the legal hounds long to catch the scent of my relationship with Jessie. I had been spending considerable time with Jessie and her three boys after The Win had moved out and into one of Detroit's swankier hotels. We soon learned that the Nuke spies had the place surrounded. Through photographs, video, and wiretaps, they kept a close watch on us. They tracked our every move, tailing

Jessie to and from her work at the Birmingham Public Library and me the nearly one hundred miles round-trip to and from my place in Lansing.

Jessie's attorney had advised her that we should stop seeing each other until the divorce was final, which I agreed this was good idea. The Win, along with his new and powerful allies, would certainly use the affair to demonstrate that she was unfit as a mother.

When I suggested that she seriously consider it, Jessie wouldn't have it. She picked up the phone and called The Win. She told him right in front of me that he had better get used to the two of us together. As she loved me, was in love with me and that once the divorce was final, she and I were getting married. Before hanging up on him she had added, *Henry spends more time with your children than you do. He always has. He's more of a father to them than you are, and he's what they need right now.*

Before then, Jessie had never so much as hinted such things to me, but it made me feel good. Afterward, I asked her if she had really meant it and if she actually did love me.

More than you will ever know, she had said. *You are the love of my life, Henry Allen. And I will marry you, if you'll have me.*

It was the rest of my life, it was forever, it was everything I had ever wanted, and it was standing there before me. I remember at that moment wanting to tell her something, something important, something unforgettable, something that she had never heard me say before.

I love you, was all I thought to say, and I remembered hoping that it would be enough. *You could lose your kids,* I warned her. *I know how these things work, Jess. They could award him primary custody if they believe you're an unfit mother. It happens all the time. I have no doubt that Winslow and Zuccaro are putting together quite a case right now.*

To hell with them, she had said. *It's just a game to Winslow. He doesn't want them. I don't believe he ever has. Even if he does get them, he won't keep them. He wouldn't know what to do with them.*

But, Jess, you have to think this through, I had pleaded with her. *He can pay someone. He can have his parents help him. You don't want to run the risk of that, do you? You could lose your children.*

No, she had said. *He won't do it. I know he won't. After all this, he'll want me to have them, to have them and to know that he's their father. He told me as much after the twins were born and I had named little Henry after you. He told me that it didn't matter. I could name them whatever I liked because the boys were his and mine, and that's the way it always would be. Now I know what he meant by that. I suppose he is right, and I hate him for it.*

But you could lose your children, I had said again.

So be it, she had said so coldly that it sounded evil. If it wasn't evil, it derived from there. Not fear, but the opposite of it—impenetrable and unfeeling, an etherizing spell cast to shield her from the demons in her world. I didn't know it, but I had been witness to it. Before, it had always come in her face and eyes, the night in the stairwell at our high school dance and then again in the moments after I had killed Spenser. It was pure indifference, and it frightened me.

By the beginning of October, Nuke had called off his dogs and things had finally calmed down enough for Jessie and me to spend some time together without constantly looking over our shoulders. I was sure it was only the quiet before the storm, and soon, there would be a flurry of motions, hearings, and orders concerning the best interest of the three boys.

Just five years old and starting kindergarten, Junior Marshall had his mother's dark hair and eyes and had already settled easily into the role of big brother to the twins James and little Henry, even though he wasn't a year older. The unquestionable playtime leader, the full-time protector and the sometimes peacekeeper, Junior also had his mother's curious nature and an inherent ability to understand the mature world around him.

Why did Daddy go away? Junior had asked his mother shortly after The Win had moved out.

Because I asked him to, Jessie had said. When he then asked why, she had told him, *because Daddy doesn't love me the way I want to be loved.*

Junior had appeared satisfied with the answer, and once while watching the boys play, I overheard him explaining it to his little brothers.

Daddy went away because Mommy doesn't like his love, he had said to them.

James, who had his father's thick features, an extremely quiet and reserved disposition, and who always appeared to know much more than he was letting on, listened intently but didn't say a word. Little Henry, who resembled neither of his parents, who was the smallest and certainly who was the most animated of the three, asked James: *why not?*

Because Mommy wants a different kind of love, he had said.

I had been there when they came into the world, known them as infants, toddlers, and now little boys. They meant as much to me as my own family, and I was glad that Jessie wanted me in their lives. To them, I was *Uncle Hen*—a reliable, trusted, and loyal friend. Much of the time I spent with Jessie, I spent with the boys. I enjoyed my time with them and loved them.

This was why I worried about Jessie losing them to The Win. Regardless of what she believed, The Win and his maverick lawyer had a real shot at winning custody, particularly when Jessie had all but refused to fight. I made a living fighting such battles, and I never had a client who had so much to lose and seemingly cared so little. It made me question whether she truly understood the consequences.

You don't know him as well as I do, she had said whenever I had brought it up. *He won't want them, even if he does win. You'll see.*

I wasn't so sure, and I was glad I wasn't her lawyer. It had to be extremely frustrating for Jimmy.

The new more fatherly Winslow had taken the boys for an entire week and was planning to take them to his parents' place in Chicago, which meant that Jessie and I would be alone. More importantly, for the first time in sixteen years, the Tigers were back in the World Series and leading three games to one with game five at the Stadium, and I had scored a pair of tickets.

I had given Jessie the news and she was thrilled, but I didn't tell her everything. To get the tickets, I had to call in a favor from Frank Harris, a retired Detroit police officer I had known since my law school days. Over the years, I had handled both his divorces and had done a fair amount of other legal work for him without charge. The work was easy, and I didn't mind doing it because I always thought that knowing a police officer might come in handy.

I didn't realize just how handy knowing a Detroit police officer could be.

Aside from getting the tickets, which he did without effort, Frank told me of a guy he knew in Dearborn that could get me an *incredible* diamond at an *easy* price, to use his words.

After hearing what Jessie had told The Win, nothing could stop me from doing what I was convinced was our destiny.

I met Frank in the parking lot of a seedy little jewelry store in Dearborn that I had never heard of before. It had been a while since I had seen Frank. To look at him, you never would have thought he had been one of Detroit's finest. With his thinning gray hair slicked back and curled around his ears and his dark squared sunglasses, he looked more like a crime boss than a former crime fighter. But back in the day, I was not sure there had been much difference in downtown Detroit. He had hugged me like a gangster, pulling my face close to his while patting me a couple times on the back.

From the front pocket of his green button-down sweater, Frank pulled out the World Series tickets and handed them to me. When I asked him how much I owed him, I was surprised to hear him say *no charge*. He then told me that as far as favors were concerned, he was long overdue and he hoped he could do me right with the ring.

Inside, Frank introduced me to the owner, a tall Arab man named Behzad who wore a thick black mustache and a Colt .44 revolver strapped to his side. Behzad went about showing me dozens of different types of diamonds and settings from the many lighted display cases.

Already engaged twice in my lifetime, I had some experience buying diamond engagement rings. Though Sara's ring had barely been a diamond at all, I did learn about quality, clarity, and shape. I had chosen a tiny little marquise, despite my minuscule budget at the time. Gina's ring was elegant enough, nearly a carat in size, emerald shaped with excellent clarity, but I paid too much for it. Gina had already dumped Sully and was married to another guy by the time I had made the last payment on the ring.

This time, though, I knew exactly what I wanted, and it wasn't long before I had poked through nearly every diamond on display at Behzad's little store.

Nothing had caught my eye.

Finally, I thanked Behzad and Frank for their time and was on my way out when Behzad told me to wait. He disappeared beneath one of the display cases for several seconds before he reappeared holding a small leather pouch. He sprinkled its contents onto the black velvet pad atop the display case, a half dozen or so of the prettiest diamonds I had ever seen.

Each one was well over a carat in size and cut in every shape. They sparkled brilliantly. I picked out a princess-shaped diamond and examined it. Behzad let me inspect it for clarity under the scope, and as far as I could tell, it was perfect.

It is best one, Behzad had said. *You know diamonds.*

I wasn't sure about that, but I knew enough to know what I wanted, and this was it.

How much? I asked him.

Behzad raised his black and bushy eyebrows and then stroked at his large mustache, his dark eyes suddenly sharp and searching. After a few moments, he held up eight fingers.

Eight, he said.

Eight thousand? I said, coughing with surprise. My law career had been going well, but I wasn't making Winslow money. I shook my head and told him I was sorry, but that was too much.

Behzad then glanced over at Frank who smiled villainously at him before motioning for me to step aside. The two men immediately began to shout, each firing a variety of vicious and ethnically charged insults at the other. At one point during the heated exchange, I remember fearing that Behzad might pull his gun. But as quickly as it had started, it ended, with Frank holding up three fingers and Behzad relaying a reluctant nod.

We sat some fifteen rows behind the visitors' dugout for game 5 of the World Series. The seats were great, Tiger Stadium was electric, and my plans had gone without a hitch.

Yes, I will marry you! Jessie screamed at me over the jubilant crowd.

Kirk Gibson had just pounded his second homer of the night, virtually assuring the Tigers the game and the Series. I then placed the ring on her finger as her face flushed with surprise.

My god. It's beautiful! she shouted. I remembered the tears in her eyes when she told me this was the happiest she had ever been.

When the final out came and the Tigers were World Champions, we watched from our seats as the team and the crowd rushed the field in triumphant celebration. I asked Jessie if she wanted to go down there with them, but she shook her head no. Then moving up into my arms, I remember her whispering into my ear: *No, I'm right where I'm supposed to be.*

We viewed the trophy presentation where they named Alan Trammel the Most Valuable Player of the Series. Afterward, we made our way through the blurring mobs of orange and blue and then out into the swarming streets of a city gone mad with joy.

Flying along Michigan Avenue high on free shots of champagne, hanging fast to the moment, I listened as Jessie laughed lightheartedly and planned our life together.

Fairbanks, she said, waving her ring near my face. *As soon as this damned divorce is final. That's where I want to marry you—in Fairbanks, Alaska. We'll cash in all that gold and throw the biggest party that two-bit town has ever seen!* I remembered she kissed me and then asked if I loved her.

Yes, I had said and then I asked her the same.

More than you'll ever know, she had said.

Although the question of custody still loomed, the months to come were good for Jessie and me. I spent every chance I could with Jessie and the boys. However, The Win and his muscle Nuke didn't make things easy. Motions regarding *the use* of the marital home as it pertained to me were still pending. As it was, I never spent the night at The Win Palace, but the latest series of motions set to ban me from the place altogether.

It was disheartening to be at the center of a domestic war knowing that The Win blamed me for his broken family, broken marriage, and broken heart—knowing that I was the scapegoat for all his misery and the focus of all his hate. Although divorce was my profession and placing blame is part of the game, and even though I sincerely believed that Jessie and I belonged together, there was another part of me that felt strongly that The Win was right.

Jessie knew that it was difficult for me and went out of her way to make me feel loved and important to her. When she didn't have the boys, she was with me in Lansing. When we were together, she only wanted to talk about our marriage and our future together. She had all but planned our wedding in Fairbanks. She had said she wanted a new house, a new career, and a new life with me, as far away from Winslow as she could be.

But neither her plans nor her intentions could make things move any faster. The rest of our life together all seemed to hinge on the divorce and, more specifically, the custody battle for her boys. A hearing had been set for late December but adjourned and resct to early February. Then for some unknown reason she couldn't quite explain, the court adjourned that hearing and reset it for early May. Rarely did she want discuss with me anything regarding the hearing, but even when she did, she only said that she was confident that the court and The Win would ultimately do the right thing.

I wasn't so sure. The Nuke himself had deposed me for two days straight with The Win at his side. All his questions seemed to focus around Jessie's relationship with the boys and me. The questions were personal in nature, often leading, and sometimes downright inappropriate. I hadn't hired an attorney to represent me at the deposition, thinking that I could handle it on my own. By the second day of questioning, I had wished I had.

So, Mr. Allen, he had said, his snake eyes biting over the top of his half-mooned spectacles, *how many times have you had sex with Mrs. Marshall in front of the children?* He glanced assuredly over at The Win before leaning back and placing his hands behind his head to await my answer.

The Nuke was clearly showboating for his client, which compelled me to give The Win his money's worth.

Never, I said directly to The Win. *We have never had sex in front of the children. It has always been in private.*

So, fired the Nuke, *if the eldest child had told us that he witnessed you and Mrs. Marshall engaging in—*

He's five years old, for crying out loud! I said, cutting him off. *And I already told you, we've never had sex in front of the children—at the home or anywhere the children were present. Although*, I had said, glaring at The Win, *I would be more than happy to tell you every place we did have sex!*

We took a break, and I felt ashamed of what I had said. When we reconvened, Nuke only had a few more questions for me, most of them civil. Afterward, I called Jessie and told her the news. I seriously began to wonder if she actually understood what it all meant. The custody hearing was rapidly approaching, and I feared the worst. It confounded me that she could be so calm.

I barely saw Jessie at all the last couple of months before the hearing. I was busy with several cases of my own, and to prevent any last-ditch maneuvers by the Nuke, we both agreed it would be best to stay away from each other.

When the day finally arrived, I set up camp at my office to await the news, my insides as twisted as the telephone cord I sat staring blankly at. It was nearly five when the call finally came, and Jessie told me that she and The Win had settled everything. She would maintain primary custody of the boys, would keep the house and most of its possessions, and would receive monthly child support payments as well as an enormous monetary settlement in lieu of alimony.

I was shocked. Not with the settlement, but the way in which Jessie delivered the news. As if she had expected it all along. She didn't seem at all excited, and when I asked her about it, she simply said that she would meet me at my house tonight and explain everything.

I had opened the bottle of Chardonnay and already Jessie was working on her second glass. She sat at my kitchen table gulping it down and fiddling nervously with her hair.

"He thought he had me, Hen," she said after taking another large drink of her wine. "He thought he could pull one over on me, but we caught him. We caught him, Hen."

"*We?*" I said, leaning against the refrigerator. "Who's *we?*"

"I did, really . . ." She hesitated. "My lawyers and me."

"*Lawyers*," I said. "I thought Jimmy was your only *lawyer?*"

"He is . . ." She hesitated again, shook her head dismissively, and then quickly finished her glass of wine. "There's something I need to tell you."

"What?" I said, suddenly anxious.

Jessie poured herself more wine.

"There's this guy who works with Jimmy."

"Another lawyer?" I asked.

"I don't think so. I think he's studying to be one. You know, like those guys you have at your office, the ones who do research and things."

"You mean he's a *law clerk* for Jimmy?"

"Yeah, that's what he is, a law clerk," she said.

"What about him?" I hated to ask.

"We've been working together the last month or so. You know, on the case. Going through the financial records, planning things. Spending a lot of time together formulating strategy

"What *strategy?*" I said.

"Winslow sent Jimmy a bunch of stuff. Copies of things—paperwork, really. You know, businesses interests, stocks, deeds to property, titles, and all those kinds of thingies. You know what I'm talking about," she said.

"*Discovery,*" I said.

"Yes, that's it: discovery. It's where we found the smoking gun," she said before taking another good-sized swallow of wine.

"What smoking gun?" I asked the question so easily. Tragically, I knew precisely where this was going. I had heard it from her a hundred times. Like the perfect storm effortlessly destroying everything in its path. It would destroy me.

"He found . . ." Jessie paused, choking on a sob. "A transaction." She began to cry but continued through tears. "He found a deposit that led to a company in Cleveland. I knew that Winslow had business there. I knew he was hiding something from me. Then we found it. Just a tiny interest in some new technology company, but it was worth more than everything we owned. We got all the details and confronted Winslow with it today. Jimmy said that he and his lawyer could get in real trouble for hiding it like they did. Winslow gave me everything I asked for and then some."

Her eyes already red from tears, Jessie came to me, threw her arms around me, and held on tightly to my chest.

"I'm so sorry, Hen!" she cried. "I hate myself for hurting you!" She slid down the length of my body still holding onto my legs. "I don't know why I do it, Hen! I hate myself. Know that I hate myself for it!"

Jessie was so beautiful to me. Beautiful in all the ways beauty is. In her hair, in her eyes, in her mouth and skin. In her laughter, her smile, her movements, or when she was still. There was beauty even in her anger and her sadness, or in the way she kissed me and loved me. In her every aspect, her beauty was there for me to worship and to love.

But never in her words. Her words were often unpleasant, painful, and cruel, belying her beauty with cutting truth—the truth was always more than I could stand.

Jessie stayed there holding my legs and crying for several more minutes. Then picking herself up from the floor, she wiped her eyes and left me alone standing there in the kitchen, staring down at the vacant chair and her empty glass of wine.

My world had stopped. I had stopped. I knew there was more to it than this, more words, more to know, more to try to understand—but ultimately, there would only be more hurt. It was hopeless, as something inside of me had already broken. Something inside of me had already died.

I grabbed a half bottle of Bacardi rum from a kitchen cabinet and, in the bathroom, located a full bottle of Percocet left over from a dental surgery. I managed to gag down the pills and finish the rum in three large swallows. Then I lay down on my bed, closed my eyes, and waited to die.

I awoke to hammering chimes—a fire alarm. No, not a fire alarm; my blurry vision said otherwise. An alarm clock, 6:30 a.m. I snatched the clock and flung it at the wall. The empty bottle of rum lay on the floor beside the bed, pointing at me, mocking me.

Then there was a smell.

"Oh, for fuck sake!" I shouted to no one there. Grave-white pills festooned across a swamp of brown and bile. Then I remembered. "Oh, for fuck sake!"

It was supposed to be easy. Pills and booze—that's the way it is done, for crying out loud. A sour stomach had left me alive and wallowing in a pool of puke and self-pity.

The phone rang, startling me.

"What?" I barked into the receiver, getting a strong whiff of the dried barf pasted to the back of my hand.

"Henry? It's me," said Jessie.

"Yeah," I said.

"Are you all right? I was . . ." she paused.

"I'm fine," I said, trying hard to sound fine.

"I'm sorry. Please tell me what to say. I don't know . . ."

"You said enough."

"Are you sure you're going to be all right?"

"Yeah," I said weakly.

There was a long pause on the line.

"I hate myself," she said finally. "I'm so sorry, Hen." her voice trembled, broke, and then she started to cry.

"All right," I said. And there was another long pause when, at some point, I too began to cry.

"Will I ever see you again?" she asked.

The question was real, but it seemed so ridiculous.

"I don't know," I said. It was all I could think to say.

"I do love you," she said.

I hung up the phone before she felt compelled to say any more.

My head throbbed, my stomach ached, and all I wanted to do was die. But I had already fucked that up, and since my death had been so shortly lived, I might as well get up.

I staggered down a revolving hallway and stumbled into the bathroom. I got a good look at myself in the mirror. What a mess. Hair matted with vomit, dark raccoon circles for eyes, my face as pale as a ghost. Hell, maybe I was dead.

I splashed some cold water on my face, spied the empty bottle of Percocet, and tossed it at the bathtub. I took a long drink of water from the tap and then lay down on the cool bathroom floor. I stared up at the underside of the toilet as the world went spinning hopelessly around me.

I thought about picking out the Percocet from the puke and washing them down with some Pepto-Bismol. Then I thought about finding my old service pistol and blowing my damned brains out. Both were fine plans, but right now I didn't have the energy, and all I wanted to do was sleep.

Chapter Forty

June 1985

I arose from the trailer's tiny bed, or what seemed tiny after all these years, and stood awaiting the pain to come. I let the scuttling thoughts of Jessie and her new man scratch their way across my aching mind.

I hadn't stayed long enough to learn any more. In a blurred haste, I had quit my job, packed up a few things, and set out on my journey here without word to anyone except for Sue and Sully who I had left with a mess of work and worry. I wouldn't go back. Whatever happened to me, it would happen here.

I stepped out into a perpetual summer's sun, not certain yet how I would use it. Last night and well into the early morning hours, I had scrubbed clean the inside of the trailer, remade the bed with the sheets washed in Fairbanks, and then hooked up the new propane tank. I was pleasantly surprised after lighting the stove when it flamed a purring blue.

I had a good look down the road at the nearby houses but still saw no one, although from the yard of the neighboring house, a lazy German shepherd did lift his head up to me. Then, without reason, I walked over to the remains of the old house and tried to recall how it used to be. *An enormous box with a sloped tin roof* was how my mother used to describe it; a wood-sucking monstrosity was the way I remembered it. Now, it was nothing more than a heap of black char and tin.

"The foundation's still good," said a voice from behind me. Startled, I turned to find a gaunt man wearing ragged jeans, a flannel shirt, and a bright orange stocking cap fast approaching. He stuck a hand out to me, which I instinctively shook. "Russ Rahall," he said with a lopsided grin. He had a hint of an accent in his words that I didn't recognize.

"Henry Allen," I said, looking squarely into his sallow green eyes.

"The foundation is in great shape," he said, pointing toward the rubble. Walking past me, he kicked at the short brick wall that surrounded it. "You see here? It's solid, just a little sooty."

"Oh yeah?"

"Sure," he said, his eyes scanning the mess. "Clear this shit away and you can start rebuilding." He paused then, glancing back at me, "if that's what you want to do."

"It is," I said, surprised that I had said it. I had no idea why or how I was going to do it, but all at once, I had made up my mind. I was going to build a house.

"That's great," he said. He shot me another lopsided grin. "I'm your neighbor." He nodded toward the house next door. "I saw you get in last night. So you bought the place, I take it?"

It was a fair enough question. Hell, for all he knew, I could be some squatter.

"No," I said. "I used to live in this house with my family. My stepfather gave me the place. I didn't know it had burned down."

"Yeah, it's too bad. They don't know what caused it. Happened in January, thought it might be vandals. So Tom Talbot's your stepfather?"

"Yes, that's right," I said. "You know him?"

"Oh sure, yeah, he and Helen. They lived here for about a year after I bought the property next door," he said. "Good people they are. What are they up to these days?"

"My mother passed a few years back," I said. "Tom remarried and lives down the California way."

"Sorry to hear that, she was good people," he said. "I tried reaching Tom after the fire, but to no avail. I even went down to the borough assessor's office, but they wouldn't give me the time of day. Sure sorry to see it burn as it did. I'm glad to hear you're going to build. It's a nice piece of land. I would've bought it myself had I the money back then. I'm a builder. I built all these houses around here. I bought the land up piece by piece, built these homes, and then sold them one by one. What kind of place do you want to build?"

"I'm not sure," I said. "I only just decided that's what I want to do. I'm not a builder, but I suppose I'm going to need one. You think you might be interested?"

"Not usually the way I do things," he said with a weighty scowl. He glanced back at the burnt remains, then out toward the road, and then back at me. "But I guess things the way they are, not real busy at the moment. I'm sure we can work something out."

"Great," I said. "I don't need much, just a roof and a couple rooms."

"That's a start," he said. "Do you know how many square feet you're thinking?"

I hadn't a clue, but I remembered when I bought my place in Lansing the realtor told me it was 1,800 square feet, and that seemed a nice size. "About 1,800 I think."

Russ nodded. "Single story, I suspect?"

"Yeah," I said, without giving it a second thought.

Russ stared skyward. When his eyes returned to mine, he said, "With the foundation already in place, and if the well and septic are still good and with labor—"

"I want to help." I interrupted. "I want to build it with you. I don't know a lot, but I'm a quick learner, and I'm darn good with hammer," I lied.

"What is it you do?" he asked.

"I'm a lawyer," I said.

Russ raised his eyebrows and then shook his head.

"Well shit, that changes everything. The last thing I need is to be messing around with a lawyer."

"I'm not licensed up here in Alaska, nor do I plan to be. I'm not even working."

"How do you expect to pay for a house if you aren't working?"

"I have some money," I said. "I'll pay it all up front if I have to. I promise, you won't have any trouble with me," I said. "You can hire anyone you want to. I just want to help, that's all."

Russ gave me a sour look, and then after another long stare at the sky, he said, "Nineteen dollars a square foot. That's fair, you can ask around. That's $34,000 and some change. I want half of it up front." He shot me a suspicious frown. "And we'll put it in writing."

"Fine," I said, offering my hand.

He took it reluctantly but shook it nevertheless.

"In writing," he said sharply.

"Of course," I said.

"I'll rustle up some plans tonight and get back with you tomorrow. I'll want to start right away, the summer's burning," he said.

"Fine," I said, smiling. "I'll see you tomorrow then."

I watched as Russ headed off toward the road, as an excitement came charging through me. I was going to build a house. There was so much to think about. In fact, I thought so much about building a house that, for the next hour, I hardly thought of Jessie at all.

Back in Fairbanks, I found a local bank where I opened a checking and savings account. I deposited between the two of them all but a few hundred dollars of my cash and walked out of there with a nifty little carryall, as a gift for my patronage.

At a hardware store, I purchased a handy leather tool belt, a hammer, measuring tape, and a host of other tools I thought handy for building a house. I also bought a mailbox and the supplies necessary to build a stand.

Afterward, I found a pay phone where I called Sue. I asked her to contact a realtor that I knew—a former client that could never stay married but could sell sand to an Arab. I was confident he would do what it would take to sell my house, including clearing out all of my shit.

"Give him the key I gave you and tell him to send the contracts to the address I gave you," I said to Sue. "He'll have to get someone to clear the place out though. Tell him to send me the bill. There might be a bit of a mess in the bedroom."

"What mess?" said Sue.

I couldn't imagine what three-week-old puke smelled like. "He'll figure it out," I said.

Following my conversation with Sue, I called my bank in Lansing and had them close out my accounts and send a check for the balance to my new address. It was pathetic how little I had saved over the years, but right now, I could use the nearly $4,000 I had there. With the money coming from the firm, my savings, and the money I had in the bank here, I had enough to start the construction. The rest I was sure I had in equity in my house in Lansing. In all, it was enough to last me through the summer and until I could figure out what it was I was going to do with the rest of my life.

On my way home, I stopped at the entrance to my road. Seven mailboxes already lined the highway, but fortunately, there was a large enough space on the platform between the *Zimmers* and the *McCalls* to put my new box. When I had fit and firmly fastened it to the platform, I neatly wrote my last name and Star Route Number on the front of the box. My box sparkled in comparison to the others. I now had an address, and I felt good for having put it there.

Back home, I was pleased to find a power line connecting the pole to the trailer. For the first time, the refrigerator hummed to life, and the electric light gave the old place a new shine.

I spent the next several hours clearing away the remains of the old house. What I could get into the back of my truck, I hauled off to the local dumpsite in Fox. The rest, I piled back behind the old boathouse. It was hard work on the body but easy on the mind, and before long, I had a good portion of it cleared away.

When finally night did come, free of the darkness and free of the shadows that so haunted my mind these last weeks, I lay in bed, tired, wanting of sleep and thinking only of a house not yet built.

My morning began with the sound of a gentle rapping from the door.

"Just a minute," I said. It was nearly noon. I had slept long and well but was still feeling the weight of the night. I quickly pulled on my jeans and pushed open the door.

Russ, standing with an armload of papers, gave me his lopsided grin.

"Afternoon," he said wryly. "Up before sunset, I see."

"Yes," I said. "Catching up on some sleep."

I invited him in, and we both sat down at the little table. Russ spread out his paperwork and placed a small brochure in front of me.

"I have an idea," he said. "Have you ever heard of a kit home?"

I shook my head.

"I have a brother who works for an outfit in Southern Idaho that makes these prefab log homes out of cedar," he said. "They have several different designs or floor plans, if you will, and once you pick the one you like, they cut the logs for everything. Then they package it all up and ship it up here." He pointed at the brochure. "As you can see, they look real nice, and they're a snap to put together. You can assemble the entire thing in less than a few weeks' time."

"They look very nice," I said. "What about the cost? Seems like that would be quite a shipping bill."

"Yeah, it's not cheap," he said, nodding. "But here's the thing. This company ships all over the lower forty-eight, and recently, their competitors have made some real headway here in Alaska. They want to get their feet wet, get a list of reliable builders up here and see if they can tap this market. Because you would be one of the first, the first in the Fairbanks area, they're willing to make you a good deal, providing you let them take pictures for their leaflet," he said, tapping the brochure.

"How good of a deal?" I asked.

Russ picked up the brochure and flipped it around to a floor plan called *Mountain Home.* "This one here," he said, setting it back down in front of me, "is a little over 1,600 square feet. It's two stories, three bedrooms, two baths—with the master bedroom and bath on the second floor. It has a giant beamed living room with huge windows that will look nice facing the creek over there. I checked, and I can have it cut for your foundation. It comes with a good-sized front deck. And here's the thing: they've agreed to cut the walls a good ten inches wide for a warm winter and a cool summer."

Russ sat back in his seat and smiled.

"And the cost?" I said.

"Oh right. The whole thing—cut, shipped, and assembled—for a little less than $30,000. Now you'll have to decide how you're going to heat it and supply all the bells and whistles like fixtures, baths, toilets, and so on—and that might run a few thousand more—but all in all, I'd say it's about the same as what we were talking yesterday."

"Will I get to help assemble it?"

"Sure," he said with a laugh. "You can do as much as you want."

I glanced down at the brochure again, pretending to show doubt, but my mind was already set, and after a few long seconds, I said, "Let's do it."

Before Russ left, he told me that it would take a good month or so for it to get here. But as long as I put ten grand down and signed the contract, they would start cutting and preparing it to ship. He also said that I was welcome to use his shower and abode, which I took him up on immediately.

A beautiful summer's day and with my dark thoughts distracted by the idea of building a house, I decided to hike some of the trails I knew in my youth. Sadly, I glanced over at the spot where Saucy's doghouse used to be. I was in Vietnam when my mother sent me the news that Saucy had died. Just a few days after Flanny's death—a bad week for me. My mother had said they found her lying next to the creek in front of the boathouse, peaceful, as if she had simply decided that was where she was going to die. Tom had buried her somewhere up near one of the blueberry fields. I would visit her, but not today.

I found the narrow path that led down the steep embankment to the creek, and twice, I nearly fell. The trail seemed smaller now. Perhaps it had grown over or, more likely, I was older and not as fleet of foot as I once was.

I had a much easier time following the creek side, and after a good fifteen minutes with my high-tops already soaked in mud, I hit the dry tailings that ran along the far side of the creek. The splash from a beaver's tail startled me, but I took it as a sign that I was close and as a sort of welcome home.

For the most part, the beaver pond was how I remembered it. Taller trees, more brush, and more grass surrounded it now, but the water was still as clear. Across the other side and up the rocky bank loomed the giant tailing pile that suddenly didn't seem so gigantic. I hiked through the forest of birch trees, crossed over the lower dam, and walked up the rocky bank to the base of the tailing pile.

Naturally, I wondered if it was still there. I had for some time.

I had worked nearly every afternoon and weekend as a bagboy at a grocery store in Pullman to save enough money to visit Jessie in Michigan that Christmas. She was still living with her mother in Flint at the time but had arranged for me to stay in a motel not too far away. She had finally gotten her driver's license and picked me up at the Detroit airport in a '55 Chevy that had seen better times.

Jessie looked as good as I had ever seen her look, and I was positively thrilled to be with her again. I must have talked her head off on the ride from Detroit to Flint. I remembered telling her about the gold and how I had buried it atop the tailing pile. Jessie had said I had done the right thing, and she was glad I hadn't let on to JT that there was more.

He'd just spend it on that fat bitch, Jessie had said. *No, Hen, it's yours. I don't want anything from that old bastard.*

I told her that I didn't want it either and had given her the key to the strongbox.

A couple months ago, she'd told me that she still had it, and if the gold was still there, we would cash it in on a big wedding and honeymoon.

On your grandpa? I had asked.

No, she had said. *On my grandmother*.

I felt a sickness in my thoughts of Jessie, so before they could overwhelm me, I climbed to the top of the tailing pile. From there, I had a good look over the valley. It was all so different now. Where there had been brush, there were trees; where there had been trees, there were forests. And there were rooftops and clearings now that I had never seen before. Nowhere did I see any sign of the Shit Towers, and I was glad for it.

To my surprise, a vigilant young birch tree stood tall atop the hill where I was sure a sapling had once been. I was sure because I knew I had buried the gold next to it. I was disappointed to find that there, within its shade, was nothing but an empty hole.

I decided to take a longer trail back home, one that I recalled continued downstream from the beaver dams and circled around to the highway. I hadn't gone too far when I came across what looked to be modern gold mining equipment floating atop a small pontoon platform in a little slew just below the dam. Chained to a large cottonwood on the bank, the pontoons nosed up to what looked to be an abandoned campsite. I couldn't help but wonder if this was the person or persons who had run across the gold. I hoped it was, as I could only imagine their elation and their subsequent tales of how they had come across a box of gold bars on a tailing pile next to their gold mine.

Although parts of the trail had all but disappeared, I managed to make my way to the highway and follow it back to the mailboxes. Not surprisingly, I had no mail, but it still felt good to have a mailbox.

A short distance from home, I noticed a white sedan parked behind my truck in front of the trailer. The white Ford Taurus was new, probably a rental, and had Alaska plates. The door to the trailer was open wide, but the screen door was shut.

Pulling open the screen door, I nearly fell over when I saw Jessie sitting in the bench seat at the far side of the table. Like out of a dream or a character from some twisted *Twilight Zone* episode, she just sat there in the dim light, expressionless, staring back at me through ghostly eyes. I sat down across from her, still unconvinced that she was real.

I blinked hard and then closed my eyes, but she was still there when I opened them. Her face seemed pale, her eyes almost black. She wore her hair pulled back into a French braid, and I could barely make out the soft pink scar beneath her chin. She appeared older than I had ever known her to be.

Then, as if a picture came to life, she blinked, her eyes shifting to the window the way they had in that lifetime before. When her eyes moved to mine, they held tears.

"Hey, Hen," she said, her voice quivering.

I did not speak.

"It's good to see you," she said. "I've been so worried about you. You just left, Hen, without a word to anyone. Sue told me you quit. She thought you might've left town, and I figured you might've come here. I saw the house had burned, so I decided to wait. I've been here almost a week waiting for you. You can't imagine how relieved I was to see your truck here today. I'm glad that you're okay," she said, forcing a smile. "I feel so bad about what I did, about hurting you. It's something I know that I'll never be able to explain, and that you will never understand. But I feel I owe you an explanation. I owe you some kind of—"

"Don't," I said, raising my hand. "Please don't. I don't want to know. Really, I'm not sure I can live with that truth."

"I'm pregnant," she said.

The words hit hard, but they didn't surprise me. I had heard them somewhere before. Still, I searched in her eyes for even the faintest of hope, but I found none.

"*His?*" I said.

Jessie nodded.

"I've agreed to marry him," she said flatly.

"The hits just keep on coming, don't they, Jess? Why did you even come here?"

It was a fair question to such blistering revelations. She had been with another man, she had gotten pregnant, she had smashed a lifetime of dreams. But Jessie didn't answer. Instead, she looked again toward the window.

"I've lost everything, Jess," I said. "You're all that mattered to me. You're all that ever mattered to me. I thought that when we were . . ." I hesitated, words stuck dry in my throat. I couldn't say any more. My eyes blurred with tears as my throat tightened.

Jessie looked over at me.

"I wanted us to be together," she said, crying. "I'm so fucked up, Hen. You've always been there for me. You *deserve* so much better. *I* did this to us. It's *my* fault, Hen, and now . . ." Jessie paused and then, staring back out the window, she said, "*I'm so afraid I may have lost you.*"

The years may as well have been seconds and Jessie a teenage girl again, telling me all the things that I hated to hear.

Jessie looked at me again, her eyes blurred behind the tears.

"Don't leave me. Please don't ever leave me. I love you so very much. You can hate me if you want, but don't leave me. I can't lose you, Hen."

I stared intently into her eyes. I saw the fear, and I knew why she had come.

I had believed in love, *our* love—in its intentions and its good. I had hung hard to the *meant to be*, to the *always*, and to the *forever*. I had reveled in the *destiny*, in the *understanding*, and in the *someday*—the type of *someday* that is spawned from hope and nurtured in dreams. My dreams were her dreams, and her dreams mine. And if timing was our foe, then time—time was our friend. And with time, the stars would surely find their rightful places and, ultimately, we would be together.

But this was *my* delusion, not hers.

I didn't doubt that Jessie loved me. She may have loved me more than she loved anyone. She may have even believed in my dream, but it was only because she knew it was what I wanted. Not wanting to lose me, she had tried to love me the way I wanted her to.

To her, I was family, a brother, her most trusted friend. It was what I had always been to her. It was the way she had always seen me.

It was what Jessie had needed me to be. Not the way I needed her or wanted her, the way other men wanted her, but in the way the mind needs conscientious thoughts or the heart needs unconditional love. She needed me to love her, free of the consuming lust that had already so depraved her soul.

Jessie had failed me as a lover, the way she had failed all her lovers, but I had failed her as a friend by falling in love. Too many times, she had warned me not to covet her, not to be in love with her. I had hated to hear it and refused to believe it.

I had ignored it because I was already in love. I had been since I was fifteen. Had we not been together, I would still be waiting for her to be in love with me. I would have waited forever.

Jessie wiped her eyes with the sleeve of her faded jean jacket and then stared blankly down at her hands. She looked older to me, as though time had reversed itself again. I thought about what Eddie had said about tigers and lambs and how experience changed people and their perspectives. Perhaps her perspective had changed, or perhaps—

And then I knew. My perspective had changed. For the first time, I saw Jessie the way she was—in darkness and in light, in good and in bad. She was no longer the girl of my dreams. She was a woman: lost and tired, broken, flawed, and looking to me now for understanding and forgiveness.

"It's okay, Jess," I said, my own eyes filling with tears. I took her hand. "It's all right."

She looked back at me and shook her head.

"No," she said.

"I mean it, Jess," I said, gently squeezing her hand. "It's all right, really."

Sliding out from behind the table, she thrust herself up into my arms.

"I do love you," she said in words and tears. "I will always love you. I never told you this before, I don't know why, but what you did the last day I was here. I was glad you did it. I never could've done it, Hen, and I was glad you did. I want you to know that you did nothing wrong."

"I know, Jess. It's one of the few things in my life that I don't need to be forgiven for," I said.

At some point, we moved from the table to the bed where we lay silently for several hours, content just holding on to one another. It was well into the afternoon before Jessie finally spoke.

"You're not coming back with me, are you?" She had been gently stroking the back of my hand.

"No," I said. "I'm home now."

She nodded. "You might change your mind after spending a winter in this trailer."

"I'm going to build a house," I said.

Jessie sat up on the edge of the bed and, looking back at me, she said, "Seriously?" Then she laughed.

"What's so funny?" I said, a little offended by it. But it was good to see her laugh again.

"I'm trying to picture you building a house. You have to admit, you're not the builder type."

"What's the builder type?"

"I don't know. My daddy maybe, but certainly not you," she said. Jessie laughed again. "Do you even know the first thing about building a house?"

"Sure," I said, "hire a builder." Then I laughed.

Jessie looked at me, confused.

"My neighbor is a builder, and I hired him. It's all there in the brochure," I said, pointing at the table. "It's a kit—has a roof and everything. They'll ship it all up here and put it together for me. I'll help, of course."

Jessie had moved over to the table and found the brochure.

"You're serious," she said, examining the front and back of it. "They can do this?"

"Sure," I said. "It's pretty neat, huh?"

"It can't be cheap," she said.

"I'll manage," I said, moving over to the table. I sat down across from her. "I've got some savings and some money from the firm coming. I'm not sure what I'm going to do for work here, but I'll figure something out."

Jessie grinned.

"You'll be fine," she said excitedly. "The *gold!*"

"I've told you before, I don't want it. Besides," I said with a sigh, "it's gone. Somebody came across it. I checked today, and it's not there."

"Somebody did come across it," said Jessie with a mischievous smile.

She reached into the inside pocket of her jean jacket and pulled out a folded piece of paper and spread it out on the table in front of me. It was a check made out to me for $250,000. "*I* came across it," she said with an enormous smile.

"I had to hire a lawyer and a small crew. They thought I was crazy until we dug up that strongbox with all those gold bars inside. You should've seen the looks on those bastards' faces, Hen. We hauled it out and cashed it in. Lost a little on the transaction, but there should be enough there to put together your little puzzle house."

I smiled at the thought of Jessie and her crew digging up the gold.

"No, Jess," I said. "This is your money, your family's money. I can't accept it." I pushed the check back toward her.

"You're such a *rube!*" she said. "Don't you know, Hen? You *are* my family."

Jessie smiled at me again and then, through tears, she said, "Please take it, Hen. I want you to use it to build your house, to build your life here. I know it's going to be beautiful. And maybe, who knows, someday you might even forgive me for the horrible things I've done. Then maybe the boys and I will come for a visit. We'll visit you here in your beautiful house and your beautiful life," she said, tears making her eyes seem brighter.

My eyes too held tears.

"There is nothing to forgive, Jess," I said.

"Take it for me then, because I want you to have it. I want you to build your house with it."

She wiped her eyes with her sleeve.

"Okay," I said, my voice breaking.

And together we cried.

Jessie had plans to leave early the next morning. We slept little and talked much. The conversation was light, reminiscent, and pleasant. Except my plans for the new house. We didn't discuss the future, nor did we discuss anything to do with her life back in Michigan. We made no plans to see each other again as I thought it best we live our lives apart for a while.

When the morning did come, I walked Jessie to her car.

"At least send me pictures of your house," Jessie said with a fragile smile. "When it's built," she added.

"I will," I said. "Take care of yourself and the boys and the . . ." I pointed awkwardly to her stomach.

"The baby?"

"Yeah," I said, forcing a smile.

"I do love you, Hen," she said and then, pulling me into her arms, she hugged me. "More than you'll ever know," she whispered.

When she let me go, Jessie reached into her back pocket and pulled out a wadded handkerchief and opened it. She placed my old moose-bone necklace around my neck.

"It holds all your luck, Hen."

I said nothing.

Jessie kissed me sweetly on the cheek, and with a quick good-bye, she was gone.

Chapter Forty-One

September 1985

Although the sun shone brilliantly, cold air bit at my ears and cheeks as I jogged across the parking lot toward the grocery store. The race with winter had begun, and I was off to a solid start. The house was finished and furnished, three cords of wood split and stacked, and yesterday, Russell and I had installed my custom cabinets, which I now had plans to fill.

Holding a door open for me at the entrance was a girl of five or six. Bundled from the toes up, she pulled the scarf from her face, revealing a toothless grin.

"One left, mister," she said, pointing to a freckle-faced boy standing behind a cardboard box.

Perhaps it was the sweetness to her sales pitch, but I peeked inside the box as the freckled boy eyed me warily. Peering up at me—one eye brown, one blue, and wobbling on two stubby hind legs—was the ghastliest pup I had ever seen. More mutt than anything else and not much bigger than my hand, the runt started yapping at me viciously.

"He likes you," said the little girl.

"What makes you say that?" I said, peeking back at her. "Because he hasn't bitten me yet?"

"He doesn't bite," she said seriously.

"You're kind of cute," I said to the dog, "albeit in that ugly sort of way." I scooped him up and held him to my face. Instantly, the little guy stopped yipping.

"He likes you," this time from a woman's voice.

I glanced back and got a glimpse of a woman standing next to the little girl, but before I could get a better look, I felt a sudden warming sensation trickling down my arm.

There came a swell of laughter from behind me, and I quickly set the pissing bandit back down into the box. I did my best to shake piss from my arm and was about to wipe it off on my pants when a woman came rushing to me with a handful of tissue.

I managed to soak up some of it, but it wasn't enough, and soon I was smearing piss all over the dry parts of my arm. I would need to find a bathroom in a hurry if I didn't want to smell like a urinal the rest of the day.

"There's a bathroom at the back of the store," said the woman, reading my mind. Then giggling, she said, "But you're going to have to buy him first, *Henry*."

It wasn't just hearing my name; it was the voice speaking it that staggered my senses. What my ears suspected, my eyes soon confirmed.

Carrie Ferguson, the grown-up version, the woman who had supplied the tissues, stood staring back at me shamelessly.

"Carrie?" I said, surprised.

She nodded. Then placing her hands on my shoulders, in little more than a whisper, she said, "My goodness, Henry."

"Five bucks, mister," blurted the boy from behind me.

Before I could respond to either of them, Carrie pulled me into a hug.

"What's it been, only a hundred years?" she said, releasing me. Her hair was longer and lighter, and there was some age to her face, which she didn't try to hide. But years had not tempered the kindness that always shone behind the blue in her eyes. Gone was all her girly prettiness, replaced with a mature and timeless beauty that resonated from within her aspect and smile.

All at once, I found her attractiveness intimidating.

"I built a house," I said. It was all I could think to say.

"Really?" she said.

"Actually, I—"

"You want the dog or not, mister?" said the boy.

Glancing back, I saw the freckle-faced kid holding the puppy, a sour look on his face.

"All right, a minute please!" I shouted.

Carrie laughed.

"I helped build it, I should say," I said. My mind was running in a thousand different directions. "I've already moved in."

"Incredible," she said. "Whereabouts is it?"

"It's my parents' old place. Burned down last winter, so I rebuilt it. Helped to rebuild it, anyway."

"Out on the Steese?" she said. "About twenty miles or so?"

"Right," I said. "How did you know?"

"I get out that way from time to time," she said. "I work for the Fish and Game. I'm a ranger, believe it or not. I've always wondered which place was yours. I remember the fire, though. Shame it had to burn like that."

So captivating she was; my eyes seemed to lose themselves in hers.

"Yes," I said.

"I'd like to see your house sometime," she said.

"I'd like to see *you* sometime," I said, instantly, I felt as stupid as the line sounded.

Carrie smiled easily, her blue eyes moving past me. Glancing back, I caught another contemptuous glare from the freckle-faced boy. I pulled a five-dollar bill from my wallet and handed it to him. For the first time, the boy smiled. I took the box holding my new best friend and set it on the floor between Carrie and me.

"It's great to see you again," I said.

"You too," she said.

There was so much more to say, but for the life of me, I couldn't find the words.

"Is there a number where I can reach you?" she said.

I should be so bold.

"Not yet," I said. Truthfully, I hadn't even thought about it. Of course, they offered service now, but in the nearly four months I had been back, I had made less than a half dozen calls, most of them from Russell's phone or the phone booth here at the grocery store. "But I should have one this week," I added after making the decision.

"Great," she said pleasantly, reaching into a small purse she had strapped around her shoulder. She took out a pen and a small notebook and jotted down a number. "Then here's mine," she said, ripping the paper from the notebook and handing it to me. "When you get a phone, call me."

"I will," I said.

"Great," she said again. She peeked into the box at the puppy. "He's very cute," she said, her smile never wavering. "Hopefully, I'll see the two of you very soon."

Then she left me with a friendly smile and good-bye.

"What you going to call him, mister?" asked the little girl.

"Call what?" I said, confused.

"The puppy, what are you going to call him?" she said, pointing at the box.

Looking down, I saw my new best friend was sound asleep.

"*Kobuk*, I think," I said.

Russell had let me help him put together my house, but I built the separate garage and shop with only Russell's gentle direction. I had fallen in love with building. Every day there was a project to start or one to finish—something to do, a solace to the routine.

The work consumed me, and although I never felt more alone, rarely did I feel lonely. The house, garage, and shop forged for me a purpose. My only fear was that once the projects ended, then so too would my purpose.

I was to build benches for the shop today and, later, a doghouse. Russell offered to help me out with the doghouse, but I told him I could handle it. After all, I had done it before, sort of. Besides, I suspected that Russell could use some time away from me. We had spent the better part of three months together building my new house and my new life, and I still wasn't sure if he even liked me.

Russell had an irrational temper that reminded me of Tom's, except that Tom never lost his temper while working. At work, Tom was patient, attentive, and the consummate teacher. Russell was not.

Russell had a cold and skeptic nature tangled within a dry and subtle humor that made him always appear irritated. He was headstrong and oftentimes moody. There was an underlying precision to his work, as though all things he did had an inexorable method to them. And there was never compromise in the method, only error in the person. Mistakes made meant blame dispensed, and in that way, he was unforgiving.

Working with Russell made me appreciate Tom. Certainly, I had taken for granted much of what he had provided for my family and me. Tom had built us a fine house, and in a land of cabins and shacks, it had been the only true house in the valley. The *Big Shitbox,* he had called it. But it was well built, it had everything, and Tom had built it by himself. I believed now that, in many ways, I had misjudged him.

The benches went together without a hitch. Before long, I was putting together the doghouse. Built in the same tongue-and-groove style as the house, it only took a few hours to finish, and I was sure that when Kobuk was ready, he would love it.

The day ended as quietly as it began. I sat alone on my new sofa, too tired to keep the visions inspired by the early night from slipping in around me. But tonight, they were pleasant. I saw my mother and her ever-mending arms reaching for my wounded face. I saw Emily too, playing quietly, but she has for me a wishful smile. And then I saw Flanny, who laughs and tells me that nothing is as bad as it ever seems to be.

Angels, all of them—tending to my soul, enfolding me in their redeeming graces and offering a promise of hope.

Wanting cries from a puppy cast me from my pensive state. Kobuk was hungry, and suddenly, so was I.

Chapter Forty-Two

December 1985

It took less than two hours for the guy from the phone company to install my new telephone. Mounted high on the kitchen wall next to the refrigerator, my new porthole to the rest of the world had an extra-long cord and easy touch-tone pad that seemed to beckon me to make a call.

When I did and my sister Gwen answered, I felt instantly connected to the world again. "It's so good to hear from you, Hen," she said, her voice pitched high with excitement. I was surprised at how much she sounded like my mother. "Just the other day, Lila was asking about her Uncle Henry. Stephanie too. We're so glad you called."

And so was I. We talked for nearly two hours. This time, I held little back and did most of the talking. Through tears and laughter, I told her about my new house, my new life, and the past. We discussed our mother, my journey back home, and Jessie. There was even talk of a visit next summer.

"Perhaps we can get a hold of Maggie," said Gwen.

"Yes, we must," I said. "A regular family reunion."

"I may even call Dad," she said. Then she paused, no doubt awaiting my reaction.

"No, don't," I said. "I'll call him."

"All right," she said.

Before our last good-byes, Gwen put Lila and Stephanie on the phone. They told me that they missed me and they loved me and they hoped to see me soon. Although it was clearly coached, it pleased me all the same.

A few minutes after hanging up with Gwen, I found myself dialing the number she had given me for Tom. I wasn't sure why I was so eager to talk to him. We hadn't spoken since my mother's funeral, and that was only a few conciliatory words lost to the anguish in the moment. I had seen him once before that, at their house in Seattle, after returning from Vietnam. We had talked little. I spent most of the time with my mother reassuring her that the war for me was over and that I would be all right—although at the time, I was still on the mend from the whole Sara debacle.

"Hello," came a mature woman's voice.

I supposed it was Tom's new wife. I couldn't remember her name. Vivian, or Veronica maybe. Surely it began with a *V*.

"Hi," I said politely. "I'm looking for Tom, Tom Talbot. This is Henry Allen, his stepson," I added weakly.

"Who is this?" she said, as if hard of hearing.

"Henry Allen," I said loudly. "I was hoping to speak to Tom Talbot."

"Oh, okay," she said. "One moment please."

She set the phone down with a sharp static click. I could hear some faint talking in the background. Then a man's voice I recognized asked, "Who is it?" There was another sharp click before the voice said, "Hello, who is this?"

"It's Henry," I said loudly. It seemed strange having to tell him who I was, but it had been a long time.

He didn't answer right away, and an awkward pause ensued. I thought I would have to repeat myself, but then finally he said, "Henry, no kidding?"

"Yeah, Tom, it's Henry."

"Well for Christ sake, what can I do for you?"

"Nothing really," I said. "It's been so long, I thought I might say hello. I'm back in Alaska, at the old place—or new place now. I wanted to thank you for the property. The old house burned down.

I rebuilt it, and I wanted to let you know that I'm up here now. And again, thank you for the property."

My words felt rushed, muddled, and insincere; and I probably should've given them more consideration before making the call. Again, there was an awkward pause.

"No kidding," he said at last. "That's swell. So, the *Big Shitbox* burned down, did it?"

"Yes," I said, glad for the question. "Last winter, I'm told. I got up here last summer and rebuilt it. Your foundation was still good, Tom. We built the new place on top of it."

"No kidding?" he said.

This time, I had words ready for another long bit of silence, but Tom surprised me. "Hell, the best thing about that place was the foundation. Good to hear you could use it. I wasn't much of a carpenter in those days, but I could put together a foundation. Did you build it yourself?"

"No, I had some help," I said hesitantly. I wanted so badly to tell him I had done it all myself. After all the time between us, I still sought and needed his approval. "I purchased one of those cedar packages. You know, a tongue-and-groove kit, and assembled it on the foundation. Your old neighbor Russell Rahall fixed me up."

"No kidding? Well, for Christ sake," he said with what sounded like a chuckle. "Russell is a good man. I'm sure it's beautiful. Sure, I've heard of them kit homes. Didn't think they would ship all the way up there, by god, but it's got to be better than that shitbox I put together."

I wanted to tell him that the house he had built for us was perfect. That despite all the anger, his and mine, I appreciated everything he had done for my mother, my sisters, and me. I wanted to tell him that I had always enjoyed our time alone together, working at the hangar and learning to fly. But there on telephone, the whirr of the long-distance line between us, I knew that it wasn't his way.

"I'm glad to hear you're back there now," Tom said, breaking another long silence. "Your mother always said you'd go back. She said that the land up there suits you. Said it's where you should be, it's where you belong. She never told me why, but I suppose she was right. She knew you a lot better than I did." His tone was as deep and as firm at it had ever been, but there was a comfort to his words. I thought back to that day outside the mine shaft, watching them carry out the sheeted bodies of Abigail Mason and the O'Brien brothers. When he had put his arm around me and let me rest my head on his.

My eyes filled with tears, and I found it difficult to speak.

"That reminds me, the old boathouse still standing?" asked Tom.

"Yeah," I said when words came. "It's still here."

"Good, good," said Tom. "You should find one of them metal army chests, you know, one of them old locker types we had back in the day. Your mother put some of your things in it for you. Said that you might like to have them if you ever returned. I told her she was crazy, but by god, she was right about that too." Tom chuckled. "I thought about putting them out there in your old trailer, but I never could tell where that old thing might end up. You may want to have some of that stuff."

"I'll look for it," I said.

"Do you still fly, Henry?" Tom asked.

"No," I said in a whisper, the volume lodged somewhere in my throat.

"They won't let me fly anymore either. Christ, I miss it though. I've been telling Victoria here that I'd like to get back to Fairbanks again. Now that you're up there, who knows?"

Victoria, I thought. That was the name. "Yes, you should, Tom," I said after swallowing hard and releasing the words caught there. "I talked to Gwen and she, Lance, and the kids are thinking about coming up in the summer. Would really like to have you and Victoria come up too."

"No kidding?" he said. "That sure is something to think about. Yes, it's certainly something to think about. I would love to see the old place and your new house. Too bad you don't fly anymore. Would love to have you take me for a ride."

"You come up and I'll find you a ride," I said.

The conversation didn't last much longer, and our good-byes were as awkward as our hellos had been.

I hung up the telephone and sat down at the kitchen table, Tom's deep voice still resonating in my ears. It was almost as though he were there, sitting across from me, telling me in his stern but assuring way that everything from now on is going to be all right.

I had one call left to make. It had been some time since our encounter at the grocery store. I wasn't sure why I had waited so long to call Carrie. Perhaps I was afraid that too much life had passed between us. She was so different from the girl I knew in school. But after reaching out to my family, I was feeling better than I had in months, and now I supposed was as good of a time as any to try and make a friend.

She answered on the second ring. "This is Carrie," she said in her pleasantly familiar way.

"Hi," I said, and then hesitated. When she didn't respond right away, I said, "Hi, Carrie, this is Henry Allen."

"Hi, Henry," she said with some excitement. "I was nearly ready to give up on you," she scolded.

"I'm sorry," I said. "It's been so—"

"I'm only teasing," she said, cutting me off. "I'm glad you did. I have been out your way quite a few times. Saw your house, it's beautiful! I almost stopped in, but I thought . . ." She paused.

"Next time you should," I said.

"I will," she said. "You couldn't have called at a better time. Some friends from my church are having a Christmas party tomorrow night. Why don't you come by? We can catch up."

"Sounds fun," I said.

Carrie went about giving me the address and the directions to the party. I discovered it wasn't too far from here. She told me to come around eight o'clock. Then with a pleasant enough good-bye, she was gone.

I left the house at 8:15 p.m. with the notion of being fashionably late to the party. I didn't count on drifting through wafer-sized snowflakes. The sketchy visibility made it difficult discerning the road from the dark and white, making the drive slow and uneasy. More than once, the truck slewed from one side of the road to the other, flirting with ditch or disaster. I completely missed the turn at Goldstream Road and went pirouetting through the intersection. I was fortunate not to find any other drivers. Of course, what kind of fools would be out on a night like this?

Sliding by the driveway, I nearly took out a row of onlooking mailboxes. Fortunately for them, the truck bounced off a protecting snow berm and then caromed back into the center of the highway. It took some nifty driving, but I managed to get the truck turned back around before nosing it down the steep driveway—anxious about my chances of ever making it out again.

It was well past nine when I pulled in beside one of four cars parked at the bottom of the driveway. There was a good chance that Carrie wasn't even here. Then what? I thought about heading back, but I probably couldn't get back up that hill without some help. I might as well make an appearance.

The house was good-sized, stained brown and, of course, had two main entrances: one on the ground floor and another atop a flight of stairs. Both looked well groomed and well lit. For no particular reason, I chose the ground floor, rang the doorbell, and stood awaiting the awkwardness.

It was a good three minutes before I pressed the doorbell again, and another two minutes after that when I set out for the other door. I had only taken a couple steps when I heard the sucking sound of the door being pulled open. I turned in time to see Carrie pop her head out from behind the screen door.

"Hi," she said when she saw me. "I can't believe you made it."

"Yeah, a little crazy to challenge these roads," I said.

"I'm glad you did," she said, holding the screen door open for me.

I walked into the dimly lit room. The warm air felt good on my face and hands.

"The party's downstairs," Carrie said, leading me through the darkness. "It's hard to hear the doorbell from down there. I thought Eric had it. He's hosting this thing, but heaven knows where he went." We passed out of darkness and into a kitchen area before heading down a creaky set of stairs.

The room was gigantic, covering the entire bottom floor of the house. It had a pool table, a projection television, a video player, and a serious collection of videotapes. A brightly colored Formica bar curling around one corner of the room fronted a series of old movie posters for *Citizen Kane*, *The Apartment*, and *The Philadelphia Story*. And at the center of the room was the largest sectional sofa I had ever seen. In the corner opposite the bar, two women stood next to an enormous jukebox flipping through the selector. They were the only other people in the room. Music came from everywhere, a new Bruce Springsteen tune. It was one I had heard before but didn't know.

"Quite a place," I said, handing Carrie my coat. She hung it up in a small closet at the bottom of the staircase. We sat down across from each other at a corner of the enormous sectional. "Whose place is this again?"

"My friend Eric's," she said. "He just had the place remodeled." She pulled at the sleeves of her cable-knit sweater and then brushed back her hair from her eyes. She seemed suddenly shy.

"Sometimes I can't believe I'm really back up here," I said, trying to make conversation.

Carrie glanced over me and then at several other places around the room.

"I lost track of you after you went to school," she said. And then when her eyes found mine, she said, "I did hear you went to Vietnam."

I wasn't sure if she meant it as a statement or a question, so I waited for her lead. But after a few seconds, she looked away and again began tugging at the sleeve of her sweater.

"Yes," I said. "I went to Vietnam."

I was surprised that she knew as much, but I supposed it wasn't a secret. I remember I had stopped writing Carrie after about a year into college. She had continued to write me, but I never responded. It was a shit thing to do, but at the time, I was stupidly in love with Sara. I wondered if Carrie was holding a grudge now.

"How did you know?" I asked.

"I heard it from Jessie," she said. "We've kept in touch over the years. Once in a while, anyway." She seemed to almost smile. "Actually, just couple of letters a year, not a lot. She let me know what you were doing from time to time." She nodded slightly. "I did see her last summer," she added.

After all the years of being Jessie's friend, her best friend, and then her lover, and after sharing so much with her, there were still parts of her I didn't know, parts to her that still surprised me. Jessie had never so much as mentioned that she had heard from Carrie. I wondered how much Carrie knew. Suddenly, I felt sick.

"Are you all right, Henry?" she said, studying my face.

I didn't realize I was being so transparent.

"I'm fine," I said somewhat dismissively.

"We only met for dinner," Carrie said. "Jessie said she was here on some family business, something to do with her grandfather's estate. She asked me if I knew any lawyers in town, and I told her of one. I don't even know if she saw him. Honestly, she seemed really distant, as though she had a lot on her mind. I asked her about you, and she said she didn't know much. She said she thought you were traveling."

I nodded. It all made sense, and I was a little relieved that Jessie hadn't said more.

"She said she would call me before we left town, but she never did."

Just then, a sandy-haired gentleman with sturdy shoulders entered the room carrying two cartons of eggnog. He eyed Carrie and me curiously as he slipped behind the bar.

"Hey, Eric," said Carrie. "This is Henry, the friend I was telling you about."

Eric's eyes shot to mine, shifting from a mild curiosity to a menacing scowl. He sent me the slightest nod before disappearing entirely behind the bar.

Carrie gave me a puzzling look and then shrugged.

"Don't know what's got into him," she said.

I had an idea, but I didn't say. It was obvious Eric didn't like the attention I was receiving from Carrie. I couldn't blame him. Carrie was beautiful. He was a fool if he didn't have something going on with her already.

"Nice to meet you, Eric," I said when he reappeared. I thought I would try to make peace. After all, the rate the snow was falling and with the steep driveway, I might be here a while. I worked my way over to the bar and offered him my hand.

He shook it weakly over the bar and sent me only another uneasy nod.

"Nice place you have here," I said.

"How about some eggnog, Eric?" said Carrie, bouncing up beside me.

Eric's stern look appeared to melt some at the request. "Sure," he said to Carrie.

"Eric's been talking all week about his eggnog," said Carrie. "Says he mixes it with something or other. Something strong anyway."

"Rum," said Eric, placing a glass pitcher of eggnog into a large microwave oven behind the bar. He smiled at Carrie, avoiding me altogether.

"Let us know when it's ready," said Carrie, moving us back toward the sofa.

I didn't have to look, as I could feel Eric's eyes burning on my neck. When Carrie and I sat back down, not surprisingly, Eric was gone.

"So, Henry," said Carrie, her eyes fixed upon me. "Since we last knew each other, you went to college, joined the army, shipped off to

Vietnam, graduated law school, became a lawyer, and that's about all I know," she added with a giggle.

"That's the long and short of it," I said.

"Surely there must me more," Carrie said, slapping playfully at my knee.

I smiled at her.

"There is," I said. "I'm not really sure where to start."

"You can start with the part where you stopped writing me," she said with a wry smile that instantly became a cheerful laugh.

Somewhere along the way, Carrie had matured into a beautiful woman, but surprisingly, the parts of her personality, the parts that I had known hadn't changed. She was still as friendly, good-natured, and as easy to talk to as she was back in high school.

"I am sorry about that," I said.

"Oh, I'm only kidding," she said, waving at me dismissively.

"It was a crummy thing to do," I said.

Carrie shook her head and then laughed.

"Well, you're here now, aren't you?" she said, slapping my knee again.

"Here's where I ended up. What about you?" I said, not sure what to make of her playfulness.

Carrie's look then tensed some, and she seemed to force her smile.

"I think so," she said. "Of course, after everything, I'm still here and I've been here a while."

"So what's it like?"

Carrie looked confused.

"Being divorced?" she said.

"I meant, living up here for so long."

"Oh," Carrie laughed. "I enjoy it up here. I moved up here after the divorce. I can tell you that it has been much easier on me than others."

"The divorce?" I said.

"No, living up here." She giggled.

"Right," I said.

"I left him," she said flatly.

I didn't speak, but waited for her to explain.

"I can tell you it was a lot easier telling Shane, my ex-husband, than it was my parents. I'm sure Shane suspected something was up. He was actually great about the whole thing. He's an engineer in Anchorage. I still see him from time to time. He's married again, has a wife and a little boy. I think he's really happy," she said in a way that suggested that she had only just now convinced herself.

"So why did you marry him?" I said, genuinely curious.

"I'm not sure, really. He was a member of the church. He seemed like a person someone like me was supposed to marry. My parents loved him."

"But you didn't?" I said.

"I thought I did. He was easy to talk to, easy to get along with—too easy as it turned out. The type of person that would always be there for you and would never let you down, so long as he didn't have to make a decision. He couldn't make a decision about anything. I felt like I was living our lives for the both of us. He would defer everything to me, from dinner to having children. I didn't want to go through life having to make decisions for the both of us. I didn't want the responsibility. It's a terrible thing to say, but he had no backbone, and I wanted somebody with a backbone, Hen. It would have been easy to stay married to Shane, but we wouldn't have been happy. We weren't happy, and I knew he'd never leave me, so I left him. Thank goodness we didn't have children."

"You don't want children?"

"I don't know. I suppose I do, but the lord knows I'm not getting any younger," she said, rolling her eyes. "My parents wish that I would settle down. They really want grandchildren."

Carrie leaned back on the sofa.

"I always knew you were in love with Jessie," she said with an impish grin.

"That obvious, huh?" I laughed.

She nodded and then giggled.

"Yeah, well she never felt the same. At least not in the way I wanted her to."

"It's funny how we spend our lives believing in the *meant to be*, the *supposed to be*. We believe in it so much that we can't see anything else. We miss what is really important, what is actually in store for us."

"A lot of wasted years," I said.

"I don't think so." She smiled softly. "In his sermons, my father used to talk about a dark road. I suppose what my father was trying to say is that we spend a lot of time in the dark before we actually see the light."

"It makes sense," I said.

"It's really crazy seeing you again," she said, leaning forward. "I have to confess that I've thought about you from time to time—where you were, what you were doing. I was really hoping that I would see you again. Jessie told me about how you joined the army and went to Vietnam."

"That was a long time ago," I said. And I wasn't going to say any more, but there was something in her tone that made me want to.

I told her about college and Sara, the engagement, and Vietnam. I told her about my life there flying helicopters and all the shit I had experienced over there. I told her about the people I had known, the *Dear John* letter, the missions, Flanny's death, and Jake's too. Carrie listened intently as my mind shed free the streams of thoughts that ultimately formed a river of words and sentences that rolled now so easily from my tongue. I half expected an interruption from Eric and his special eggnog, but one never came.

I went on about life after the war, my return from Vietnam, and my confrontation with Sara (or, more truthfully, her Neanderthal of a husband). I imparted to her all my stories of Michigan State and law school, as well as Sully, Gina, Jessie, and The Win. There were parts Carrie knew, but most she didn't. The more I talked, the better I felt. And at some point, I even talked of my mother's death and Tom and my family. At last, I told her about Jessie and our short time together, then apart, and my long and tempestuous journey home.

It was well past ten when I finished with tears blurring my vision.

"I'm sorry," I said, wiping my eyes. "I've said too much. I should go."

"Please don't," she said. "There's no reason to be sorry. Thank you for sharing that with me. It couldn't have been easy." Her words were soothing and light, and she placed her hand on my knee. "I was only telling someone the other day about the formal we went to back in high school," she said, obviously changing the subject. "What a night, huh?" she added, smiling.

"It sure was," I said, nodding.

"I remember old Spenser driving us home that night. I'll never forget it, Hen. I never was so scared in all my life. I was just glad you were there with me," she said.

I nodded again.

"Yeah, that was quite a night," she said thoughtfully. "I remember hearing all sorts of creepy things about that old man, and Jessie." She paused and then shook her head.

"So you're here all the time," I said, changing the subject again.

"Yeah, I don't get away too often. I was seeing this guy in Delta Junction for a while, but . . ." She hesitated then, rubbing her hands together, she said, "It just wasn't working."

"Why?" I said. Then hesitating, "Sorry, it's really none of my business."

"Oh, not at all." She laughed and then got up and went over to the bar and pulled a bag of tortilla chips from one of the cupboards. She poured the chips into a large ceramic bowl. "It's just that my social life is, well, complicated these days." She laughed again. "Let's just say he was a piece of work. You know something, Hen? I don't mind being by myself. I've got my work and my friends here. I don't need the headache," she said, sounding as if she had had the conversation before.

"No," I agreed, not knowing what else to say.

Carrie brought out the bowl of chips along with a dish of salsa. She set them on the coffee table and then went back to the bar and took a couple bottles of beers from a small refrigerator. She popped the tops and came back over and handed me one of the beers before sitting down.

"I guess we aren't getting any eggnog," she said.

I talked more, mostly of my new house and Kobuk. She agreed to come for a visit sometime soon. I told her what it was like being a divorce lawyer. I explained to her some of the particulars of the trade and the types of clients I represented. I even went so far as to defend the profession, and once I caught myself telling her that there were times when I actually found the work rewarding. But whatever it was I wanted to talk about, she seemed to enjoy listening.

It was nearing midnight and I began to think we were all that was left of the party, when Eric appeared before us. His face was serious, and his hands were shaking.

"Carrie," he said firmly, but then appeared to lose some nerve. "I think I was hoping that we could . . . that we could spend some time together. I mean, I thought tonight we were supposed to be together. Here together. I have liked you for so long, and I really was hoping that we could be . . . well, you know how I feel about you, Carrie. You know I love you to death," he said, tucking his hands into his pockets.

Chivalry has had better spokesmen, but listening to the poor sap spill his guts like that, I couldn't help but be impressed.

Carrie shot me a puzzling glance before sending him her most sympathetic one.

"Oh, Eric," she said sweetly. "I'm so sorry. I suppose I misunderstood your intentions." She then turned back to me and said, "Excuse us, please, Henry."

And then she led Eric out of the room.

I waited for nearly an hour for her to return, but she never did. And as I didn't see another soul, I grabbed my coat from the closet and showed myself out.

Outside, it had stopped snowing, and the truck started without a hitch. It took three good tries, but I was able to make it up and out of the driveway, glad not to have had to call on the young and gallant Eric for assistance.

I found the road to be clear and dry, but the drive home through the darkness uneasy. It wasn't until I saw the bright of porch light high above the backdoor of the house that I knew I was safe and I could finally relax.

Chapter Forty-Three

March 1986

The weather outside was warm, nearly forty degrees. Still, we'd had some snow the night before, and Kobuk was bouncing around the house as if outside was where he needed to be. He had nearly quadrupled in size over the past few months and was still adjusting to his big new body that always appeared a half stride behind his notions. Still a puppy, he had already chewed up one of my high-tops, a leg of the coffee table, and had done some modest damage to the new telephone cord. I wasn't sure he was ready yet for the doghouse, but his restless and curious nature might just earn him an early exile.

"Let's go, boy," I called after opening the front door. Kobuk went bounding through much too fast, lost control, and then slid across the icy deck where he went ass-end-over-teakettle into the snowbank on the other side. He recovered quickly but stood draped in wet sticky snow, his off-colored eyes searching me for more instruction. When he got none, he shook himself off and flopped on up to me.

"Slow down, boy," I said, patting his head. He darted toward the steps and hopped down to the driveway. I pulled shut the door and hurried after him.

Kobuk paused at the end of the driveway and then plopped down on his hindquarters to wait for me.

"Come on, boy," I called when I passed by him.

Kobuk didn't move, but testing my resolve, and his own, he let me walk a ways without him. I hadn't gone too far before I heard his squeaky cry. Looking back, I called him again. This time, he leaped up and pranced after me.

We received several reproachful woofs from the neighborhood dogs before reaching the highway. This convinced Kobuk to stick close to my heels. At the highway, I checked the mailbox and endured the type of melancholy associated with not receiving mail six days in a row.

I discovered a well-traipsed snowmobile path paralleling the highway. The trail was an easy walk, and Kobuk had little trouble keeping up with me.

The old two-tracked driveway I once knew to lead up to the Shit Towers was no more. A recently plowed roadway was in its place. Across the highway from that stood a neat little mailbox shaped like a barn, its diminutive red sidewalls displaying the name *Wendell*.

Curiosity moving me forward, I ambled on up and around the bend, fully expecting to find signs or at least remnants of the old place. But surprisingly, I found none. There was nothing to suggest that Spenser Mason and his ramshackle cabin or any of the heaping piles of shit had ever been here. Instead, the cleared roadway continued on into the distance, and I could make out a modern-styled house and a large red barn protruding above a winter-bare tree line.

Had I not known of Spenser then, from the look of the place now, he may very well have never existed.

The thought delighted me, coaxing from my face a pleasant smile.

―――――――

Back at home, I plodded my way through the crusty snow to the stone steps that wound down to the creek and the old boathouse. There, Kobuk waited for me to make my way to the bottom before tossing himself over the edge where he performed two complete summersaults and then slid across the frozen creek on his belly.

"Take it easy, boy," I said to the dog.

Back on his feet, but clearly shaken, Kobuk let loose a series of woeful little whimpers. But before I had any cause for concern, he began nosing back up the trail searching for whatever culprits there may have tripped him.

Shut tight, but not locked, the door to the boathouse was frozen at its base. With a couple of swift kicks and one good shove, the door broke free of its icy frame and wiggled open easily.

The boathouse was a one-roomed log cabin that was twice as long as it was wide and had an extra large door that made it ideal for housing a boat. Of course, Tom never owned a boat, nor had he ever housed one here. Instead, the place served as a type of storage facility for outdated furniture and other obsolescent items my mother no longer wanted inside the house.

When I shined the flashlight inside, I expected to see such a collection of items, but to my surprise, the place was empty except for the metal army chest and an ancient-looking armoire.

As Kobuk sniffed about, I pulled the chest out from the dark cabin and into the daylight. The lid unlatched easily and opened with a gentle pop. Inside the chest were three separate packages, each securely wrapped in a thick black plastic.

The first package contained three pairs of mukluk boots that I knew my mother had handmade. For years, she had belonged to an arts club in Fairbanks where she learned to craft them in the Yupik, Inuit, and Athebaskan clothing way. When Maggie, Gwen, and I were young, it was all we ever wore. These boots had never been worn, each having been made from a different type of fur (reindeer, moose, or bearded seal), each in a different style, and each a different size. But they all had had been intricately sewn and ornately decorated by my mother with the finest precision and touch.

The next package was the largest of the three. When I pulled it from the plastic, a sudden surge of nostalgia came so strong, it knocked me to my knees. There in my hands, I held Tom's old overcoat. I pressed it to my cheek and, through tear-struck eyes, I saw my mother's face, calm, certain and forever forgiving—forgiving me for all the worry I had ever caused her. I cried hard into the overcoat until Kobuk's damp and consoling nose nudged at my ear.

It was a while before my eyes dried and I could open the last package. When I did, I thought I might have dreamed it all. But the orange-flowered tunic, the *kuspuk* I knew Emily to wear in a dream, lay before me as certain and as real as I had ever known anything to be. My body shivered as my mind slowed trying to decipher truths from fantasies, dreams from memories, before settling reluctantly upon the tenuous notion that somehow, *I must have known of it before.*

I set the items aside and carried the chest back inside the boathouse. On my way out, I noticed narrow streams of light squeezing through cracks in the wall beside the doorway. The streams, when traced together, formed a perfect square where once there might have been a window—a *window* Vladimir Verden remembered next to a door in a cabin that faced a creek. I glanced out beyond the open door and watched Kobuk stumbling along a patch of bare ice on the frozen creek. The *rendezvous*, Frank and Abigail's secret spot, right under my damned nose all these years. I hadn't given the boathouse a thought.

I shined the flashlight's beam at the cabin walls, floor, and ceiling, but the only thing of interest was the armoire. Built from an ebony wood long since faded, the simple two-door, two-drawer armoire stood forgotten at the back wall of the boathouse. Above the drawers, the cabinet was empty. Its doors hanging open and clinging to brass hinges turned green with time.

It took some effort to open the first drawer. Its handles broke off in my hands after the first good yank. By pulling at it from the sides, however, I managed to pry off the front of the drawer. Scattered about the bottom, I discovered the head of a claw hammer and a handful of rusted six-penny nails.

The second drawer opened easily. Stuffed inside, I found pale linen curtains adorned with barely discernible blue and yellow flowers—the *flowery curtains* Vladimir had said covered the window and matched the bedspread and the rug.

I removed the curtains and began folding them when light from the doorway glinted off something at the back bottom corner of the drawer.

Several inches long, a few inches wide, and bound in light brown leather was a notebook. Etched across the front in dark-brown block letters was a single word: *THINK*. I flipped it open and found a thick pad of lined paper that appeared blank at first glance. After a closer examination with the flashlight, however, I could make out a few lines of faded handwriting. I thumbed through the pad and discovered many of the pages contained the same handwriting. I gathered up the curtains, the notebook, and the items from the chest I had left outside before calling Kobuk and heading back to the house.

While Kobuk snored lightly beneath the stove in the living room, I opened the notebook beneath the white light of a desk lamp. The notebook was a message log of sorts containing short informative notes regarding past and future meeting times. Not all of the entries were dated, but those that were indicated the year 1938. Mostly, Abigail Mason and Francis O'Brien authored the entries, but Jules O'Brien had written a few as well.

I spent the next hour reading the entries. There wasn't much to them. Phrases like *looking forward to* and *missing you* crowded the lines on the pages, Abigail signing with a scripted *Abby* and Francis always with a capital *F*. Fishing, hunting, hiking—Frank and Abigail did everything together, reminiscent of Jessie and me. The two of them were certainly in love, all under Spenser Mason's cold and contemptuous nose. No doubt, Jessie would have found it all very romantic.

However, the last two entries caused my heart to race and my throat to tighten. The messages themselves read harmlessly, but taken with the knowledge and manner of the lovers' ultimate demise, the entries read like the latter act of a Victorian tragedy.

Abigail had written the first, her usual stylish penmanship appearing sloppy or rushed.

Dearest F

I know we were not supposed to meet until tomorrow, but I had to tell you—I did it! I told Spense I was leaving him and that I was taking James. I realized that I could not spend another moment pretending to love him—pretending that he loves me and pretending that I don't love you. I know this is sudden, but it's what I want and what I feel is right. I didn't tell him about us, but he suspects as much. He asked me if James was your son. Oh god, how I wish that were true!

Spense seemed to take it well—I told him that I was going back to Flint to live with Charlene. He was angry and left, but before he did, he agreed to send me back there. It's probably for the best.

Oh, Frankie, how I wish you were here right now. There is so much I need to say. I will be by tomorrow like we planned, and we can sort this out together.

All my love,
Abby

The last entry was from Francis O'Brien.

Abigail,

It has been three hours and you still have not arrived. I fear the worst and am off to find you. If you are reading this, please stay put. I will return for you.

Love,
F

Never before had Abigail Mason and Francis O'Brien been so real to me. I always envisioned them as characters in an ill-fated story rather than real people with real lives shattered by a heartless monster. I hadn't read much of the diary, nor had I read much into their affair. I had hated Spenser for Jessie's sake—and for Jessie's sake alone, I had killed him. But Jessie had lived with him, and she had understood.

Suddenly, I felt sick to my stomach, as if someone close to me had died. I located a pen and some paper and wrote to Jessie. I explained to her about the cabin and what I had found. I tucked the letter into the notebook and wrapped the notebook in brown grocery paper.

I would mail it to Jessie in the morning.

Chapter Forty-Four

June 1986

The enduring sun shined hopefully over the latter days of spring. With the lengthy winter nearly forgotten, my attentions were now set amongst the eddies of the Chatanika River and the grayling I knew loitered there. I longed for the first cast of the season, not from my pole but from the second fly rod I had recently purchased for Carrie.

Not long after the holidays, Carrie had called to apologize for abandoning me at the Christmas party. She explained that Eric had misinterpreted her friendship for something more and that, although she liked Eric, he could be nothing more than a friend to her. Apparently, that was not enough for Eric, as he had not spoken to her since then.

I had seen Carrie several times throughout the winter, but I feared that our relationship had also settled into that safe, easy, and implicitly defined syndrome known otherwise as friendship. But perhaps a warm day on the banks of the Chatanika would change all that.

An early call from Carrie burst my angler's bubble, as she said that she'd been summoned to investigate an accident involving a moose northeast of Fairbanks somewhere on Chena Hot Springs Road. She did promise to come by afterward, but couldn't say for certain when.

I would wait. I thought about fishing alone but didn't want to ruin the chance of missing her. Instead, I hung around the house and did paperwork. A few months ago, Russell and I had gone into business together for the sale and assembly of kit homes. We had already secured twelve contracts for this summer and three for the next. Working with Russell wasn't easy. It certainly wasn't a beautiful friendship, but that didn't mean it couldn't be successful.

I spent the morning shoring up the business's organizing documents and the afternoon drafting the corporate bylaws. It was important to define the terms of our relationship carefully so as to appease Russell's overabundance of concerns and my own peace of mind.

I had nearly finished when the phone rang.

"Hello," I answered.

"Hen," said the familiar voice, "it's me."

Her voice sounded strained, but perhaps it was the distance.

"Jess?" I replied.

"Yes, it's me," she said. "How are you?"

Her call took me by surprise. I hadn't spoken to her since she had left here last summer.

"I'm fine," I said. "This is a surprise."

"I received the notebook," she said. Her tone was definitely strained. "Thank you for it. It meant a lot to me to know. It's sad how they were so close to being together."

"Yes," I said, swallowing down words I wanted to say.

"Did you ever finish your house?" she said.

"Yes, it's beautiful, thanks in part to you," I said, referring to the money she had given me.

"That's great. I'm so happy for you. Really, it's what I wanted for you."

"What's wrong, Jess?" I said.

And then she began to cry. "I've ruined everything, ruined it for everyone," she said between sobs. "I'm sorry, Hen. Please know that I'm sorry."

"Of course," I said, not sure what else to say. "Everything will be all right."

"I miss you . . ." She hesitated.

"Everything will be all right, Jess," I said again.

Jessie continued to cry.

"Is everyone okay?"

"The boys are fine, but Winslow never sees them. And *Sean* . . . he's never here either."

The name pinched at my heartstrings some. She had never used it in my presence and lit a small fire within me.

"Did you have your baby?" I said with some bitterness.

There was a long pause. Then I heard her sniff.

"Yes," she said, "another boy."

I still loved her. I would always love her. Nothing would ever change that. But I knew a life without her now, and I had lived without her.

"That's good, Jess," I said. "You're a wonderful mother." It wasn't what she wanted to hear, but it was all I had to say.

I would have liked to believe that she understood. Because after another long pause, she said yes and then muttered something with the word *love* in it before the line deadened, and I let her go.

Carrie arrived a little after five, her hair pulled back and dressed in her evergreen-colored Department of Fish and Game uniform now spattered with what I soon learned was moose blood. She greeted me with a smile and an apology for missing our date. Apparently, the situation with the moose had evolved into a small fiasco. No one had been hurt, except the moose, whose carcass blocked both lanes of the highway. Because no vehicle could be readily obtained to remove the beast, it had to be skinned and quartered while traffic waited.

Carrie had brought a change of clothes, so I offered her a glass of chardonnay and the use of my shower. She gladly accepted both. While she was in the shower, I baked a red salmon Russell had pulled from the Copper River while dip-netting down in Chitina, Alaska.

She appeared from the shower dressed in jeans and a tee shirt and free of animal blood. Her wet hair lay gently on her shoulders, her deep blue eyes sparkling against her soft white skin.

"H-h-have a seat," I stuttered, motioning her to sit down at the table. I had prepared rice and green beans to go along with the salmon. "I hope you like salmon," I said anxiously.

"Yes, of course," she said. "I'm not sure I would be in the mood for moose tonight." She laughed.

The salmon was surprisingly good—surprisingly because I didn't cook much for anyone other than myself. But Carrie ate all that I served her and even requested a second helping of salmon and rice. After dinner, we fed a lobbying Kobuk the leftovers before relocating to the sofa in the living room where I refilled our glasses of wine.

"Jessie called the other day," said Carrie easily before taking a sip of wine. Her eyes seemed to jump over her glass at me in flagrant anticipation of my reaction.

Neat and orderly thoughts in my mind suddenly shuffled chaotically.

"I . . . really? What did . . ." I said, as thoughts mixed with words made sputter from my mouth. "Oh yeah," I said finally when words only came. "What did she have to say?"

Carrie smiled at me.

"Not a whole lot," she said. "We didn't talk for long, but mostly we talked about you."

My blushing face kept no secrets.

"Is that so?" I said.

"Yes, I told her that I had been seeing you," Carrie said.

"*Seeing me*," I said, not wanting it to sound so much like a question. "I mean that you see me, that you saw me." My face burned.

Carrie laughed cheerfully. "Jessie said the same thing, but I told her we were just friends."

And there it was, stated with all the declaration and condemnation of a life sentence. I thought about asking Carrie if we could invite Eric over.

"She just wanted to make sure you were okay. She wasn't sure whether you were all right. She's going through a tough time right now. She and her new husband are not doing well," said Carrie, her eyes jumping at me again.

"I wouldn't know anything about it," I said. "There's nothing I can do for her anymore."

"She's been through so much in her life. You know, I heard about what her grandfather did. It was so horrible," she said, shaking her head. "It's hard to imagine people could do such things. What a horrible, horrible man he was. She had every right to kill him."

My mind skipped back the near twenty years to that dreadful day. I could feel the tight swell of my face, the sickness in my gut, and the bat in my hands. Never since that day had I been so close to it.

"Jessie didn't kill him," I said. I never said it aloud to anyone other than Jessie, but for the first time, I wanted someone else to know the truth about that day.

Carrie seemed to look right through me.

"She didn't? But I thought—"

"No, she didn't," I said, cutting her off.

"But then . . ." she said, her voice fading.

"I did it. I killed Spenser Mason," I said.

For a long while, we sat in silence. There was nothing revealing in Carrie's expression. She stared blankly at the floor, as if she were waiting for something else from me.

"Jessie found out that old Spenser had killed her grandmother and the O'Brien brothers. She had put it all together. I didn't believe her at first, but after a time, she convinced me and it all made sense," I began. And for the next several hours, I rid my soul of every bloodstained detail regarding Spenser Mason's death.

Carrie listened intently, the same way she had at the Christmas party. Her expression never wavered. When I finished, I waited for her reaction—her judgment even. It was what I wanted, and I welcomed it.

But none came. Instead, Carrie sat quietly, her eyes still set in their attentions somewhere on the floor. I felt a sudden awkward silence arise between us, compelling me to speak again.

"I don't have any regrets," I said decisively. "I'm not sorry, and I'd do it again."

With that, her eyes lifted to mine. She took the last drink from her glass of wine. "It's late," she said, standing up.

I gave my watch a confirming glance. "Yes," I said. It was nearly midnight.

"Are you tired?" she asked, setting the empty glass down on the end table.

"I don't sleep much," I said honestly.

"Someone does," she said, pointing to Kobuk sprawled out on the floor next to the stove. "I'm a night owl myself. *No rest for the wicked,* my father tells me." She laughed and then sat back down beside me on the sofa.

Brushing blond hair from her face, she lifted her eyes to mine. In them, I saw a hint of the young girl I once knew.

"I don't want to be friends," I said.

Carrie looked at me intently, her expression verging on a smile or a scowl, and I felt the need to explain. But before I could, she kissed me—softly and sweetly—on the lips.

"What was that for?" I said.

"I don't want to be friends either."

"Then what do you want to be?"

"I'm not sure, but we'll sort it all out in the morning," she said with a giggle.

"Are you saying that you want to spend the night?"

Carrie kissed me again, this time with such a force and fever that there was no doubting her intentions.

"What would your father think?" I said, grinning.

With the back of her hand, Carrie gently touched the side of my face and laughed.

"Well, you know what they say about preachers' kids."

Edwards Brothers Malloy
Thorofare, NJ USA
October 24, 2012